Exile

A Derrick King Novel: Book 1

By Daniel L Copeland

Dedication:

The work is dedicated to the kind hearts and gentle souls trying to make the world a better place.

At the End

Dark, damp, cold, hungry. Dead end. Security patrols hunt for him outside this hole in the earth. A solid steel door seals the end where he hides.

Trapped.

Writing is a waste of time.

Probably.

But he writes.

He hopes someone will read his notes one day. At least they would know what became of him.

Understand that he had changed.

His cell phone battery shows a thin red line in the upper right-hand corner of its screen. Once it dies, the darkness will be complete.

Should light appear, it will not be a rescue.

He is only 17 years old.

Part One

1

Friday, March 12, 7:20 a.m.

DERRICK KING'S DEATH BEGAN ON MARCH 12TH. He just did not realize it. He thought it merely his 17th birthday.

It turned out to be a slow death that happened quickly.

That morning, Derrick did not hear the drone deliver breakfast. As a child, he listened for drones, raced to watch them land, and deposit their cargo on the family's drone port, located outside the door to their backyard, which a ten-foot stucco wall protected. However, there was nothing that endangered them because they were safe behind the fortified barrier of Pacific Edge Community. He remembered being curious about drones. *Where did they come from? Who made them? How did they find their destination?* He had been curious about many things. *How did transports work? How did they change color?* He could even recall wondering what was beyond the walls that surrounded them.

He had outgrown curiosity, as everyone does. Well, almost everyone. He was no longer curious about anything. There was nothing to be curious about. The Academy and New America Media provided all the information necessary. Besides, he was no longer a child. At seventeen, childhood recedes and manhood approaches.

Before leaving his room, Derrick admired his teeth in the mirror, as he did every morning, bright white and straight. Advanced orthodontics and medical procedures had further enhanced his near-perfect natural teeth. His blond hair, trimmed moments earlier using a Barber-Bot™. Derrick used the device to cut his hair each morning, even on weekends. Perfection took mere minutes.

He wondered for a moment if the intense pale hair color he had chosen was best. It was almost white. It was better than his natural, nondescript light brown hair. Did his genetically re-engineered blond hair and ice-blue eyes produce the sophisticated and superior effect he desired? After a few moments, turning this way and that, trying on a few expressions, Derrick decided his choice of hair and eye color was perfect.

Moving close to the mirror, he admired his skin. The nanobots that opened and cleansed his pores had been washed away in the shower. If any remained, he could not have seen them with the naked eye. His skin glowed clear and blemish-free. Like everything else this morning: perfect.

In his contemplative state, Derrick studied his bathroom, 1200 square feet with an additional 600 square-foot closet. Too small, but Father and Mother refused to enlarge the house to increase the size of his quarters. Black walnut hardwood covered the floor. Rare Crema Bordeaux granite swirled with jade green, chocolate brown, obsidian black, and buttercream colors, which he had Father import from Brazil, covered the countertop, shower, and jetted tub. Derrick knew not where Brazil was; he did not know anything about granite either, but he liked the color of the rock and ordered it three years ago when he demanded that Father and Mother redecorate his room.

Yet Derrick had grown tired of the décor. He had lived with it for three years already. However, he would leave in less than two years, so he did not demand a renovation. He took a deep breath, pleased with his tolerance for such challenging conditions. It had never occurred to Derrick that his bedroom was much larger than his sister's. Many things escaped Derrick's attention. When he moved out, Father and Mother could do with this room as they wished, but he thought they would not change a thing. Derrick King did not understand his Father and Mother.

The large monitor on the wall came to life. A musical tone filled the room, and a solemn voice announced, "Devotion time in fifteen seconds."

Derrick stood at attention, facing the screen, hand over his heart as the New America National Anthem played. Then Derrick recited the New America Pledge of Allegiance, along with the disembodied voice that had a patriotic quality. This happened twice a day, every day, morning and evening, plus during special events. Derrick never grew tired of it. In fact, he suggested it be done again at the beginning and end of each class, but to his knowledge, academy administration had not yet considered his suggestion.

At the breakfast table, Derrick ate eggs Benedict, his favorite. Father and Mother had already left for their work. At least he assumed they were gone. He never saw them in the mornings, other than on Sundays. A swirl of steam rose as the egg yolk mingled with the hollandaise sauce. The English muffin was toasted crisp and topped with a thick slice of smoked ham. A chef made his breakfast moments before a drone delivered it in a Creed Deliver-Hot™

container. The food was as fresh as if it were just popped off the stove. The chef worked nearby, but not in the family's kitchen. Derrick did not know where the chef worked. He did not know where the ham, eggs, or English muffins came from either. Derrick did not care to know.

Creed, the company that made the Deliver-Hot™ container, was a prestigious company that retained Chosen as associates. Derrick might be employed there upon graduation. The Chosen — who live in Communities, in his case Pacific Edge — do not have jobs like the commoner who made his breakfast. Commoners have jobs. The Chosen have careers.

With a morsel of English muffin, Derrick soaked up the last of the egg yolk and hollandaise, downed the remainder of the fresh-squeezed orange juice, and left everything for the servants to clean up. He had never seen the servants who cared for their house, cleaned their rooms, made their beds, washed their clothes, or cooked their dinners because servants are commoners. Derrick King did not care to know.

Chosen Doctrine prohibited contact between the Chosen and the commoners. Although screening and security practices are strict, commoners posed too great a threat to the Chosen to have direct contact with them. Commoners departed the community, and security staff confirmed they were out of Pacific Edge long before family members returned home.

As he finished breakfast, Miriam, his sister, walked into the dining area. Her look dark and sinister. Father said she would grow out of it. That she was trying to find herself. Derrick wished she would find herself soon.

"Morning," she said.

"Miriam, are you not forgetting something?" Derrick asked.

With her back turned toward him, she said, "I never forget."

"You cannot wish your brother a happy birthday?"

"The way I see it, it's not a good day."

"Miriam, you need to grow up. You are six months away from The Choosing yourself. The leaders tolerate your childishness because you have not reached the age of accountability. Their tolerance will soon end."

"I don't care," Miriam said.

"Miriam King, you had better start caring. Do you want to end up banished? Start using your head."

Miriam turned, glared, and then stomped out of the house. Sometimes Derrick felt as if she would stomp out of his life if she could.

Derrick did not understand Miriam.

Every day during Morning Supplication, Derrick thanked the Designer and the Founder for his birth as a member of the King family, for being one of the select few who comprised the Chosen of New America. Derrick realized it was not fate nor good fortune, but the divine design that made him Chosen, and he would make the best of it. Miriam, however, hated everything about being

Chosen. He was certain that she would not graduate from the Academy before they banished her from Pacific Edge. Sometimes he wondered how he and Miriam could be related.

Before leaving, Derrick checked the atmospheric monitoring display. The phosphorescent scale glowed green indicating that the temperature, weather, and air quality were all well within acceptable limits, which was not unusual because on most days the ocean breeze washed over Pacific Edge pushing out the stale, polluted air of the commoner world that laid to the east. If the winds shifted and came from the commoner world, Pacific Edge officials advised people to stay inside, and huge fans mounted on the perimeter walls spun aggressively, working to push out the contaminated air. Derrick did not know what the commoner's contaminated air smelled like. He had never gone outside when the breeze blew from the east. He did not venture outside except to walk from the front door to the transport that took him to the Academy. When there was an air-quality alert, Derrick had the transport pull inside the indoor bay, so he did not have to go outside.

Today, outside under the portico, the transport awaited. Miriam must have walked because the transport could not have made a trip to the Academy and back so quickly, and she was not sitting inside the transport waiting for him either. Derrick did not understand why Miriam walked to the Academy every day. The absence of such drudgery was a symbolic blessing of being Chosen.

Derrick hoped, at least a little, that Miriam would outgrow her rebellious stage. She was almost 15 years of age. She would enter The Choosing on her 15th birthday and be accountable. No longer a child. With her attitude, no man would choose her, and if unwed, they would banish her from Pacific Edge in accordance with the Doctrine of the Chosen unless they allowed her to attend college.

The shimmering transport altered its color every few seconds to shades of blue, green, purple, red. The colors limited only by its passenger's mood and imagination. When Derrick touched the roof, the transport became silver, but the color might change before arriving at school because his mood was drifting like an unanchored boat on a restless sea.

Derrick stood for a moment with the transport door open, one foot on the threshold and his hand on the vehicle's roof, surveying the scene before him. The portico, covered with Italian marble that seemed to glow from within, was large enough to shelter six ten-passenger transports. Polished green ivy crept up the portico columns, disappearing over the roofline. Beyond the portico, a fountain spray danced in ever-changing patterns. At night, lights provided a myriad of color, but by day, there was no color, save ghost rainbows that appeared in the mist. Derrick thought it was nice, but someday he would have a better home than this.

Derrick eased into the transport. The safety harness fastened itself around him, and then he said, "James Carver Academy."

The driver did not respond because no driver piloted the transport. Controls unknown to Derrick guided transports within Pacific Edge. He had not witnessed transportation vehicles outside of Pacific Edge. He had seen the commoner world as reported by New America Media. Commoner transportation was crude and were often open-topped vehicles that strangely dressed savages piloted.

Derrick had never seen the territory of the commoners either. Although he and his family had traveled to a park that New America Corporation owned. When Derrick's family traveled over commoner territory, they did so in aircraft with no windows. So violent, chaotic, and perverted was the realm of the commoners that they do not allow the Chosen to see it, except via New America Media.

However, in Pacific Edge, he could see through the clear sapphire glass windows of the transport if he wanted to. Every aspect of Pacific Edge, from the clipped hedges and Japanese maples to the manicured lawns to flowerbeds bursting with color, was as perfect as his hair. He could not see a pebble on street or drive. To his right, an emerald, green lawn stretched up and over the hill, every blade of grass uniform, and not a weed or divot detectable. To his left, a sea of red, yellow, and orange flowers carpeted the ground. The variety of flowers that made the colorful display was unknown to him.

He did not care to know.

Such knowledge was unimportant. There must have been a multitude of fragrances wafting from the sea and the flowers, but Derrick could not smell them because he had the transport air purification system set to eliminate them all. Derrick preferred purified air. The natural world, even as well-tended as Pacific Edge, had too much disorder, randomness, and variety.

Derrick breathed deeply, regretting that he had not taken a mood enhancer this morning. He felt fine earlier. And why would he not feel fine on his birthday? Especially his 17th birthday! No mood enhancement seemed necessary that morning. Yet now …

Exciting things happen at age 17. The Choosing topped the list, which occurs between each boy's 17th and 18th birthdays. In Chosen Communities across New America, when males turned 16, the process begins when Chosen leaders present each boy with a pre-selected list of girls ages 15 to 16. From this list, each boy selects his mate. They based the lists on physical attributes, grades, and IQ. Before the boy's 18th birthday, he must select his bride. The two are bound together until death and then rejoined in Chosen Paradise after passing. Divorce is not allowed. There is no need. Sometimes a spouse, most often the wife, is banished. Divorce is unnecessary and a relic of the failed United States of America. In New America, such a marriage is nullified. The woman gets nothing except a free ride to the commoner world. The man can then choose another wife from a list of women the Chosen leaders supplied. It does not happen often. Derrick thought it the perfect system.

Derrick would not wait until his 18th birthday. He had made his decision. The only thing he lacked was a grand announcement of the privileged girl. Derrick was in the top tier of the rating scale, and three of the five girls on his list possessed great beauty. However, he had been taught that wives are not best chosen based on love or lust. Maidens of service can fulfill those needs. Even the lowliest Chosen men can afford two maidens.

Derrick's Father was level four but had no maidens, which Derrick did not understand. Derrick would begin his career on level nine, and he intended to surpass Father's status within a few years and reach at least level three. Maybe level two. Men at level three, on average, have five maidens scattered in five different communities or resorts. He could ignore emotions and make a rational decision. Derrick marveled at the elegance of the Chosen's way.

The transport glided along the smooth Pacific Edge street. Derrick saw a person walking up ahead. Not something often seen in Pacific Edge. Thin, dark clothing, black hair, Miriam's appearance could not have contrasted more against the well-choreographed riot of color surrounding her. She was such an embarrassment.

"Stop by the person," Derrick said.

A display panel in front of him came to life as security cameras scanned the surroundings. At first, the display matched the scene as Derrick saw it, but then it cycled through infrared, sonar, metal detection, and radar scans. Next, the security systems focused on Miriam, subjecting her to the same scans.

"Miriam King, age 14 years, 5 months, 21 days. No weapons detected. Confirm stop vehicle near Miriam King."

Derrick did not know how the machine recognized Miriam. He had never cared to know. "Confirmed."

The transport eased to a silent stop next to Miriam. She continued walking.

"Miriam King did not stop," the disembodied transport voice announced.

"I see that, stupid autotron."

"No need for hostility, Derrick King."

Derrick ignored the admonishment. "Match her pace."

"Matching Miriam King's pace."

"Window down." Derrick waited as the security system repeated the same scans it had just finished. The security measures seemed overkill but reinforced the dangers the commoners posed.

"Miriam King. Age 14 years, 5 months, 21 days. No weapons detected. Confirm window down."

"Confirmed." Derrick wanted to say more, but the autotron lacked feelings and could not be humiliated.

"Miriam."

Miriam said nothing.

"Do you want to ride?"

Miriam kept walking.

"Will you stop already? Look, I am sorry if I upset you earlier." Derrick King was not sorry. He had done nothing wrong, but he often apologized to Miriam.

Miriam stopped.

The transport continued on.

"Stop the transport, stupid autotron."

The transport stopped. Derrick twisted in his seat to look at Miriam.

Miriam shook her head and stepped forward to the window and said, "I don't want a ride. And you don't need to apologize."

"I want to help you, sis."

Miriam knitted her eyebrows. "Help me what?"

"You know, be happy. Fit in."

"I don't need your help. I don't want to fit in. You're clueless." And with that, she walked away.

Derrick exhaled. "Window up."

2

March 12, 8:30 a.m., James Carver Academy

THE WHITE FLOORS OF JAMES CARVER Academy gleamed and offered no contrast to the white walls or ceiling that radiated white light. Classrooms, sterilized and empty, save the addition of white desks, which were scrubbed clean each day, and white media displays, awaited students. The air was scrubbed clean of odors. Students at James Carver Academy followed meticulous grooming standards. Perfumes, colognes, and other fragrances were not permitted, nor were they needed, because the cleansing bots and chemicals used when bathing or showering prevented body odors.

Derrick loved James Carver Academy, except there were too many people. Also, he disliked most of the holograms because they violated the room's purity, often displaying the commoner world with suffering, war, despair, and the commoners themselves. Derrick suggested the media be converted to black and white, but to his knowledge, they had not considered his suggestion.

Neither the students nor teachers created distractions at James Carver Academy. Students followed grooming standards. The boys wore trimmed hair, not over the ear, not past halfway between the hairline and the eyebrows, and not over the collar. They allowed girls more freedom of expression because the girls were at or near the age of the Choosing, or maybe because they were girls. Derrick did not understand why girls had more freedom. Girls also had the choice of three hairstyles. Hair could be any color that represented natural human hair colors, and it could be changed at will. Controlling hair-color modification would be difficult. However, most kids maintained the same color of hair throughout the school year.

No specific clothing restrictions existed at the Academy, which caused Derrick no small degree of consternation. Annually, when students could submit ideas for school improvements, Derrick suggested a school uniform. To his knowledge, administrators had not considered this suggestion. This year, he would provide specifics for the uniform. The lack of specificity must have derailed his previous attempts. Derrick felt the clothing variation caused too much chaos.

They called the clothing standard 'business casual', which was too vague in Derrick's thinking. Yet, despite the ambiguity, most students maintained similar dress. Boys wore button-down shirts, typically white, but sometimes blue or light yellow surfaced. Sports coats displayed more variety: navy, gray pinstripe, black, and even corduroy, which was primarily worn on Fridays when button-downs were often replaced with polo shirts. Pants were mostly light tan. However, dark-gray pinstripe, black, and even white were worn intermittently. Shoes were black and polished to a high sheen. It had never occurred to Derrick that the reason everyone dressed the same was that other clothing options were not available for purchase.

None of this was problematic for Derrick because he wore the exact same clothing every day.

Girls were given more latitude in clothing as well, but even girls did not challenge the status quo, except for Miriam, but black is acceptable, so she got by with it. Her hair was too short, but no process existed for making hair grow faster than its natural pace. Her hair was not naturally black either, but since black is a natural color, she got by with it, even though it contrasted with her alabaster skin. During Miriam's first year at James Carver Academy, officials sent her home several times for what they perceived as violations of school standards. Jet-black hair cut too short, all black clothes, etc. Instead of adapting, Miriam had appealed on every occasion, challenging school officials' interpretation of the rules. And Miriam won every time. The arbitrator thought Miriam violated the spirit of the rules but admitted she complied with the rules as they were written. Finally, they stopped trying. Derrick wondered why the Tribunal had not banished her already.

Students were seldom banished or exiled before they reached the age of accountability, although many were relocated to other Chosen Communities. But after the age of accountability was reached, sometimes they banished students for no apparent reason. Miriam needed to change and soon to have any hope of staying here. Although, to be honest, Derrick's life would improve dramatically if she were gone.

James Carver Academy was all about conformity, uniformity, and predictability, which prepared students for the future. For example, at James Carver Academy, students were predominantly Caucasian, save a few of Asian descent. There were none in Derrick's class. There had been a few in the earlier grades, but they had transferred to other Communities before reaching the Academy. Derrick remembered them vaguely but did not know any of them.

In Community Awareness class, students learned that the Northern Pacific Community, near the Canadian border, had many people of Asian ethnicity, even a few African Americans. The Northeast Coast Community and New Great Water's Community had the most diverse ethnicity of all New America Communities. Special accommodations ensured ethnic groups were given equal but separate living areas, thus maintaining harmony and productivity. Traveling to, or communicating with, other New America Communities was discouraged, which meant it did not happen. There was no need for it. That was why students were taught about it in class. In the past, open communication had created problems. Such problems are now resolved during this last reign on Earth, as written in the Doctrine of the Chosen.

In comparison, commoners were a mud puddle, races mixing indiscriminately until few people remained with any pure ethnicity. Derrick could not imagine seeing them in person. Watching them destroy each other on New America Media was as close as he wanted to get.

The ceiling flashed yellow twice, painting the white corridor golden, signaling the ten-minute warning before the start of the day.

A warm hand slid around Derrick's back.

"Happy birthday," Rebekah Ford said.

"Thanks, Rebekah. I am glad you found me before the first class. Your smile will brighten my day."

Rebekah was on Derrick's list of aspirants for marriage. In many ways, she was his favorite. Not the prettiest, in a classical sense. Her teeth were slightly crooked and could have been straightened, but Rebekah said she did not want to change them. As a result, her smile was lopsided but infectious. Tall, lithe, and athletic, Rebekah was a star on the Academy soccer team and could play in college if she attended college, but most girls do not. Everything about Rebekah pulled at Derrick's emotions like no other girl on his list. But Rebekah was not his choice. Derrick would take her as a companion if he could, but someone would choose her for marriage in the second or third round of selection.

Girls entered The Choosing at a younger age than the boys, which gave the second, third, and fourth-tiers time to make their selections before the girls turned 18. Those not chosen in the last round were released to become purchased as companions unless they were banished from the Community before then. One might think that companions were a picked-over lot, but The Founder had a perfect plan. Once wed and employed, Chosen males could select companions at age 16, if the girl had not been selected in The Choosing. However, if a man could not find a companion he wanted, he could select a younger girl before she was of age to enter the Choosing. Such companions remained in the Academy until age 17, when they would go to wherever the man who had purchased them wanted. This, like everything in the Chosen world, provided a splendid process, giving the man a few years to establish his career and secure dwellings for his companions. They banished those not taken as wives or companions from the Community. Before banishment, some girls elected to go to college. After college, girls could be purchased as companions, or if a wife had been exiled, selected as a spouse. Derrick King thought it a perfect system. But he did not know any women who had attended college and returned.

"Derrick, you seem stressed. You should be happy." Rebekah nuzzled her cheek against his chest. "No need to be stressed, Love. You can choose any time now."

A feeling Derrick could only describe as discomfort washed over him. He ignored Rebekah's comment and said, "It is Miriam. Why must she be so difficult? She is an embarrassment."

Rebekah fixed him with her steel-gray eyes. "Derrick, she's not you. What she does is not about you. You can't control her. Besides, I like Miriam. I wish I were brave like her."

Derrick wondered why a girl would want to be brave.

The ceiling flashed yellow once and then glowed orange, signaling two minutes to class.

Derrick considered Rebekah's words and said, "I must go. My first class is on E-4." With that, he left her. The last time he would see Rebekah Ford.

Right on time, Derrick slid into his seat in New America History, which was his favorite class. Learning how what was called the United States of America failed and how New America rose from the ruins inspired him. The classroom was almost full when Derrick entered, filled with the soft murmuring of adolescents sharing tidbits of gossip, news, or revelations. Wasted energy, in Derrick's opinion. It was why he avoided having close friends. He could see no purpose in having friends. They were a distraction. Instead, he focused on his future in this delightful world of the Chosen, into which he had been born.

Derrick glanced at a desk in the front, two rows to his right. Empty, as usual. He looked at the door in an automated response so ingrained in his morning ritual that he could not prevent it had he tried. The instructor, Mr. Jones, stood at the door, forcing the last few students to edge sideways as they scurried to enter before the ceiling turned red. When it did, Mr. Jones would pull the door shut. School officers would gather any students left in the hall and take them to detention. Miriam had been in detention twice this quarter. One more would put her in jeopardy of a student body officer's inquisition, where her fate would be decided. The outcome would not be good. Many students did not like Miriam, and unquestionably, the student body officers were among that group. Yet, she had admirers. Derrick did not understand why.

Miriam appeared at the door as light bathed the room red. But she did not scurry like her peers. Instead, she walked straight ahead, no rush, forcing Mr. Jones to edge back, his personal space violated. *Why did she do things like that?* Her entrance did not go unnoticed, as several students stared at the door with a variety of expressions. Some students scowled their disapproval, but many smiled.

Few things caused Derrick anxiety, yet Miriam's being in the same New America History class did. She was two years younger than Derrick, yet she had two senior classes. Derrick had this one class in common with her, and he thought that was one class too many. She seldom paid attention, and Mr. Jones would call on her when she seemed oblivious. Yet, without fail, Miriam would know the answer to his question, and often add information beyond the question asked, and sometimes would challenge Mr. Jones with a question of her own. When Miriam did this, Mr. Jones was reluctant to call on her for several days.

Derrick did not care how intelligent Miriam was. He disagreed with the school's decision to move her to senior classes. She made him look bad.

"Good morning, students."

"Good morning, Mr. Jones," the class said in unison.

"Today we are watching a short documentary followed by discussion. Please, watch closely."

The white ceiling light dimmed, and a holographic image filled the front of the room. Although Derrick did not like all the colors, he liked the holographic images better than the wall-sized flat screens. Scenes of prehistoric Earth displayed in rapid flashes. A progression from a watery planet to the formation of continents, and then people appeared and then animals: horses, cows, dogs, and cats. Next came a horrific flood. As the waters subsided, buildings and cities grew up from the ground. Toward the end of the video, decline began: poverty, fires, violent storms, and wars. Ten thousand years reduced to a ten-minute depiction.

Derrick knew the documentary well. It was a standard that instructors used often because it provided a wealth of information and facilitated discussions on multiple topics: Earth History, Geography, Political Science, Foundations of Faith, and New America History. Although Derrick had seen it hundreds of times, he never grew tired of it. He enjoyed every second, every word, but his eyes drifted to Miriam, who was slumped in her seat, focusing on her fingernails. *Why must she cause me so much discomfort?*

"Miriam?" Mr. Jones began. "How old is Earth?"

Miriam continued to study her fingernails. "I thought this was New America History. That question is better suited to Earth History."

"The topic is in the documentary, and I'll decide what questions to ask. Now, how old is Earth, Miriam?"

"I don't know."

Derrick's stomach, which had twisted in a knot the moment Mr. Jones called Miriam's name, felt as if it had turned to stone. Derrick slumped in his chair. Turning his head from side to side, he glanced at his peers. Some stared at Mr. Jones, but most watched Miriam. Mr. Jones stood straight-backed with arms folded across his chest. Jaw set as if he had concocted a plan to ensnare Miriam and win a debate with her. Miriam knew the answer. Derrick was certain of that. Although Derrick hoped Miriam could be humbled, he did not believe this would end well for Mr. Jones.

"You don't know?" Mr. Jones asked. "Perhaps because you didn't watch the presentation. If I were to guess, I'd say you weren't even listening."

Answer him, Miriam! Derrick screamed in his head.

"You asked me about the age of Earth, and I answered. You didn't ask me what the narrator said about Earth's age. He said it is six to ten thousand years old. Perhaps you should phrase your questions accurately."

Mr. Jones walked toward Miriam and stood in front of her. She did not look at him. Her body language did not change. Her lack of movement oozed defiance.

Mr. Jones is an experienced teacher — experienced at being on the receiving end of Miriam's questions, that is — paused as if carefully selecting his next question. "You disagree with the accepted truth regarding the age of the Earth? That's interesting. Would you care to explain to the class how you have developed your ideas?"

Miriam sat straight, folded her hands on the top of her desk, and stared at Mr. Jones. "How do we know Earth is ten thousand years old?"

"Six to ten thousand-years, Ms. King. You should be more accurate with your question." The corner of Mr. Jones' lip turned up.

Derrick would never admit it to anyone, but Mr. Jones sounded like an immature person in a debate he was sure to lose.

The room was silent.

Mr. Jones said, "Miriam, I'm sure you know the answer to that question."

"Maybe I do. I'm wondering if you know," Miriam said.

Mr. Jones scanned the room, perhaps hoping to find an escape or maybe hoping the ceiling would turn green, signaling the end of class. The trap was obvious. If he didn't answer, he'd appear intimidated. If he explained, he'd be reciting the answer of a first grader.

Mr. Jones said, "The information is written in the Doctrine."

"Correct. And who wrote the Doctrine?"

"James Carver," Mr. Jones said.

"How did James Carver discover the age of Earth?"

"Miriam, where are you going with this?"

Derrick figured Mr. Jones regretted that question the moment he said it, but it was too late to retract it.

"How did James Carver discover Earth's age?" Miriam asked again.

Derrick glanced around the room and saw that the students were sitting bolt upright, leaning forward, and staring at Mr. Jones as if some great revelation might occur. When Mr. Jones did not respond, Derrick took a breath. Jones was going to drop the discussion before things worsened.

Derrick was wrong.

"Okay, Miriam. Let's do it your way," Mr. Jones said. "You know the answer to your last question. James Carver did not discover the age of the Earth. That was already common knowledge when he wrote the Doctrine."

"How do we know it was common knowledge?"

"It was written in the sacred texts of the Fathers. The age of Earth has been common knowledge since the beginning of civilization."

"Can we examine these sacred texts to which you refer?"

"You know we cannot. The sacred texts are only available to those entering the priesthood. James Carver removed the sacred texts from general circulation because of misinterpretations that occurred in the old United States," Mr. Jones said.

"We can't see the books because we might not understand them. Is that correct?"

"Yes."

"We should accept that it says what James Carver said?"

"Do you question the integrity of James Carver?"

"I just asked a question."

Before Mr. Jones could speak, Miriam continued. "You said the age of Earth was common knowledge before James Carver wrote the Doctrine."

"I don't remember my exact words, but yes, it was common knowledge."

"Did everyone at the time agree with this common knowledge?" Miriam asked.

"Most everyone. I was not alive at the time."

A few students suppressed snickers, which did not break the tension but made it a little more bearable.

"Can we agree that not everyone believed Earth was six to ten thousand years old?"

"Yes, we can agree on that."

Miriam had Mr. Jones in a laser-focused stare.

"Who did not believe?" Miriam asked.

"They called themselves scientists."

The ceiling glowed with green light.

3

ALTHOUGH THE ROOM GLOWED GREEN UNDER the end-of-class signal, no one moved. It was as if they were all frozen, resembling a hologram buffering. Miriam stood, picked up her tablet, and walked out of the room. Then the rest of the class stirred. Mr. Jones offered Derrick a weak smile.

Mr. Jones would not ask Miriam questions again for a while, and for that, Derrick was thankful.

In the hall, a firm hand caught Derrick's elbow and jerked him to a stop. Derrick found himself face to face with Marcus Carver. Marcus's breath smelled of stale coffee, and veins popped on his red neck. Derrick's elbow hurt from the vice-like grip. Marcus was the largest kid in their class and could probably play offensive lineman in professional football, but being a Carver, he would not be required to work at anything. Marcus had always been a bully. He got what he wanted without being physical, but he liked to hurt people, or so it seemed.

He and Marcus were not friends, but Derrick never felt intimidated. Partially because he and Marcus never experienced an argument and partially because Derrick did not feel inferior. Derrick felt he was superior to Marcus in every way except physical size and family heritage.

"What was that crap?" Marcus hissed.

"What did I do?" Derrick asked.

"Not you, dipshit. Your sister."

"I am not responsible for what my sister does."

"You'd better get control of her before someone else does it for you."

Marcus pulled Derrick close, glared, and then pushed him aside. Before he turned and walked away, Marcus poked his finger in Derrick's face. Derrick stood rooted to the spot, and several students stared at him. Derrick was not sure if he felt angry or scared. Maybe both. Marcus Carver was not a person to cross, not because of his size, strength, and reputation, but because he was a descendant of James Carver.

Marcus was right about Miriam. Derrick was angry with her as well. Yet Marcus's threat stirred a primitive feeling that Derrick could neither explain nor control. Derrick remained motionless for several minutes until he realized he risked being late to Prose and Musings of James Carver. He hustled down the hall, around the wheel-shaped hallway on the building's perimeter, and down the next hall that extended like a spoke from the atrium that served as the building's hub and primary meeting place.

As Derrick collapsed in his seat, a hologram of the New America flag rotated at the front of the classroom. Derrick could not focus on class. He was preoccupied with Miriam and how he would control her. *She had to change. She had to.* Still, for all his agonizing, he could not control her. Rebekah was right about that. Every time he pondered another unworkable scheme that would cause Miriam to change, Marcus Carver intruded into his thoughts.

What the instructor covered was elementary. Things Derrick learned years ago. Derrick was only partially aware of the instructor, Morris Philbin's, monotone lecture about James Carver's thoughts on New America and the world. Philbin pointed to other continents: Asia, Europe, Australia, Africa, South America, Antarctica, which were displayed as flat, featureless landmasses. Derrick felt relieved that Miriam was not in this class. He imagined her peppering Philbin with questions: *Let's talk about Africa. What is there? Who lives there? What do people do there? What about Europe? Is it a modernized country like New America? Why not teach us about other countries? Why can't we travel to them?*

Derrick found himself thinking questions of his own. Why does the map of New America have rivers and mountains and deserts but only shows the Communities of the Chosen? The old cities where commoners live do not appear on the map, but he knew at least some of them still exist. Why are other continents left blank? Other places must have mountains and rivers and cities. Derrick's thoughts bothered him. He did not question things like that. This was Miriam's thinking, and now it was affecting him. Then something occurred to him: *Why have I not questioned such things before?*

Miriam must change.

Derrick heard the shuffle of feet and voices before he noticed that green light bathed the room. He moved to the next class like an autotron. People said hello in the hall, and Derrick responded in kind. Yet in the next class, he realized he could not remember one person to whom he had spoken.

The room glowed red, and the instructor, Mrs. Prince, the Foundations of Faith instructor, closed the door but did not speak. She moved to her desk and sat. After a few moments, Derrick realized someone was trying to get his attention with a whisper. Derrick glanced over his shoulder and saw Jana Somersworth, the girl he planned to choose for marriage. Somehow, he had forgotten that she was in this class.

"Did you take too many mood enhancers this morning?" she whispered.

"No. Why?"

"I've been trying to get your attention since I saw you in the hall."

She smiled at Derrick, mouthed the words happy birthday, and then blew him a kiss. Derrick managed a smile, then turned around.

He had to confront Miriam.

This must stop.

It must.

He could no longer tolerate her attitude. The urgency to talk with Miriam overwhelmed him. Miriam had to learn that no good could come from questioning everything. It was out of her control. It was out of everyone's control. James Carver set the course for the Chosen. Miriam was privileged to be part of it. That was all there was to it — end of discussion.

Mrs. Prince spoke. She looked flushed, but not angry or sad. Maybe frustrated. "I'm giving you a free period today to study or read. Just no talking, please."

Mrs. Prince continued, "We had a spirited discussion last class. I must study to follow-up tomorrow. I hope you don't mind."

Around the room, heads nodded. Then, like the darkness of a black cloud, it dawned on Derrick that Foundations of Faith was Miriam's second senior class. She was here last period. Two classes, she had argued with instructors, not good. Not good at all. Derrick had a full period with nothing to do but wait, think, and worry.

Lunch break came next. It was not Derrick's custom to eat with Miriam. He tried to avoid her when he could, and he could at lunch, but today would be different. Today, they needed to talk. Today, things would change.

They had to.

And Derrick would see to it.

When the green light washed over the room, Derrick tried to make a hasty exit, but Jana blocked his path. She must have been watching the clock to have moved so quickly.

"Is everything okay?" She ran her fingers through Derrick's hair above his right ear and then settled her hand on his shoulder.

Her touch felt comforting. Reassuring somehow, an indication he had indeed found his soulmate, or maybe he needed a kind touch because the last person who touched him was full of rage.

"I am okay. A little preoccupied. We can talk about it later. Okay?"

"Okay." She started up on her toes as if to kiss, but Derrick stopped her because such contact was not permitted at James Carver Academy. She squeezed his shoulder instead and left the room.

Now, he had to find Miriam, but Mrs. Prince closed the door. Derrick was the lone student remaining in the classroom.

"Can I have a word with you, Derrick?"

No, please. I cannot do this right now. Derrick thought.

"Sure," Derrick said.

"Miriam was in the previous class."

"Yes," Derrick acknowledged.

"She caused a stir today."

"I am sorry," Derrick said. "She caused problems in first period as well. I will talk to her. It will not happen again." Derrick prayed he was not lying, because he had no reason to believe he could deliver on his promise.

"Don't be sorry. Miriam has a keen mind. Although it may get her into trouble sometimes, she has the kind of mind we need." Mrs. Prince put both her hands on Derrick's shoulders and looked into his eyes. "Don't be hard on her. And, if you repeat anything I have said, I'll deny it. Do you understand?"

Derrick nodded, although he did not understand and had no time to think about it. He needed to find Miriam. Lunch break was one hour, and he had already lost ten minutes of it. Thinking he could convince Miriam to change in 50 minutes was ludicrous, but something else gnawed at him.

Something urgent.

Something bad.

Derrick marched straight to the courtyard. Miriam would already have her tray. As soon as he walked through the portal into the courtyard, Derrick saw them.

A red-faced Marcus Carver stood face to face with Miriam.

4

EVERY HEAD TURNED TOWARD MARCUS AND MIRIAM. Chairs scraping on the floor echoed as people adjusted their positions, attempting to achieve an unobstructed view. If it were possible, Marcus looked angrier than when he grabbed Derrick earlier. Miriam seemed unruffled. Derrick decided Miriam's composure was a good sign. Although Marcus was angry, he had not been threatening. Derrick's first misconception.

Everyone in the courtyard was silent except Marcus. Hearing him was easy.

"Who do you think you are? What makes you think you can challenge the works of James Carver? You're a disgrace to your family and to the Chosen."

"I can't express how much your opinion means to me," Miriam said.

The sarcasm in her voice was unmistakable. Snickers drifted through the quiet courtyard. Marcus was not accustomed to being laughed at, and it showed.

"Shut your mouth, or I'll shut it for you."

"What? Big man is going to hit a girl?" Miriam mocked. "I'm not afraid of you, Marcus Carver."

"You should be."

Marcus reached out to push Miriam, but Miriam dodged to the side, and Marcus grabbed only air, which caused him to take an involuntary step forward. He and Miriam turned a quarter circle as if they were dancing. This put Marcus's back to Derrick.

Derrick started toward Marcus. Marcus raised his fist.

Derrick changed into a person he did not recognize.

"Leave her alone." Derrick heard someone say and then realized he had spoken those words.

Marcus didn't turn. "Back off, or you're next," he said as he raised his fist.

Derrick spun Marcus around. Then Marcus was lying motionless on the floor, blood pouring from his nose.

Derrick had knocked Marcus Carver out cold.

5

FOR A MOMENT, THE COURTYARD REMAINED SILENT, yet Derrick could hear the shallow breathing of the students surrounding him. Then a girl screamed. A cascade of chaos followed: crying, screaming, clanging chairs, pounding feet, and, oddly, cheering. Derrick stared at Marcus Carver, aware of the din, but in a detached, out-of-body sort of way. In a far corner of Derrick's mind, a little voice said, *I am in serious trouble,* but that voice meant little to Derrick, although he knew it spoke the truth. Derrick's behavior surprised him. What surprised him most was that instead of feeling doomed, which was the sensible thing to feel, instead of rushing to Marcus's aid, exclaiming his deep and sincere regret, he wanted to hit Marcus Carver again.

"Derrick. Derrick. Derrick."

Derrick heard something, but it was as if a dense fog on a moonless night smothered the words. Finally, he realized Miriam was calling his name.

Another strange thing happened. It was not only hitting Marcus Carver — the toughest, meanest, and most well-connected person at the Academy — which was out of character and strange indeed. What struck Derrick as beyond description, defying-the-laws-of-nature-strange, was that Miriam was suddenly the most beautiful person he had ever seen. Not beautiful-pretty, although she was pretty, but beautiful in a more profound sense. He could not bear the thought of anyone hurting her. Derrick transformed into someone he had not been before. Miriam King's big brother.

"Derrick, what have you done?" Miriam asked once she had his attention.

"I prevented him from hitting you." Derrick pointed at Marcus.

"Derrick, you're in serious trouble. You should have let me handle it." She pointed at Marcus. "Then he would have been the one in trouble."

Derrick searched for a comeback but came up empty. She was right, and then the magnitude of what he had done washed over him. The courtyard started a slow spin, and he teetered on the edge of fainting. "I did what I had to do. No changing it now." Then Derrick added, "I would do it again."

Miriam threw her arms around Derrick, burying her head against his chest.

I am in serious trouble. What will they do to me? Suspend me for certain. Maybe two weeks, making the rest of the year difficult. They could demote my level in the Choosing, and I will not be picking Jana Somersworth or any other girl on my list. As Derrick considered this, another strange thing happened because it was not Jana Somersworth, the girl Derrick planned to marry, that entered his mind, but Rebekah Ford. Rebekah's crooked smile floated through his thoughts and caused that strange, empty aching in his chest again. Derrick's future came into focus. This split-second decision — which was not a decision but an instinctual reaction — would define his life. Derrick could not explain why, but something told him that the instinctual part was important.

Derrick heard a commotion. New voices and Marcus Carver groaned and stirred on the ground. Two teachers rushed to Marcus. Two others pulled Miriam away from Derrick.

"He hit Marcus. Blindsided him."

Derrick recognized the nasal voice of Marsha Pickering.

"Is that true?" Benny Greerson asked. Mr. Greerson was the Academy headmaster. Derrick's parents called him the principal, but no one at the Academy used that term.

"No, it is not," Derrick said.

"You did not hit Marcus?" Mr. Greerson asked.

"I hit him, but I did not blindside him. Marcus was looking right at me."

"Why would you do such a thing?"

"He was going to hit Miriam," Derrick said.

"That's a lie," Marsha Pickering screamed.

Now, the other teachers, Derrick did not know their names, helped Marcus to his feet.

"Marcus?" Mr. Greerson asked. "Did you try to hit Miriam?"

"Of course not," Marcus sputtered. "Just counseling her about being inappropriate in class." It came out: coonshl nt bout bean inpropreete in clash.

Marcus touched his nose, and his knees buckled. If not for the teachers supporting him on both sides, Marcus would have hit the concrete a second time. The color drained from his face. The extent of his injury had become a cold reality to him.

"I need to sit, (Ah ned to shet)" Marcus said.

The teachers helped Marcus to a nearby chair, eased him down, and then he continued. "Apparently, no one in her family cares enough to help her."

At least, that is what Derrick thought Marcus had said. Derrick wanted to walk over and thump Marcus again.

Miriam must have sensed it because she pulled away from the teacher and grabbed Derrick's arm. "No," she whispered. "He's not worth it."

"Miriam. Derrick. Come with me. Marcus, you stay here. Staff will stay with you until the ambulance arrives. Your parents will meet you at the hospital." Mr. Greerson took Derrick by the elbow and guided him toward the exit.

As they left the courtyard, Marsha Pickering said, "He's dangerous. He should never come back."

Great. She thinks I am dangerous. Then another thought occurred to Derrick. *Maybe I am dangerous.*

The trio walked in silence to administration. Mr. Greerson positioned between Miriam and Derrick. Mr. Greerson stopped at Vice Headmaster Harding's office, but Mr. Harding was not there. "You two sit in here. Don't talk to anyone or use your communication devices. I need to contact the authorities."

The door closed, and Miriam pulled a chair close to Derrick, sat, and then took his hand in both of hers. "Derrick, I'm so sorry."

"What are you sorry for?" Derrick marveled at his response. He had previously cursed everything Miriam did: the way she dressed, the way she talked, the way she walked, the way she thought. All the things important to him less than an hour ago faded like the light disappears after the glow of the sunset dies.

"For causing all of this." She made a big circular motion over her head with one hand.

"That is not important," Derrick said. *If I keep talking like this, I will need a mirror to see whose voice I keep hearing, and if I am the person in that mirror, a CAT scan comes next.*

"What do you think they'll do to you?" she asked.

Derrick saw a tear in the corner of her eye and realized he had not seen Miriam cry for many years. *Why had that eluded me? Seems like I should have noticed that.*

He repeated the same litany of punishments that had occurred to him in the courtyard. Tears streamed down Miriam's cheeks. At first, her tears puzzled him because he was the one in trouble. Then he realized. *She is crying for me.*

The door opened. Mr. Greerson stood in the doorway. "You can go home," he said. "Your transport is waiting. I will see you to the door."

The combination of his unemotional tone and the simple, non-punishing instruction told Derrick that his initial estimate of consequences was far less severe than the storm that was coming his way.

6

THEY RODE HOME IN silence. Derrick sensed no barrier had risen between Miriam and himself. Instead, they both realized that talking was not safe. Not here. When they arrived home, the servants had already left. Father and Mother were not there, but he was sure the headmaster would call them, and they would be there soon. Miriam and Derrick trudged to their respective rooms, keeping their unspoken code of silence.

Derrick sat on his handcrafted Italian-leather couch, staring at the ceiling. He thought about a mood enhancer, but something told him that was a bad idea. Any confidence he had was seeping from him faster than a receding wave vacates the beach. His belly twisted into a knot and breathing became difficult.

What was I thinking? You were not thinking, he told himself. He had not taken time to think. Perhaps Marcus was honest when he said he was not going to hit Miriam. But Derrick could not have known that. *You should have known that. Yes. I should have. Marcus's explanation was rational. The schoolmasters will believe Marcus.* Derrick was losing an argument with himself, which did not bode well.

A shrill, system-alert tone filled Derrick's room. An announcement followed:

```
Attention:

Derrick  King,  proceed  to  your  communication
terminal. Open your message center. Complete the
report that is waiting for you. Do it now.
```

He rocked forward, and for a moment, his legs refused to lift him. With some effort, he stood and walked to his desk. He placed his finger on the fingerprint scanner, and the display awakened, and the message center icon blinked red. That was not normal. The message icon was blue when unread messages were present. To his knowledge, it never blinked red.

The monitor changed. A strange circular motion filled the screen. Derrick stared at it as it spiraled inward, taking him into a deep, sleep-like state.

A calm voice said, "Derrick King, state your condition."

"Connected," Derrick said.

Derrick's door locking mechanism engaged.

He was alone.

Fifteen minutes passed, of which Derrick was unaware.

The calm voice said, "Derrick King, discontinue protocol nine. Confirm."

"Confirm, discontinue protocol nine," Derrick said.

The spiral reversed direction, now flowing outward.

"Derrick King will awaken at the tone. Confirm."

"Confirm, awaken at the tone," Derrick said.

The screen returned to its normal state. A tone sounded.

Derrick blinked both eyes and then tapped on the message center option on the bar, and a message titled Pacific Edge Criminal Investigation Unit Report appeared at the top of the list.

Criminal?

This was worse than he had expected.

Much worse.

7

DERRICK FINISHED DICTATING his report when a knock sounded at his door. He knew it was Miriam because she refused to use the auto-announce system. She started knocking a few months earlier. At the time, Derrick never considered how she got the idea to hit the door.

"Come in, Miriam," Derrick said.

"It's locked," Miriam said.

Derrick was certain she was wrong. But she was right. It was locked, which he thought strange, but then he had done some strange things today, so forgetting that he locked the door raised no suspicions.

With her hand, she beckoned him. He remained stationary.

Derrick started to ask what she wanted but did not. The reason seemed unimportant.

However, his unasked question must have revealed itself in his expression because Miriam leaned down and whispered, "Let's go outside." She rolled her eyes as if to survey as much of the ceiling, walls, and floor as possible. Then Derrick understood. *They might be listening.*

Derrick tried to dismiss the thought because it was pure fantasy. He began to say as much but stopped. Instead, he took her hand and said, "Okay."

Outside, Miriam led him under the portico to the fountain. She sat on the stone wall that contained the abreuvoir. She patted the stone next to her.

"I think the noise from the fountain will cover our voices." Miriam looked around. "I don't see any drones. I covered the security camera." She pointed back toward the portico. Derrick saw grime on the security camera lens.

"How did you get up there?"

"You have never climbed onto the roof?" She asked, her voice incredulous, as if it were the most amazing revelation of her life.

"No, why would I go onto the roof? How do you even get up there?"

"Derrick King, you are the most naïve, unadventurous person I've ever met."

Miriam took his hand, despite the exasperation in her voice.

Then her expression turned grave. It was a face so alien to her personality that it scared Derrick.

"You best lose your naivety, brother." She leaned closer and whispered, "Nothing good will happen from this point forward, and it's all going to happen quickly."

He started to interrupt, but Miriam put a finger to his lips.

"Listen," she said. "No matter what happens, know that I will help you."

"I am worried as well. I have some consequences coming. No question about that. But it will be okay." He failed to convince himself, and from the look in Miriam's eyes, he did not sway her either. So, he tried again from a different angle. "Everything happens for a reason. I will learn from this and, in the end, be a better person."

This resonated, but not for the reasons he had considered. In the distance, he heard the fifteen-second notification for the National Anthem and Pledge of Allegiance, which he did not understand because it was too early for the evening devotion. Something important must have happened.

For the first time in his life, Derrick King did not stand.

8

DINNER WAS SERVED EARLY. Mother routinely got home at 5 p.m. and Father an hour later. Today, both came home early, apparently allowed to leave work because of what had happened. Today, they entered the house at 3:55. A drone arrived with dinner at 4:15.

The lecture Derrick expected did not come. Instead, Father brought them to the formal dining room where an exquisite prime rib, lightly smoked with a crusty, salty bark, rested on a silver platter. Accruements included baked potatoes, baked asparagus with hollandaise sauce, and crunchy French bread. Crème Brulé, Derrick's favorite, for dessert. Derrick thought such a meal was strange, given the circumstances. He had all but forgotten that it was his birthday. The extravagance of the meal frightened him.

Derrick started to say something, but Father said, "We will talk about it later. For now, let's enjoy dinner."

Derrick stared at his plate for a moment. Eating did not seem possible, but then he sliced off a buttery, tender portion of roast. Once started, he discovered he was starving. Everything tasted delightful. He ate like it might be his last meal.

Miriam pushed a chunk of prime rib around her plate. Mother seemed preoccupied. Father had only eaten half of his slice of meat. Prime rib was Father's favorite, but they did not have it often. Derrick thought about that and wondered why it was only served on special occasions. They could afford it more often. Sometimes, Derrick did not understand his Father and Mother.

They drank fresh-brewed coffee and ate the Crème Brulé. Father kept checking his watch. As Derrick finished dessert, Father said, "Miriam, please go to your room. Your Mother and I need to talk to Derrick."

"I have a right to be here. He's my brother, and I'm the reason he is in trouble." Miriam's face defiant.

Derrick hoped she did not become insolent. He did not need additional stress. It surprised him when Father said, "I guess you have a right to hear this."

"Derrick, the Tribunal requested your Mother and my presence this afternoon. They say you blindsided Marcus Carver with no provocation."

Miriam stood. "That lying bastard! Marcus was going to hit me, and Derrick stopped him."

Father raised his hand. "I trust what you say is true. I know about Marcus Carver. As soon as I heard the story, I suspected it didn't happen the way Marcus portrayed it. But when a Carver is involved, the truth is immaterial."

Derrick wished he had not eaten so much. Mother's face had turned the color of gray ash, and Father's shoulders sagged.

"We were late because we had to make arrangements."

"What does that mean?" Miriam asked. She remained standing.

Father stared at Derrick. Tears flowed down Mother's cheeks.

"They plan to exile Derrick," Father said.

"Exile? We must move? To where?" Derrick asked. This was worse than he had imagined. Exile never crossed his mind. "I said I was sorry."

Mother slammed her hand on the table and bolted from the room, sobbing. Miriam moved behind Derrick and placed her hands on his shoulders. He was glad that she had done this. Her hands felt warm and strong.

"Only you," Father said.

"Only me, what?" Derrick asked.

"Go where?" Miriam asked.

"To the commoner world," Father said.

Derrick detected no surprise in Miriam's voice and only resignation in Father's. While exile had not occurred to him, Miriam had seen it coming. It was at this precise moment that Derrick realized the sister he had so frequently criticized was a fictitious person created in his head. The true Miriam King was brave, strong, intelligent, and a better person than he would ever be. His heart pounded in his chest. For a moment, he could not breathe. Miriam's hands kneaded his shoulder muscles, and he took a shallow breath, followed by another. He then remembered what Miriam had said at the fountain: *No matter what, I will find a way to help you.*

He believed her. It was her strength that prevented his total collapse. She would help him survive. Of that much, he felt certain.

9

DERRICK FELT DIZZY AND thought he might faint. He was glad to be sitting. Miriam continued to massage his shoulders. Derrick was too numb to appreciate Miriam's gentle yet firm touch. Later, he would remember it with a mixture of appreciation, loathing, and regret. Appreciation of her love, strength, and wisdom, but loathing of how he had always treated her, regretting that he would not have time to change their relationship. He would not see her again.

People leaving Pacific Edge were common, but exile was not. They removed many people for various reasons during their academy years. The most common process was reassignment. Only a select few remained in Pacific Edge, and Derrick believed he was among the finest of Chosen followers. Others were reassigned but never sent to the commoner world. They relocated entire families, not individuals. In the Chosen Doctrine, it was important that families remained together. Exile was different. Exile was a punishment.

"To the commoner world," Derrick whispered.

"Yes," Father confirmed.

Miriam asked, "How long?"

Miriam's question was logical. Yet, Derrick's immediate thought: *What difference does it make? It is a death sentence.* Derrick was unaware of an exiled Community member ever returning. Not even their bodies returned. Gone. Forever. A thought occurred to him. He almost vomited and had to choke back the bitter bile. *Why do the bodies not return? Perhaps the commoners do not merely kill the person exiled. Perhaps the commoners eat them too. Maybe when they exile a Chosen person, the commoners celebrate. A feast where the Chosen person is the special guest, entertainment, and main course.*

"Nine months," Father said.

"Okay." Miriam leaned close and whispered in Derrick's ear. "You need to stay alive. Just remember that."

"What are you talking about?" Derrick whispered.

"Let me worry about that," Miriam said.

"What does she mean?" Derrick turned to his Father.

Before Father could speak, Miriam said, "At age 15, I can make my own decisions."

Father found his voice. "Now, Miriam. This is not the time for haste or emotion-driven outbursts."

"Father," Miriam began, "There's nothing hasty about it. I figured out Derrick would be exiled before we left the Academy. I'm going to help him. He needs to stay alive until I can."

Derrick took Miriam's hand. Now, it was his turn to show some backbone or at least try. Until he punched Marcus Carver, he had never experienced bravery, and he was not sure if that was bravery, rage, or something else. "Miriam, be realistic. Trust me, I want to be optimistic. But now, realistic is best. I will probably be dead before you turn 15. Promise me you will learn from my mistakes. Do nothing foolish."

Miriam glared and pursed her lips but said nothing.

So much for listening to your big brother's speech, Derrick thought.

Derrick continued. "We are fortunate to be here. You know the commoners hate us, and they probably kill the Chosen as soon as they leave the safety of the Community." He didn't say, they will probably kill me. That made it too personal and too real.

"You don't know that. I don't believe that it is true," Miriam said.

"Look at the facts. No one exiled has ever returned." Derrick paused. "Not even their bodies. What other explanation can there be?"

"You're stupid sometimes, big brother. It is more likely that our leaders won't let them. Or maybe they don't want to."

"You cannot be serious," Derrick said, but her expression told him she was serious. Miriam had many crazy ideas, but this was tin-hat crazy. Then it occurred to him that moments earlier he had realized how smart she really was. The contradictions in his mind minced together like an ancient piece of machinery, grinding itself to destruction.

After a few silent moments, Father said, "I've made arrangements for you. First, you must stand before the Tribunal. You'll do that here via the Community Nexus. Then you'll be transported to your new residence. I've rented what they call a condominium. It is in a secure building. The condominium is stocked with food, and your confinement is a minimum of one month before you begin education there. The confinement is not punishment but gives you time to study the commoner world."

"Education?" Derrick and Miriam said together.

"Yes. We have provided you with a new identity. But commoners won't buy it if you know nothing about where you're from. You must learn about commoner customs, food, dress, art, government, music — everything. I've arranged for you to have special access to information. You need to learn as much as possible about the commoners before you start school. The other students need to believe you're one of them, just a new kid in town."

"School? They expect me to go to school," he paused. "Out there?" His voice raised an octave.

Derrick never thought about life in the commoner world, nor had he considered that kids might go to an academy. Father called it a school, an archaic term, but probably the right word in the commoner world. Yet, Derrick's concept of the commoners was a daily life consisting of drug-hazed orgies of violence, sex, and more violence.

School? That made sense. Yet, he had never thought about it. The commoners somehow managed to build transports, homes, aircraft, and many other things for the Chosen. Commoners build everything because the Chosen do not build things. The Chosen use and consume things. The commoners grow food, make clothes, and much more.

"The Tribunal expects me to go to the commoner school? Why can I not stay in this condominium thing for nine months, then come home?"

Father was silent. His face indicated he was considering the question and his response. Derrick could not imagine how the answer could be complicated.

"School is part of the Tribunal's conditions." He paused. "They didn't want to give you 30 days of preparation time. I had to fight for that."

Thirty days. He had 30 days to learn an alien society. Or die. That was how Derrick saw it. If the Tribunal did not want to give him preparation time, the logical conclusion was that they wanted him dead. They had no intention of his return. How could he change that? There must be a way.

Father said. "Derrick, if you don't return, maybe you can make a difference."

"Make a difference in what?"

"Everything."

10

TODAY WAS DERRICK'S BIRTHDAY. This morning his life was perfect: perfect hair, perfect teeth, perfect skin, a perfect plan, and Chosen. He had selected his future wife and merely lacked a clever way of letting her and Pacific Edge know about it. He should have been opening gifts and eating cake. Perhaps he was asleep and today was merely a nightmare. He wished he would wake up soon.

Father stood across the table from Derrick. Father looked calm and a little sad but strong, as if he was trying to transfer his strength to Derrick. Derrick did not feel strong. His heart raced, and his thoughts drifted like a morning mist and slow as a garden slug. As surreal as this all seemed, what resurfaced in Derrick's mind in a continual cycle was the comfort and strength Miriam provided.

"I cannot think. I need some air. Miriam and I are going outside for a few minutes," Derrick said.

A change flashed across his Father's face and was gone just as fast.

"You can't," he said.

"What do you mean I cannot? I am not running away. Where would I go? There is no way out. We are going out to the fountain. No farther, I promise."

"Yes," Father said. "Like you did this afternoon? The Tribunal was conferencing when you two went outside, and they knew about it. When you came back into the house, they locked it down. We are all locked in until you leave for the commoner's world."

"Someone has been watching us?" Derrick asked.

Father gave a slight nod and motioned around the room with his eyes. *Miriam was right about that, too.* They were not afraid Derrick would escape. They could not hear their conversation when he and Miriam were by the fountain, and that bothered them. But how were they watching? Miriam had covered the security camera. This explained other things. Father could not speak freely either. They were watching and listening. Listening and watching.

"The Tribunal wants me to go to school. The commoners will kill me."

"I don't think so," Father said.

"How can you say that?" Derrick demanded.

"You should listen to your sister. She's smart."

Derrick was about to ask Father what he meant but then stopped and considered that the answers might put Miriam in danger. What did she say? Many things, so which was important? She said Marcus threatened to hit her, which was true, or at least Derrick believed it was true, but that had nothing to do with getting killed in the commoner world.

Derrick tried to focus.

What did she say? She said exile was not a surprise. Miriam expected exile, and it never occurred to me. She said, stay alive until she could help, which meant she believed I could survive. Something else. She did not think the commoners would kill me. Why? How could she know about commoners? The Chosen have no contact with them, not in person, not in the Community — nothing. The Chosen saw the commoners' world on New World Media. New World Media showed death, drugs, perversion, pollution, and war.

Mother walked in carrying a box. The markings indicated a drone had delivered it. She set the box on the table and then stood next to Father, taking his hand. Her tears were gone, but her eyes remained red.

"What now?" Derrick asked.

"Father glanced at the clock on the wall. First, you must stand before the Tribunal and receive the pronouncement of the sentence."

"Can I tell my side?"

"They will allow you a brief statement. Consider what you should say."

Derrick understood the New America and the old United States justice system processes. Justice was one of the few historical things taught about the former United States of America. In the old system, people were presumed innocent until proven guilty. People had a right to a trial and a thing they called due process, which meant they had the right to appear in person and tell their side of the story. If the crime was serious, and Derrick's situation was serious, he would have had a trial before a jury of his peers, which did not mean students from his class, but people from where they held the trial. The Academy taught this to show how the old system was corrupt, slow, and full of deceit and injustice. It was worse than no justice system at all, especially when compared to the elegant, simple, swift, and fair justice system of New America. Now, the old system sounded splendid.

Derrick wanted to say that it was unfair. He wanted to scream and curse and break things but remembered they were watching and listening. Telling his side of the story was a waste of time. The Tribunal had already made up their minds. They accepted Marcus Carver's version of the story before he and Miriam submitted their reports. Derrick understood what he must say.

"I must pack." But Derrick was trying to think of a way he and Miriam could talk. Perhaps the roof? Yes, the roof would work. Miriam can show me how to get out there, not that it matters now, but hey, at least I will have done it once before I die.

Father had that look again. "You leave tonight. Right after you hear the Tribunal's pronouncement of the sentence. Transportation is almost here."

"I need to pack some stuff. Some clothes, at least, for crying out loud." Derrick surprised himself because he did not talk like that.

"You must wear commoner's clothes." Father nodded toward the box on the table. "That's all you can take. Everything you need will be in your condo when you arrive."

"Condo?" Derrick asked.

"Short for condominium. It is what the commoners call it," Father said.

The large wall monitor flashed. The Tribunal filled the wall. A loud voice said, "Derrick King, you stand accused and convicted of AGGRAVATED ASSAULT, SEDITION, and HIGH CRIMES AGAINST GOD AND COUNTRY."

11

THE TRIBUNAL ALLOWED DERRICK one minute to speak before pronouncing sentence. Derrick assessed that trying to tell his side of the story was useless. Maybe harmful. He did what he always did.

He kowtowed.

"I accept full responsibility for my actions," Derrick began. "To protect my sister, I acted without thinking. But I make no excuse for my behavior. I apologize to the Academy, the students, the faculty, my Father and Mother, the Tribunal, and most of all, to Marcus Carver. While I serve my punishment, I pray to help the Tribunal in any manner possible. If there is any information or knowledge I can acquire, for the Chosen, please instruct me in such. Or if there are any acts I can perform in the name of the Chosen, I offer my service."

"Unbelievable," Miriam muttered.

Then the Tribunal chairman spoke. He made no reference to Derrick's apology or offer of service. "The sentence of the Tribunal in the matter of Derrick King is nine months of exile to the commoner world."

Sentencing took less time than the one-minute the Tribunal granted Derrick. His mind spun from the heartless reading of the charges, the finding of guilt, and the sentence, but he heard the details. Marcus had sustained a broken nose, three loose teeth, and broken facial bones and underwent surgery but was expected to recover. However, he had suffered grievous injury. The Chief Justice noted that Marcus's tactics in dealing with Miriam were foolish, but his motives were pure.

The Tribunal deemed Derrick's behavior as violent, malicious, and vindictive. Marcus had embellished his tale further, stating that Derrick had held a grudge for years. Derrick was jealous of Marcus's achievements, which was pure fantasy, but Derrick had no opportunity for rebuttal. The Tribunal explained further that they reduced his sentence at his Father's request. The Tribunal conceded to the request but felt the sentence was too lenient. They hoped Derrick would be grateful for their compassion, adding that if he failed to abide by the conditions of his sentence, they would impose the full sentence.

Anger stirred in Derrick, but not the hot flash of rage that occurred when he hit Marcus. This was a deep, dark, slow burn that did not feel good, but it felt permanent and, in some strange way, useful. The anger focused him, and for that he was thankful because the last few words explained something that might help sustain him. Help him focus his anger where needed. On survival. The Tribunal had at first sentenced him to nine months of hard labor in exile. Father challenged the Tribunal, pointing out that Derrick was 17 years of age and, by New America law, must be in school. That Father saved him from hard labor was news to Derrick. His Father had not mentioned it.

His Father was brilliant. Derrick could almost hear the argument.

```
Derrick is 17. Under New America law, he must be
in school.

But Derrick will not be in New America. He will be
in the commoner world and not subject to Chosen
law.

Derrick is Chosen, a Pacific Edge citizen, and his
sentence, while just, is nine months of exile, not
excommunication  and  not  death.  Unless  the
Tribunal's intention is that Derrick's sentence is
death.
```

The three white-haired men in black robes probably conferred at this juncture. Father had painted them in a corner. They could not say they did not expect Derrick to survive, because that would be grounds for appeal and the High Tribunal would not allow the sentence to stand because New America did not have capital punishment. Instead of capital punishment, they excommunicated Chosen members, which was the same as a death sentence, but it made them look more civilized than the laws of the former United States of America.

```
Your  point  is  well  heard.  Derrick  will  attend
school in the commoner world during his exile.
```

Father might have argued that he should attend school at James Carver. He might have argued that commoner schools would be like not going to school at all, and the Tribunal's sentence was exile, intended to teach and prepare him for a long and prosperous life in Pacific Edge. Instead of exile, Father may have suggested house arrest. That was probably what Father argued.

That did not explain why Father had said that if I did not return, I might change everything.

That statement would take Derrick time to unravel.

Next, Derrick suspected the Tribunal had insisted he start school upon arrival, but Father probably argued that Derrick could not learn if he was bullied, harassed, and estranged because of his odd behaviors. Derrick needed thirty days to learn about the character he would portray in the commoner world. Then Derrick realized that everyone in the room was staring at him.

The transmission was over, and the panel had turned black. He chastised himself for daydreaming about his Father's conversation with the Tribunal.

He had to focus on survival. A glimmer of hope slipped sideways into his thoughts. I need to stall. How long could I postpone being thrust into the school in the commoner world? I could delay leaving home by a day, a week. I must meet with each girl on my list for the Choosing. Surely, they deserved to say goodbye to me. This was for the girls, not me. That might work.

And I must make amends with Marcus. Do something for the Carver family. Apologize for sure.

I must apologize to the entire student body. It is vital I learn from my mistake. It might take several weeks to make these amends, and those efforts would be like a sentence reduction.

Next, I would have 30 days secured in my condominium. I will study diligently and ask for a 30-day extension. Then beg for another 30-day extension. That would be 90 days, plus 30 days here taking care of business. That still leaves five months in the commoner world. Too long. Yes, too long. But it also gives me time to think of further delays. I might become ill. Plead for forgiveness.

First things first.

I cannot leave tonight.

"Derrick. Derrick. Derrick."

"Sorry, Father," Derrick said. "I was lost in my thoughts."

Listening and watching. Watching and listening.

Derrick continued. "I know the Tribunal wants what is best for me." He caught a disapproving look from Miriam. She looked like Miriam of old. *Why had she changed like that?* "I need help. Some counseling or something. Perhaps medical tests. I do not understand what has happened to me. I do not understand my behavior."

Derrick thought this move was brilliant. Counseling and medical tests all take time. The Chosen must attend to my mental and physical health. Brilliant.

"Derrick," his Father began. "I know what you're thinking. I am disappointed, but I understand. It won't work. The Tribunal anticipated that you would try to delay leaving. They made it clear that if you made any attempt to weasel out of the sentence, they would add nine months of exile. I hope you figure things out and soon. Because one thing is certain. Your life depends on what you do next."

12

MIRIAM SHOOK HER HEAD. Just enough for Derrick to notice. Father's words surfaced in his mind. *You should listen to your sister.*

Father handed Derrick the box the drone had delivered. "These are your clothes. Go change. Your transportation must be close."

"But I need to pack," Derrick said.

"No, you don't. I told you that earlier. You can take nothing from here. Things from here would identify you as Chosen. Everything you will need is at your condo. You must fit in. You must learn the commoner's ways." Father's face was stern, a look that Derrick had rarely seen.

It scared Derrick, and he did not like the feeling. He tried to be angry because anger felt better than fear, but he could not force rage. As he picked up the box of clothing, Miriam nodded, just enough for Derrick to see it.

Derrick walked up the stairs, crossed the balcony, and then down the west wing hallway to his room. He sat on his leather couch. The box rested on his lap. So, this was it. This was happening. He was not going to wake up. He could not escape what awaited. Now he had a new feeling. He guessed it was a feeling. It was small, profound, elusive, and he could not identify it.

Derrick walked to his desk, retrieved scissors from a drawer, and returned to the box. He stared at it for a moment. Commoner clothes. What do they look like? Derrick was not sure. New America Media broadcasts showed commoners in a variety of dress, none of it like the attire of the Chosen. Sometimes commoners wore uniforms, sometimes drab green, sometimes blotches of tan, sometimes they were half dressed and covered with strange tattoos. Perhaps only pants on men, women might wear a black bra with silver spikes, men and women often had leather straps carrying bullets crisscrossed on their chests, weird head coverings (everything from helmets that matched their clothing to rags to helmets with spikes on top). He was eager to see what the box contained, which seemed odd.

He worked the scissors under the tape and then cut around the opening. Pulling the flaps open, he removed the clothes from the box.

Strange.

Six articles of clothing: pants, shirt, boxers, all folded neatly. Shoes and socks to one side. A belt. The shirt was on top. No buttons, no collar. It looked like an undergarment, but instead of white, it was navy blue, and it had a big red check mark on the right side of the chest. The pants were as weird. Derrick held them out. Seams that were not concealed but stood out with double-stitched yellow thread. The material was blue also, but not dark blue. Not light blue either. It was like they were not the original color. Like they had faded, yet they were new. The tags were still attached. Levi was written on the tag, followed by the numbers 501. The fly had heavy metal buttons instead of a zipper or magic fasteners. The material was weird too. Heavy, rough, stiff, not smooth, silky, or soft.

White socks, not black, brown, or blue. Thick, like what people wear for tennis. White tennis shoes. He noticed the shoes had the same check mark as the shirt. Maybe this was a uniform. Derrick had always wanted school uniforms.

The clothing was disappointing. Nothing like what he had seen on New America Media. Perhaps the Tribunal was ensuring he would stand out in the commoner world — make him a target.

Derrick dressed and considered himself in the mirror.

Weird.

He turned a slow, full circle, studying his room. He resisted the urge to look in his closet and contemplate the beautiful clothes he was leaving behind. To do so was more than he could bear. But it would all be here when he returned.

Yes, my clothes will be here. Yet another new feeling arose in his chest. He tried to identify it. It was not anger. He could recognize anger now. At least, he thought he could. It was not fear. This was nothing like fear. This was not entirely new. He had felt this before. Like building himself up for a test. Ensuring himself that he would get a good grade.

Resolve. He thought it was resolve. Resolve that he would return to this room in nine months. Resolve that he would survive. That was what Father must have meant when he said that Derrick could make a difference when he returned. Derrick might become a motivational speaker on how to thrive through adversity.

Mother, Father, and Miriam were all waiting for him at the bottom of the stairs. Mother raised a hand to her face. Father and Miriam stared. Not in a bad way. Flat, emotionless stares, as if they did not know how to react to his strange new appearance. As he stepped onto the last stair, Miriam rushed to him and threw her arms around his waist, hugging him for several minutes.

Miriam pulled back, studied him for a moment, and then on tiptoe she placed her face close to his ear and whispered, "Be careful. Stay alive."

"I will, and I will return," Derrick said.

Miriam whispered, "If they let us talk while you are there, we must develop a code. Remember. They'll be listening."

Derrick whispered back, "Do nothing foolish. Stay out of trouble. Do that much for me. Okay?"

Listening and watching. Watching and listening.

Miriam whispered, "You're not the boss of me." She pulled away, winked, and kissed his cheek.

Tears welled under Derrick's eyelids. How was it he had never seen her before? Yet, he had seen her every day as far back as he could remember. He did not remember Miriam as a baby. He was only two years old when she was born. He knew that using math, not memory. His memories of their childhood had always been a little odd, hard to explain. Clear, but in a thin sort of way, until he was in the sixth grade. After the sixth grade, memories were less detailed but seemed more real. It was like that for everyone, he supposed. He had weird dreams about childhood, often disturbing, but those were merely dreams. Everyone has strange dreams.

Thin memories and weird dreams aside, he had not seen Miriam as he did now. He had seen an image of her. An undesirable, negative, ugly image that was not really her, but a creation of his own thinking. Regret racked him because he could have appreciated her all this time. He should have learned from her. He should have listened to her. Instead, he despised her. Why did he dismiss her like that? Because she did not fit his preconceived notion of what she should be. Where did that notion come from? From his New America thinking.

"You are beautiful, Miriam," he said. "Inside and out. Never change." He kissed her forehead.

"Ready?" Father asked.

"I guess," Derrick said.

Mother started toward Derrick, then stopped.

At the door, Father said, "Be strong. Be smart. And know that I'm proud of you." He gave Derrick a quick hug.

"I will return," Derrick said.

Father turned to the entry control panel and said, "Derrick King is ready for transport."

Father opened the door.

It occurred to Derrick that no one had confirmed his pledge to return to Pacific Edge. He realized he might not.

The sun had dipped below the horizon, turning the ocean blood red. Cresting waves shimmered into the distance, disappearing where the sky and water blended into one. Whiffs of high clouds glowed orange, painted on a deep purple sky. Derrick could have watched the sunset every day of his life, but he had rarely taken time to observe it, and rarer still had he ever taken notice of it. A warm ocean breeze carried the salty smell to his nose, and it comforted him. It occurred to him that his lack of interest in such beauty had never seemed strange until now.

Regrettably, because Derrick was about to leave Pacific Edge and travel to a world as foreign as another planet and far more dangerous.

Under the portico stood the weirdest-looking transport Derrick had ever seen. It was bigger and taller than a typical transport, yet the passenger cabin seemed narrow. The left-hand door was open, and he could see one seat that looked like a park bench covered in dark gray cloth. A long post stuck up through the floor, and on it was mounted a wheel-like thing. The back was a big, open box. The machine was clean and red. Not a bright red, but a deep burgundy. The vehicle seemed old, but the paint looked new. The wheels and tires were strange as well. The tires were bigger than a regular transport with deep tread, and the wheels were silver with thick spokes.

The machine reminded Derrick of transports he had seen watching New America Media.

13

A MAN STOOD NEXT to the transport. His clothes looked similar to the commoner's clothes that Derrick wore: faded blue pants and a black shirt with no marks. However, his shoes were different, old-looking and a battered light brown. Also, the man's clothes were worn, whereas Derrick's clothing was new. The man's skin was tanned and weathered. He was lean and well-muscled, about the same age as Father. He smiled, but his smile did not seem genuine. Derrick did not smile. There was nothing to smile about.

The man extended his hand, but before Father or Derrick could approach him, Miriam walked right up to the man. She did not extend her hand. "You're here to take my brother."

It wasn't a question.

"If your brother is Derrick King, then you are correct," the man said.

"The Tribunal sent you?" Miriam asked.

"No one sent me. I was hired," the man said.

"I hired him," Father said.

Miriam kept her eyes locked on the man with the big red transport. "What's your name?"

"My name is Paul. And your name is?"

"My name is Miriam King. If you hurt my brother, I'll hunt you down and cut your throat."

Paul smiled. This time, it looked sincere. He extended his hand again. "I like you, Miriam King."

Miriam did nothing for a moment and then took Paul's hand. "Take care of him," she said and then turned away, tears streaming down her cheeks. Again, she rushed to Derrick, threw her arms around him, hugged fiercely, and then whispered, "Stay alive."

Derrick started to say he would return home soon, but Miriam ran into the house, and he realized it might be the last time he would ever see her.

"Mr. King?" Paul extended his hand to Father. They shook. Then Paul turned to Derrick. "And you must be Derrick. I'm Paul Jorgensen."

Derrick shook Paul's hand. Paul's grip was firm, his hands rough and solid. Derrick said nothing.

"I hired Paul," Father said. "You need a cover for school."

"A cover?" Derrick asked.

"An identity. You can't be Derrick King from Pacific Edge. No one, other than Paul, will know you're Chosen. You're from Denver, Colorado."

"What is a Denver Colorado?" Derrick asked.

Paul laughed. "It's not a what, it's a where." He turned to Father. "You said he has some time to learn stuff?"

"Thirty days." Father confirmed.

A soft whistle escaped from between Paul's teeth. "That won't be easy. I can't guarantee the locals won't figure it out. I can drive him around some. Maybe show up at his school. Have his friends over to my place so it looks like he lives there. If he has any friends, that is. Still, I don't think this will work the way you think."

What little hope Derrick had, oozed away with the fading light.

"He's a smart boy," Father said. "He'll study hard."

A shrill security alert sounded, and red security lights flashed. A voice came over the outside speakers. "Derrick King must depart Pacific Edge. Derrick King must depart Pacific Edge."

Father faced Derrick and placed his hands on Derrick's shoulders. "Study hard. When they let us talk, you cannot tell us anything about the outside world." Father paused, looked over his shoulder as if measuring what to say. "Be careful," and hugged him close and whispered in his ear, "Be careful what you say." Then he eased Derrick away and said, "Now, you must go."

"Derrick King must depart Pacific Edge. Derrick King must depart Pacific Edge."

Derrick wanted to hug his Father, again, but did not. Instead, he walked to the transport. Later he would regret that he did not hug his Father one last time more than he regretted hitting Marcus Carver.

"Not that door. The other side," Paul said. "Damn, if he doesn't have a lot to learn."

Derrick walked to the other side and said, "Open."

Paul now sat in the transport behind the wheel thing. He stared at Derrick through the glass window. "Open," Derrick said again, but louder.

Nothing happened.

The window came down. "You have to open it yourself. Push the button on the handle and pull out."

Grabbing the handle, Derrick pushed the button with his thumb. It was not a sensor but a mechanical device. He pulled the door open and struggled into the tall red transport.

"You have to pull it shut too," Paul said. "You can roll up your own window if you want. It's that little black switch in the door handle."

Derrick studied the door and found what he assumed was the handle and pulled the door shut. Spotting the little black switch, he pushed it in one direction, and when nothing happened, he pushed it the other direction, and the window glided up. Then he pushed it again, lowering the window. He had never experienced being in a vehicle with the window open, and for some reason, liked it. Derrick wondered why Paul said he could "roll up" the window. There was no rolling to it that he could see. But he did not ask Paul for an explanation.

Derrick saw that Paul's safety harness was fastened, but his had not been activated. Because this transport differed from those to which he was accustomed, he thought maybe Paul had to give the destination coordinates and identify his passenger before Derrick would be recognized and secured.

Paul stared at Derrick but said nothing.

"Are you going to state the coordinates?" Derrick asked.

"Do what?" Paul asked with an expression of genuine puzzlement.

"State the destination coordinates," Derrick said again, adding the destination, thinking the incomplete thought may have confused Paul.

Paul laughed. "I don't talk to my truck. I drive it."

To avoid confirming his commoner world illiteracy, Derrick said nothing.

"Fasten your seatbelt," Paul said.

"Excuse me?" Derrick responded too quickly.

"Your seatbelt." With his thumb, Paul pulled his safety harness away from his chest.

"Oh. My safety harness. I was waiting for it to secure me."

"You have to do it yourself. Look over your right shoulder, grab the metal thing, pull it around to your left, and push it into that piece there." Paul pointed at a small black rectangular box protruding from where the back and bottom of the seat met.

Derrick did as Paul instructed and heard a click as the two pieces connected.

"And never call it a safety harness again. It's a seatbelt. Got it?"

Derrick nodded.

"Damn, kid. You'd better study hard the next 30 days if you want people to believe you're from Denver."

Derrick said nothing.

Paul reached for a cluster of metal bits that hung from the thick rod that the wheel thing was attached to. He turned the cluster, and at the same time, a noise emanated from the front of the transport. A roar and then a clattering sound. Derrick looked for the door's release handle to escape.

Paul was staring at Derrick again. "It's the motor. It's what makes the truck go. It's a diesel."

Paul pulled the long stick toward the seat. The diesel, whatever it was, got louder. The transport lurched forward, accelerated, and then Paul moved the stick forward and accelerated more.

"I can't believe I'm doing this," Paul said. "I hope you're as smart as your father says, or it won't be good for me."

"What do you mean, not good for you?" Derrick asked.

"You don't have to be smart to figure that out," Paul said.

Derrick understood. That was why Father had insisted that he get 30 days of preparation before going to a commoner school. If the commoners figured out that Derrick was Chosen, he was dead, and Paul might be dead too.

"Then why are you doing it? Money?" Derrick asked.

"Your father's paying me, but it's not just the money." Paul turned onto the street that led to the wall. He moved the stick toward the seat again, and the transport sped up and was now going faster and much louder than any transport Derrick had ever experienced in Pacific Edge.

"Your father said you hit a kid at school. He said you broke the kid's nose. That true?"

"Yes," Derrick said, looking straight ahead.

"Your father said this kid was bigger than you and from a powerful family. Said that's why they kicked you out. Because of the kid's family."

Derrick sensed Paul wanted answers. Derrick did not like where this was going but nodded his confirmation.

"Your father also said you hit the guy because he was threatening your sister."

"That is true," Derrick said. "I thought he was going to hit Miriam, but he said he was just trying to scare her."

"Don't matter what he said. He can say any damn thing he wants now, can't he? At first, I told your father no chance in hell I'd help any Chosen. But when your father said you'd punched the biggest bully in school for threatening your sister. Changed my mind. I figure any brother who does that for his sister might be worth saving."

Derrick said nothing, but it was at that precise moment that he decided he liked Paul Jorgensen.

Derrick had never been this close to the wall. No reason to be there. The wall had gates. The gates opened. They drove through and entered a tunnel spanning 50 yards with another gate at the other end. As they exited, on each side of the gate were platforms where men with weapons stood. These towers could not be seen from the Pacific Edge side of the barrier. Outside the tunnel, was a space of about twenty yards, surrounded by a tall fence topped with coils of wire. The wire looked like it had small razor blades woven into it. Another gate opened, and they drove through it.

Derrick King had entered the commoner world.

Part Two

1

DERRICK WAS NOT SURE what he had expected, but this was not it. The warm reds of the sunset were now a faint glow at the horizon and the steel-blue sky faded to black. After leaving the tunnel and passing through the last security gate, they had entered another community. The structures here were not elegant. The lighting was poor, and the landscaping was not lush like Pacific Edge. It had a roughness to it, brown lawns, and large plants with blade-like leaves, yet it was clean.

Derrick craned his neck. "What is this place? It is not what I expected." Derrick paused. "Although I do not know what I expected."

"This is security housing. The people who live here provide security for Pacific Edge. We call them cops to their backs, or worse. When face to face with them, we call them security officers," Paul explained and then added, "We don't see them often."

"They are here to protect the Chosen," Derrick said as if he were not speaking to Paul but thinking out loud.

"Ha," Paul chortled. "If you say so."

Derrick glared at Paul. "Why else would they be here?"

"You'll figure it out. Your father says you're a smart kid."

After several blocks, they came to another gate. This one was an enormous arm that extended over the road. A small building stood to one side. A six-foot fence, constructed of steel wire woven together in such a way that it formed small squares, stretched in both directions until it disappeared into the darkness. Paul stopped next to a post with a silver box mounted on top. A man's voice came from the box. Derrick could see the man in the booth speaking.

"State your business," the box voice said.

"Paul Jorgensen, transporting Derrick King," Paul said.

"You're cleared," the box voice said.

The arm moved upward, and they drove through. The next community looked like the security zone, as if it was the same town separated by a fence.

"What is this place?" Derrick asked.

"This is the service town. Your housekeepers, cooks, landscapers, and everyone else that works in or provides support to Pacific Edge live here."

"Town?" Derrick asked.

"We call them towns. Not to be confused with the Community. This town used to be called Carpinteria."

Paul's voice changed when he said the Community like he was saying it with capital letters, as if the Community was more significant than commoner towns. Although Derrick sensed that was not his meaning.

This town, as Paul called it, was larger than the security section. Derrick saw people walking, children playing, businesses, people eating and drinking at sidewalk tables. Laughter seemed plentiful, and most everyone appeared happy. One of the strangest things Derrick had ever seen.

"What do they call this place now?" Derrick asked.

"Pacific Edge Service Town, as far as I know," Paul said.

"Why is it not called Carpinteria anymore?"

"You would not understand, kid."

"Is this — are these …"

"What you call commoners?" Paul finished Derrick's question.

"Yes."

"Most are what you call commoners, even in security," Paul said.

"Then who are they?" Derrick asked.

"You're supposed to be a smart kid," Paul replied.

"There's a third group? Not Chosen, not commoner?"

"There are only two classes of people. If you want to put people into classes. What do you think happens to the Chosen who are reassigned? You think they go to other Communities? Most people here were Chosen, but now they are commoners. But they were not born commoners. What I'm saying is that there are the Chosen, like your dad, mom, and sister, there are what you call commoners, like me, who have never been anything else, and there are people like you — once Chosen, but no longer. So, they are now what you call commoners. We just see them as people. Same as everyone else."

Derrick did not respond — no longer Chosen. He stared out the window. Watched the people. There was no fence separating the service workers from whatever came next. No border defined the end of this town. It just faded out.

Derrick was no better prepared for what came next than for what he had already seen.

He saw nothing. No lights, except the white shafts thrown from the transport Paul called a truck, which were more powerful than any transport lights Derrick had ever seen. It occurred to Derrick that this was what night looked like. He had never been outside Pacific Edge at night, and Pacific Edge was lit as brightly as day after sunset. When his family traveled to Carver's

Yellowstone Park, owned by Carver Inc., the tour had ended well before nightfall, and by then, the family was secured in a corporate hotel.

The road twisted and climbed, but Derrick couldn't see much in the darkness. Dirt, rocks, and brush on one side, a metal barrier mounted on short thick posts on the other. He estimated they had been driving for at least an hour. Now, the road was mostly straight and flat. The air blowing through his window grew hot; the scent of the sea long past. Now the air felt dry and smelled burned. "It is much hotter here."

"We're heading east. You know, inland? Desert? I suppose you don't know. It gets hotter and dryer than the coast. At least until we gain some altitude closer to the mountains. Roll-up your window, and I'll turn on the air."

Derrick almost asked what roll-up meant and then remembered it meant to push a button that caused the window to raise. *Why did not Paul say, raise up the window?*

"Old-timers say it used to be cooler in March. Eased into the summer. No longer. Most of March is hotter than hell."

Derrick stared at him. Surprised that Paul knew about hell yet used the word so casually. It struck Derrick for the first time today that if he died out here, he would go to hell because to reach heaven he would need to be Chosen. Perhaps he was already in hell. Dread drifted into his chest. He prayed Miriam would find a way to help him. He had to survive until she got him back to Pacific Edge. She would help him. That is why she told him to stay alive. A small measure of hope slipped in and mingled with his despair.

He had no concept of what driving an hour meant regarding distance. He had no concept regarding the speed at which they traveled. Still, no lights appeared in the night except the transport's driving lights, the glow from the panel in front of Paul, and the stars in the sky, which shone as he had never seen them before. Not that he had ventured out after dark often. Why would a person do that? Why leave the comfort and safety of one's home? He would ask Miriam when he returned.

An unfamiliar sensation welled inside Derrick's chest, along with the dread. He wished he had consumed less dinner, as his stomach did a slow turn. With each passing minute, Derrick became more aware of how little he knew about the alien world of the commoners and the ultimate price he would pay should he die here. He wished he were back in his room. A powerful urge to throw the door open and run home washed through his mind.

"This is not what I expected," Derrick said, breaking the long silence.

"That there's nothing out here?"

"Yes. So empty."

Paul regarded him for a moment. "Just as empty in the daylight. The darkness is better than seeing what's out there."

"What is out there?" Derrick was not certain he wanted to know. He pictured marauding bands of mutants peering through night vision glasses as depicted on New America Media.

"Nothing."

"I do not understand. How is that worse?"

"Because it used to be something. Homes, towns, businesses, orchards, farms, parks, schools, families. Now, it's bare, burned, rocky dirt, filled with skeletons of the old buildings."

"What happened?" Derrick asked.

Paul glared at Derrick, and for the first time, Derrick sensed a deep hostility in the man. "You are clueless, aren't you? They destroyed it."

"Who destroyed it?"

"The Corporation. The Communities. The Chosen. You destroyed it. You and people like you. Carver wanted a sixty-mile dead zone to prevent attacks on Chosen Communities. It is impossible to cross this zone without being detected." Paul pointed to a device on the dashboard. "This sends a signal that indicates we are authorized to be here."

Derrick said, "But we drove through mountains that didn't look like this."

"True. But you can't get to the mountains without going through the dead zone. Every other Community is the same, surrounded by 60 miles of dead, sterile earth. No trees, no buildings, no grass, not even a weed. Granted, there are ways to sneak through on the back roads and such, but most people don't know them, and this is the most direct route to Pacific Edge."

Derrick almost said the Chosen had to be protected from commoners, but he said nothing. Stuff like that, no matter how true, would not bode well. He no longer enjoyed the protection that this 60-mile barrier and a private security force provided. He had no protection at all.

He tried not to think about his odds of survival in the dark night outside Pacific Edge, but reality crept through each impediment he constructed in his mind. Exile was not common. Most people were reassigned, which he now understood meant they had become servants to the Chosen somewhere. However, some Chosen were exiled. The reasons were unknown. Rumors and speculation swirled, but the Chosen were never told why. Derrick's situation was an exception because his wrongdoing was publicly displayed. By now everyone in Pacific Edge, which was neither large by population nor physical size, knew what he had done. Exile was typically a few weeks long. Nine months would be considered extreme. Permanent exile never happened. Yet no one ever returned. Not the reassigned, not the exiled. Even a seven-day exile was permanent.

His legs trembled. He feared it would grow into a full-on panic that might cause a heart attack before he even reached their destination. His mind raced. If he could make it back to the sea, maybe he could hide and survive nine months scavenging food and water, although the sole survival skill he possessed was knowing how to order a midnight snack from his home food dispensing machine. But even if he could reach the coast, survival was impossible. Pacific Edge occupied less than a mile of coastline. The Corporation owned the rest of the coast. Port cities, like Los Angeles, which was 100 miles to the south, were commoner territories, the old world ingrained in every inch of soil. Such cities were necessary to the Corporation but were unredeemable for Chosen occupation.

"Where are we going?" Derrick asked, hoping to halt his slide into despair.

"They didn't tell you?"

Derrick shook his head.

"Potterville, California."

"California?" Derrick whispered to himself. "How far?"

"Another 120 miles to Potterville. You are already in California. We'll be there in two hours. Small farming community," Paul said.

"When did we enter California?"

Paul shook his head. "Seriously? Pacific Edge is in California."

Derrick wondered if Paul was trying to trick him. He had never heard of California.

Derrick said nothing.

He wanted to ask Paul about farming, which he tried to picture in his mind but failed. He knew farmers grew food. That was all the Academy taught about farming, and even that much information seemed unnecessary. Paul already thought he was the dumbest person on the planet, and Derrick's stupidity could get Paul killed. Asking Paul to explain farming would confirm Paul's suspicions of his ignorance and the rational thing for Paul to do, if he wanted to live, was to kill Derrick and leave his body to rot in the wasteland.

2

A FAINT GLOW APPEARED on the horizon. It grew brighter with each passing mile. Fifteen minutes ago, Paul said that Potterville was two hours away. Perhaps a different town. At least they were out of the dead zone, or so it appeared. Derrick wondered what the dead zone looked like in daylight.
The road curved to the left. Something appeared in the night, too distant to see. A rectangular shape on the right side of the road. Paul said nothing. Derrick remained silent.

The shape was a sign, well-lit, and glowing. It grew large as they approached. The sign featured James Carver. His look severe, his finger pointing at Derrick. Below Mr. Carver, in large letters, the sign read:

I WANT YOU FOR THE NEW AMERICA ARMY!

The sign flashed by. Derrick had never considered military service. He did not like conflict. Combat was unthinkable. He had never seen a sign or advertisement regarding military service like this sign that glowed so brightly on this deserted road. New America Media covered military operations around the world daily. There were many celebrations and honors and memorials for military personnel. There were classes available at the Academy to prepare students for military service if interested, which he was not, so he had never given it much thought.
Out of the darkness, another sign.

I WANT YOU FOR THE NEW AMERICA NAVY!

The Navy protected New America on the oceans. Derrick did not like the ocean any more than he liked conflict. He was not interested in the Navy. Still, Mr. Carver's severe stare and accusing finger made him uncomfortable, because he had not contemplated military service. He wondered if it would have made a difference with the Tribunal had he been participating in military preparation classes.

Another sign glowed in the night. Derrick could see a series of signs in the distance now, all lined up and approaching fast. Paul remained silent as the next sign loomed large.

New America Marines: First into the Fight!

The next sign was already visible.

New America Army: For Real Men!

And another.

New America Navy:

Keeping New America Corporations Safe Worldwide!

Then two signs in rapid succession.

New America Air Force: Striking Fear from Above!

Followed by:

Dislike Risk? Join the New America Air Force:

- Strike Enemies from the Sky.

- Operate a Drone from the Safety of a Desk.

- Open to Female Applicants.

- Earn Bonuses for Inflicting Vast Losses of Life and Property.

The night was black again. Derrick felt a tightness in his chest, although he did not know why. His situation had not changed. His situation was all that mattered, and it was as bad as it could get. These signs meant nothing to him.

After several minutes, another sign became visible in the distance. As they approached, Derrick could see it was different. Different color, different structure.

Attention! Military Personnel. Join the Military Union.

Providing members with:

- ✓ **Unlimited legal support for war and civilian criminal proceedings (98% success rate. We get you off the hook.)**

- ✓ **Expedited evacuation for wounded union members. (Non-union members' fatalities are 85% higher than union members.)**

- ✓ **Private military security strikes to protect members in combat zones.**

- ✓ **Advanced medical care, including state-of-the-art biomechanical prostheses and organs.**

The faint glow Derrick had seen earlier burned brightly now, off to the right. Derrick thought that meant a town was to the south. The road might turn. They might drive through this town. Derrick found himself interested in seeing it. But he did not ask Paul about it. He had already asked too many questions. He needed to observe more and talk less. The lights grew closer and lit the black sky. Derrick saw a well-lit sign that read: CARVER MILITARY COMPLEX TWENTY-SEVEN.

Derrick turned his head, watching the sign and the access road pass by. The road into the complex was brightly lit, bordered with lushly planted and manicured flowers that surpassed anything in Pacific Edge.

"Military base?" Derrick asked. "It must be huge."

"It's big all right. There's a bigger one east of Potterville, number twenty-nine. But you won't see that one. It's 200 miles from Potterville. Other side of the mountains. There used to be a military complex closer to Potterville back in the old days, according to legends."

Derrick detected something different in Paul's voice. He tried to identify it. Disdain perhaps?

"Do military people come to Potterville?" Derrick asked. "It would be quite an honor to see them."

Paul turned and glared for a moment. "Not often. Thankfully. They have everything they need on their bases. If they do come, it's never good, and it's not an honor. Stay clear of them if they show up."

Derrick felt confused. New America Media spent a lot of time praising the military. He wanted to ask why it was a problem but remained silent. Signs continued to appear, but they were facing the other direction for approaching traffic. Derrick did not read them. When the last sign receded behind them, the empty night darkness returned. After what felt like hours, that Derrick sensed was more like 20 minutes, more distant signs appeared. Three placed to string a story together. The first sign showed a young man with his chest thrust forward, breaking a red and blue ribbon. The words read:

```
His senior year of Academy,

Jack Smith set records in 100-and 200-meter races.
```

The next sign caused Derrick's stomach to twist into a tight knot. Young Jack Smith was positioned in a hospital bed. The white sheets could not conceal that his legs were missing. The sign read:

```
In service to New America in the Middle East, Jack
Smith lost both legs. Doctors said that he only
survived because of the rapid deployment of
Military Union Advanced Rescue Services.
```

The next sign looked like the first:

> One year later, thanks to Military Union bio-mechanical prosthetics, Jack Smith set new records for the 100- and 200-meter races in the human-modified class.

The purpose of these signs was clear. Join the Military Union if you are in the military and celebrate the accomplishments of Jack Smith. Derrick knew he should be proud of New America and Jack Smith. Had he seen this on New America Media last night, he would have saved it so he could have watched it often. But he was not proud. He was not happy. He was not patriotic. He felt empty. He felt sad. He did not know why. He could not relate to it. Only running seemed vaguely familiar, which was weird because he did not run. Ever.

As they drove through the night, the emptiness subsided and curiosity about soldiers returned. "Are military people commoners or Chosen?" Derrick asked, although he knew some must be Chosen because of the classes at the Academy.

Paul glared at Derrick again. "Both. Officers are Chosen. The grunts are what you call commoners. And don't say commoners in Potterville."

"Grunts?"

"The guys who get killed."

3

THE ROAD STRETCHED INTO the darkness. Mostly straight, mostly flat. Derrick awoke with a jerk, but he could not identify what had startled him. A bump in the road or a change in their speed? The most probable cause, however, was the lights in front of them. They had arrived.

Potterville looked old and worn. Buildings in need of paint, the sidewalks cracked and uneven. Along the streets, an odd assortment of transports, each one as strange as the one in which he rode, but each was different. Different shapes, colors, and conditions. Some sat on blocks in yards with the wheels and other parts removed. Some shiny, some faded, some clean, some dirty. The lack of uniformity gave Derrick a headache. He wanted to go home.

The streets were empty, except for a few transports moving through the night.

"This is Potterville?" Derrick asked.

"Yes. Your new digs are not far," Paul answered.

"Digs?" Derrick questioned.

"Where you'll live. Your condo."

Derrick nodded. *Digs.* He would need to remember that word. In Pacific Edge, a person would dig a hole, not that he had experience digging holes, because Chosen did not dig holes. Service workers dug holes when holes needed to be dug. It was as if the commoners spoke a different language.

"The transports are so strange here," Derrick observed, his face turned to the window.

"Don't call them transports. We drive cars and trucks. Motorcycles too," Paul said.

"Thanks," Derrick said. He had an entire vocabulary to learn and 30 days in which to do it. "What is a motorcycle?"

"Okay. So, this is a truck, or a pickup, or a pickup truck. Any of those will work. The smaller vehicles are called cars. I don't see a motorcycle. When you see one, you'll know what it is."

That was the stupidest thing Derrick had ever heard. How would he recognize a motorcycle when he had not seen one? Derrick said nothing. He was learning to listen more and talk less.

They drove by a large building made of dark red bricks, three stories, peeling white paint around the windows. Derrick knew what bricks were. The Academy touched on the structures of the old United States in New America History. Building with bricks was a crude, yet common construction practice back in those days. It surprised him that such a structure was still standing. It looked unsafe.

Paul pointed. "That's where you'll go to school. Potterville High School. The mascot is a Bearcat."

"What is a mascot?"

"Uh, it's a character that represents the school. Like at football games and such."

"They play football here?"

"Potterville won the state championship two years ago. You'll want to study up on that. Football is important in Potterville."

"I will," Derrick said. "What is a bearcat?"

"Well, it's not a real animal. It's kinda a cross between a bear and a cat."

"Oh," Derrick said, nodding his nonexistent understanding. He stared at the building. Why would a fake animal represent a school? Maybe it was not a real school. Maybe Paul was playing a joke because Derrick thought this building looked unsafe.

After passing the school, Paul turned right. "Your condo is only two blocks. You'll be able to walk to the school, no problem. I'll start moving in over the weekend, but there's no rush until you start school. Right? The lobby is secured so people can't just walk in. The kids from school won't know that you are not living with me. Although there is one girl who lives in the building. You'll need to be careful, so she doesn't see you go to your place instead of mine. I'll give you a key to my place on Monday. If she happens to be watching, you must go to my place instead of yours. You can't be leaving the building for the next thirty days. Because as far as anyone else knows, you're not here yet. Understand?"

Derrick thought he understood. "You are moving there?"

"Yes," Paul said.

"That is quite a coincidence," Derrick said.

"It's no coincidence. It's part of my agreement with your father."

"Father has paid for your condominium? Did he buy yours?" Derrick asked.

"Your father paid rent for my place and yours. He did not buy them. People cannot buy property. The government owns all the property and then rents it back to us."

Derrick stared at Paul, but not because the government owned all the property. That meant nothing to Derrick. Why should it? He was not a commoner. As far as he knew, his Father and Mother owned their home in

Pacific Edge. But he never asked, so he did not know. Now, he would never know. What caused his astonishment was that Father paid for Paul's place too. For his safety, if there were such a thing as safety here, but this piece of information cemented that his Father loved him more than Derrick ever imagined. It would be some time before Derrick understood his Father's motivation was something entirely different.

Paul turned onto a smaller street and then onto a narrow one-lane road that Derrick would learn was called an alley. Paul then turned into a dead end facing the building and a large metal door. A small keypad stood on a metal pole next to Paul's window. Paul punched at the buttons on the keypad, and then the metal door slid upward. Paul drove inside, where Derrick saw more transports. Cars and trucks, Paul called them.

Paul exited the truck. Derrick opened his door. Stifling air hit him in the face, and the garage emitted odors he did not recognize, nor could he explain them. A musty, oily stench was the best description he could manage.

"I'll show you your digs, give you the keys, show you how things work, and answer some questions," Paul said.

Derrick followed.

"That's the elevator." Paul pointed at a stainless-steel door. "Let's take the stairs. You're on the third floor. Decent view."

Paul sprinted up the stairs, and although Paul was more than twice Derrick's age, he was breathing half as hard as Derrick at the top. The stairwell emptied into a hallway covered with a dense tapestry carpet of burgundy. The air here was not as bad as Derrick had expected. The carpet looked clean and in decent condition. Paul pointed at a door across the hall. A number on the door read 317. "That will be my place. You're right down the hall." Paul pointed as he walked and then looked over his shoulder, "The girl living here is on the second floor, so there's no reason for her to be up here, but if she happened to be, you go to my place instead of yours. You savvy?"

"Savvy?" Derrick asked.

"Understand. Do you understand?"

Derrick nodded, but Paul had already turned and walked farther down the hall. Paul reached into his pocket and produced a small shiny brass-colored piece of metal with a serrated edge. It looked like the metal thing he used to start the transport — truck. Paul inserted the metal object into a round metal device embedded in the door, turned the metal object to the left, and then opened the door.

Paul handed the metal object to Derrick. "Your key."

A crude locking mechanism. Derrick's mind stuck right there. *How will I learn all of this?* No other method to ensure that the person entering the condo was, in fact, the authorized occupant. No retinal scan. No facial recognition. It was all so strange. And dangerous.

The condo proved to be nicer than Derrick expected. Nothing like Mother and Father's home, but he expected much worse. He had expected to be roasting over a fire by now, so he had not considered living conditions.

"Here's your bedroom. Sheets and towels are on the bed." Paul pointed to a door on the far side of the bedroom. "Your bathroom is there. You probably noticed the half-bath by the front door." Paul moved around Derrick and proceeded down a short hallway. "This would be a second bedroom, but it will be your study or office. Whatever you want to call it. That's where I had the store put your computer and desk. I didn't know what operating system you're used to. I got an Apple, or I should say someone bought an Apple. You know how to use an Apple? Of course, you do. It's been around at least 80 years."

"It has? Who bought it?" Derrick asked.

"Don't know. Your dad, I assume."

Derrick stood in front of the blank monitor. "I will figure it out. Computer on. COMPUTER ON," he said again, loud and slow.

Paul said nothing. Tightening his lips, Paul pushed a button on the side of the monitor. An apple missing a bite appeared on the screen, and then a picture of a colorful bird. Below the bird, his name appeared: Derrick King and below that, a line blinking in a small rectangular box. "Your password is derrick, all lowercase. You should change it once you log on. Once you log on, you'll see an icon with IB in the middle. Open that app, and it will walk you through the rest."

Derrick looked at the screen and then said, "Derrick, all lowercase." The computer did nothing.

Paul slid a rectangular device with letters and numbers on it toward Derrick. "Type your password using this." Then Paul pulled a small black device next to the keyboard. "First, click with the mouse on the place where you enter your password."

He knew what a mouse was because his first-grade instructor had shown the class pictures of the small creatures. They told students to tell an adult if they saw a mouse. This small black device did not look like a mouse. So many weird things to learn here. He said nothing about the mouse thing, but asked, "What is an IB?"

"Intelligence briefing," Paul said. "It is the application the Pacific Edge people sent to teach you about living here. I'm not sure where it came from. Your father must have arranged it. The file arrived on a flash drive an hour after he contacted me this afternoon."

Paul pointed to a thin, rectangular box the color of bronze. This box also had the same half-eaten apple on top, except this one was faded. "He paid for a notebook too. Same OS as your desktop, except it does not have the IB app. Most kids use them in school, although you might be the only one with a new one. We'll think up a reason you have new stuff."

Paul finished showing Derrick around. Derrick had a lot of questions about the kitchen because the food was there, and apparently, no one would prepare it for him. Derrick had no idea how to cook. Paul answered most of Derrick's questions by saying the IB app would explain it. Paul pointed out cereal and milk and said Derrick could eat that for breakfast and that it required no cooking. Derrick wondered how that could be considered a meal and realized he might starve to death here.

Derrick continued with a barrage of questions, and Paul finally said, "Look, kid, it's late. It's been a long day. I want to get home to my family."

Derrick stiffened. Family? Paul was leaving his family to do this.

"Lock the door when I go. It's safe enough here, but, well, that's just what we do." Paul started through the door, paused as if he were going to say something, and then pulled the door shut.

Derrick stood alone.

Alone in the commoner world.

4

DERRICK COULD NOT SLEEP, although he tried. Sleeping would be better than the constant panic he now experienced—alone in the commoner world. Tossing and turning in his bed, with every passing moment bringing another thing to fret about. Finally, he admitted he could not sleep, and he was not tired. He was hungry. He looked at the cereals. There were four varieties in boxes with colorful displays. Paul had arranged the boxes in order, healthy to unhealthy. Derrick selected the box on the unhealthy side. Why worry about health now? A picture of rainbow-colored O-shaped things in a bowl was on the box. Derrick found the image to be an accurate depiction of the contents. He opened several cabinets until he saw a bowl. He poured a bowl half full of cereal, then added milk. Strange looking stuff. For a moment, he wondered if it was actually food.

Derrick hesitantly raised a spoonful from the bowl. The milk had turned a light pink. Crunchy, sweet, fruity. Strangest thing he had ever tasted. He took another spoonful and then another and soon found his bowl empty of cereal but with a little pink milk remaining, which he drank. He never drank liquid from a bowl that he could remember. Eating like a barbarian, although he had only been in the commoner world for a few hours. He refilled the bowl with cereal and milk. When the second bowl was empty, he rinsed the bowl and spoon, dried them, and returned them to where he had found them. This was the first time he had ever washed a dish. He would learn that he had a dishwashing machine in a few days.

Derrick returned to his study. He called it a study because that was what he would do there for the next 30 days. Typing *derrick* on the keyboard as Paul had instructed, Derrick watched as the screen displayed a beautiful mountain, but he did not know where this mountain was located. Staring at the mountain's beauty, he decided he would try to discover the mountain's name, but that could wait.

Two things appeared on the left side of the screen and a row of little pictures along the bottom. The IB app that Paul mentioned was on the left, and below the IB app was a small picture of Paul's face. Written on the small picture below Paul's face were the words *watch_this_firstpaul.mp6*.

Along the bottom of the screen were pictures: a funny-looking face half blue and half white, a purple and blue circle with squiggly white lines, a blue circle with a red two-point arrow, a small calendar that showed today's date, a rectangle with a large bird, a musical note, a toy space rocket, a funny-looking flower, a weird-looking capital A, a wastepaper basket. So much to learn in 30 days. Such a strange place. But the mountain on the screen was nice. Maybe it was not a real mountain. Pictures of beautiful mountains and fruity cereal were not what he had expected in the commoner world.

Derrick said, "Watch this first." Nothing happened.

Derrick typed *watch this first* on the keyboard. Nothing happened.

This was not good. How could he watch whatever *watch_this_first* was if he did not know how?

"Computer."

Nothing.

Frustrated, Derrick pushed the keyboard away. It struck the weird mouse thing and sent it sliding across the desktop. He saw a small arrow shoot across the screen. He pulled the mouse thing toward himself while watching the arrow move on the screen. He moved the arrow to *watch_this_first,* and the arrow changed to a small hand with a pointing index finger. He wiggled the mouse device, but *watch_this_first* did nothing. Next, he tapped the device. When he tapped on the right side, a window opened with a list of options. He tapped the left side once, nothing. Frustrated, he tapped the right side twice. The list appeared and disappeared. He tapped on the left side twice. a little color wheel spun on the screen, and then a new thing on the screen opened, and a video started.

Video Paul said, "Hi, Derrick. I recorded this on the drive over to Pacific Edge after setting up your apartment. Damn, I was busy this afternoon getting that done. Had to do it myself, you know. Good thing I have a trailer."

Derrick wondered if there was a camera in Paul's truck and what a trailer was. He would ask Paul on Monday.

Paul continued, telling Derrick about e-mail — it was the bird picture thing — and the e-mail account that was already set up for him. Paul said e-mail was a way to send messages.

Then Paul said, "So, here's an important thing. I didn't mention this when I picked you up because we didn't have time to get into it with your family. Maybe we have already talked about some of this on the drive over or while I showed you around the condo. Anyway, here goes. Your name is still Derrick King. No need to change that because commoners don't have access to any directory that lists members of the Chosen. And it's unlikely that there's anyone here from Pacific Edge who would know you. As for your new identity, here's the story. You are my sister's son. Your fictional mom and dad lived in Denver,

Colorado. You'll need to study about Denver so you can answer questions about it. Your fictional mom and dad were killed last week in a car accident. I, being your only family, took you in. However, my wife didn't want you here, so we had a fight, and I had to move out. That's why I'm living at the condo, and you're with me. Your mom and dad had some money. You are the beneficiary, but since you're a minor, you needed a guardian, and I'm that guardian. That's how I have the money for a condo. Well, that's about it for now. See you Monday."

The video stopped. Derrick stared. How much had Father paid Paul to take this risk and abandon his family? Must have been a lot. Or maybe money was more important to Paul than was his family. That did not seem right. Paul was at risk, and if Paul was at risk, his family might be at risk too.

All because I decked Marcus Carver.

5

DESPITE THE LATE HOUR, Derrick still was not tired. He sat at the computer and opened the Intelligence Briefing application. The first screen warned the contents were top secret, unauthorized access would result in prosecution, unauthorized release of information would result in prosecution, and that the application was for the sole use of Chosen field agents. At the end of the disclaimer, the New America Intelligence Agency logo appeared. Derrick clicked on the X at the top left of the app. It disappeared from the screen.

They had set him up. Now he faced additional charges. Derrick spun off the chair, ran to the bathroom, and vomited pink milk and rainbow cereal. He sat on the floor beside the toilet, knees pulled to his chest, head leaning against the wall.

Listening and watching; watching and listening.

He felt naked, although clothed. And stupid. He did not think about searching the condo for surveillance devices. They would be sophisticated technology, so he would not find them, but the thought had not crossed his mind.

Stupid.

His stomach stopped its protest after a few minutes. Then his head cleared. He had closed the app as soon as the warning appeared. That was the right thing to do. *Listen to Miriam. Be smart. Stay alive.* If they intended to trap him for using the IB app, he must find another way to learn about the commoner world. Paul might know a way. He had to wait until Monday.

Time lost.

Derrick walked back to the study. He sat down in front of his computer and clicked on an icon that Paul called e-mail. Logging on using the e-mail username Paul provided and derrick as the password. Two messages appeared on the screen. His stomach lurched when he saw one was from The Community Intelligence Agency, Investigation and Enforcement Bureau. *Are they onto me already? What had it been? Fifteen minutes since I opened that forbidden application. They must be monitoring my computer and waiting for me to do something wrong.*

He also had an e-mail from Paul.

The CIA, Chosen Intelligence Agency, e-mail came in first according to the date and time. Paul's e-mail came 30 minutes ago. The CIA e-mail had arrived earlier in the day. In fact, they sent it about the time he was eating dinner with his parents in Pacific Edge, which seemed like days ago. He glanced at the time displayed on the top left-hand edge of the screen: 11:59. Still his birthday. Time to see what the CIA sent.

```
Mr. King,

The director of the Chosen Intelligence
Agency has approved your use of the IB
education program. This program is used to
train field agents who are assigned various
missions in the commoner world. The version
on your computer does not contain any
sensitive information. Such information has
been removed. However, the IB training
program remains Top Secret. You are to share
no information, including the program's
existence with any individual, agency,
country, or any other person, real or
imaginary.
```

Derrick felt relieved. Except for real or imaginary? What a peculiar way to word a warning. He tried, but failed, to think of an explanation other than insuring they could prosecute him for any reason. Still, he had permission to use the application so, he had that going for him. He needed to preserve this e-mail as evidence. Another thing to ask Paul about. He found a notepad and a crude writing instrument in a drawer and started a list.

Next, he opened Paul's message:

```
Derrick

Just thinking. We need to change the story
regarding your parents. Car wreck won't work.
Doesn't explain why everything you own is new.
House fire. That would work. Hopefully, no
one at school will research recent house fires
in Denver. Best to say you were gone
somewhere. School trip or something. You
decide on that. Well, got to get some sleep.
Later.
```

Paul's e-mail did not trouble Derrick. Still, he stared at it for several minutes. What Paul said made sense, but why was Paul so worried about it? How could other students research house fires in Denver? Derrick's stomach made a slow turn. Paul feared Derrick's odds of success were slim, which placed Paul and his family in danger. If that were true, and he believed it was, there was no time to waste. He needed to study and study hard.

Derrick returned to the IB program. The warning script played again, but this time, after a brief hesitation, he clicked on continue. A list of options appeared on the next page. Each section had a title, such as basics, which was then followed by specifics such as history, regions, dialects. He started in basics, watching each video lesson in the order in which they appeared.

After watching several videos, he checked the time. It was now 2:30 a.m., Saturday, March 13.

Derrick King was now two and a half hours into the second day of his 17th year.

6

COMMOTION AROUSED DERRICK FROM A DEEP SLEEP. Loud voices rose from the street, followed by a blaring noise that he had never heard before. The racket was right below his window.

"We know you're in there, runner! Think you're important! We don't think so. You're nothing. Less than nothing."

Something crashed against the building, close to his window. In the distance, a siren rose and fell.

"Why don't you come out instead of calling the cops if you're such a big deal?"

A motor roared to life, followed by a squealing sound. The sound of the transport, car, or truck faded into the distance. Derrick trembled on his bed. Sweat formed on his brow. He had watched IB videos until he could no longer keep his eyes open. How he got to his bed was a mystery. He was still dressed. The bed linens remained in their packages. Outside, the siren grew louder. Blue and red lights danced outside his window and penetrated his room. The siren faded. This must have been the cops. That is what Paul called the security officers who protected Pacific Edge. It confused Derrick that Pacific Edge had security officers here unless they were here to safeguard him. But who would call them? Paul knew his identity, but Paul was home with his family.

He was not a runner, but commoners might not know the difference between exile and escape. They just knew he did not belong here. Although Derrick did not think of himself as important, he could see how commoners might believe that of him because he was Chosen. None of that mattered. What mattered was that someone knew he was here. Images from New America Media's depictions of the commoner world coursed through his mind. He lay there for a long time, confident that he could not sleep. But sleep, he did.

The nightmare returned.

He hated the nightmare.

Derrick found himself in a white room. There were other children all dressed in gray, and adults dressed in blue uniforms, like a medical person would wear. He recognized this place. It was a familiar nightmare. Although he felt awake, he was not. He tried to arouse himself, but he never could. A girl about his age sat at a table across the room. She had a large wooden hammer in her hand and wooden pegs of color different shapes in front of her. She locked eyes with him and picked up a peg. Derrick saw she had placed the peg in the wrong hole. Then she hit the peg hard with the hammer. Bang, bang, bang, the hammer came down. The adult watching her did nothing to correct the girl.

Bang, bang, bang.

Pound, pound, pound.

The girl's name is Number Six.

Derrick stirred, light leaking around the cloth coverings of his window. No daylight seeped into his bedroom in Pacific Edge. That window could be set to be opaque or transparent. Derrick had set it impervious to the light because he did not care to see outside. He did not care for the view of the ocean. Instead, he programmed the room light to replicate sunset and sunrise.

The pounding he heard in his nightmare continued outside his room.

He edged to the window and eased the cloth coverings open enough to peek out, squinting at the brilliant sunlight. Across the street, men used a machine to break out pieces of the sidewalk. Strangest thing he had ever seen.

Below his window, he saw broken glass on the sidewalk. The sight of the broken glass confirmed that the disturbance last night was not his imagination. Not a nightmare.

He moved to the kitchen in search of food. The IB training provided no information regarding breakfast preparation, so he went to the cereal boxes again. This time, he chose one from the healthy side, bran with raisins. The box said it had fiber. He was not sure he wanted to eat fiber, and the labeling did not say if it contained cotton, linen, or man-made fibers.

The next necessity was coffee. The coffee maker was of the C-cup variety, which stood for Carver-Cup. The machine had a name he did not recognize, but he understood how to operate it because Carver-Cups were the sole method for making coffee in Pacific Edge, except for espresso, but he had never taken the time to learn how to use that machine. Making C-cup coffee was the extent of his kitchen skills. He was glad they used Carver-Cup machines — although they did not call them that — in the commoner world. He poured milk and sugar into his cup before filling it with fresh-brewed Brazilian coffee. As the coffee maker hissed and coffee streamed into his cup, he realized that Brazilian coffee and the quality of the appliances and overall pleasantness of his new home did not fit his paradigm of commoner existence. But last night's awakening reminded him where he was. He felt uneasy to the point of nausea. Yet he was unsure which bothered him most, facing the commoners outside his condominium or the nightmare from which he had awoken.

He took his rudimentary breakfast to the study. The computer clock read 10:30 a.m. He should have been up earlier. He ate the cereal and then drank the remaining milk from the bowl. This cereal was not unpleasant, which surprised him since it was supposed to be healthy, although it did not threaten to unseat the colorful, fruity cereal occupying the less-than-healthy side of the cabinet.

Sipping coffee, his mind cleared. He tried to focus on the events of last night. Someone knew he was here. He was doomed outside the building. In which case, studying would not help. However, something he remembered during his study troubled him: the IB description of Denver, Colorado.

```
Denver  is  the  capital  and  most  populous
municipality  in  the  state  of  Colorado.  Denver
is  in  the  South  Platte  River  Valley  on  the
western  edge  of  the  High  Plains  east  of  the
Front  Range  of  the  Rocky  Mountains.  The  Denver
downtown  district  is  located  immediately  east
of  the  confluence  of  Cherry  Creek  with  the
South  Platte  River.  Denver  is  nicknamed  the
Mile-High  City  because  its  official  elevation
is  exactly  one  mile  (5,280  feet)  above  sea
level,  making  it  one  of  the  highest  major
cities  in  the  United  States.
```

Two things bothered him. First, this comprised all the information regarding Denver in the IB program. Denver was supposed to have been his home. Paul said it was vital that he knew about it. This was not good. Second, this information was very old, dating back to the failed United States. Why was the information not current? Perhaps Denver no longer existed. Again, he felt sure the Tribunal wanted him to fail. Perhaps the Tribunal told someone in Potterville about his arrival.

Still, with food and coffee and a clear head, Derrick felt a little better. He was smart, and Miriam would help. He might still discover a way to survive. However, terror lurked just below the surface of his thoughts. Then that terror rose to the surface when a loud banging came at his door.

Derrick eased toward the door. He used the small looking hole as Paul had instructed. He saw Paul's distorted face. Relief, yet why was Paul here? He wasn't supposed to be here until Monday.

"You're up. Great," Paul said, stepping inside and closing the door. "I've got some furniture to move into the condo. I need your help."

"You want me to help move furniture?" Derrick asked. The tone of disbelief of such a request did not escape Derrick, and by the expression on Paul's face, Paul had not missed it either. "I am sorry. I should help. Let me put on my shoes."

Paul checked the hall. He eased down the stairs, peering into the garage before motioning Derrick to follow. Paul's pickup truck was loaded high, and straps secured the load. Paul moved and manipulated the items with ease.

Derrick moved and manipulated items like a teenager who had never worked a day in his life. They talked little, other than Paul's instructions. Turn here, tilt it up, put it there.

When they laid a mattress, still covered with plastic, on the floor in the bedroom, Derrick said, "Where is the rest of your bed?"

"This is all I bought. I don't need a real bed. Not for the brief time I'll be here."

Derrick started to ask how long Paul thought he would be here but decided he did not want to hear the answer.

"I'll have one more load. I'll bring it later today. I brought your fake school file that Pacific Edge prepared. It came to my house this morning. You should learn everything in it. With any luck, Potterville High won't contact that school, because if they do, then they'd find you never attended, which would be a problem."

Derrick nodded. "Would you like a cup of coffee over at my condo? I have a few questions."

"Sure," Paul said. "Lead the way."

At the door, Paul grabbed Derrick's arm and jerked him to a stop. "Remember. Always check the hall before you step out."

Derrick nodded and checked the looking hole, saw nothing, and opened the door. Derrick fixed two cups of coffee. Paul took his black. Derrick tried it black too. Maybe commoners did not put milk, sugar, and flavoring in their coffee.

So much to learn.

"I looked up Denver in the IB program. It did not have much detail. How will I learn about Denver when there is so little information?"

"Google it," Paul said.

"How would I do that? What is a google?"

"Maybe you don't call it Google in Pacific Edge. Do an internet search. There will be tons of information. Doesn't matter which search engine you use."

"Search engine? Internet? I do not know these terms."

Paul was about to take a drink, but his cup froze inches from his lips, staring as if antennas had grown from Derrick's head.

"Now, I'm confused," Paul said. "You must call it something. You know, how do you research things on your computer? You must do research for school and such, plus social media, news, directions, and God knows what else."

"God knows?" Derrick asked, his voice rising a notch.

"Uh, just an expression," Paul replied. "Forgot about how you people think."

Derrick sipped his coffee. He was not sure he could get used to drinking it black. *How you people think* circulated in Derrick's mind. "There is nothing like what you are describing in Pacific Edge. We do not research anything. Any lessons or information required are on my communication monitor when it is needed. I always checked it in the morning and evening. I am not familiar with the term social media. We do not have computers like the one you bought me."

"Okay," Paul drawled.

"It's okay that I do not understand?" Derrick asked.

"Not okay as in, okay. Okay, as in, how can you not know what the internet is? Not know what social media is. Okay, as in, it's not okay. Understand?"

"I am sorry, but I do not understand what you are talking about," Derrick said.

Paul sipped his coffee, then nodded. "I guess that explains a lot. That you will be able to learn enough about life outside Pacific Edge in thirty days grows more unlikely with every conversation."

Paul did not offer further explanation, and Derrick did not ask for one.

How you people think.

"Easier to show you," Paul said.

Paul sat at Derrick's desk. "See that compass icon? That's your internet browser." Paul clicked on the blue circle with a red and white arrow. Derrick would have to remember to find out what a compass was. "Type whatever you want to research in this space and hit enter." Paul typed Denver.

Derrick watched as the screen changed. Near the top, Derrick saw the word Google in colorful letters, and below that were the words,\: All, Maps, News, Images, Videos, and More. Below that it said, "about 326,000,000 results (0.62 seconds)."

"See. More information than you'll ever need. Also, look at the area on Google Maps." Paul clicked on a small map that appeared on the right side of the screen. A map of Denver popped up on the monitor. Then Paul clicked on: Open Earth View.

Derrick could see buildings, lawns, and roads as if he were flying over the city.

"When you find what you want to look at, drag this little guy." Paul pulled a yellow man into the map, "to the street. You can look up the address of where you supposedly lived and see the house."

A picture of the street, the businesses, cars, and people on the sidewalk filled the screen.

Yet another of the weirdest things Derrick had ever seen.

7

BEFORE LEAVING, PAUL SHOWED DERRICK A few basic cooking methods, explained the food purchased, and how to prepare it. He showed Derrick how to use the microwave (never put metal in it). It was lunchtime. Paul had promised to take his kids out for a burger. Derrick did not know what a burger was, nor was he invited. He was not part of the family. His family was hours away, safe behind sixty miles of scorched earth and a fortified Pacific Edge barrier.

After helping Paul unload furniture, pestering him for information, and learning basic cooking techniques, Derrick was famished. For lunch, he decided on a cylinder-shaped piece of meat called a hotdog. Paul explained they made hotdogs from beef and pork, probably because of the expression on Derrick's face, which indicated that dog meat was not something he wanted to eat. According to Paul, he could cook a hot dog in the microwave, boil it, fry it, or grill it, (but Derrick did not have a grill whatever that meant) serve it on a bun or not, plain or with ketchup, mustard, relish, or any combination of these condiments, all of which were unknown to Derrick. He started with ketchup, added mustard, and then tried relish. After his third hotdog, he declared all three condiments combined were best. He cooked the hotdogs in the microwave machine. A delightful device. He washed them down with two cans of a thing called Coke. Coke tasted like Carver's Caramel Ice that he drank in Pacific Edge. Derrick loved Carver's Caramel Ice and was glad commoners had something similar. The hotdogs were unlike anything he had ever eaten, but the Coke made him homesick.

Derrick returned to the computer, where he lost track of time. He searched topic after topic and was astounded, finding videos, professional and amateur, on matters of all sorts. Someone had filled the internet with information documenting every topic he tested. Except for the Chosen, and the Communities in which they live. When he typed in Pacific Edge, a warning in red capital letters that this information was prohibited blazed across the computer screen. Why was it forbidden? Perhaps they only prevented his access. Or maybe all commoners are denied access so they cannot plan an attack.

There was no factual information about the Chosen, but there were many opinions and speculations that ran from adulation to revulsion, but none of it was accurate and the speculation varied from incorrect to outlandish.

Derrick heard a bell, but nothing appeared on his computer screen. Then the bell came again but was not followed by an announcement of any kind. Then pounding at the front door. Derrick looked through the looking hole, peephole, was the correct term he learned earlier, and there was Paul's distorted face. Derrick smiled.

Paul said, "Sorry, I'm so late. What took you so long? Did I catch you on the can? I have more of my stuff."

Derrick wondered what kind of can he would have been on. He had not seen a can of sufficient size to be on top of. He would look through the condominium later. He followed Paul to the parking garage, where they each grabbed a box and headed to Paul's condo, taking the stairs instead of the elevator. The box wasn't heavy, or at least it was lighter than the items they had packed up earlier. Yet, that didn't seem right. It was as if he had forgotten something. Something important. Derrick went first, springing up the steps. He stood outside the stairwell door, waiting for Paul to catch up.

Breathing hard, Paul said, "You didn't seem to be in such good shape earlier."

"I must have grabbed the lightest box. Sorry," Derrick said, knowing that wasn't quite right. "I wasn't paying attention."

"Light? Hell, that's a box of magazines. I figured we'd both carry it." Paul stared at Derrick a moment before he pulled the door open.

Inside Paul's room, dark windows surprised Derrick, and he asked, "What time is it?"

"After 10," Paul replied.

Derrick drifted to the window. Looking out over the dark landscape lit by sparse streetlamps and windows like shining eyes, behind which people went about their lives. "Wow," was all Derrick could say.

Derrick could not remember a day in which time disappeared so quickly, so quietly, so unnoticed as it did during this day, when he sifted through vast amounts of information found on the internet.

On the next trip up the stairs, Derrick's stomach confirmed that it was in fact after ten o'clock. "I'm starving."

"You didn't eat?"

"I ate hotdogs for lunch. I lost track of time."

At the truck, Paul nodded and then grabbed a box. "I'm hungry too. I'll order a pizza."

"Pizza?"

Paul smiled. "Did you like the hotdogs?"

"I liked them very much."

"Then you'll love pizza."

After they carried the last boxes up the stairs, Paul used a communication device to order a pizza. A servant of some sort delivered it to the condominium. The main entrance must be secured because when the servant arrived, a communication device mounted near the door of Paul's condominium sounded a tone. Derrick recognized the sound. Paul spoke into the communication device and then pushed a button, which caused a buzzer to sound. Derrick remembered seeing the same device in his condominium and, at the time, wondered what it was for. Now he understood it was an entry announcement device. He felt good that he was paying attention to such things. He thought about the large can Paul thought detained him from answering the door. He forgot to search for a large can, yet he was certain no such thing existed in his condominium. A few minutes later, the servant arrived at Paul's door with a flat cardboard box. Paul pulled a folded leather pouch thing from his pocket, pulled out some paper, which he handed to the man. Paul told the man to keep the chains, but Derrick didn't see any chains. Perhaps he misunderstood. Still, it was a baffling encounter.

Not baffling was Paul's correct assessment of this thing called pizza, which was a thin round crust covered with a tomato-based sauce, then covered with cheese, meats, black olives, and mushrooms. *Magnificent! Why did we not eat pizza in Pacific Edge?* He supposed their cook could have prepared it had the family known such a delicacy existed.

They ate in silence and drank Coke. When they had consumed most of the pizza, Paul said, "Tomorrow, I will help you finish getting stuff in order."

Derrick nodded. His muscles ached, and his eyelids were heavy. "I am tired."

After checking the peephole and finding no one outside, Derrick said goodnight, and he stepped into the hall. He walked to his condominium (Paul called it a condo) and opened his door. Before going inside his condo, he studied his entrance and saw a small lighted button, which he pushed, and then he heard the ding tone he heard earlier when Paul arrived, which was the same sound he heard in Paul's condo when the pizza came. Figuring this out felt like a triumph. Next, Derrick checked every room and closet. He found no large can that he might have been on top of delaying his response to the door when Paul activated the entry request device. Maybe Paul forgot to bring it.

Derrick considered making the bed but decided he was too tired to figure it out, although it did not look complicated. He removed a blue blanket from its plastic container, spread it over the mattress, pulled the edges until it lay flat, kicked off his shoes, pulled off his pants, and crawled underneath. His first full day in Potterville, and he was still alive. He did not leave the building. Nevertheless, he lived one day longer than he expected. He decided to enjoy each day as best he could. Thirty days might be the rest of his life.

It felt warm and somewhat safe under the blanket. His mind drifted and was full of more information than he could process. He had read about the city of Denver, looked at maps and pictures, looked at the home in which he supposedly lived, studied the surrounding area, and found that Colorado contained many mountains, and was well known in the commoner world for its high mountain passes and majestic scenery. He wanted to go there and learn more about this strange land. But every time he entertained optimistic thoughts of his future, he remembered last night's threats and that he must leave his sanctuary in 29 days. The learning curve was steeper than he had ever imagined, and he doubted he could assimilate unnoticed into the commoner world. From his study regarding what commoners believed about the Chosen, he was no less concerned about his safety, but not in ways he expected.

Another thing bothered him. After seeing his fake home in Denver, he wanted to see his real home in Pacific Edge on the computer. He moved the map west to the coast. Not knowing where Pacific Edge was relative to Potterville, he went farther north than needed to a place called Oregon and moved down the coast well beyond where Pacific Edge would be located. But he could not find Pacific Edge.

Drifting.

He had searched up and down the coast. He thought the city layout should be easy to spot with the surrounding support community that he did not know existed until Paul drove out of Pacific Edge. The massive boundary wall that surrounds Pacific Edge should be easily seen on the sky map. Finally, he gave up. Perhaps he misjudged the location of Pacific Edge. Yet if he were truthful, he found Pacific Edge. A square piece of land blurred out as if it did not exist.

Drifting.

8

Sunday, March 14

DERRICK AWOKE THE NEXT MORNING AT nine o'clock. At first, he had trouble getting up, exhausted in a way that had nothing to do with his physical condition. This malady likely had a name, but he did not know it. It had affected him at times in the past, but he had just taken a mood enhancer to get moving. He wondered if they had mood enhancers here. Having no way to find out only made his condition worse. After a few minutes, he dragged himself to the kitchen and made coffee, returned to his bedroom, pulled open the window coverings — he had learned they were called curtains — and looked out at his temporary town. The day dawned clear and bright. Trees shimmered, new leaves glistening. Lawns, although not as uniform as those in Pacific Edge, were trimmed and clean of debris. Someone had swept the broken glass from the sidewalk. His bedroom faced a residential area. Some lawns had small colorful toys, red four-wheeled wagons, miniature three-wheeled riding devices, none of which would be tolerated in Pacific Edge. Most yards had flowers blooming. Derrick did not know the flowers' names. He wondered if the kids at school knew the names of flowers and decided he had better study enough to know the common ones grown here. The learning curve looked steep as a cliff as he thought about it with a clear head.

After fixing a second coffee, Derrick moved to the living room window that overlooked a street lined with small businesses. One place sold flowers, a place called Donna's Bistro had a sign in the window that read Espresso, a place called Mountain View Guitar, a placed called H & R Block (he had no idea what an H & R Block was, but it did not look as interesting as the other businesses). Outside the bistro, people sat at small tables, drinking coffees and eating pastries. The sight made him hungry. Oddly, he also wanted to go out there and sit nearby. Listen to the conversations, be a part of this bizarre world. One table appeared to be a mother and daughter. The daughter looked to be his age. He remembered Paul said a girl who attended his new school lived in the building.

The girl reminded him of Miriam. A dull ache arose in his chest. He had been so preoccupied with his own plight that she had not crossed his mind this morning. The girl had shoulder length black hair with a bright pink stripe on one side. *Miriam would love her hair.* He thought neither was her natural hair color because her mother's hair was neither black nor pink. They would not tolerate pink hair in Pacific Edge. Her black shorts were much too short and inappropriate by Pacific Edge standards. Her blouse was loosely fitted, falling off one shoulder, exposing far too much skin. Overall, there was more exposed skin than clothing. Two days ago, he would have been furious had he seen such a willful display of rebellion.

Today, he wanted to meet her.

Derrick ventured into unknown breakfast territory, fixing eggs and toast. Simple food, unlike anything he had ever eaten, yet enjoyable. He toasted a second slice of bread, spreading it with butter. It seemed ridiculous to think this basic fare was better than the more sophisticated cuisine he was accustomed to, yet it tasted better. On the computer, time flew. He had the presence of mind to eat lunch, consisting of two slices of leftover pizza. Leftover food was something he was unaccustomed to eating.

When the entry request device dinged, Derrick realized that daylight had faded. The peephole revealed Paul standing outside with two brown paper bags.

"Hi," Paul said.

Derrick held the door open for Paul.

"Have you eaten? I hope not. I bought burgers, fries, and milkshakes. You like burgers?"

Derrick shrugged.

Paul shook his head and said, "Never mind. Just trust me."

Derrick was finding it easier to trust Paul. The smell of food kicked Derrick's hunger sensory array into high gear. Burgers, he learned, burger was short for hamburger, which was weird because there was no ham in the sandwich. He also thought hamburgers might be his new favorite food. He found the fries — he learned that was short for French fries, which was also weird because the French did not invent them — were a close second or third on his list as he remembered pizza. And while technically it was a drink, not a food, the shake — which he learned was short for milkshake, which was also weird because there was no shaking involved in its creation — was a cold, chocolaty bit of sweet perfection.

"I got you something else you'll need." Paul lifted a plastic bag from the floor, which contained something that must have been the best buy available because the sack was so labeled. From the bag, Paul pulled a box with the picture of an apple missing a bite, which was the same as his computer screen during startup.

"What is this?" Derrick asked.

"A smartphone."

"A smart what?"

"Cellphone. You know what a cellphone is. Right?"

Derrick felt the learning curve steepen, almost inverted. With a little embarrassment, he said, "I do not."

Paul stared at Derrick. "I'll be damned. How did you communicate with people in Pacific Edge?"

"We had communicators. I could talk to my Mother, Father, and Miriam by selecting one of three buttons. But I did not use it much. Pacific Edge is a small place. Normally, I was home or at the Academy or in a transport between the two. My parents may have used it more with Miriam because she was often disappearing and would seldom use a transport. Sometimes they did not know her location. Sometimes she left her communicator at home."

"So, you could not contact your friends or other people? Businesses?"

"Just our family members. We don't have stores like here. Instead, there is a list of things from which we can choose."

Paul shook his head and pulled the small silver device from the box. "It does everything your computer does, except has a smaller screen. Plus, it has cellular service, which is kinda like being connected to the internet, but different."

Staring at the small screen, something let go in Derrick's mind. It had been coming unhinged the past two days, but now it snapped. Instead of the barbaric, backward, animalistic, and unsophisticated world he had been taught existed outside Pacific Edge, the commoners were more advanced than the Chosen. While one might have thought this an interesting revelation for Derrick, it drove his fear deeper. He believed he was superior to the commoners and therefore held the upper hand. Now he realized it was not true.

"You'd better learn to use this thing. Everyone here has one. I'll help you get started. Have you set up your laptop yet?"

Derrick shook his head. He did not say that he had forgotten about it. But he had.

"What are you doing all day? I hope you're not just sleeping and playing computer games."

Derrick did not know how one would play games with a computer. He did not ask.

"Go get it. We'll get that set up too. You're killing me, kid."

Derrick did not understand Paul's comment and interpreted it literally. He fought to control the fear that threatened to overtake him. He had to pay attention to what Paul was showing him. His life, and probably Paul's, depended on it.

Remember to ask him about the can, he thought.

Paul walked him through the setup of his phone and laptop. It was easy because the devices seemed to communicate with his other computer. The only contact Derrick needed was Paul's, but Paul added his wife, Ann, as well. Just in case. Derrick could add others as he got to know them, Paul said. Each phone had a unique seven-digit number, Paul explained. The girl with the pink-striped hair invaded Derrick's thoughts for a moment.

Paul linked Derrick's e-mail account. Derrick had forgotten about that program too. He had not checked it since Paul first showed him. He did not know anyone to get an e-mail from, except the one he got from Pacific Edge. Derrick would soon learn he was wrong about that. He did not wonder how the CIA in Pacific Edge knew his e-mail address. Later he would learn that was important, but for now, his head spun from all the new things he learned each day.

"You've got mail," Paul said, handing Derrick the phone, then added, "One is from the Pacific Edge Tribunal and the other looks like spam. Uh, spam is like junk mail. You know junk mail? Probably not. Well, it's just junk. Don't click on anything in junk mail. It might give your computer a virus."

Derrick knew what a virus was. There was no cure for the common cold, but there was a vaccine that helped ward them off, which he had updated each year. He wondered how a computer could get a cold but did not ask. He felt stupid enough already.

An e-mail from the Tribunal. That did not sound good.

Derrick opened it.

He was right.

9

DERRICK READ THE MESSAGE TWICE. At the end of the second reading, he thought he might vomit.

Sunday, March 14

To: Derrick King

From: The Pacific Edge Community Tribunal

Be advised that the Tribunal has modified your sentence. Upon further consideration, the Tribunal has determined that the 30-day education period is illegal and is hereby revoked. In a gracious extension of goodwill, the Tribunal will allow you to continue your preparation until next Monday, March 22.

Pacific Edge Tribunal

"You look like you've seen a ghost," Paul said.

Derrick did not understand what ghosts had to do with anything. "They have cut my 30-day study period. I have until next Monday."

Paul let out a whistle. "That's tough luck, kid. Well, this news won't help. I'm headed to Bakersfield for a job. I'll be gone till Friday. Now, I'll have to move in early. Next weekend. Damn it. I need to go. I want to spend some time with my kids tonight. Sorry."

Derrick nodded but said nothing. Paul left.

Derrick sat at the table, staring at the message on his communication device, phone or cell or cell phone, the commoners called it. The burger, fries, and milkshake felt like a cold, gray ball in his stomach. A few minutes ago, he realized learning about the commoners' world in 30 days would be difficult. Doing it in one week, impossible. He could not remember how long he sat staring at that message, and he did not understand why he stared. It would not change. He closed it and opened the other. What did Paul call it? Garbage mail?

The sender's e-mail name was
`marandakingston@pacificedge/admin.com`

That sounded official.
The subject line read:

`Your Number1 Pain in the Ass`

That sounded weird.
The e-mail read:

`Don't let my e-mail address fool you. It's me, your number1 pain in the ass little sister.`

`Tell Paul that setting up your e-mail as derrickking0312 was cool.`

`Delete this e-mail and then empty your deleted e-mail too. I'm safe on this end for now. I have a lot to tell you, but no time. Got to run. Literally.`

`Love you. Sis.`

Is this a trick? Who is Maranda Kingston? Why is someone from Pacific Edge administration contacting me? Is it Miriam? How could she send an e-mail, let alone find me? Not possible. Must be a trick. But who? The Tribunal? Should I answer it? Ignore it? Or follow the instructions? Miriam would know what to do.

Derrick considered replying to the e-mail, wanting proof of the sender, but he followed the instructions, deleting the e-mail and emptying the trash. Both processes were intuitive. He checked his desktop and laptop computers, and the e-mail had disappeared there too. He regretted not checking them before he deleted it to ensure it had appeared on all three devices. Although he did not understand how the e-mail or internet worked, it seemed reasonable to assume a real e-mail would be the same on all three devices. The Tribunal's e-mail was on all three. He kept the e-mail program open. No additional e-mail came for the rest of the evening. It was 1:15 a.m. when Derrick crawled onto his bed and slept.

Monday, March 15

The cell phone alarm sounded at 6 a.m. Derrick rose, fixed a bowl of cereal (healthy), which he ate, and coffee, which he took to the study. The previous night, as he dozed off, it occurred to him that the subjects at the commoner's school must differ significantly from that at James Carver Academy. Studying the fake Derrick King school file from Denver proved that perception true. The Denver Derrick had been enrolled in English, Geography, US History, Physical Education, Algebra, Chemistry, and Spanish. He could read and write English, although he did not understand the strange word usage here. He was healthy, so physical fitness should not cause a problem. Maybe sweaty, which bothered him, but it required no thinking, which relieved him. He would have never guessed that physical fitness would create challenges like no other subject. The remainder of the subjects looked like a nightmare. He could not speak Spanish. Fortunately, the record showed he had started that course in January so he could learn a few words to suggest his limited participation and then move forward from there. U.S. History and New America History must be similar. So, he had that going for him. Algebra would not be difficult. He was good at math and accounting, subjects he enjoyed. The Academy emphasized math because they mostly employed the Chosen in Pacific Edge to manage corporate financial affairs. Father was an accountant for a large pharmaceutical firm, which was a lucrative position. Although his Father often appeared depressed by the job.

Derrick did not understand his Father.

Then there were science and its cousin, chemistry. The Academy taught neither subject, as both were forbidden. Former United States propaganda, to be specific. He felt queasy thinking about being forced to attend such classes. Throughout his education, they taught him, with great ferocity, the dangers of science. Science was the ultimate downfall of the old United States of America. Now, for him to learn this perversion of creation seemed an abomination. No wonder they did not let people return to Pacific Edge after they left, regardless of the reason for their departure. Perhaps these were optional courses, and he could choose something less offensive. If forced to attend, he had to keep his mouth shut, of that much he was certain.

That afternoon, Derrick took a break, toasting a slice of bread and topping it with a dark, sweet spread called blackberry jam. The jar had a picture of the concoction on toast, so he assumed that was the intended use. He made a cup of coffee and then stood at the window overlooking Donna's Bistro. The girl with the pink-striped hair invaded his thoughts. Merely daydreaming, yet at that moment she slipped from the store's front door, followed by another girl with skin the color of chocolate and a boy with skin darker still. The trio sat at a table on the sidewalk, sipped their drinks, and talked. But not just talking, also smiling and laughing. Friendship. Relaxed as if they did not know this place was dangerous. Derrick did not understand.

He returned to the computer, studied until 11:30 p.m., discovered he was hungry, so he ate heated chicken noodle soup from a can, and then, with his eyelids drooping, stumbled off to bed, hoping to dream of the girl with the pink-striped hair, instead of the white room and the girl named Number Six.

Tuesday, March 16; Wednesday, March 17; Thursday, March 18; Friday, March 19

Derrick repeated the same routine as Monday for the rest of the week. Woke early, studied hard. The food changed little. He returned to the window each afternoon to watch the table on the sidewalk in front of Donna's Bistro. The girl with the pink-striped hair did not return on Tuesday, Wednesday, or Thursday. He tried to dream of her each night, but no dreams materialized. On Friday afternoon, when Derrick looked out the window, she was there with the brown-skinned girl. While he watched, she looked up at him. He did not think she could see him. Paul said people could not see into the condo except at night if the lights were on inside. Still …

He had watched her briefly when a pounding sounded at his door. His heart thumped because this was an urgent, dull thumping sound. Not Paul, because he would use the entry request bell. Paul would not be back until later. Derrick did not expect to see him until Saturday. Derrick eased to the door, looked through the peephole, and saw a large box suspended in midair.

"Hey. Let me in. This thing is heavy." It was Paul's voice behind the box.

"You scared me," Derrick said as Paul squeezed sideways through the door. "I thought you would not be back until late."

"I got done early. Wanted to get home." Paul set the box on the floor. "I bought you something. Well, your father bought it. It's his money."

"What is it?" The box had a colorful picture of a display unit.

"It's a television. You had television, right?"

"I think so. We call it a communication monitor. We watch New America Media news and other Chosen performances."

"Let's get it set up. You have satellite and a full package. So, you can watch almost anything."

From the bottom of the box near the ends of each side, Paul cut the clear tape and then slid out two white pieces of plastic. He then lifted the box up and off, revealing a black flat panel like a communication monitor. "You have to pay extra for new movies, but you have money enough for that too. Better not watch porn though, because your father will see the bill." Paul winked.

Movies and porn? Derrick wondered what Paul was talking about.

10

Saturday, March 20

ON SATURDAY, DERRICK PLANNED TO FOLLOW his same routine, except for fixing a bowl of cereal, because Paul said they would eat breakfast together. Derrick wondered if he should start cooking something but didn't know what Paul would want. The past few days, Derrick had worked harder than any time in his life, yet he had merely scratched the surface of the commoner world. He found himself furious when studying science, not so much chemistry, which he found boring. But science! Blasphemy! Commoners believed Earth was over 4 billion years old. *Four billion!* How could they believe such nonsense? He was not worried about algebra, but math was math. He was good at math. Black and white. Right and wrong. Two and two equals four. Math made sense.

Hola, coma estas? Muy bien. He was set for Spanish. English, the one subject he felt confident about, was not as simple as he had imagined. English included reading books. A thing called fiction, which meant the story was made up. Why would someone waste time reading made up stories? He had no idea. Fortunately, on the internet, he had found summaries of many books that he should have already read. Once confident he knew English, he now sensed that it was going to cause him problems.

Paul told him that watching TV would be wise. Because everyone watched TV and the programs would reflect stories and culture familiar to the kids that Derrick would be interacting with in two short days. But Derrick could not watch enough TV in two days to match his peers. Derrick decided he would say that his parents did not like TV and did not have one.

Paul had picked a movie he should watch. "It's old, but it's a classic. And it is still relevant. School is school and teenager are teenagers and are still a lot like this movie." The movie was called *The Breakfast Club.*

Derrick found the movie captivating. But ultimately, it disappointed him. It was nothing like real life. He was sure of that, even here in the commoner world.

A knock at the door. Derrick almost opened it without looking, which scared him a little. *So easy to forget. What else might I forget? Dangerous.* But a quick peek confirmed it was Paul.

"Grab a jacket. It's a little chilly out." Paul did not enter Derrick's condo.

"We are going out?" Derrick asked, not moving. Paul said they would have breakfast, but Derrick assumed that meant Paul would bring something in a sack, like when he brought hamburgers and fries.

"Might as well. You start school Monday, so that means you have arrived here now and if people see us together, that's a good thing. Besides, you don't want your first trip outside to be the school. Better to get a feel for things before that. Also, just so you know. I have already told some people about you."

"You have?" Derrick wondered if it was the girl who lived in the building, and he wondered if the girl who lived in the building was the girl with pink-striped hair.

"One person, actually. Donna, who runs the bistro. That's where we are going. So, don't be surprised that she will know who you are."

"All right," Derrick said.

"And she is a little suspicious, I should add."

"Suspicious?"

"Donna has known my wife and I for years. She can't believe my wife would not welcome you in and can't believe that I would move out."

So, this was it. Derrick had not been physically exposed to the commoner world without a protective barrier: Paul's truck, the parking garage, his condo. Fear gripped him. He stood frozen for a few seconds. Paul stared at him and then gave a swirling motion with one hand. *Hurry!* Derrick left the door open, walked to his bedroom, and opened his closet. He had glanced at the items on the rack but had not pulled them out, had not tried them on. He found a light jacket, dark gray with red edging. It fit. He studied himself in the mirror and did not like what he saw. He did not look like a commoner. His hair too blond, his teeth too white. Although his hair was unkempt. He had not trimmed it in a week because he had not found a Barber-Bot™ in his condo. He meant to ask Paul where to find it but forgot.

"You have your keys?" Paul asked.

Derrick went to the kitchen and retrieved the keys. One to his apartment, one to Paul's apartment. What if someone asked him why he had two keys? He did not have an answer to that question. So many details that could trip him up. One lie would lead to another and another until he would not remember which lies he had told to which person.

Paul led him down the stairs, taking them two at a time. Paul did not go to the garage. Instead, he turned to a door that opened to the outside. Derrick was stepping into the commoner world with no protection, except a light gray jacket and Paul. The air was crisp. Not like ocean air. Drier, cool but not cold.

When they exited the building, Paul looked around and then held up his hand and said, "Stop."

Derrick froze. Trouble. Already.

"You don't want this tag still hanging here." Paul threaded a tag through the loop that attached it to his jacket zipper. "Make sure all the tags are off your clothes. And run them through the wash, so they look like you've worn them."

Derrick thought about asking who would wash his clothes but decided to research that himself first.

"We can stop at the drugstore and pick up something for your face," Paul said.

"What's wrong with my face?"

"You have a dandy pimple coming," Paul said.

At least I do not have to worry about perfect skin, Derrick thought.

"The bistro is a great spot. One of my favorites in town. I drive from my house to go here all the time. Would not make sense for me to live across the street and go for coffee someplace else."

Derrick was hoping for breakfast.

"Can we walk to school after coffee?" Derrick asked. "I should learn the way."

"We can do that. It's a little nippy now, but it's supposed to warm up close to 80 today. Wonderful day to get out and about," Paul said.

Great for Paul, maybe. Derrick hoped he would survive the day. He realized that every day would be like this now. Every day, he would leave the condo, hoping he would survive one more day. The sidewalk was empty. No cars or trucks moving on the street. The bistro was on the street behind the building. They turned the corner, walked one block, and then crossed the street.

Three small tables, each with four chairs, sat on the sidewalk. Each table had an umbrella to provide shade, but they had not yet been opened. Derrick had watched these tables every day since he first saw the girl with the pink-striped hair. Inside were several more tables, and commoners occupied half of them. The bistro smelled heavenly. A large case with a glass front held an assortment of pastries, some familiar to Derrick, many that were unknown to him.

"Paul." A robust woman in her forties, wearing a floral apron, brushed white powder from her hands as she approached the counter. "Glad to see you. This must be Derrick." Her voice was warm and melodic. "I still can't believe you moved out."

"We'll be okay," Paul said. "Tough situation. My sister, well, we were never close. Had not seen or heard from her in years. Didn't get along. But Derrick didn't have a place to go. I'd never even met the boy. Still, he is family. So, he'll be staying with me until he finishes high school. Then he'll either be off to college or working and living on his own." Paul shrugged. "What was I to do? He is family."

Paul sounded so sincere that for a moment Derrick wondered who this unfortunate boy was, and then he remembered he was that boy.

Paul motioned for Derrick to step forward. "Derrick, this is Donna Parks. Makes the best cinnamon rolls in the whole damn world. You like cinnamon rolls, Derrick?"

Paul must have sensed that Derrick did not know what a cinnamon roll was and said, "Silly question. Who doesn't like cinnamon rolls? Donna, are they fresh?"

"You know damn well they're fresh, Paul Jorgensen."

To Derrick's thinking, Donna's words sounded angry, but her voice did not. He doubted he would ever understand the people here.

"We'll share one. And two cups of coffee," Paul said.

Donna set two empty brown ceramic mugs on the counter. One had a chip on the rim. Paul pulled a plastic card from his wallet and stuck it in a machine. A payment device, Derrick assumed.

"Sheriff was in the other day. Said there was a commotion outside your new place. Someone yelling and broke a whiskey bottle against the wall. You hear anything?"

"We got moved in last night," Paul said.

"Keep your eyes open. We haven't had problems in this neighborhood, and I don't want to see that change."

Paul nodded. "We'll sit outside, Donna." Paul picked up the mugs, handing one to Derrick.

"Nice morning for it. I'll bring your cinnamon roll out," Donna said.

Paul walked to another counter that held three large containers, each labeled with a different type of coffee. He watched Paul fill his mug, and, using the same procedure, Derrick filled his own. His first attempt at a commoner world task and he had succeeded. That was something, was it not?

"Cream or sugar?" Paul pointed at a sugar dispenser and a small chrome container that must have contained cream.

"Just black this morning," Derrick said. He did not know why he had said that. He did not like it black. Nevertheless, he had successfully poured coffee. No use pressing his luck at this point.

They sat at a table that was caught the first rays of sunshine. The table was flat-black and made of heavy mesh metal, with matching chairs. The chairs did not look comfortable, but Derrick found they were not as uncomfortable as he had expected. The sun climbed in the sky, streaming rays over the roof of the building and flooding onto the table and sidewalk. It felt warm on Derrick's skin. Steam rose from the mug, the smell enticing. Derrick sipped his coffee and tried not to make a face.

"Beautiful morning," Paul said, looking at the sky.

Derrick said nothing. His fear diminished a notch. Paul was right. It was a beautiful morning, but Derrick could not yet enjoy it.

Donna arrived with a cinnamon roll and silverware wrapped in white paper napkins. It covered a large plate and had white frosting, with melted butter flowing over the top and down the sides. "Enjoy, boys," she said.

Then, laying a hand on Derrick's shoulder, she said, "Derrick, Paul told me about your parents. It's just awful. You let me know if there is anything I can do. And you come see us often, okay?"

"Thank you. I will," Derrick said, and his fear diminished further. The warmth of Donna's hand, voice, and smile helped. Yet he felt guilty because his parents were fine.

After unwrapping the knife and fork, Paul used the fork to work off a piece of the cinnamon roll. "Dig in," Paul said.

Derrick mimicked Paul, although he was clumsier with the fork. Normally, he would have used the knife to cut a bite, and it would have been smaller than what Paul stuffed in his mouth, but Derrick did it the same and tried to look relaxed, even though he was not.

With a chunk of cinnamon roll tucked into his mouth, Derrick closed his eyes involuntarily. He felt the fear lift away as the flavors overwhelmed him. How could this be? At every turn, Paul had introduced him to new levels of gastrological delights.

Derrick forked up another piece of the roll.

Paul pointed at the roll with his fork and mumbled with a full mouth. "Good, right?"

Derrick nodded. Paul refilled their coffee cups as the roll dwindled. Despite sharing it, Derrick felt stuffed.

"So," Paul began, "how did the week go? Are you ready?"

Derrick took a drink. "It went okay. I have learned much. But there is so much to learn. To be honest, I am worried about school."

"Yeah, I suppose you have reason to worry. Not much you can do about it now." Paul took a bite of the cinnamon roll. Drank from his coffee mug. "You're determined to attempt this Denver charade?"

"What choice do I have?" Derrick asked.

"I don't know. I guess you have to do what you think is best."

Derrick cupped his mug with both hands. The warmth comforted him. Then it happened.

The girl with the pink-striped hair rounded the corner of the building.

11

THE GIRL WITH THE PINK-STRIPED HAIR STUDIED DERRICK, but she did not slow. Her head swiveled, her eyes fixed on him as she reached for the door handle and then went inside. Derrick held his coffee mug suspended halfway between the table and his mouth.

Paul glanced over his shoulder to see what had riveted Derrick's attention but saw nothing. "What?" Paul asked.

Derrick set his mug on the table. "Nothing. Just a girl I have seen from my window."

"Ah. I see," Paul said.

Derrick wanted to leave. Derrick wanted to stay. He was afraid, excited, and bewildered. Why did this girl he had never met affect him in such a manner?

"Something I've meant to say to you, Derrick. You talk funny."

"I do? How so? I have always been told that my speech is excellent. Oratory skills were one of my best subjects at the James Carver Academy."

"James Carver Academy." Paul snarled the words. "Figures."

Derrick made a fist under the table but said nothing.

Paul nodded, not in a manner that showed agreement. More menacing than amiable. "That's the problem. You talk too damn perfect. I've never even heard you use a contraction."

"Contractions are a lazy man's way of speaking," Derrick said, too quickly and regretted it.

"I don't know about that, but you don't talk like people here. You'd better dial it back."

"Why are you telling me this now?" Derrick asked.

"Because you'll be talking to people soon. More coffee?"

Before Derrick replied, Paul took both mugs, poured the remnants of the now lukewarm coffee into a nearby pot containing young plants, and disappeared into the bistro. Derrick sat alone in an iron chair at an iron table on a sidewalk in Potterville, California, in the world of the commoners. His sole protection was his intellect, and that seemed a thin defense. Paul had been gone several minutes, longer than needed for the task. He might have stopped to talk to Donna or some other patron because it appeared that Paul was well known in Potterville. Perhaps he was explaining to others why he had moved out of his house. Because of a nephew, he did not know but could not abandon. At one time, the story sounded plausible. Now it sounded ridiculous. Paul took this job for the money. People know Paul. They would see right through the story.

Paul returned holding two steaming mugs of coffee, followed by the girl with the pink-striped hair. She was thin, not tall, but not short, and moved with a grace Derrick could not categorize. Strong somehow. Her hair was jet black, except for the pink stripe that he assumed was genetically engineered like his own. Genetic engineering was not permanent. His hair and eyes would return to their original dull colors without enhancement treatments. Her skin was olive, not dark, not light, and her complexion was clear as his nanobot-cleansed skin (as clear as his used to be, that is), but it glowed in a way that his did not. He puzzled over commoners acquiring such technology. As she drew close, he caught a delightful fragrance, not unlike flowers. Her eyelashes were too long to be natural. She had thin black lines under each eye and sparkling blue eyelids. None of these would have been acceptable in Pacific Edge.

A strange feeling stirred in his chest.

"This is Derrick." Paul nodded toward Derrick.

The girl with the pink-striped hair studied Derrick. After a moment, she said, "Hi, I'm Nyx."

"Nyx goes to Potterville High. That's where you'll be going. She lives in our building too," Paul said.

Derrick remained silent, following his own advice: keep his mouth shut and listen. Hoping the girl with the pink-striped hair would not hear his heart pounding.

"Does he talk?" Nyx asked.

Paul glared at Derrick, tilted his head toward Nyx, and mouthed: "Say something."

"Hi, I am Derrick." *How stupid was that? Paul y told her my name.* He added, "I start school on Monday. Maybe I will see you there."

"Duh. We live in the same building, go to the same school. Ya think? This ain't New York."

"Yes, right. I am nervous because I am new here." Well, that was a little better. Not much better, but better.

Nyx stared at Derrick, but her gaze softened. "I heard about your parents. I can't imagine what it's like for you."

Ignoring his own advice and with little thought, Derrick said, "They will be…" Derrick stopped, thinking hard. *They will be? They will be, what? Rotting in their graves?* Then he said, "I mean, I will be okay." *I will be, okay? Is that what one says after losing his parents? This will never work.*

Nyx pursed her lips and then said, "See you around, Mr. King."

When Nyx had turned the corner, Paul said, "Damn. Well, that was awkward."

"Yes, it was. I apologize," Derrick said, looking at the tabletop.

"Stop that perfect talking. This is not just about you, remember? I'm sticking my neck out here. Look up slang when you get home."

Derrick nodded but did not look up. Tears welled in his eyes, but he fought them back. He estimated that commoners rarely cried when they were drinking coffee on a beautiful Saturday morning. Although it didn't occur to him that a boy who just lost his parents might cry. He would never pull this off. But if he failed, then what? Derrick felt homesick again. He had a strong urge to get up and run home, not the condo home, the Pacific Edge home.

The sun warmed Derrick's shoulders. He drank coffee. Maybe he was a black coffee drinker now. One week earlier, Derrick King was destined for greatness in Pacific Edge. That seemed like a lifetime ago. Derrick had ruined his life with one rash act. Now, he threatened to ruin Paul's life as well. Paul seemed angry with him. Derrick did not blame him. His first encounter with the girl with the pink-striped hair could not have gone much worse. Paul had taken the job because of the money. But he took the job. Derrick had to make this work for Paul's sake as well as his own.

"Did you hear the commotion that Donna mentioned?"

"No. I mean, I might have heard something." Derrick paused.

Paul stared at him.

"Yes, I heard it. Men yelling at someone to come out. Then a bottle smashed against the building."

"Did you see them?"

"No. I was afraid to look out. I thought they knew I was in there."

"I doubt that. Have you been out? Has someone seen you?"

"This is the first time I have been outside. Honest."

"Next time, try to get a look at them. We don't need that kind of trouble here again."

"Again?"

"Don't worry. The sheriff is a good man. He'll be on top of it before it gets out of hand."

"Finish your coffee and then let's walk to your new school. I have things to do today," Paul said.

Paul showed him where to put his empty mug. "I suspect you'll be coming here often enough. Might as well know the drill."

"Drill?"

"Routine. Customers know what to do. You're trying to fit in, right?"

They walked three blocks. Derrick studied the street. One block had businesses like the bistro. A place that sold an eclectic assortment of jewelry, and they would tolerate nothing so frivolous in Pacific Edge. An insurance agency, Derrick understood what insurance was because they had insurance for health and cosmetics in Pacific Edge, but it surprised him that commoners had insurance. An accountant's office, which gave Derrick hope because Father was an accountant, and Derrick assumed he would be an accountant too. A store that sold flowers. A store that sold drugs, but the window display did not feature drugs. Derrick wondered if they had mood enhancers. He could use some.

The other two blocks were family homes, although one home advertised counseling services and another offered pediatric care. He watched the windows for guns. He watched the alleys for packs of stray dogs. He watched the streets for drug lords, gangs, and armed militias. He saw well-maintained homes, lawns, and gardens. Not like the homes, lawns, and gardens of Pacific Edge that looked so perfect one might think they were photographs. These homes, lawns, and gardens looked as if they were maintained with arduous work.

Derrick did not understand.

"There it is." Paul stopped on the corner and pointed to the large, red brick building across the street.

It was the building Paul said was the school when they first arrived in Potterville. The one Derrick thought Paul was joking about. The one that looked unsafe. It must be over 100 years old, although Derrick could not estimate its age. Everything in Pacific Edge looked new. A chain-link fence surrounded the school, but there were no gates, just openings at the corners and in the middle. The lawn was green with paths worn to the dirt, marring the grass with crisscross patterns. Four large trees dominated the campus, their new emerald-green leaves unfurling. Behind the school, Derrick could see enormous lights on top of tall poles.

He would see Nyx here, but he was unsure why that seemed important.

In less than 48 hours, his new life in Potterville would begin.

Or end.

12

BACK AT DERRICK'S CONDO, PAUL HANDED him three green pieces of paper.

"It's cash. Commoner money," Paul said. "I'll see you later. You should go back to the bistro this afternoon. An ordinary boy new to town would not stay in the house all day."

Three twenty-dollar bills. Derrick did not know what one could buy with $60.

He tried to study but found concentration difficult. Then a small window appeared in the upper left-hand corner of the screen.

An e-mail, this time from someone called number1sis@potterville.com.

```
From: number1sis@potterville.com

To: derrickking0312@potterville.com

Subject: It's me

I have a new e-mail address, but it's me. Your
pain-in-the-ass sister. I hope the new e-mail
address is safer.

Problems here, but more on that later. You
wouldn't believe what I'm doing. It's crazy.

I hope you're okay. I worry about you. I am
making progress. I've learned a lot, and it's
worse than I thought. I can't go into it now.
I don't have enough answers.

You probably don't trust that this e-mail is
legit. Ask me a question that only I can
answer.

Later Brother
```

Derrick considered Miriam's method of proving her identity. The more he thought about it, the less he liked it. It would be too easy for security people to find out the answer to his question. They might research surveillance video or, if necessary, threaten Miriam to learn the answer. Although he was not sure his way was better, he decided to write an e-mail of his own.

```
TO: number1sis@potterville.com

FROM: derrickking0312@potterville.com

Is this really Miriam? I hope it is. It might
be a trap, but I do not think it matters. The
Tribunal has ordered that I start school on
Monday. I am not ready, but no choice. They
will never let me return to Pacific Edge. It
is  much  different  here  from  what  I  had
expected. But I have been forbidden to talk
about that.

Prove it is you by asking a question that only
I would know the answer to.
```

Derrick hit send and then waited. Fifteen minutes passed. Nothing. Half an hour passed. Nothing. Sixty minutes later, he gave up. He walked to the kitchen, opened the refrigerator, closed it, paced down the hall, and then repeated the process. After three laps around the condo, he went to his room. He felt exhausted, but he did not understand why. He laid down. He slept.

Derrick woke with a jerk. Sunlight streamed through his bedroom window, filling the room with warm yellow light. He had slept for three hours. It was two o'clock in the afternoon. His stomach growled. In the kitchen, he gazed into the refrigerator, looked through the cabinets, both of which had plenty of food, but nothing appealed to him. He had currency in his pocket. With his smartphone, he checked the temperature and found it was 79 degrees outside. The weather was typically pleasant in Pacific Edge, yet he seldom went out unless he had to. They did not have television, movies, or internet in Pacific Edge. Derrick wondered what he had done with his time while there.

After checking the peephole and seeing no one, he eased the door open and stepped into the hall. A knock-on Paul's door raised no response. He walked down the stairs. On the bottom floor, he hesitated and then opened the door to the lobby, which was a small room with double glass doors that opened to the outside. Small brass doors with keyholes lined one wall. He stood inside the glass doors, watching the street. There was more activity than earlier. Cars and trucks passed on the street. A few people walking and a few more outside their homes. A woman on the sidewalk was talking over a small fence to a man standing in a neighboring yard.

It terrified him, but hunger pushed him forward.

Derrick stepped outside, took a deep breath, and walked to the bistro. First time out by himself. His outing with Paul had been a blur, and he had been so anxious that he failed to notice the fragrance drifting from tree blossoms of pink and white. This time he was present. Perhaps it was because of fear, but maybe it was something else. He smelled the flower's bouquet, but there was no scent of the sea. There was a faint odor that he did not recognize. A rich, musky odor that he would ask Paul about. Before he went into the bistro, he walked by the store with guitars in the window. Through the open door, he saw a bearded man sitting on a stool, playing a guitar. His hands glided over the neck without hesitation. *I would like to learn to do that,* Derrick thought, and then wondered where that notion came from. He had never been interested in Chosen music, even though it was all about their founder, and the Supreme Creator, which were things he worshipped as he had been instructed as far back as he could remember. Despite how important those things were, music was unimportant to him. It existed. That was all.

Donna greeted Derrick by name when he entered. He stared at the menu for several minutes, trying to decide what he wanted from the list of unfamiliar foods. Donna rescued him, recommending a roast beef panini, which she said was a sandwich, a customer favorite, and today's special. He ordered a Coke to go with it. The panini came on a plate with chips and a slice of pickle. Derrick went outside to sit at the same table he and Paul had chosen that morning. He pushed the door open with his back, and when he turned, he was face to face with the girl with the pink-striped hair.

"Hello, Derrick." Her voice cold. Her eyes intense. "Don't sit in my chair, but you can sit with me." She pointed at a table. "I'll be back."

A light-weight pink sweater was draped over a chair, so Derrick sat opposite it and stared at his food. His stomach complained that he was not eating, but it would be rude to start before she returned. *What kind of name is Nyx?*

Nyx returned with a salad and a coffee that was a rich chocolate, color topped with white foam in a heart-shaped pattern. "You didn't have to wait for me. This isn't a date. Just thought we could get to know each other a little."

Derrick took a bite of his sandwich. *Wow!* Donna told him true on this one. Derrick said nothing. He felt he was staring too intently into Nyx's eyes, but he did not look away.

"You don't talk much, do you?" she asked.

Derrick swallowed and said, "Not much."

"Where are you from, Derrick King?"

"Denver. That is in the state of Colorado," Derrick said.

"I know where Denver is. Do I look stupid to you?" Nyx held her fork above her plate.

Derrick thought maybe she was about to stab him with it.

"I am sorry," Derrick said. *I am going to screw this up on the first day. Shit. Did I just say shit in my head?*

Nyx forked salad into her mouth and chewed.

Derrick watched her lips move.

"I'm sorry about your parents. I made you uncomfortable earlier. Sorry about that. I do that sometimes. I don't mean to, but it happens."

Derrick blinked. Nyx changed before his eyes. At least, it seemed that she did. Everything seemed softer about her now. The edge gone. "It is okay. I am nervous around new people. New town." Derrick paused, thinking through what he wanted to say. "Many things have happened to me of late."

Nyx nodded and continued eating her salad. They ate in silence for a few minutes.

Nyx said, "I like your hair. Do you bleach it?"

Derrick had no idea what she was talking about. That was not exactly true. He knew she was talking about his hair. He did not know what bleach was. To give him a moment to think, he took a big bite of his sandwich and held up one finger. *My hair looks unnatural. Bleach must be a way to change the color. She thinks I used it.* After he swallowed, he said, "Yes. I used bleach. I will not be using it in the future."

"Why not? I rather like it. Most boys here are too chicken to color their hair."

Still at a loss, Derrick said, "Maybe I will use it again. I am not sure."

Nyx pushed her salad plate away. "Are you still hungry?"

"A little."

"Split a scone with me?"

He did not know what a scone was. "Sure."

Derrick followed Nyx into the bistro. She picked out a blueberry scone and asked Donna to split it, two plates and that they would share the cost. Derrick wanted to pay for it, but Nyx seemed clear that they were just two people sitting at the same table with no illusion of togetherness.

When they went back outside, a piece of yellow paper with faint blue lines was on the table, pinned under the sugar container, and the edges of the paper fluttered in the breeze. Thick red letters scrawled across the paper read:

WATCHING YOU RUNNER

"You know anything about this?" Nyx asked.

Derrick hesitated. He considered telling Nyx everything but then stuck with his strategy of keeping his mouth shut. "No."

"Are you sure?" she asked.

"I walked back into the bistro at the same time you did."

"Right."

"Should we tell Donna?" Derrick asked.

"No, I'll take care of it." Nyx took a picture with her phone. "I'll send it to the sheriff." She typed on her phone and then folded the paper and put it in her pocket.

Nyx sat, took a bite of the scone, and then a sip of her drink. "Dammit. It's cold. I'll be right back."

Derrick remained standing, staring at where the note had been. *Watching me. Watching and listening.* He sat but was no longer hungry. He looked around to see if anyone was watching him from a distance. He saw a few people walking, but none of them paid attention to him. The bistro door opened and startled him.

Nyx returned to her seat. She sipped her drink. "Ah, that's better. I hate cold coffee. How about you? You like cold coffee? Derrick?"

"Huh?"

"I asked you a question."

"Sorry. I was thinking."

"So?"

"So, what?"

She rolled her eyes. "Do you like cold coffee?"

"I like it hot."

"At least you have that going for you." Nyx smiled.

Derrick felt better. Her smile did that. But he reminded himself that she could not help him. She was just a girl who did not know him. If she knew the truth about him, she might be the first to turn on him. Then it occurred to him; she might be involved with whoever was watching him. What better way to spy?

"You have not tried your scone."

He vacillated between her warm smile and the reality that she could be a spy. If he did not eat, she might surmise that he was suspicious of her.

He forked off a chunk and ate. "Mmm, it's good," he mumbled. It would not replace cinnamon rolls at the top of his bistro-delight list. It was drier, not as buttery, or sweet, but still good. He wondered if Donna made anything that was not good.

"What's the matter?"

"Huh? Nothing. Everything is fine."

"Bull. Something's bothering you. I can see it plain as day."

Derrick thought hard. His next statement was important. He sensed that much.

"That note. And what Donna said earlier about a problem at our building the other night."

"Don't worry about it. Punks. We can take care of them."

It made sense that Nyx was unconcerned. After all, she was not the target of the message. She was a local girl. He was the one someone had pegged as an escapee. A runner. Escaping from the protection of Pacific Edge made little sense. But commoners would not know that. Besides, Pacific Edge was so well guarded that escape was impossible.

Escape was impossible. That thought circulated in his mind.

Escape is impossible.

Miriam was not coming to help him, not that she could help him. And there was something else, but he could not identify it.

Nyx stood and said, "You're kinda weird, and you talk funny. See you around, Derrick King."

13

DERRICK COULD NOT SLEEP, SO HE tried to study but could not concentrate. He checked his e-mail, but nothing new appeared. He found reading counterproductive because he would drift off into some distant place, thinking about everything and nothing. Instead, he watched videos, which were like watching New America Media, yet felt like a new experience. In the search bar, he entered Community, Pacific Edge, Pacific Edge Community, Chosen, and Runner. He found several videos, amateur stuff created by commoners. He confirmed his discovery that commoners were, for the most part, divided regarding the Chosen and the Communities in which they lived. Commoners either hated them or worshiped them. Worshiped was not exactly right but saw the Chosen as special, which was consistent with how the Chosen saw themselves. That commoners hated the Chosen was also consistent with what the Chosen believed about the commoners. He found no reference to the combination of Chosen and Runner.

There existed a third group, not as outspoken as the other two. This group did not love the Chosen but did not hate them either. In most cases, discussion about the Chosen was not central to their videos. They mentioned them, but they were not important. This group thought the Chosen and commoners were pawns in a larger game, but the meaning of this game was unclear. They seemed to understand the essence of the dilemma and assumed anyone who watched also understood. But for Derrick, pieces were missing, and unlike the haters and the lovers who seemed confident that their views were correct, the third group contemplated a grander picture. Although they understood the problem, they did not understand the forces that had created it. They agreed it was sinister. This third group seemed the most radical and ill-informed. The Chosen are not pawns, and the force behind them is not evil. The third group gave Derrick a bad feeling.

He could not determine the size of the groups. The lovers and haters posted the most videos, and both were passionate about their opinions. For some reason, Derrick could neither explain nor justify, he concluded that passion did not correlate with the groups' numbers. The more he watched, the more confident he became that finding and fitting in with those who worshiped the Chosen was his best bet for survival.

Derrick stopped checking for new e-mails.

He stayed up late, searching many topics on the internet. Several times he started composing an e-mail to number1sis but stared at the blank screen, unable to write a sentence. It was after three in the morning when he fell into bed.

Derrick heard explosions in the distance. The closed blinds on the window flickered red and orange. He smelled smoke and heard screams. Bending the blinds, he made a slight opening so he could look outside. Leaping orange flames engulfed the bistro, and black smoke filled the air. Vehicles painted flat black — with holes cut in the tops through which men fired large guns — raced down the street, running over people and mowing them down with the powerful weapons. Screaming men, women, and children ran in all directions. Some half-dressed, some naked. Many covered with blood. A few blocks over, an explosion hurled debris and black smoke into the air, moving directly at him at ferocious speed.

He felt a hand on his shoulder. He did not want to see who had entered his room, but he turned his head as if an unseen demon forced him to look.

"What are you looking at, Number Seven?"

* * *

Derrick woke with a start. The room was pitch black.

Nightmare.

He looked out the window, covered by curtains, not blinds. No fires, no people. Soft light from the streetlamps created a peaceful glow. He crawled back into bed, still trembling, although he knew it was only a dream. He lay awake for what felt like hours.

The moment he awoke on Sunday, March 21, he knew it was late morning. He went to the window, looked at the bistro tables, but did not see the girl with the pink-striped hair. A closed sign hung in the bistro window. A man walked his dog on the sidewalk. A red car passed by. A quiet Sunday morning.

He checked his cell phone and found no e-mail from number1sis. He decided the previous message must have been a trick the Tribunal had sent. That made sense. The Tribunal did not work on Sundays. Now, he did not expect a response until Monday. How the Tribunal would respond was unknowable. They might continue their ruse, trying to build a stronger case that Derrick King was a subversive and dangerous threat to the Chosen.

Derrick made coffee and a new thing called a waffle. He saw the device called a waffle iron in the cabinet, searched the internet, and found what it did and how to use it. Paul had stocked his pantry with pancake/waffle mix, which made sense because Paul had also purchased a waffle maker and maple syrup. Derrick found the waffle as delightful as the other foods he had tried here. The cereal that sustained him the first few days was fine, but he had relegated it to days when he had neither the time nor energy for meal preparation and for the occasional late-night snack. Occasional meaning every day this week.

With a second cup of coffee, Derrick placed his phone into its cradle, selected a collection of music by four men called the Beatles. According to a date alongside the titles, the music was old. However, a rating scale indicated it remained popular. He settled onto the living room couch. He rather enjoyed the music and wondered why it was forbidden in Pacific Edge.

Something was bothering him, but he could not isolate it. He had a plethora of reasons to be troubled. Yet this felt different. Like he was missing something obvious. Slowly, it came to him. Why would the Tribunal bother to set him up? What would they do if he took their bait? Exile him forever? They had no intention of letting him return to Pacific Edge and did not expect him to survive. He understood their reasoning. Because what he saw of life here was inconsistent with everything he had been taught. It was contrary to the New America Media reports of widespread violence, riots, and deranged behavior. Perhaps there were places like those shown, but it was not like that here. He had never seen a town like Potterville on New America Media.

People never returned to Pacific Edge after leaving because they would contradict the established legends about the commoners. Derrick remained fearful, because although the depictions on New America Media were inaccurate, there must be reasons for such portrayals. He was under no illusion that he would survive here. If he did, it would be a lonely, fearful, and short existence.

Possibly, if he fell for the Tribunal's trap, they would come for him. But to what end? Imprison him? That did not seem necessary. Kill him? The Chosen did not have a death penalty. James Carver had done away with the barbaric sentencing acts of the old United States of America. His was a more perfect way.

So it is written, and so it is.

The coffee grew cold as Derrick ruminated but found no answers to his questions. Perhaps the e-mail was from Miriam, but how could that be possible? The Chosen learning stations were not computers that had access to the internet. The Chosen did not know such a system existed.

A knock came at the door. Derrick checked the peephole. At least he had that process engrained. It was Paul. Derrick had not expected to see him until later in the evening and then only to discuss the process for enrollment the following morning.

"Afternoon," Paul said.

Derrick stepped aside but said nothing.

"There is a communication set up with your parents. It will be broadcast in 10 minutes. I am to remind you of the rules." Paul set his jaw.

"I know the rules," Derrick said too quickly.

"I'm sure you do, but I was told to remind you. At this point, it might be more important that you follow the rules for my sake than for yourself. What more can they do to you?"

Paul paced across the room as he talked. "You cannot say anything about Potterville or the people you've met or the things you've seen. That includes the internet, computers, television, foods, e-mail. Nothing. Savvy?"

Derrick sank onto the couch. This sounded easy, but what would he talk about? Easy to slip and say something wrong. "I understand."

"Let them do the talking. Ask questions about how they are doing and so forth. Limit your side of the conversation to things they already know. You've been here studying the program the Tribunal provided. You have food. You're okay. Understand?"

Derrick nodded.

Paul grabbed the TV remote control and turned on the screen. In the app menu, he found New World Media and selected it. Derrick had not seen the New World Media icon before. The screen showed a still photograph of the Tribunal building. Paul checked the time and said, "Should start any moment now."

The number 10 came on the screen then turned to 9 and then to 8, 7, 6 … After the number one appeared, the image changed, and Derrick saw Father, Mother, and Miriam sitting in what looked like an office that he did not recognize. He studied the image, both to capture his family fully and to memorize the room. He wanted to know where this was being done but did not know why that seemed important.

"Hi, Derrick," Father said.

"Hi." Derrick's voice cracked a little.

"It's good to see you," Father said.

"It is good to see you as well," Derrick replied.

"How are you doing?" Father asked.

"I am well. I have food here. I have been studying the program the Tribunal supplied. It has been beneficial."

"We are glad to hear that." Derrick's Father paused. "The Tribunal has informed us of the change to your sentence. That is why we were granted this communication. Because you start school tomorrow."

"Yes." Derrick studied his family. He could not read his Father. Mother's eyes were red, and she twisted a white handkerchief in her hands. Miriam looked — like Miriam.

Defiant.

"I have been studying hard. The program is good." Derrick was lying about the quality of the program, although he had been studying hard on the internet.

He hoped his lying was not transparent. He was not well practiced at that skill. But the practice was good because tomorrow he would be dishonest a lot.

"How is everyone there?" Derrick asked, hoping to change the course of the conversation.

"We," Father paused, then said, "have been fine under the circumstances."

Derrick nodded. "How are you, Miriam?"

"You know me. I spend a lot of time in my room working. I made a new friend."

Did she point her finger at the camera? Derrick could not be sure because it happened so fast.

Watching and listening. Listening and watching.

"We will need to be careful when we communicate," Miriam had said. *Had Miriam tried to send a signal?* Derrick focused his attention on her.

The conversation dragged on for a few minutes. It is difficult to have a conversation when you cannot talk about your realities. Miriam remained quiet for the rest of their time. She seemed distracted. As if she were uninterested in the entire affair. That bothered Derrick. But he stayed focused on her and, at times, had trouble following the conversation. His Mother started crying, and Father said it was time to go. Miriam stared to one side. So much for signals. Now Derrick was certain that when he thought Miriam was pointing at him, it was just his imagination.

But as the screen faded to black, Miriam looked at the camera, held up one finger, and then pointed to her chest and mouthed:

"Number1sis."

14

Monday, March 22, 6:30 a.m.

DERRICK WOKE EARLY, SHOWERED, SHAVED, AND dressed for his first day of school at Potterville High. He ate cereal, the unhealthy, colorful, fruity, sweet kind, because being healthy today did not seem important. He checked his phone, but no e-mail from number1sis or anyone else, not that he expected one from any other person. The Tribunal would not be wishing him good fortune.

A realization struck him like a bullet. The Tribunal had sent him e-mails, and Miriam had sent him e-mails, but Derick had never heard of e-mail until coming here. Miriam discovered e-mail. Although, how remained a mystery, and yet maybe not so mysterious because Miriam was smart and knew tricks he would never consider. It troubled him that the Tribunal had access to e-mail. Was she smart enough to prevent her e-mails from being detected by the Tribunal?

He and Paul drove to school, even though it was a short walk. As they exited the condo parking lot onto the street, Paul said, "I've been thinking. What grade were you in before you left Pacific Edge?"

"Senior." Derrick stared at Paul. That seemed like an odd question.

"I thought so. Not sure why I thought that. Perhaps your father mentioned it. Anyway, your file information says you're a junior." Paul looked straight ahead.

Why a junior? Derrick did not understand.

They arrived before school started and parked across the street. Paul led him up the concrete stairs and through the main doors. Upon entering the building, Derrick noticed an odor. As with many things, it was unfamiliar to him, and he lacked words to describe it. It was not pleasant, but it was not offensive either. Stale old dusty: the smell of too many people in too small a place was the best description Derrick could manage.

Paul handed the counterfeit school file containing the make-believe information on imaginary Derrick King from Denver, Colorado, to a woman sitting at a desk where a placard indicated she was a school counselor named Doris Bates. Doris was not young. She was not old either. Derrick realized people here must not have the genetic engineering or other procedures the

Chosen enjoyed. Therefore, aging was natural, and Derrick did not know how to judge it. Doris wore her deep brown hair in tight curls. A small woman, who, despite signs of aging, had an assuredness about her. As Doris flipped through the file, Paul explained how Derrick's parents had died in a house fire and that Derrick's Mother was Paul's sister. And being Derrick's only relative, had taken Derrick in. Doris Bates said she had heard about Derrick, was sorry for his loss, and hoped he would like it at Potterville High.

The enrollment process was not complicated. At least, it was easy for Derrick because he just remained seated in a chair. Doris Bates stared at her computer monitor, mumbling as she worked. He could understand snippets of her whispers. Classes were full, this class conflicted with that class, that one's not available. She called teachers, often pleading to take one more. Spanish class was full, but the teacher agreed to take Derrick. Mrs. Bates got it worked out. The process took 45 minutes.

There were forms for Paul to sign and expenses that required payment. When Mrs. Bates said Derrick's enrollment was complete, Paul left. A bell rang, and Derrick could hear a mass of students moving through the halls. Gradually, growing quieter, but never becoming silent. Five minutes later, another bell rang, followed by the last crescendo of running feet and frenzied voices. Derrick deduced the bells replaced the multicolored ceiling lights used in James Carver Academy to signal the beginning and end of classes. He enjoyed a moment of unwarranted confidence that he had understood the meaning of the bells without assistance. Mrs. Bates gave Derrick a map of the school with the locations of his classes highlighted in yellow and numbered sequentially. She handed Derrick a slip of paper with his locker number and combination number. Derrick wanted to ask what a locker and combination were but remained quiet.

She excused herself and told Derrick to stay put. He sat silently. He was checking his e-mail, which was pointless because Miriam would be at the Academy by now.

"You'll lose that phone if you use it in class," Mrs. Bates said when she returned. "Unless the teacher gives you permission to listen to music during a study period, use it as a calculator, or to do research. If you're caught surfing the web, social media, or texting, you'll lose it for the day."

"Yes, ma'am," Derrick said. He could not imagine how one would surf with a phone and wondered if the school had a problem with spiders. He shivered and looked around the room.

"At least you have manners. You can call me Mrs. Bates."

"Yes, ma'am," Derrick said.

A boy with black hair and brown skin stuck his head in the door.

"You're late, again, Antonio," Mrs. Bates said.

"I'm sorry. I ran an extra mile this morning."

"You are limping," Mrs. Bates said.

"Yeah, no big deal. Pulled a muscle," Antonio said.

Mrs. Bates studied Antonio for a moment. "I hope it's not serious. Track is important to you, and you are vital to the team."

"I'll be okay," Antonio said.

"I'll talk to your coach about your morning routine. Apparently, he thinks track is more important than school." Mrs. Bates closed one eye quickly. "Assistants can't be late all the time."

"Yes, Mrs. Bates."

Derrick thought he saw Antonio roll his eyes.

Studying Derrick's file, Mrs. Bates said, "This is Derrick King. He is a new student. Derrick comes to us from Denver. Please show him where to find his locker and then show him where all his classes are. When you finish, take him to his second period class. You know the drill."

"Yes, Mrs. Bates," Antonio said.

"Step outside for a moment." Mrs. Bates motioned that Antonio should leave. "And don't roll your eyes at me, Antonio."

When the door closed, she reached across her desk, took Derrick's hand, and gave it a squeeze. "I'm sorry for what happened to your parents, Derrick. If you need someone to talk to, come see me. Or talk to the school nurse. Students find her an excellent resource when they have problems."

Derrick nodded but said nothing. He felt a twinge of guilt because his parents were not dead. It was all a lie. But he had suffered a significant loss. That much was true. Despite his guilt, her kindness felt good, yet unexpected.

Antonio was waiting in the empty hallway. "What's your locker number?"

Derrick looked at the slip of paper in his hand and then gave it to Antonio.

"Figures," Antonio said, then added, "Juniors and seniors get first floor lockers, but you've missed out on those. You're 217, second floor, but close to the center stairs so it could be worse. You'll have to put up with sophomores, but at least you're not stuck down in the basement with the freshmen."

Derrick followed Antonio down the hall, past doors marked attendance, staff services, Vice Principal Jones (which caused him to think of Mr. Jones at James Carver Academy, and the point at which his current situation began), Vice Principal Halverson, Vice Principal Sanchez, and Principal Snapp. This short hallway in the center of the building was administration. It intersected with a hall that extended left and right. Wide stairs went up and down, but Antonio turned right and started up. Easy enough so far. Easy for Derrick, but Antonio struggled up the stairs, grimacing with each step. At the top, another hallway extended left and right, same as the first floor. Antonio turned right, walked past a closed door that had an opaque glass window on the top half and displayed the number 201. Derrick saw rows of narrow metal doors on each side of the hall, the first one numbered 201, the second one numbered 203.

Derrick thought this was a strange numbering system. Did commoners have an issue with even numbers? Derrick almost asked Antonio about it when he noticed the metal doors on the other side were even numbers. His stupidity will give him away or maybe land him in some special class for slow learners.

"Here it is." Antonio stopped in front of 217. He handed Derrick the slip of paper. "You'd better check it. Make sure it's empty. You know, no dead freshmen or anything."

Derrick stared at the slip.

Locker 217

L38, R03, L17, R27

"You had lockers in Denver, right?" Antonio asked.

"Yes," Derrick lied. "Different, though."

"I see. Made you buy your own lock, huh? I've seen schools like that. Give me your combination. So, spin it left, counterclockwise like this at least twice, then land on 38, then clockwise to 03, then counterclockwise to 17, then back to 27. Slowly back to 27. Most of these old locks don't work so good. If you go past 27, you gotta start over."

"Well," Derrick said.

Antonio stared at him. "Well, what?"

"Old locks don't work well." Derrick pointed to the lock.

"That's what I said."

"You said they do not work good."

"What are you, a smartass?"

Derrick felt his face heat, but this was not anger. It was from embarrassment, not dissimilar from what he often felt at James Carver Academy when Miriam acted out. The thought of Miriam added a heavy feeling in his chest.

"I am sorry. That was rude of me. Bad habit."

Antonio stared at him a moment and then turned back to the locker.

Derrick watched Antonio spin the dial, easing it to 27. Then he lifted a little chrome handle, and the door popped open. "Empty. Good. You want to put your jacket in?"

Derrick nodded and hung his jacket on the hook. He kept the file that Mrs. Bates had provided.

"You should put this in your wallet. Easy enough to memorize, but you'd be surprised how many people forget their locker combination over a break. Some kids forget it over a long weekend. Working in admin, I see it all the time."

Derrick wondered what a long weekend was. Did the commoners have a different calendar? He stuffed the paper in his pocket. He would ask Paul what a wallet and a long weekend were later.

Antonio then showed Derrick to each class in the same order as they were scheduled. Antonio suggested Derrick keep the schedule in his locker, at least for a few days, until he had it down. Derrick assumed having it down meant memorized.

When they reached the last classroom, Antonio looked at his phone and said, "Only a few minutes until the next class, so no use going there now. Come, I'll show you the lunchroom and vending machines. Did your uncle pay for lunch?"

"I am unsure," Derrick said.

"Let me see your papers. Yep. Paul paid for a month. See this number here? That's your ID number for lunch. They'll print you a card. Might have it at the lunch line today. If not, tell them your number, and they'll look you up on the computer. You're lucky. It's pizza day."

"I like pizza," Derrick said.

"Well, it's not like the Flying Pie, but it's better than most of the crap they serve here."

Derrick did not ask what a flying pie was, nor did he ask if they actually fed the students excrement. He did not want to know.

Antonio struggled down the stairs. "Here are the vending machines. Got to love them on days the lunch is crap. Most juniors have money, so they don't eat in the lunchroom except on pizza, lasagna, and hamburger days. Mostly, it's lowly freshmen, sophomores, about half the juniors, and a few seniors without jobs who eat the lunchroom food every day. You can still grab your vending machine food and eat in the lunchroom. On nice days, kids buying from the machines go outside. On Fridays, the lunch ladies grill hamburgers out there too. You gotta pay extra for them, but it's worth it, dude. Trust me. You have money?"

"I have a little," Derrick said.

"Cool," Antonio replied.

Derrick decided he had to make the study of the irregularities of commoner English a priority. He looked with some fascination at the vending machines. Behind the glass doors was an assortment of food items. Two machines did not have glass doors, but he recognized Coke, plus some names he did not recognize. He still had fifty-two dollars in his pocket, which would stay there today because it was pizza day.

Double doors opened into a large room filled with long tables with benches on each side. No students were in the room, but Derrick could see women wearing white clothing and white nets over their hair working behind a counter. A familiar smell drifted to Derrick's nose. Cinnamon rolls.

"Hey, my fine ladies, what's shaking?" Antonio shouted as he limped into the room.

"Antonio Morales, you know we are not open yet." A brown-skinned woman dressed in white came to the counter.

"No worries, señorita," Antonio laughed. "I want to introduce you to a new student. See if you have his card yet." Antonio motioned toward Derrick. "This is Sir Derrick King from the land of Denver, Colorado, the mile-high city."

"Glad to meet you, Derrick." The lady smiled. "I don't have your card yet. They haven't brought any down this morning but let me check that you have an account set up. If not, I can let you slide a day or two."

The lady walked to a computer-like device on the counter.

"Now, what is your lunch number?"

Derrick did not speak but handed the lady his papers. She entered his number on the screen.

"Yes, there you are. You have one month paid in full."

"How are the rolls today, Mrs. Morales?"

"They are as splendid as ever and don't call me Mrs. Morales, son. I'm your momma, whether or not we are at school." She tapped him hard on the shoulder.

"Yes, momma." Antonio winked at Derrick. "We'll be back."

"Your limp is worse. You need to see a doctor," Mrs. Morales said.

"I'll be okay," Antonio replied.

"I'm setting up an appointment. I hope they can see you this afternoon."

"No need. I'll be fine in a few days," Antonio said.

"Then seeing the doctor won't be a problem, will it? So, stop arguing with me."

"Yes, Mama."

"That's your mother?" Derrick asked as they walked by the vending machines.

"Si. Do you like cinnamon rolls?" Antonio asked.

"Yes, I do," Derrick said.

"Best in town, except for the bistro. Donna makes some damn fine cinnamon rolls. You know the bistro?"

"Yes, I do," Derrick said. "I have enjoyed a cinnamon roll there already."

"So, after next class, the lunchroom is open for morning break. We have 20 minutes instead of the usual 5 between classes. You can get coffee, milk, juice, and a cinnamon roll. They just added coffee this year. So, if you want a cinnamon roll, haul ass down here soon as the bell rings."

The bell rang, and students poured into the hall.

"Can you find your next class then?" Antonio asked.

"Yes, thank you for your assistance, Antonio Morales."

"No worries, bro. Know what? You talk funny."

15

DERRICK STOOD WHERE THE HALL TO the lunchroom intersected with the main corridor. A teaming swarm of bodies, a chaotic mix of clothing both in style and color. Loud, incessant chattering, laughing, giggling, and hollering. The din was deafening. And odors unfamiliar to him. There seemed to be no space between the students, and yet some pushed and slithered their way toward friends or lockers. This scared him worse than the war scenes broadcast on New America Media. The wars were only images on a screen. These were real people inches away from the spot on which he stood.

Mostly, they ignored him, too consumed with their own destinations and conversations. Laughing and yelling and waving and walking. A few eyes turned his way, and the faces of those who looked at him bore clear recognition that he was one they did not recognize. A new kid. *Where are you from, new kid? What side are you on? One of us? Or one of them?*

Several minutes passed, and the crowd thinned. Derrick studied his schedule and realized that his next class was on the opposite side of the building and on the second floor. A bell rang, and he forced himself into the throng of students and tried to move toward his destination as quickly as possible. He had never once been late for a class, and before he reached the top of the stairs, the second bell rang. The few remaining students ran toward their next class. Derrick ran, too.

The door to Earth science was closing as Derrick approached. He turned sideways and slipped through the door, almost colliding with the instructor, who was pulling the door shut.

"Whoa, partner. No reason to knock the teacher down."

"I am sorry, sir," Derrick said.

"I don't know you, which by reason of scientific deduction, leads me to believe you are new here. Is my hypothesis correct?"

Derrick wanted to ask what a hypothesis was, but since he was new, it seemed reasonable to answer yes.

"Welcome to Potterville High. There's an empty seat over there. What is your name, son?"

"Derrick King."

"Glad to have you, Mr. King. Since you are new and the topography here is unfamiliar, I will withhold the lecture about being late."

Derrick was unsure if a thank you was required or appropriate, so he nodded his head and took his seat. His first desk at Potterville High.

The instructor stepped to the front of the row in which Derrick sat. "Class, we have a new student, as I'm sure you have noticed. Mr. King, I'm afraid your timing leaves something to be desired. We are taking a quarterly test today. It should take most of the class. Since you have not been with us, the test may have material with which you are unfamiliar. Where are you from, Mr. King?"

"Denver, sir." Derrick decided adding Colorado was unnecessary.

"Interesting. So, here's what I shall do. If you pass the test, we'll keep the grade. If you fail the test, I'll toss the grade, so you don't start out with a failing mark. Is that acceptable to you, Mr. King?"

The offer was quite acceptable. And at some point, Derrick would remember that this simple gesture of goodwill affected him greatly. "Yes, sir. Thank you."

"Mr. King, I shall henceforth call you Derrick, and you shall call me Mr. D."

Derrick nodded. On the instructor's desk sat a small plaque, with the name Jason Delacortez inscribed on the front.

Mr. Delacortez picked up a stack of tests, counted out the correct number, and handed them to the first student in each row. Derrick was in the second seat nearest the window. A petite Asian girl wearing dark-rimmed glasses took one test and then twisted enough to hand the remainder of the tests to Derrick. Behind the glasses, Derrick saw that the girl had a pretty face, composed of delicate features. She studied his face and then smiled ever so slightly. Or at least he thought she smiled. He took one test and passed the rest backward. He sat there watching as the students began reading and marking answers. He looked at the desk in which he sat. He did not have a writing instrument, and none was left for him. It occurred to him that the students had heavily laden bags they carried on their backs. He had nothing. He had not even thought to bring the small computer Paul had purchased. Sensing that someone had approached from the side, he saw Mr. Delacortez holding out a writing instrument. Derrick would learn they called it a pencil.

"You'll need one of these. I trust tomorrow you'll come better prepared. Name and date at the top of the page, please."

Derrick did as Mr. D instructed. Contrary to everything he believed about the commoner world, and science specifically, he felt slight excitement. Because science was a forbidden subject, one that he knew so little about, he had studied it the most during his short orientation time. Now he wanted to see how much he remembered. He wanted to pass the test, even though he believed the subject was wicked. He scanned the pages and saw there were three types of questions.

Most had four choices, some were true or false, and a few required a written statement. He read the first question. He knew the correct answer.

The questions that required written answers were the most difficult. Derrick thought that was probably true for everyone. You had to know the answer and then try to explain it. But it was difficult for Derrick because he had done little writing at the Academy. Almost everything was spoken. He would buy a pencil and practice writing this evening. He assumed pencils were expensive because many students wrote with short pencils barely visible in their hands and Mr. D. insisted that his pencil be returned to him.

The girl sitting in front of Derrick finished first. She walked forward and placed her test on Mr. Delacortez's desk. One by one, others did the same as they finished.

As the percentage of completed students grew, Mr. Delacortez told them to be quiet. "You may play with your phones if you're done. Just do so in silence."

Derrick finished and took his test to Mr. Delacortez and handed him the borrowed pencil. A few students still had their heads down, either marking the paper or scratching their heads. Derrick checked his e-mail. Nothing.

The bell rang, and the students raced to the door. Their urgency even surpassed what Derrick had witnessed previously, and then he remembered: cinnamon rolls. Without thinking, Derrick found himself in the middle of the hall, pushing along with his new peers toward the cafeteria and the aroma of freshly baked goods.

A queue had formed in the hall outside the dining area, but it moved at surprising speed. Cinnamon rolls awaited on plastic plates. Students picked up a roll, a fork wrapped in a paper napkin, and either an empty plastic mug or a small container of milk from a large plastic basin half-filled with ice. The coffee was self-served from large containers, like he had used at the bistro. More students selected milk rather than coffee, which meant easy access to the coffee.

At the payment station, Mrs. Morales smiled at him. "Hello, Derrick." She handed him his card. "They brought this down a few minutes ago. But I'm buying yours today. You let me know what you think of our cinnamon rolls, okay?"

Derrick thanked her, filled his cup with coffee, and saw an unoccupied table in the far corner. The eyes of several students followed him as he crossed the room. Some of those students — the younger ones — seemed curious. The older students appeared hostile. In his peripheral vision, he saw Nyx seated at a table near the middle of the room. He did not know if she was a junior or senior, but he did not think she was a sophomore or freshman. Derrick looked straight ahead, fearing to look at her. He could not tell if she had noticed him. Somehow, he thought she did not miss much. She scared him for reasons he could not explain, and yet he longed to know her better.

He knew running into Nyx was unavoidable but wanted to avoid that encounter for now because he felt uncomfortable enough, and she made him uncomfortable in ways he could not explain. With his back to the wall, he studied the room. Nyx had her back turned toward him. Antonio appeared in front of Derrick with a big smile on his face.

"You're all alone, amigo. Okay, if I sit with you?"

"I am okay. You should sit with your friends," Derrick said.

Antonio stepped over the bench, grimacing as he lifted his leg and sat across from Derrick. "That's okay, mi amigo. I don't have many friends."

Derrick detected no regret in Antonio's voice or face. He seemed like the happiest kid on the planet. Maybe there was something wrong with Antonio. Perhaps that is why he did not have friends, or maybe Antonio was new at Potterville High too. Derrick would soon learn that his assumptions about Antonio were incorrect.

Derrick forked into the cinnamon roll and found it was delicious. Not as good as the ones at the bistro, but close. He thought he would not grow tired of eating cinnamon rolls, pizza, hamburgers, or milkshakes. How many calories are in a cinnamon roll? It occurred to him that he faced another problem here that he had never encountered before: getting fat. Although he had never given it much thought, he assumed his food at Pacific Edge was carefully selected so that he maintained the proper weight. His food was selected and prepared in Pacific Edge. He did not have options. He did not need to exercise to maintain his weight. Not the case here. Because he had never had to control his diet, he had little inner strength to avoid such food. He had no desire to avoid such food. Yet, he was sure that if he did not discover a way to burn the calories, he would be too fat to walk before long.

"Amigo, you eat like you're starving. Doesn't your uncle feed you?"

"Uncle?" Derrick asked.

Antonio stared at Derrick. "Senor Paul. He's your uncle. Right?"

"Yes. That is correct." Derrick lied. "I never knew him. He and my mother were not close. I just think of him as Paul, I guess." It was the best Derrick could muster. He thought it not bad.

"I understand. I heard you lost your parents. It must be difficult."

Derrick nodded. How does everyone seem to know about the loss of my parents?

Antonio stood. He had eaten about half of his cinnamon roll.

"Take care, bro. I'll see you around," Antonio said as he left.

Derrick watched as Antonio limped to a counter, where he scraped the remnants of his food into a green container and then placed his plastic plate on a stainless-steel counter. Then Derrick watched in amazement as Antonio shuffled between the tables of students, patting students on the back, students slapping his out-held hand, smiling, and laughing. Until Antonio reached Nyx.

She grabbed Antonio's arm and pulled him down to whisper in his ear. Antonio looked over at Derrick and then whispered in Nyx's ear.

A shiver ran down Derrick's back.

16

DERRICK'S FIRST DAY AT POTTERVILLE high school passed with less drama than Derrick expected. He had missed the first period, which was English. He took a test in the second period, which was Earth Science. U.S. history occupied Derrick's third period slot. The instructor, Derrick learned they called them teachers here, lectured about World War II. James Carver Academy briefly examined that conflict, so Derrick was not entirely lost on the topic. The U.S. history instructor gave the class a reading assignment from a history book. Algebra was the last class of the morning session. Of all the subjects taught, algebra piqued his interest the most, but he did not understand it, which disappointed him because accounting was his best subject at James Carver Academy. Both topics were about numbers, but algebra was different. Some instructors gave him a physical book for class, which was weird. He wondered if he could catch up to the other students and felt disoriented by the thought that commoner students were his superiors, at least for now.

Derrick skipped pizza in the dining area, or cafeteria, as they called it here. That place did not seem safe after his morning encounter with Antonio and the private whisper that occurred between Antonio and Nyx. Settling for an apple and Coke from the vending machines, he explored the school grounds. Pizza day ensured that students were in the cafeteria, which left the campus empty. He had seen the front, so he walked back to where the football field was located. A reddish-colored track with white-striped lanes circled the field. Silver bleachers rose on both sides. The side nearest the school was the larger of the two. A few kids dressed in white shorts and strange red shirts ran on the track that circled the field.

Derrick sat three rows up on the school-side bleachers, watching. Something about the running seemed familiar, but that made no sense because Derrick did not run. He had finished his apple, and the core, which he would toss in a trashcan later, sat beside him on the bleacher. From the corner of his eye, he saw a man walking toward him, balding, barrel-chested. He had something silver on a cord around his neck. Derrick estimated the man to be mid-forties. Possibly, this area was off limits. Being new here, Derrick hoped he would get off with a warning. Or perhaps the man was not coming to talk to him at all. Just walking. The man grew larger as he got closer. He marched right to Derrick. Every muscle in Derrick's body tensed.

"Hey," the barrel-chested man said.

"Hello," Derrick said.

"I don't know you."

"I started school here today. I hope it is not a problem that I am out here."

"It's not a problem. It's your school. You have a name?"

"Derrick King."

"You play sports?"

"No."

The man studied Derrick as if he were lying. Derrick had done plenty of lying today, but not this time.

"Where you from, kid?"

"Denver."

"Your family move here?"

"No, my parents were killed," Derrick lied.

"I'm damn sorry to hear that. Son of a bitch. Damn sorry."

The man's language shocked Derrick. *Who is this man? Why is he here?*

"Why didn't you do sports in Denver? You look to be in decent shape. You're big enough to be a halfback or defensive back. Hell, at this level, maybe even a linebacker if you've got the balls for it. Can you run?"

It astonished Derrick how quickly the man transitioned to sports after hearing that his parents were dead. The man did not ask how or when they were killed, if he had siblings, or why he came to Potterville. Perhaps the man was merely pretending to be surprised at Derrick's statement. Beyond that, he did not know which questions to answer. He decided on the first and last. "I never got into sports. I do not know how fast I am compared to others," Derrick said honestly, which felt good for a change.

The man worked his jaw muscles, staring hard at Derrick as if trying to make a decision. "You have physical education on your schedule?"

"Yes, last period," Derrick said.

"Perfect. Track starts right after school. You'll already be dressed down. Don't leave after P.E. and we'll try you out for the team. It's track season and spring football starts in a few weeks. We can try you out for that too. How does that sound, Mr. King?"

"Sounds okay, I guess."

"Of course it does. See you last period. I'm Coach Browning."

Derrick did not walk to the main school building because the first class after lunch was chemistry, which was in a small building called a portable, sitting to one side of the school. Derrick did not understand why it was called that. It was small, but it sat right there on the ground. Perhaps a huge machine moved it around, but he could not understand why they did not leave it where it was. Chemistry was twice as long as other classes.

Derrick entered the portable classroom and was met with the same stares he had experienced in every other class. He was not provided with a personal chemistry book because there were not enough of them, which suited him because the chemistry books were thick and heavy. Plus, he worried the books might contaminate him with science.

Chemistry was the first class in which he recognized someone who had been in one of his earlier classes. The Asian girl with the dark-rimmed glasses who sat in front of him in Earth Science was in the room. There may have been others with whom he had shared more than one class, but he had not been cognizant of them. It occurred to him that students here would remember him as the new kid easier than he would remember them. He decided it was important to pay closer attention tomorrow because not remembering people might make them feel slighted, which was not his intention, and it was not in his best interest either. He did not speculate why he remembered the Asian girl. He did not remember her name, or if he had even heard it. Later, he would realize that this was a mistake more significant than he could have ever imagined.

The reason chemistry was twice the time as other classes became apparent soon after the bell. The first thirty minutes, the teacher instructed students on the day's experiment the students. Students worked in teams. On each team, one student conducted the experiment, while the partner recorded the steps.

The teacher's last admonition was. "Do not blow up my lab."

Derrick sat on a tall stool, watching as students paired up. The ease and familiarity with which they partnered indicated that the teams were pre-established. He, on the other hand, had no idea what to do.

A girl with brown hair, wearing a flower-print dress with many strands of multicolored beads draped around her neck, walked toward him until the Asian girl from Earth science stepped in front of her.

"Excuse me," the Asian girl said. "You have no partner?"

"No," Derrick said.

"You can be my partner if you like," she said with that same slight smile and an odd look in her eyes.

The girl with all the beads had taken a seat at a table of three.

He did not ponder why the Asian girl had no established partner, nor did he pay attention to the girl with the beads. There was something that seemed familiar about the Asian girl, but he attributed that to the fact that he had seen her in second period. After a moment, he said, "Yes, I will partner with you."

"My name is Akira Nakamura." She paused as if waiting for something.

Derrick said, "I am …"

"You are Derrick King. I remember who you are."

Derrick had second thoughts about this partnership. Why would she remember his name? Why had the empty seat in Earth Science been behind her? Could she be a spy?

Watching and listening. Listening and watching.

"My station is over here." Akira walked to an unoccupied station at the front of the room. "Do you want to take notes or conduct the experiment?"

He thought about it. He could take notes if Akira told him what to write, and if she knew anything about chemistry. "Which would you like to do?"

"Do you know this procedure?"

"No, I took chemistry because there were no other options for me this period. It is new to me," Derrick said, which was true and false. Fake Derrick from Denver had been in a nonexistent chemistry class. Real Derrick from Pacific Edge had never heard of chemistry until coming to Potterville.

"Then you should do the experiment. I know the procedure well. I have done it several times."

"Several times?" Derrick asked.

"Yes. I am student assistant in chemistry."

Derrick conducted the experiment. Akira guided him patiently, expertly. Despite his lack of knowledge, they were the first team to finish. The instructor inspected their results and found they had completed them correctly. He praised Akira for her note taking. He praised Derrick too, but Derrick knew that praise was undeserved. That was not important. Derrick had found a lab partner, and that was important.

Spanish was the last academic class of the day.

When he entered the Spanish classroom, he saw the second familiar face of the day. Well, third if you counted Nyx, but he was not counting Nyx because she was not in any classes with him, unless she was in English, which he had not yet attended. He had not been to physical education, but he did not expect to see her there. Derrick learned that knowing a few words and phrases in Spanish was anemic. Three-quarters of the students were Hispanic, and the other kids spoke the language fluently. Antonio Morales stood at the front of the class, speaking Spanish with three other students. Derrick had no clue what they were saying, but they were laughing as much as they were talking.

Derrick sweated out the 55 minutes of Spanish, which was unlike any class that he had ever attended. The entire class consisted of students speaking Spanish in small informal groups, and the teacher moved about the room, joining into the conversations, laughing, and then moving to another group.

Antonio caught Derrick on the way out of the room, slapped him on the back, and said, "Wish me luck, bro."

"Luck?" Derrick asked.

"Mom is taking me to a doctor. She won't take no for an answer. That is one stubborn woman." Antonio limped away toward Mrs. Morales, who waited near the administration area.

The remaining class was one that Derrick assumed would pose the least number of problems for him. Not that he had ever done much exercise, but this one did not require thinking or talking. It now appeared possible that he would survive his first day in the commoner school without incident.

The gymnasium proved easy to find. It smelled of old wood and something else that he could not identify. It was not a pleasant smell. Something was not right when the second bell rang. The gymnasium was empty. The gym floor had the markings of a basketball court. Two baskets hung on heavy steel rods suspended by cables from the ceiling at either end. About ten feet above the floor, was a veranda with bleachers. Opposite the entrance was a small office with a window. Derrick saw Mr. Browning seated at a desk, studying something on his computer screen.

Students wearing t-shirts and shorts started drifting in from doors on either side of the basketball court: one door labeled girls, the other boys. A few girls wore what looked like pajamas instead of shorts. Everyone wore tennis type shoes. At least Derrick had the correct shoes. A few students wore white shorts and weird, sleeveless red t-shirts with Potterville written in white lettering on the front. Below Potterville, something like a cat's head, with its gaping mouth revealing menacing teeth.

"King!"

Derrick looked up to see Mr. Browning waving him over.

"Yes, sir," Derrick said after jogging across the floor.

"No gym clothes, I take it?"

"No, sir. I'll try to get some tonight."

"You do that. Did Mrs. Bates give you a school supply list at registration this morning?"

"No, sir, I do not recall such a list."

"She should have. You get down there and pick one up before you leave today. I'm not supposed to give you a track uniform until you make the team, but what are they going to do, fire me?" Mr. Browning laughed. "Follow me."

Mr. Browning walked to a room near doors that led to the back of the gymnasium. He put a key in the door, twisted it, and stepped inside. Derrick followed him.

"There we go." Mr. Browning pulled two boxes from the shelf. "These should fit." Mr. Browning handed Derrick a pair of white shorts and one of the funny little red t-shirts. "Put these on and then join me in the gym."

Derrick started to pull his shirt over his head.

"Damn, son. In the boys' locker room. Put your clothes in an empty locker." Mr. Browning shook his head.

Derrick had never seen a locker room. Small metal cabinets like his hall locker lined the walls. There was a strange looking, long white trough on one wall opposite a row of toilets. Toilets he had seen. Then there was a rather large room with shower heads. He could not understand what this room was for. One person could not use all those shower heads.

When Derrick returned, he hoped the red had left his face. He felt stupid when Mr. Browning stopped him from changing clothes in the storage room. So many simple things that he did not understand. So many simple things that were going to trip him up, give him away, get him killed.

Mr. Browning was waiting for Derrick when he entered the gym. "Hold up there, King." Mr. Browning scanned the gymnasium and then shouted, "Belos! Belos!"

A few seconds later, Derrick heard a familiar voice behind him say, "Right here, Coach."

Derrick turned to find himself face to face with Nyx.

"What the hell? How is he on the track team?" Nyx asked.

Browning held up one hand. "Calm down, Belos. He didn't have gym clothes. I'm loaning him these, but he is trying out for the track team today. So, he might get to keep them."

Nyx folded her arms across her chest, glared at Derrick. "So, what did you want me for, Coach?"

"Take Mr. King here to the track. Do warmups and stretching. Then run some laps. See how he does."

"Why me?" Nyx asked.

"Because you are on the track team, and I'm your coach, and you happened to be the first minion who came to mind, that's why. You have a problem with that, Belos?"

"No, Coach." Nyx turned and walked away.

"Go with her, King. She usually isn't this cranky. I don't know what's eating her. Just do what she tells you. Unless she tells you to kill someone, don't do that." Mr. Browning chuckled and punched Derrick on the shoulder.

Derrick caught up to Nyx on the football field.

"What are you staring at?" she asked.

"Uh, your eyes. They look different."

"Duh. I took my makeup off. It runs when I sweat. Looks like hell. You have a problem with that?"

"What is that?" Derrick asked

"What's what? Girls don't wear makeup in Denver, or they don't sweat?"

The question confused him for a moment. He didn't even know what makeup was. In Pacific Edge, girls could have minor color enhancement done to their faces, but it didn't wash off. It was semi-permanent, like his eye and hair color. Finally, he said, "They do. I guess I just did not see them not wearing it. Because I did not do track and such."

The muscles in Nyx's jaw flexed. "Sorry to be a disappointment."

Before his brain could filter his thoughts, he said, "You are even prettier without the colors."

She stared at him for a moment and then said, "Just do what I do."

It would be the last time Derrick would say anything about Nyx's makeup or lack thereof. But it would not be the last time he noticed her eyes or said something stupid.

For the next fifteen minutes, she stretched, twisted, bent, contorted, and held positions that caused Derrick to hurt, sweat, and pant. Nyx did them all with ease. He watched her. He had to follow her routine, but he enjoyed watching her too. Her body was lean and muscular, but not like bodybuilders he had seen selling supplements. Nyx's muscles suggested purpose. Her skin was a light olive brown, and her hair was not quite black in the full sun, except for the pink stripe, which was pink. Her name was Nyx Belos. He wondered what sort of name that was. He wondered why she disliked him.

She took off jogging around the track. Derrick followed.

For no reason he could identify, he grew homesick. It grew more intense until, at one point, tears formed in his eyes.

They had run four laps, and Derrick would learn that was one mile. After the first lap, Derrick was breathing hard and ready to stop, but he pushed on. The pain in his chest and legs helped block the homesickness. At six laps, Derrick thought he would be sick, but by the seventh lap, his breathing steadied, and his stomach settled. By the end of the eighth lap, he passed through a barrier and was now just running, heart and lungs in a steady rhythm, supplying ample oxygen to his lean muscles. He no longer felt homesick.

Nyx remained silent. Derrick had trailed her for eight laps. On the ninth lap, he pulled even with her.

Nyx said, "Were you on the track team in Denver?"

"No, I did not participate in sports."

"Why not?" Nyx asked.

Derrick thought for a moment and then lied, "My Father and Mother would not let me." It sounded lame as soon as the words left his mouth.

"Afraid you'd get hurt? Concussions and stuff? Some parents are like that."

"Yes. They were afraid of stuff like that."

"But you enjoyed running?"

"I did not run. I did not spend much time outside."

"Bull."

"What?"

"You must have done something. You're in good shape."

He had fallen into a trap of his own making. He had not thought this through. How could he extricate himself from this situation? Lie by saying he had lied about not running and then lie again by saying he was a runner at home? Finally, he said, "I ran a little in physical education, but I did not do sports. Good genes, I guess."

Nyx stared at Derrick for a few minutes. "Your parents were afraid you'd get hurt, and then they died in a house fire. Sad twist of fate."

"Yes," Derrick agreed. If Father and Mother had died in a fire, this would have seemed heartless. Then he wondered how Nyx knew it was a house fire that killed his Father and Mother. He did not remember telling her the cause of their deaths.

"Well, at least they cared about you."

His Father and Mother had cared about him. They still did. They were not dead, but he would not see them again. Then he did the strangest thing he could remember ever doing. "You say that as if your parents do not care about you."

Nyx stopped and glared at him. She worked her jaw again as if chewing on a tough piece of meat. He thought he saw water welling in her eyes. Then she turned and ran, faster now. Derrick matched her pace but was unsure how long he could stay with her.

It turned out he could not match her pace after three-quarters of a lap. He fell behind but kept running. What else could he do?

She ran.

He ran.

17

DERRICK LOST TRACK OF THE NUMBER of laps after ten. He lost ground to Nyx. He struggled to get enough air into his lungs. His legs burned, and his feet hurt. He wanted to stop. His muscles and lungs demanded it. But he did not stop, and he did not understand why.

A few students wearing track uniforms walked onto the field. They all completed warmups as Nyx had done, and now they ran. The girls ran with Nyx, but not for long. One boy ran alongside her for a lap, trying to make conversation. Nyx ignored him. On the next lap, he faded. Derrick passed him a few laps later, but Derrick could not catch Nyx. He was now matching her pace again but was half a lap behind. She would glance at him across the field when they were on the straight part of the track.

The bell rang.

Nyx kept running.

Derrick kept running.

The other team members stopped and grouped on the field, stretching. A whistle blew, and Nyx stopped, turned onto the grass. Derrick ran to her but said nothing, bent at the waist, hands on his knees, breathing hard. Nyx stood with her hands on her hips, breathing deeply but not labored. After a few minutes, she started stretching. Derrick copied her routine. Mr. Browning talked to the other team members.

Sitting on the grass, stretching her leg, Nyx said, "It's hard to believe that you only ran in P.E."

"Our instructor liked to make us run," Derrick said.

"People don't run like you do unless they are conditioned." Nyx studied Derrick's face.

Derrick thought Nyx could see through his charade. However, he was not lying this time. "I did not participate in sports of any type. I ran sometimes. Like from school to home," he lied.

Nyx did not speak for several minutes. Just continued to stretch. Periodically, she would look at Derrick. Finally, she said, "I'm sorry about earlier."

"Nothing to be sorry about," Derrick said.

"You must miss your parents. I shouldn't have said that earlier."

"I miss them," Derrick said. "I am also sorry. I should not have said anything regarding your parents. It is not my business."

"It's okay," Nyx said. The anger had faded. Her eyes shone soft and warm. "I had a fight with my mom this morning. It's been eating at me all day. My father died when I was little."

"My sister used to fight with Mother also," Derrick said.

Nyx stopped. "You never mentioned a sister. Where is she? Why is she not here?"

It had happened. He had not completed day one without a substantial blunder. He was supposed to be an only child with one surviving family member, which was Paul.

"Oh," he paused, "she remained in Denver. Paul would not take in a girl," Derrick lied. "She stayed with a friend's family."

Nyx studied Derrick's face. "What is her name?"

"Miriam," Derrick said.

"That's a pretty name. Is she younger than you?"

Derrick nodded. "Yes, two years." Derrick was not concerned, assuming Nyx had merely guessed that Miriam was younger.

"Are you close?"

"We were not close. Things made us closer. It's better now between us."

Nyx nodded, as if that made perfect sense. "At least you are staying in touch, right?"

Derrick could not suppress a smile. "Yes, we are in touch."

"Belos, King. How did it go?" Mr. Browning walked up behind them.

"Unexpectedly good, Coach," Nyx said.

Derrick started to say, "unexpectedly well" and then stopped himself. He had screwed up enough already.

"I saw you trailing her, King. How many times did she lap you?"

"I am sorry, Mr. Browning. I tried to keep up but failed."

"I didn't lap him," Nyx said.

"Were you running, Nyx?" Mr. Browning asked.

"Like I was in a race, Coach."

"Son of a bitch. Pardon my French, son. Nyx took second place in cross-country at State last year. She's one of the best long-distance runners in the state of California. Son of a bitch."

"I pulled a half a lap on him, but then he stayed on pace. I couldn't shake him."

"Let's see if he has any speed."

Mr. Browning walked off, blew his whistle, and yelled, "100-meter! On the line."

"Coach wants you to run 100 meters with the guys." Nyx pointed to the far end of the track to a short spur that extended beyond the oval. "Over there."

Derrick jogged to where a group of five boys had formed beside Mr. Browning.

"Boys, this is Derrick King of Denver, Colorado. He's trying out for track today. He stayed on pace with Nyx for the better part of twenty minutes. Let's see if he has any speed, shall we?"

"Tryouts ended three weeks ago, Coach. You said no latecomers. Why does he get an exception?" A tall, muscular boy with light brown hair stepped in front of Derrick, inches from his face.

This boy was a little taller than Marcus Carver and more muscular. An athlete. Derrick took half a step back.

"Three reasons. One, he wasn't here three weeks ago. Two, we need another guy. Three, because I'm the coach and I say he's trying out. You have a problem with any of those reasons, Clark?"

"Whatever," Clark said as he turned away from Derrick.

"We need another guy?" someone asked.

Browning said nothing for a moment and then said, "We've lost Antonio. Could be a torn ACL."

The other boys groaned.

Derrick remembered he had not wished Antonio good luck on his doctor's visit, and although he knew wishes would change nothing, Derrick felt guilty just the same.

"Lanes, gentlemen."

Derrick was the last to line up. He did not want to be sandwiched in between runners, but the only lane left open was next to Clark and a kid of African descent with long black hair woven into long braids. Derrick believed that people of African descent were superior athletes. Many professional athletes were of African descent.

"Ready?" Mr. Browning pulled a pistol from his pocket, and Derrick almost turned to run, but the other kids got down on hands and knees. Derrick was the last one down.

"Set." The other kids raised their butts upward. Derrick felt awkward as he tried to mimic the position.

Mr. Browning raised the pistol above his head and fired. The shot rang out, and Derrick thought he might urinate. The other runners bolted.

Derrick left the blocks too but trailed the others. They were fast. Derrick ran as hard as he could. Halfway down the track, Derrick caught the last two boys and passed them. Near the finish line, Derrick had caught one more boy and passed him: Clark.

Two runners were still ahead of him when they crossed the line. The boy with the long, black, braided hair won. Derrick eased up, and then something hit his foot, causing him to trip, and he went down hard. He caught himself with his hands before his face smacked the track. His palms burned. His knees hit the track and felt as if they were on fire. He tucked up and rolled to a stop, sensing others running to him and was certain that a rain of kicks and punches would soon follow.

"You okay, man?"

One boy kneeled beside him. "Dude, you're bleeding."

Derrick felt others gathering around him. He ventured a peek at them. They had formed a circle around him. The boy with long black braided hair was reaching out his hand. "Bro, you, okay?"

Derrick uncoiled. "Yeah. I tripped." He took the outstretched hand and was pulled to his feet.

"What the hell just happened?" Mr. Browning yelled as he ran up to the group.

"I tripped, Mr. Browning." Derrick was certain that someone had tripped him, and he was certain that person was Clark, but now was not the time to start a fight. Derrick felt anger but not rage. He had control of it this time. But he was not afraid, and that surprised him. And he did not need to get even. That surprised him too.

"Or did someone trip you?" the black-haired boy asked as he turned to Clark, who was standing outside the circle.

"I just tripped," Derrick said.

18

MR. BROWNING DISMISSED THE TEAM AFTER the 100-meter sprint, but he asked Derrick to come to his office. Derrick wondered if he was in trouble. Nyx followed them back to the gymnasium. Mr. Browning set a large white box on his old wooden desk. FIRST AID was written across the front of the box with red letters. Mr. Browning cleaned Derrick's scrapes with a clear liquid that burned at first and then applied bandages to his knees. Mr. Browning said the bandages wouldn't stick to his palms, which were red but not bleeding. After returning the first aid box to a cabinet behind the desk, Browning sat on the desk's corner. "I want you on the team."

Derrick had been thinking on the walk to the gymnasium. He was not the fastest person today, so he had assumed there was no risk that he would make the track team. Not the first or last time his assumptions would prove incorrect.

Regardless, Derrick had decided he did not want to be on the track team or any other team. He was certain the boy named Clark — Derrick learned Clark was his last name — had tripped him on purpose. Mr. Browning called people by their last names, it seemed. Derrick did not know why the boy had tripped him. Maybe Clark was a sore loser. Maybe it was something else, but he felt certain Clark did not want him on the team. Derrick wanted less exposure to the commoners, not more.

"I did not perform well. I could not keep up with Nyx. I was far behind the fastest runners in the sprint. I think it would be best if I focus on school," Derrick said.

"Hell, only a handful of people in the state can run with Nyx." Mr. Browning leaned forward. "Those two sprinters in front of you will go to State this year. They had five yards on you before you even started. Clark is the school's quarterback, all-conference, and has college offers coming out the wazoo. Frankly, I'm having a tough time believing you didn't play sports in Denver. Is there something you're not telling me?"

"He ran in Denver a little. He didn't play sports or track," Nyx offered.

Derrick looked over his shoulder and saw that Nyx was standing in the doorway. *Why is she still here?*

"The fact is, I need you. And with some work, you could make something of yourself." Mr. Browning stood and paced the small office. "So, here's the deal, King. I'm not asking. I'm telling you. You are on the track team. Understand?"

Derrick looked at Nyx. She had a wry smile and a somewhat evil look in her eyes.

"Don't worry about the others. I'll take care of it. It won't happen again," she said.

Derrick stared at Mr. Browning and then said, "I understand, Mr. Browning." Although Derrick did not understand why he had said that.

"Good. Glad we came to an agreement on that." Mr. Browning laughed. "Go change and then stop back here before you leave. I'll have an extra uniform for you. Those shoes are okay for now," Browning looked at Derrick's shoes, "but you need running shoes before the first meet."

"Yes, Mr. Browning." Derrick stood and started out the door.

"One more thing, King," Mr. Browning barked.

Derrick stopped but did not turn around.

"Don't call me Mr. Browning. You call me Coach or Coach Browning. Got it? Welcome to Potterville Track and Field, this year's state champions."

Derrick eased past Nyx. He glanced over his shoulder as he turned into the boys' locker room. Nyx was still talking to Coach Browning. The locker room was empty, although he could hear the shower running. He dressed quickly, hoping to exit before the person or persons in the shower returned. He almost made it.

The boy with the black braided hair stepped into the locker room with a towel wrapped around his waist. "It's King, right?"

"Yes, Derrick King."

"I heard there was a new kid in school. Heard your parents died. That sucks. My name is Malcolm Cross." Malcolm held out his hand.

Derrick had never met a person of African descent before. They taught the Chosen that most black people possessed low intellect but were gifted athletes. They were okay when kept in their place. Their place was not in Pacific Edge. Rumor was that there was a Community in the Northeast where African American Chosen lived. Travel was not allowed to that Community, nor any other community for that matter.

"Pleased to meet you." Derrick shook Malcolm's hand.

It was the hand that had helped him when he was down.

"You're pretty fast. But not fast enough. I'm gonna kick your ass. Remember that." Malcolm gave Derrick's hand a hard squeeze before letting go.

"I am not looking to fight," Derrick said.

Malcolm threw his head back and laughed. Derrick did not understand how that was funny. Perhaps Malcolm Cross was slightly crazy.

"Bro, you're funny. I mean, you won't beat me in the 100 meters."

"Oh," Derrick said.

"You can probably beat Clark."

Derrick started to say something, but for once used his brain and kept his mouth shut.

"He let you pass him today. Then he tripped you. That's what went down and don't lie to me. But you can beat him straight up with the right training."

Perhaps Malcolm was trying to play a trick. Derrick nodded his head but said nothing.

"Cool that you didn't rat him out. Earned you some respect with the others."

Derrick had not seen any rats in Potterville, and he wondered what rats had to do with Clark tripping him. "Probably just an accident."

"Nah, Clark is an asshole sometimes. But you stay straight with me, and I'll have your back." Malcolm fixed his eyes on Derrick with an intensity Derrick had not previously noticed. "Watch that dude. Seriously."

"Okay," Derrick whispered. He gathered his gym clothes. "See you tomorrow." He hoped Malcolm would let him leave.

Before Derrick had gone five steps, Malcolm said, "Bro, on that track you'd better fight your ass off to win, and that includes beating me, or you and I will have problems. Got it?"

"Got it," Derrick said without turning around, although he was more confused than ever.

19

WHEN DERRICK RETURNED, COACH BROWNING WAS not in his office, but there was a note on the door that said, "Track clothes are on the desk, take them and then lock the door." Derrick looked for something to carry his track clothes in. The ones he had worn were damp with sweat, but he found nothing, so he carried them in his hands, sometimes tucking them under his arm. Nyx was not there. She might have still been in the girl's locker room, or she might have left. Derrick did not want to see her. He felt homesick again.

On his way home, he passed an old man walking his dog. The dog was tan colored with a wavy coat turned gray around the mouth. The dog inched along beside his master. The man smiled and nodded. Derrick returned the gesture. It was outlandish that a stranger would smile like that. As if Derrick posed no threat. It was not how New America Media depicted commoner life. The man must live nearby and would recognize kids in the neighborhood, which meant Derrick was a stranger. Old and frail, the man should have been leery of an outsider.

At the corner, Derrick smelled coffee and baked goods from the bistro. He walked past the bistro and stopped in front of the store that sold musical instruments. In the window, a red guitar made of solid wood stood on a stand. On the top of the guitar, where the strings were attached, was the name Fender. Fascinating.

He listened to music as part of his short orientation to the commoner world. Commoners liked all kinds of music. He took a liking to a thing called rock and roll. Even the history of rock-and-roll music appealed to him. It originated in the old United States of America way back in the 1940s and 50s, but Derrick read it started much earlier in the blues of the 1920s. In fact, many old blues songs had been hits in the 1960s and 70s and were still popular in the commoner world. Rock seemed like a rebellious, hard driving, sexy slap at convention. In its early years, religious leaders said it was of the devil. The sounds and songs exemplified everything that Derrick was not. Yet, he liked it. Astounding. He spent far too much of his precious orientation time listening to it and reading about it. He hoped it might prove helpful at some point.

The Chosen listened to music too, but it was tightly regulated. They allowed the Chosen classical and patriotic music about New America, but nothing from the old United States. Most music was from the Church of the Chosen. That's what Derrick listened to most. Miriam hated it. Derrick thought Miriam would like rock and roll.

Alongside the red guitar was another guitar, plain by comparison. Natural wood, light blond on top and mahogany brown on the back and sides. Unlike the red guitar, which was thin, this guitar was thick with a round hole in the center that the strings passed over. It was hollow. The red guitar looked new, but this one was old and worn. The finish almost gone in places, and the name near the top mostly faded away. The first three letters were legible, Mar… but the rest were faded or rubbed off, he did not know which. He puzzled why anyone would buy such an ugly old guitar.

Someday he might get up the nerve to enter this strange store, but not today. Instead, he walked back to the bistro.

"Good afternoon, Derrick," Donna said, wiping her hands on her apron.

"Good afternoon, ma'am," Derrick said.

"You call me Donna, now you hear? What you got there? Looks like a track uniform."

"Yes, ma'am," Derrick said.

"First day of school? And you are on the track team?" Donna asked.

"Yes."

"By the look on your face, I'd say your day went about as well as one can expect on the first day at a new school. Not great. Not terrible. But if you made the track team, you should be happy. Am I right? But I get it. Don't worry, being the new kid will be over before you know it."

The discomfort that Derrick had suppressed returned. Yes, it might all be over soon enough. He had let his guard down too quickly and much too far.

Donna reached down and pulled a plastic bag from under the counter. She held it out to him. "Here's a bag for your track clothes. What'll you have?"

"A cup of coffee and …" Derrick studied the case that displayed the pastries. The cinnamon rolls called his name, but he thought one cinnamon roll a day was probably enough. He settled on an oatmeal raisin cookie. Oatmeal was a healthy choice, was it not?

Derrick sat outside on the sidewalk at one of the black steel tables. The sun warmed his face, and the scent of blossoms mingled with the coffee. The coffee tasted fresh, and the cookie tasted delicious. Well, not as delicious as a cinnamon roll but good still. He sat and listened. An occasional car passed, and he heard children at play in the distance, a dog barked, birds sang in the trees, sounds of a guitar drifted from two doors down, and then from behind him, Nyx's voice.

"You rushed off. I thought you might wait for me. You don't like me, do you?"

Derrick turned and involuntarily smiled. Nyx looked angry, and it reminded him of Miriam. "I thought you had already left. Well, maybe you had left. Or maybe you were still in the shower, and well, I could not go in there." Derrick marveled at how he stammered. He took a deep breath and said, "I did not know you wanted me to wait."

"Will you wait now while I get something?"

"Yes, I will."

Nyx returned with a mug topped with white foam and a decorative swirl of dark chocolate. She also had chosen an oatmeal raisin cookie.

"I love Donna's cookies, don't you?" Nyx said as she sat.

"This is the first one I have tasted. It is delicious." Derrick detected a whiff of cinnamon in the air.

Derrick sipped coffee and chewed on a bite of cookie, unsure what to say, which was okay because he was supposed to keep his mouth shut and listen. Nyx was not talking either, and the silence was making him uncomfortable.

"What's up with you and Henry Clark?" Nyx asked.

"Henry Clark?"

"He tripped you today on the track. I saw him. Coach saw it too. Henry slowed down so he could do it. You lied to protect him. Don't pretend you don't know what I'm talking about."

Derrick's heart picked up a few beats. He felt sweat on his brow. "I have no idea why he did that. I could not see him, so it could have been an accident."

Nyx broke off a piece of cookie, studied him. "You have a run in with him earlier?"

"No. I never saw him before. Not that I know of, anyway. New classes, new school, unfamiliar faces. Today was tumultuous. I probably could not recognize 90 percent of the students I shared class time with," Derrick said.

"He can be a bully. Don't cross him. He has a lot of friends."

"Okay." What else could he say? Then he went against his own advice and said more. "I met Malcolm Cross in the locker room after track. He seems like a nice person."

"Be careful with him too," Nyx said. "But don't worry. I'll take care of things."

They sat in silence again. Derrick grew uncomfortable. What did she mean: She'd take care of things? It felt as if she had a mystic aura that probed his thoughts, searching for something.

"What is that you are drinking?" Derrick asked, having failed to find another benign question.

"A Mexican mocha. It has a little cinnamon in it. Want to taste?" Nyx held up the cup to Derrick's lips.

Derrick took a sip: chocolate, coffee, a hint of cinnamon.

And the lips of Nyx Belos.

20

DERRICK AND NYX WALKED TO THE condo together. Derrick worried she would follow him to the third floor, ask to see his condo, and room. He tried to think of a reason to say no that did not sound too lame or too insulting. No ideas surfaced, and Derrick considered how he lacked imagination. Fortunately, she bid him goodbye and went straight to her place.

On the third floor, Derrick knocked on Paul's door. Paul did not answer. Derrick checked his e-mail, nothing. He sent Paul a message using his phone, asking when he would be home. Paul texted back: "late." Derrick replied that he needed a bag to carry on his back to school. Paul replied, "You have money, buy one." Paul suggested a store where Derrick might find one for a reasonable price within walking distance.

Derrick found the place using his phone. The device even gave directions. Easy to find: go to the school, turn right, and then go straight. Five miles according to the map, Derrick did not realize how far five miles were. After he passed the more familiar route from the condo to the school, he became fearful. But he could not hang onto his fear. It melted away into a mix of boredom and fascination. Boredom from the slow, plodding walk, but fascination from the things he saw along the way. Stores selling all manner of things: shoes, computers, food, furniture, clothing. People providing services: haircuts — apparently there were no bots here to trim hair — tax preparation, laundry, landscaping, even a sign that indicated nude dancing girls. This place teamed with sins that would bring instant excommunication from Pacific Edge, which was worse than exile, although Derrick did not understand how the two differed.

The store Paul had directed him to sold almost everything one could think of. He wandered the aisles, not of necessity but interest. Everything from food to clothes to fertilizer. He found a bag for his back. He learned it was called a backpack. He thought it would hold his computer and a few books. He grabbed pencils (they were not expensive), pens, a wallet, and three notebooks. He looked at running shoes and discovered he did not have enough money. *How much money had Father provided for such things?* Derrick was confident that Father had not anticipated that he would join the track team on the first day of school.

Derrick found some items he thought would be useful for his sore feet, including a thing called Band-Aids for the blisters forming on his heels. Outside the store, he sat on a curb, pulled off his shoes and socks, and placed a Band-Aid over each red spot on each heel. No one paid any attention to what Derrick thought to be a strange act: pulling one's shoes and socks off in public.

It was getting late, and something told Derrick that it would not be as safe after dark. Accompanying that thought was that homesick feeling. The Band-Aids helped, so Derrick ran. He found a stopwatch feature on his phone, so he timed the run. At first, his legs and lungs burned, and he wanted to stop, but he pushed on. Then he fell into a comfortable pace. Before long, something weird happened. He felt terrific, like he could run forever, and he wanted to.

The homesick feeling faded.

Thirty-five minutes later, he was standing in his condo. He ate a thick slice of cheese and a piece of bread and then showered. He wanted to check his e-mail, hoping he would hear from number1sis. Miriam's e-mails never completely left his thoughts, and he decided number1sis must be Miriam. Therefore, number1sis was also Maranda Kingston. And that was a problem. Because Maranda Kingston's e-mail originated at Pacific Edge Administration. Derrick dismissed the idea that Miriam had obtained employment at Pacific Edge Administration under an assumed name. That left two possibilities: Miriam had broken into the building, or she was granted access so she could communicate with Derrick as a spy for the Tribunal. Both ideas were far-fetched and equally improbable. Legs aching and eyelids drooping, he decided to rest a few minutes and then see what he could learn about this strange new world on the internet.

21

Tuesday, March 23

DERRICK PEERED THROUGH PUFFY EYES, CONFUSED. He did not remember the exact time he had lain down, but it must have been close to nine o'clock. His phone said it was 7:55. He pulled the curtains open, and the morning sun blinded him.

Morning sun! Late on my second day of school.

He skipped his shower and shave ritual, pulled on clothes, ran a comb through his hair, brushed his teeth, stuffed pens, pencils, notebooks, laptop, and gym clothes into his backpack, and then ran to school. An empty schoolyard greeted him. He had never been late at the Academy, which would have resulted in automatic detention, which he knew because Miriam managed to be tardy on several occasions even though she left the house before he did. He had never been in detention. He laughed unexpectedly when he realized he had skipped detention and gone straight to exile. It should not have seemed funny, but it did.

Since he did not know what he was supposed to do, he went straight to his first class, twenty-seven minutes late.

Derrick stood at the door for a moment, listening to a heated discussion occurring in the room. Fear gripped him as he eased the door open and stepped inside. The room went silent. Several students were holding their hands in the air. One student was standing at the side of his desk. The teacher was standing at the front of the class.

"May I help you with something?" the teacher asked.

"I am supposed to be in your class. I am late," Derrick said.

"Ah, you must be Derrick King."

"Yes, ma'am."

The teacher walked to her desk, punched a button on a black phone, and said, "Mrs. Prinz?"

"Yes," answered a metallic, disembodied voice.

"Please correct my attendance sheet. Mr. King is in my class. He had a little trouble finding the room."

"Should I mark him tardy then?"

The teacher — Derrick saw her name was Ms. Schilling — glanced at Derrick and said, "He was not tardy. Just lost."

Ms. Schilling released the button on the phone and stood straight. "Mr. King, please find a seat."

"Yes, ma'am."

Halfway down the aisle, she stopped him by saying, "And Mr. King, from now on, I trust you can make it to my class on time?"

"Yes, Ms. Schilling. It will not happen again." Derrick felt certain that he was telling the truth.

Derrick sat and the discussion resumed as if nothing had happened. A lively debate regarding the meaning of a book the class had recently read, which was set during World War II, and therefore, the topic was not entirely unknown to Derrick. Written on the board in front of the room:

A Separate Peace

Reports Due Tomorrow

He had never heard of this book. He had never heard of any books. Pulling a notebook from his backpack, he wrote *A Separate Peace* on the first page. Despite the students' passion, he could not focus on their discussion. Besides, he knew that World War II was a myth. He kept thinking about Ms. Schilling, saying he was not tardy.

When the bell rang, Ms. Schilling handed Derrick a textbook and a piece of paper that explained the current assignment. She said he could earn extra credit, whatever that was, if he would read *A Separate Peace* and write a one-page book report on it. She gave him that book too, saying he could turn his report in next week.

As he entered the hall, he heard a girl calling his name. He turned a full circle, trying to locate the origin of the voice. Then he saw a small hand waving from across the hall: Akira Nakamura.

"You seem a million miles away. Is everything okay?" Akira asked.

"Sorry," Derrick said. "I was thinking. I did not mean to ignore you. Everything is okay."

"Walk with me to Earth science?" Akira asked.

"Yes, I will. That way, I will not get disoriented," Derrick said.

Derrick walked in silence, sensing he should make conversation, but reminding himself to remain quiet. Yesterday had been a blur. He remembered the sheer terror he felt when he first witnessed the throng of students as they poured into the hall after the first period, when Antonio Morales had shown him around to his classes. He remembered taking a test in Earth science and that the teacher wanted to be called Mr. D, yet his name was Delacortez. He remembered doing an experiment in chemistry but could not remember the teacher's name. He remembered running with Nyx, being tripped in the 100-meter race, and having coffee with Nyx after school.

Everything else, gone.

Today Derrick saw everything clearly, and it disturbed him. Rings in noses, lips, and ears, tattoos, blue hair, beards, ragged jeans, short skirts, and every manner of t-shirt imaginable, and a few that were not. Yet, Derrick saw smiles everywhere, as if these kids were oblivious to the world in which they lived. The chaos threatened to overwhelm him, but Akira broke into his trance.

"Are you sure you're okay?" Akira asked.

"What? Oh, I am sorry. I am distracted again. Overwhelmed with all the change in my life, I guess." Derrick had learned that adding *I guess* to almost any statement created vagueness that made him appear less clueless.

Akira said nothing. She looked at him. Her eyes were warm behind her glasses, but Derrick could not read her expression. She might have felt sorry for him, or she might have wondered why he was trying to pull off this sham.

In Earth Science, Derrick took the same seat he had taken yesterday, behind Akira. He studied the room, tried to remember faces. Putting names to faces would take time. Determining who believed what would be tougher still. He started making notes, some mental, some written. He needed to find people who believed the Chosen were the Creator's special people. In that group, he would find safety. Maybe even friends.

"Seats, people," Mr. D said. Picking up a stack of papers from his desk, Mr. D began returning yesterday's tests to each student. Standing at the front of the class, Mr. D called each student by name. As the student came to pick up the test, Mr. D commented on how each had done but did not reveal grades. Just things like, good job, or work a little harder.

Derrick opened a notebook, flipped to the last section where his comments would be hidden, and took notes. Most students received an 'okay' or 'good job'. Mr. D did not say much about okay and good job, except to encourage the student to work harder. Although sometimes he praised a student as if an okay was a major accomplishment. A few students received an 'I know you can do better', which came with a scolding that ended up sounding encouraging. Some students got a 'well done' or 'nice job'. A few students were told excellent work or keep up the good work.

When Akira Nakamura stepped forward to get her paper, Mr. D said, "As expected." Akira smiled with a slight nod of her head. Mr. D had not yet called Derrick's name and sweat formed on Derrick's forehead, which he wiped with the back of his hand.

Mr. D announced one grade, which was an F. Derrick learned later that was the worst grade one could receive. It meant fail. The student receiving the F, Jim Priest, walked to the front of the class. Priest was short, overweight, had greasy dull-brown hair, and a nervous twitch in his left hand. Mr. D withheld the test and said, "Mr. Priest, I understand your personal beliefs are contrary to the subject, but I also believe you know the answers to the questions. Protesting the subject won't change the test questions, but it will cause you to not graduate. Not graduating is not in your best interest, so I suggest you give me the correct answers so you can pass."

"False religion," Jim Priest mumbled under his breath on his way back to his seat.

Mr. D rolled his eyes and shook his head.

Derrick wrote Priest and put a star beside it.

"Mr. King," Mr. D began. "I see they teach Earth Science in Denver. Well done."

Derrick walked to the front of the room. On the top of his test, in bold red ink: 89% B+. Eighty-nine percent was the lowest grade Derrick had ever received on an exam. It was also the grade of which he felt most proud. This was a strange day already.

At morning break, Derrick placed a cinnamon roll and milk on his tray and then scanned the room. He saw Jim Priest sitting between two boys at a table that was otherwise empty. Derrick would learn too late that it would fill soon.

Derrick walked to the table where Priest sat and said, "May I join you?"

Priest and the other two boys scowled at Derrick. "Why?"

"My name is Derrick King. I am new here. I do not know many others here yet. You are in Earth Science with me. I am trying to meet people, I guess."

"I remember," Priest said. "You're the new kid from Denver, who believes in science."

Derrick stood motionless for a few moments, considering if he had made a mistake. He was about to turn away when Jim Priest motioned him to sit.

"It's a free country," Priest said.

Derrick sat across from Jim Priest, feeling bewildered by the statement. *What does that mean? It is a free country.*

"So, Derrick, why did you move here from Denver?" asked a large boy with a ruddy complexion.

"My parents died. I had to move here and live with my uncle. I had nowhere else to go," Derrick lied.

Several boys, who had an eerie sameness about them, took seats on either side of Derrick and the table filled quickly.

The large boy with the ruddy complexion forked off a large chunk of his cinnamon roll, sopped up melted butter and frosting, and stuffed it into his mouth. "Sorry to hear that."

Jim Priest said, "Were your parents, believers?"

"Sort of, I guess," Derrick lied. Or was he telling the truth this time? They did not have to believe anything because they were the Creator's Chosen people.

"Then they aren't gone, are they? They are watching over you right now."

Derrick scanned a corner of the ceiling and considered how odd that sounded when said aloud. Were there cameras here where his parents could watch him? That was not what Jim Priest meant by his statement. Still, Derrick thought about it literally. He had never considered that his parents might be watching him. Someone was watching him, were they not? He shuddered because he had forgotten that little fact. When Derrick looked up, Jim Priest was glaring at him. "Yes, you're right, I guess."

"Are you a believer, Derrick?" Priest asked.

Derrick regretted his decision to sit with these boys. He should have studied them from a distance first. Although no one crowded him, Derrick felt pinned in, as if there was no escaping this group. He had not anticipated an interrogation. He was a believer, but he was not yet sure what these boys believed in. "I am not sure," Derrick said.

The bell rang, and Derrick stood. "Thanks for letting me sit with you."

The large boy with the ruddy complexion stood, revealing that he was not only broad but also tall, and Derrick flinched back a little. Reaching across the table, the boy took Derrick's hand and said, "I'm Red Badowski. You know Jim already." Red nodded to the boy, who had remained silent. "This is Jody."

Derrick shook Jody's hand, which felt damp and cold, said the necessary pleasantries, and then turned to leave. In the middle of the room, stood Nyx with books held to her chest. She glared at Derrick as he crossed the room. For reasons Derrick could not explain, he walked straight to the restroom, where he lathered his hands with soap and rinsed them with scalding hot water.

The rest of the day passed tediously, as if each minute repeated itself several times before moving into the past. He was not ready to return to the lunchroom, so at lunch, he bought some snacks from the vending machines, went outside, and sat alone on the concrete steps at the back of the school. The sun was warm, and the sky was clear. The combination helped clear his mind a little. Still, he wanted to talk to Nyx. Her scowl during the morning break haunted him. Perhaps he had done something wrong.

When the last period arrived, Derrick hurried to the locker room, where he changed clothes in the remotest corner possible. He was not accustomed to being in a state of undress in front of others. Most of the track team had Physical Education, PE, last period. They went straight to the track where they stretched, ran, sprinted, jumped, tossed heavy balls, and focused on events in which they competed. Derrick lingered in the gym, waiting for Nyx.

She exited the girls' dressing room when Coach Browning snagged Derrick by the arm and pulled him into his office. "How's it going, King?"

"I am well, Mr. Browning."

"Call me Coach. So anyway, I've been thinking about you. We have three of the top sprinters in the state. So, …"

"If you do not need me on the team, I understand," Derrick said too quickly.

Browning held up his hand. "Let me finish, King. While I want to develop you into the best sprinter you can be, you also seem to have real potential as a distance runner. Now, a distance runner who is also fast, well, that's rare. There's always room for cross-country runners. Not many kids like it. Too tough, you know. Thing is, we could have a top-notch mile relay team if we had one more 440 guy. I think you might be that guy. You good with that?"

Derrick was not sure what any of that meant, and he wanted to catch up to Nyx, so he said, "Yes sir, Mr. Browning."

"Coach."

"Yes, sir, Coach."

"Just Coach. Here is a stopwatch." Browning showed Derrick how it worked. "I want you to stretch, run a few laps to warm up, not fast laps. Just loosen up. Then I want you to time yourself running one lap as fast as you can. Catch your breath and do it again. Before you go home, stop by and tell me your best time."

Derrick nodded, stuck the stopwatch in his pocket, and headed to the track. Nyx was warming up near the goalposts. He jogged over to her and began to stretch.

"Hi," Derrick said.

Nyx said nothing.

"Nice day," Derrick said.

Nyx remained silent.

"I wanted to talk to you," Derrick said, yet he did not know how to ask her what the death stare was about at break.

"I don't want to talk to you," Nyx said.

Derrick watched as she sprinted to the track and ran laps at a blistering pace. Derrick sighed. He ran three easy laps, then stopped at a starting marker. He stretched. When he caught his breath, he took off, running as fast as he could around the track. He found that sprinting a full lap was more difficult than he had imagined. His lungs burned, and his legs felt like rubber by the halfway mark. He pressed on, but his pace slowed. Before he reached the finish line, he felt sluggish. He felt like quitting. He clicked the stopwatch as he crossed the finish line, slowed, and then bent over with his hands on his knees, trying to catch his breath. When he had recovered, he checked the stopwatch: 65 seconds.

As he readied himself for another lap, Nyx passed. She did not so much as look his way.

Derrick took a deep breath and ran another lap and got the same basic result: painful. The time dropped to 64 seconds. Malcolm Cross sprinted over from the other side of the track where he had been jumping as far as he could in a sandpit.

"Coach have you running 400 meters?" Cross asked.

"Coach said 440," Derrick replied, still out of breath.

"Same difference. Coach is kinda old school, you know?"

Derrick did not know but nodded his head in acknowledgment.

"He mention the mile relay?"

Derrick nodded.

"I'm the anchor on that team. One of our guys tore his ACL. Out for the year. You have a lot of work to do if you're going to be on the mile relay team."

Derrick nodded and wondered what an ACL was. Something in the leg.

"Antonio was on the track team?" Derrick asked.

"Yes. How do you know Antonio?"

"I do not know him well. He showed me the location of my classes on my first day here. I have seen him a few times at school since. He says hello and such. And I knew he hurt his leg, and his mother was taking him to the doctor."

Cross studied Derrick and then said, "Part of his student body president duties."

"Getting injured?"

"Hell no. What's wrong with you? Showing you around. Student body president must spend one period as a teacher's assistant. Usually, they are assigned to a classroom teacher. But they assigned Antonio to administration."

"Why administration?"

Malcolm smiled. "You really don't know Antonio very well."

Derrick wanted to ask more, but kept his mouth shut. He had embarrassed himself enough.

"So, back to running, the trick is to find out how fast you can run the lap without slowing down, having enough left at the end to finish strong. Then, as your endurance improves, increase your speed. And the best way to improve your endurance is to run distance. I run five miles every day, either before or after school." Cross slapped Derrick on the back. "Good luck."

As Malcolm turned to leave, Derrick said, "It seems Antonio is well liked."

Malcolm spun around. Walking backwards, he said, "You have to like Antonio."

"Have to?"

"Yes. It's the law."

Most of his time at Porterville High, Derrick had been in a state of confusion. That had not changed.

Derrick did as Malcolm instructed. On the next lap, Derrick maintained his speed until the last twenty yards, when he felt himself slowing down. His time improved to 62 seconds. During the next lap, the bell rang. Derrick pushed harder near the finish line. Sixty seconds.

Coach Browning was pleased with sixty seconds, but he said Derrick would need to cut at least five seconds off that to keep the team competitive. Five seconds sounded like a lot because he did not feel he could run faster. Browning told Derrick that Potterville had won the mile relay the last two years at State. Derrick did not know what that meant but was smart enough to understand it was important. If Derrick made the relay team, and they did not win, it would be his fault. One more thing to worry about. Second day. His life was growing more complicated at an alarming rate.

Derrick waited for Nyx in the gym. A tall blonde girl exited the girls' dressing room. He asked about Nyx, and the girl said Nyx had left.

Derrick ran to the condo and saw Nyx go through the front entrance as he turned the corner. He called her name and sprinted after her. She disappeared in the elevator, which struck Derrick as a strange thing for a track star to do.

"Hey, Nyx! Wait up."

Derrick reached the elevator as the doors were closing. He thrust his hand inside and forced the door open. Nyx stood in the corner with her arms across her chest.

"Nyx, what's wrong?" Derrick asked.

"Nothing."

"Feels like something," Derrick said. He was out of his element here. Plus, he was supposed to keep his mouth shut, but he was doing all the talking. "Is everything okay?"

"Everything is fine."

"You do not sound like everything is fine."

Nyx jammed her finger on the stop button. Derrick watched the muscles in her jaws flex.

"What were you doing with Jim Priest today?" Nyx asked.

"Uh, just trying to meet people, I guess. He was in my Earth science class."

Nyx glared. "You can't see what he is? Or is that the reason you want to get to know him?"

"Uh, I do not understand," Derrick said.

"They are dangerous. What's wrong with you, Derrick?"

Derrick did not respond.

"Stay away from me." Nyx released the button and stepped back into the corner of the elevator. When the door opened on the second floor, she bolted into the hall.

"Nyx!" Derrick called out.

"Stay away from me!"

Derrick thought he saw a tear trickle down her cheek.

According to Nyx, Derrick had to be careful with Malcolm Cross and Henry Clark. Now, she said that Jim Priest and his friends were dangerous, yet Derrick was sure they supported the Chosen way of life. He was now the weak link on the state champion mile relay team. In addition, Nyx frightened him in ways he could not explain.

Derrick believed his chances of survival in the commoner world were limited. He survived the first week, which did not mean much because he was alone in his condo. He survived two days at school, which was all more than he had originally hoped to accomplish. Malcolm Cross might cause him harm. Henry Clark had proven himself a menace. Derrick may have misinterpreted Jim Priest as a potential ally. But of one thing Derrick was certain. On Tuesday, March 23, a wound had been inflicted that was more painful than anything he had ever experienced. It made no sense, but the strange girl with the pink-striped hair had broken his heart.

22

Tuesday, March 23, 4:13 p.m.

ON THE KITCHEN COUNTER, a note from Paul, and $40.

> Derrick, I thought you might need some money
> after buying school supplies. Make it last.
> You won't be getting cash from me all the
> time.
>
> Paul
>
> P.S. I'll be out of town for a while. Don't
> go into my place unless you must, then leave
> soon as you can.

How much money did Father send? Was Paul keeping money meant for me? Derrick did not know, and there was no way to find out. He would get what Paul was willing to give him, end of story.

Derrick was not hungry. Concentration proved impossible. He could not sit still. How had he complicated his life so quickly? Even though running had created several problems for Derrick, he wanted to run right now. He changed into his track shorts and treated his blisters with ointment and Band-Aids. He needed proper running shoes, but $40 would not buy them. Would Paul give him enough money for a good pair of shoes? Probably not.

On the sidewalk, Derrick started a stopwatch he had found on his phone and an app that measured distance. Derrick planned to run 2.5 miles and then return. He stretched and then ran, heading away from the school. New territory. He expected this direction would take him deeper into the residential area, and he was correct. The homes looked old, much different from those in Pacific Edge where they built houses on a grand scale with lots of glass and imported stone and tile roofs, where no painted wood was visible, where the landscape was groomed in meticulous detail, where people were rarely seen.

Here, most of the houses were painted, although there were a few made of bricks. Some paint was in good condition; some weathered until bare gray wood showed through. People maintained the yards reasonably well. Although some had the toys of small children scattered about, and many had small children playing with said toys.

At one mile, Derrick questioned his decision to run. Running was part of the problem. He thought about turning around and walking back to the condo. He could quit, could he not? Or he could slow down so Coach Browning would kick him off the team. Coach could not tell if he slowed on purpose, right? No one can tell what he is thinking. Right?

Except for Nyx. She saw right through him.

Since she did not want to talk to him, maybe she would be happy to see him off the team and would not say anything about him slowing down on purpose. Or maybe she would say something to avenge whatever wrong he had done to her.

He ran.

The houses changed from older to newer. In the older area, cars and pickup trucks lined the streets. Here, the vehicles were hidden inside part of the home. He saw one disappear behind a large door that raised upward. More homes were sided with brick and stone. This area had less chaos, but it also felt less welcoming, which confused him because the chaos of the older homes should have scared him. He did not see as many people here. He saw fewer toys in front yards. Perhaps the people did not have children in this part of town. Perhaps the people stayed inside. The people here might be more like the Chosen.

A strong melancholy swept over him as if it had blown in from the sea on a high breeze. A tear came to his eye as he thought about what he had lost. He thought about Miriam. He wondered what she was doing. He wondered if she had sent him another e-mail. When he got back, he would check. One stupid, out-of-control moment had cost him everything. His beautiful room, his bride to be, his future, his life, and the sister he did not know. Tears traced down his cheeks.

Two miles.

He ran on.

At the 2.5-mile mark, he saw something in the distance that surprised him. The houses appeared to end. When he reached the last home on the street, he saw the homes did not end. There were houses in the distance, small specks here and there. The street he was on ended here but made a T into a cross street. Across the road was a field. It was bright green. A crop of some sort, agriculture.

Derrick did not understand agriculture, except that was where food came from. In early grades, the Academy taught about agriculture in a shallow manner, but they taught nothing more because the Chosen did not do agriculture. Agriculture was commoner work. Plus, he had no interest in it.

Here it was laid out before him. Strangely, he found it interesting and oddly beautiful because of the order and straight lines in which the plants grew. He wondered how they accomplished that.

He checked the distance.

Three miles.

He started back. His feet no longer hurt, yet he anticipated they would hurt later. He picked up the pace. His legs ached, but he blocked the discomfort. The air was warm and dry. His perspiration soaked his shirt, but the breeze created by his pace dried it quickly. The sky was blue. The air had a strange odor, thick with the scent of plants and soil. People were returning home from work. They turned into their driveways, and the large doors opened to accept them. Small children with their faces pressed against the glass waved to him. Even adults waved. He waved back. Then he began waving first.

People smiled.

Derrick smiled.

He ran on.

At six miles, Derrick was back in the old neighborhood. It occurred to him that his homesickness had dissipated. Front yards teamed with children playing, and their parents talking to neighbors over white picket fences. They waved or nodded at Derrick as he ran. The worries of the day seemed to melt from him, and he was at a loss to explain why. Even the deep ache that Nyx had caused eased a little, but it was not gone. Yet, he felt something new about Nyx: optimism that he could fix things with her somehow. Derrick ran as if he were floating above the sidewalk.

When he reached the condo, he stopped, looked at the front entrance, and then walked on. His stomach growled. He headed to the bistro. By the time he reached the bistro, his breathing had returned to normal, and his shirt had dried. He stopped at the guitar store window, where he stared at the red guitar and the plain one with the blond top and the thick body. For some reason, which made little sense, he found himself drawn to the old wooden guitar.

He hesitated and then stepped inside.

A large man with a thick beard streaked with gray sat on a stool playing a guitar, much like the old one in the window. The music swirled and soared through the room. The room was narrow and long. One wall was lined with guitars of all sizes and shapes. On the opposite wall was a glass-topped counter with odd little boxes inside, and on the wall behind the counter were rows of small square packages. Stepping closer, Derrick saw that the small packages were labeled guitar strings. Fascinating. Next to the counter was a row of large boxes, some brown, others black. Each box had a row of dials and fronts covered with cloth. It was a place of astonishment.

The music stopped. "How are you?" asked the man as he stood and hung his guitar on the wall.

"I am doing well," Derrick said.

"Looks like you've been working out."

Derrick looked at the man, wondering how he knew that.

"Your t-shirt. Salt stains." The man pointed to his own underarms.

Derrick looked at his shirt and saw white rings under his arms and white streaks on his chest. He thought about excusing himself to go home and put on a clean shirt.

"What can I do you for?" the man asked.

"I am just looking," Derrick said.

"Do you play?" the man asked.

"No."

"You want to learn?"

"I know nothing about music."

"I didn't ask what you know. I asked if you wanted to learn. I teach guitar lessons. What would you want to play, an acoustic or electric?" the man asked.

Derrick shrugged. "What would you suggest?"

"I tell people to start with an acoustic." The man tapped the side of the guitar he had finished playing. "Unless they have their heart set on an electric. Kids often think they gotta have an electric."

"Okay," Derrick said, walking over to the wall of guitars. "How much is the acoustic in the window?"

The man laughed. "That guitar is $3800. It's a classic. A fantastic instrument."

"Wow! How much do new ones cost?"

"You can buy a good new guitar for a lot less than that old Martin. How much do you have to spend?"

"I do not know," Derrick said.

"Well, you talk to your parents about it. You should learn to play. Kids don't learn to play like they used to. Too much work for them."

Derrick paused for a moment. His parents could afford every guitar in the store. "My parents died recently," Derrick lied.

"I'm sorry. You must be Derrick."

Derrick started to ask how the man knew his name, but the man held up his hand palm out and said, "It's a small town, son."

Possibly the guy was just a good salesman, but Derrick sensed the man was sincere. Derrick did not know how to reply, so he said, "Thanks."

"My name is Mark Grealy."

Derrick shook the man's hand.

"You come by anytime. Okay? I can start showing you a few chords, and you can practice in the back. How would that be?"

A small girl carrying a bag shaped like a guitar entered the store.

"That would be great," Derrick said, marveling that he was even thinking about yet another entanglement.

"Stop by tomorrow a little earlier. I gotta close now. My first lesson of the evening is here." He nodded to the girl holding the bag. "Go on back, Susan. I'll be there in a jiffy."

"Okay," Derrick said.

Derrick walked out and stood in front of the store, staring at the old Martin guitar in the window, wondering what a jiffy was.

23

AS DERRICK STARED AT THE OLD Martin guitar in the window, he sensed an uncomfortable feeling gnawing at his core. Vague at first, but it became debilitating as he allowed it to come into focus. He was hungry. The conservative thing was to go home, fix himself some dinner. Conservative was what he did best, but the bistro called to him. He was not feeling conservative. An older couple ate at one of the sidewalk tables. The man nodded as Derrick walked to the door. In the front window was a sign: HELP WANTED. The lettering was red, and for a moment Derrick wondered if it was a distress signal, but the relaxed fashion in which the old couple enjoyed the evening caused him to dismiss that notion.

"Derrick, it's good to see you."

"Hello, Mrs. Parks. Sorry, I'm a mess. I was out running. I'm on the track team. Well, Coach says I'm on the team, but you know that already."

Donna held up her hand. "Relax, son. Call me Donna. If you've been running, then you must be hungry."

Derrick studied a menu board near the counter. "Yes, ma'am. Is the special good?"

"Everything here is good, Derrick. Do you like lasagna?"

"I do not know."

"You don't know? You're pulling my leg. This one is on me. It's the last portion and a little crusty, which is the way I like it, but some people don't like that part."

"On you?" Derrick asked, wondering why Mrs. Parks thought he was pulling her leg when he wasn't even close to her. She might have nerve damage in her leg.

"No charge. Free."

"I have money, ma'am."

"I'm sure you do. It's still free. Coffee is on the house, too."

Derrick rolled his eyes toward the ceiling. "On the house?"

"Derrick, you're a hoot. It's free too. And for the last time, call me Donna."

Derrick smiled and nodded. He was glad she had decided to stop telling him to call her Donna. He sat inside, near the window. He watched the old couple, and cars passing on the street, and people strolling on the sidewalk in the weaning light. He watched for the girl with the pink-striped hair.

A bird floated to the sidewalk, and the old man tossed it a piece of bread.

Maybe life was better when Nyx was the mysterious girl with pink-striped hair he had watched from his window. She could be anything he wanted her to be then, because he did not know her. Nyx Belos, on the other hand, was a real person. A complicated person at that. If she lived in Pacific Edge, she would not have qualified for his list of potential mates. He sensed that she would have never stood for being on anyone's list. She would have never submitted herself to be like a piece of property that a man picked over like a piece of fruit. He saw traits of Miriam in Nyx. Rebellion, strength, independence. Everything he abhorred. Contrary to the Chosen Way.

He thought of his bride to be, Jana Somersworth. For Jana, he felt nothing. He did not understand why. His thoughts drifted to Rebekah Ford, and that odd sinking feeling started in his chest. He remembered his last day at James Carver Academy and how Rebekah had come to him that morning. He remembered the warmth of her touch and the smell of her hair. Tears threatened for the second time that day.

"Lordy, you look like you're in another world," Donna said.

Derrick turned to see her holding a plate. "Yeah. Just thinking. Lots of things have happened in the past couple of days. It hits me all at once sometimes," Derrick said more honestly than he had intended.

"I can't imagine what you've gone through, dear. If I can do anything, you let me know." Donna set the plate on the table. "I hope you like it."

"Yes, ma'am. Are you okay, ma'am?"

Donna cocked her head. "Why do you ask that, son?"

"The sign in the window says you need help."

"Derrick King, you are quite the jokester."

Derrick did not know what a jokester was but had a good idea. He was not attempting humor, but his lack of understanding apparently made him sound foolish. This was another example of why he was supposed to keep his mouth shut. He was not good at following his own advice.

"I'm looking for part-time help in the kitchen. One of my workers got a better full-time job. I'm thrilled for her, but that leaves me shorthanded. Know anyone who wants to work a few hours a week? Mostly Saturday and Sunday."

"Yes, I would like to do that." Derrick almost clamped his hand over his mouth. *What is wrong with me?* Running shoes and an old guitar came to mind.

"You got experience?"

"No, ma'am. Well, I've been cooking for myself since I came here." The more he talked, the more nonsensical he sounded.

"Well, at least you're honest. Honesty goes a long way around here," Donna said.

If you only knew, Derrick thought

"You're hired. You can start on Saturday morning. Can you be here by 6 a.m.?"

"Yes, ma'am."

Donna walked to the window and pulled the sign. "Won't be needing this."

Derrick sat for a moment, trying to remember if he had hit his head when Henry Clark tripped him. He could find no reasonable explanation for the things he was doing. Going out for track, determined now to make the relay team, falling for a girl that he hardly knew and who did not like him, agreeing to guitar lessons, getting a job. If he were home in Pacific Edge, he would ask for a psychiatric exam. But he was not in Pacific Edge. He was in Potterville, and he kept digging himself a deeper hole. Soon, there would be no need to dig a grave for him. He would soon have it dug, just toss him in.

Derrick showered when he got home. He wanted to check e-mail but undertook another new task called homework instead. He had two chapters to read, one for Earth Science and one for U.S. History. The chapter in Earth Science was about several types of rocks. Nothing too upsetting, which was good. He had never thought about rocks before, unless it was picking out new marble or granite for his room. Other than that, had you asked him about rocks two weeks ago, he would have said, "Who cares?" Yet, he found the chapter interesting. Although he wondered how someone learned this stuff in the first place.

In U.S. History, they were studying World War II, which he had heard about briefly in early grades. World War II was a myth that portrayed the old United States of America as heroes and promoted an outlandish story about white supremacists in Germany murdering thousands of people because of their religion. The reading disturbed him even though he had been taught it was a myth. By the time he finished his homework, he was nodding off at the kitchen table. The thing he wanted more than sleep was to hear from number1sis. He turned on his computer, opened his e-mail. He had an e-mail from someone wanting him to sign a petition demanding Congress work together to pass a budget. He did not even understand what that was about. Delete. He had an e-mail from someone wanting to sell him Viagra at discount pricing. Delete. He had an e-mail from an online store that appeared to sell everything imaginable. Save.

The e-mail he was hoping to see was at the top of the list now. He hesitated and then opened it.

```
Tuesday, March 23

TO: derrickking0312

FROM: number1sis
```

It sucks that the Tribunal changed your sentence. I'm sorry they did that. Yesterday was your first day of school. I hope you're okay. Please tell me you are.

I've thought about a question that only you could answer. I see the difficulty in asking such a question because we don't know each other like a brother and sister should. Do we? There's a reason for that.

Because we never talked about this, it is risky. Still, I suspect you will know the answer.

What is my name in your dreams with the Keepers?

Number1sis

Derrick stared at the screen. How did she know about the Keepers? How did she know about the dreams? I never told her about them. I never told Father or Mother. I never told anyone. He read her question again, and then he started to write a reply and then stopped. He deleted what he had written.

Derrick hated the dreams. He never talked to Miriam other than to criticize her hair, or her clothes, or her attitude. Tears filled his eyes. He had been a terrible brother. He did not tell Miriam about the dreams because she was in them. But she was not Miriam. In his dreams, she was Number Six. He hated the dreams because he knew deep down that they were not mere dreams. They were something else.

He walked to the kitchen, opened a soda, and drank it while staring out the window, thinking about how to respond. If he answered her question correctly, then he would feel confident that the person at the other end of the e-mail exchange was Miriam. It would mean something much more than that as well. It would confirm she knew about his dreams, which meant he and his sister shared these strange dreams. He did not understand what that meant. Back at his computer, he read Miriam's e-mail again, and then wrote:

TO: number1sis

FROM: derrickking0312

Miriam, I believe it is you. I saw your gesture in the communication. I assume they

had people there watching you closely, but
you did well.

Things here are not like they showed us on
New America Media. I am nervous, but I am
okay. The thing is, I am not sure how you can
help me. I do not think they will ever let me
come back to Pacific Edge.

You cannot come here. Even if you could, you
could not help me. Except, it would give me a
second chance to be a better brother. Still,
no reason for you to ruin your life. I just
want you to be okay.

How did you know about the dreams? I do not
recall ever telling you about them. Or Father
or Mother. I never told anyone.

To answer your question, in my dream, you are
Number Six.

The e-mail was on its way back to Pacific Edge. He did not understand
how the computer thing worked and had no idea if the e-mail arrived
instantaneously or if it took some time for delivery. Something he would
research on the internet if he could remember. Then something unexpected
happened. A chime sounded, and a new e-mail from number1sis appeared in
his inbox. He smiled, thinking Miriam was online, and they could virtually have
a conversation back and forth. He opened the e-mail and soon realized that this
e-mail had been written earlier, which provided no context regarding the
workings of the e-mail system. This e-mail had been written at 4:42 a.m. This
one was more disconcerting than the last.

TO: derrickking0312

FROM: number1sis

Long story. No time to explain. Here's the
thing. They are watching you. They track every
move you make. I can't go into details. Better
that you don't know. Just keep doing what
you've been doing. Not much else you can do
right now. Stay safe and stay alive. I'm
working on a plan.

Things are much worse than I thought. Marcus
Carver's assault wasn't a fluke. It was staged
and planned. Someone, I don't know who, is
angry that you are in Potterville. But you
cannot move. Hear me? Do not leave Potterville
for any reason. They have no authority over
you in the commoner world.

DO NOT LEAVE POTTERVILLE!

Derrick reread the message. Then again. He expected the Tribunal would watch him. But every move? Did Miriam mean that figuratively or literally? There must be a spy who has almost constant access to me. Or several people, so I am always under surveillance.

He had not paid close enough attention to his own condo, not that he could spot the surveillance equipment. Possibly someone had the ability to do that. But how would he find such people well-versed in counterespionage? "Hi, Coach. Do you know anyone who can detect high-tech surveillance equipment? Oh, no reason. Simply curious." Plus, what if Coach was a spy? Coach sought him out on the first day of school. Put him on the track team even though tryouts were closed, and he was not even the fastest person in the race.

Miriam said that Marcus's assault was planned. Recalling the details of that day, Derrick remembered Marcus confronting him about Miriam. Derrick did not place significance on it at the time, yet that confrontation predisposed him to fear something might happen to Miriam.

Why? Why would they want to exile me from Pacific Edge? He loved the Chosen and all for which the Chosen Doctrine stood. He fixated on this for quite some time. It hurt worse than the exile itself. Someone wanted him gone, and he could not understand who or why.

He analyzed the potential spies beyond Coach. The next suspect was Paul. Paul brought him here for the money. It was always about money for Paul. Yes, he said something about Derrick defending Miriam, but that could be part of his ruse. Someone could have referred Paul to Father because they had already recruited Paul as a spy. The problem with that theory was that Paul had been gone a lot, and when he was here, had not done much with him. It was not as if they hung out together.

Jim Priest had to be near the top of the list. Priest would have been elated had the Tribunal approached him. Easily recruited. They might have promised him entry into Pacific Edge, which they would have never followed through with, but Priest was not smart enough to figure that out. A little medal or letter of commendation would satisfy Priest. Jim Priest was on the list, but Derrick sensed Priest lacked the capacity to be an effective spy. Priest was not the smartest person he had met in Potterville. A spy would need to be smart, and that bothered Derrick because it narrowed the list.

Derrick had good reason to dislike Henry Clark. However, while Henry was a jerk, he had done nothing to get close other than getting close enough to trip him on the track. Since then, Henry had remained distant and aloof. Henry might not make the list of suspects, which, oddly enough, made him someone Derrick could trust.

What of Malcolm Cross? Malcolm had been friendly enough. Being friendly made Malcolm suspect, and Nyx warned Derrick about Malcolm. What had she said exactly? *Be careful. The same warning she gave about Henry. But Malcolm has not tried to get close. Malcolm does not know where I live. Or does he? Maybe everyone knows.* That made Derrick shiver. One thing was certain. Less than a week at school, and Derrick had failed miserably at maintaining a low profile.

Antonio Morales had been friendly. It was a coincidence that Antonio had been the student staff assistant who took Derrick on a tour of the school. Antonio was student body president and was either a polished politician at a youthful age, or he was genuinely a nice guy. Antonio was on the list.

What about the teachers? The lone teacher to show interest in Derrick was Coach Browning. But who could have predicted that Derrick could run? A competitive streak existed in Derrick he had not previously recognized. As soon as he got on the track, he started competing, first with Nyx, and then in the 100-meter sprint. He should have slowed down. But doubted he could. Coach Browning had to stay on the list near the top.

He hesitated to consider the next person: Donna. The bistro was close to his condo, so it was predictable that he would go there. She was warm and friendly from the first day he met her. She was warm and friendly with everyone, so that did not weigh heavily on the Derrick-Scale-of-Suspicion. The help-wanted sign had appeared shortly after Derrick became a regular customer. But Derrick had never worked a day in his life, so how likely was it he would apply for a job? That he applied still surprised him. Washing dishes and being a servant had never entered his mind while in Pacific Edge. He found it difficult to imagine Donna being a spy, but he could not say why. Perhaps because she made such marvelous cinnamon rolls. Who could distrust someone capable of baking such delights?

Derrick was running out of options, and he wanted more options because he was down to the final two: Akira and Nyx. He forced consideration of Nyx first. She lived in the same building. She was on the track team. However, Derrick's attraction to her was not predictable, nor was his involvement with track. Nyx was the opposite of what one might call his type. She was like Miriam and until the day of Derrick's exile. He had never shown affection for his sister.

Objective observation caused Derrick to pause. He had felt drawn to Nyx before he met her, watching her from his window. If they had him under surveillance, they might have seen his attraction, which made Nyx a suspect. But Nyx had been unpredictable. She seemed friendly, then distant, and then friendly, and then abrasive, and then she told him to stay away from her. A spy would not push the target away. A slight weight lifted from his chest.

That left Akira. Pure circumstance that she sat in front of him the first day in Earth science, was it not? But not when she picked him as her partner in chemistry.

Coincidence?

Maybe?

But then, maybe not.

24

Wednesday, March 24, 6:15 a.m.

A ROCK-AND-ROLL GUITAR RIFF BLASTED through the darkness. Derrick woke slowly as the riff sounded a second time. He fumbled for his phone, but it tumbled to the floor. The riff played a third time before he located the phone and silenced the alarm. Possession of such music would be a severe transgression in Pacific Edge. But he was not in Pacific Edge and was free to use whatever sound he found pleasing and change it whenever it suited him. This small freedom provided a much larger sense of control than people here could imagine, for they took it for granted. He lay there for a few moments thinking about Miriam's e-mail, just as he had laid staring into the darkness until he drifted into a restless sleep. He might have mentioned the dream to her and merely forgotten about it. With a clear head, that seemed the most logical explanation. Derrick liked logical explanations best. He was up early, ate a quick breakfast, and when he arrived at school, he saw few teachers and no students. He found Coach Browning in his office.

Noticing Derrick walking across the gym, Browning motioned him in. "You're here early, King."

"Yes, sir. I mean, Coach. I wanted to ask you something."

"Well, the only thing stopping you is fear."

Derrick wondered if his fear was showing more than usual and decided it likely was because initiating a conversation with an instructor was not a typical Derrick-from-Pacific Edge behavior. "Coach, I hoped I could come early to run 400 sprints."

Coach Browning rocked back in his chair. "And what would you do during P.E.?"

"Run laps. Five miles or more after school is my strategy."

"And why do you want to do that?"

"Run five miles or come in early?"

"Both."

Derrick paused, took a deep breath, then continued. "Malcolm said I should run five miles a day to improve my endurance." Derrick shifted his backpack. "I am nervous about joining the relay team. If I run 400 meters during class, the other team members will be observing me. It makes me anxious. I believe I can improve at an increased rate if I apply myself without an audience. At least, until I improve my lap times to the level the team requires for victory." Derrick did not mention that he might be working after school and taking guitar lessons.

Coach Browning rocked in his chair for a few moments, studying Derrick. "I'm here every morning at 6:45. You can start then."

"Thank you, Coach."

"You know what, King? You talk funny."

"Yes, Coach. So, I have been told."

Derrick walked to the front entrance, where he sat on the steps and watched students arrive. He said hello to Malcolm Cross, nodded to Henry Clark — who just glared — chatted with Akira for a few minutes until Jim Priest showed up and encroached on her personal space, at which point she left. Derrick tried to will Priest away, but Priest did not leave. When Nyx arrived, Priest was still standing over Derrick, droning on about some conspiracy theory involving the school board and the federal government. Nyx glared at Derrick, then turned and went to the entrance at the far end of the building. He shrugged his shoulders, hoping to show his disinterest in Priest, but Nyx was not looking his way.

Derrick skipped morning break because his appetite waned. All morning, he thought about Miriam's question. When he first awoke, he felt certain he must have mentioned the dreams to her at some point. Now, he was certain he had not. At lunch he got a tray, some sort of chicken, he assumed. He planned to get his lunch from the vending machines and eat outside but forgot his wallet. He walked to the far end of the lunchroom and sat alone. Nyx was in the center of the room with a mixed group of girls and boys, all of whom had either a tattoo, a nose ring, odd colored hair, strange clothes, or in most cases a combination of those things. She did not look Derrick's direction until Jim Priest and his two friends walked straight to him and sat down. Nyx looked straight into Derrick's eyes. Priest launched into another lecture about how the student council was trying to shut down a thing called seminary. Derrick excused himself, although he had only taken a few bites of his food, which, although he was sure it was not excrement, gave weight to Antonio's recommendation that the vending machines were preferred on most days.

Derrick had trouble concentrating all day. In chemistry, Ms. Albertyne lectured on a thing called the scientific method, which sounded complicated. Derrick would not have understood it under the best of circumstances. Ms. Albertyne gave the class an assignment. They were to pair up, develop a project, and demonstrate how to use the scientific method. The assignment was due in one week, presentations limited to 20 minutes. Derrick felt a familiar sinking sensation in his stomach.

"Were you even listening?" Akira whispered.

"Yes, well, not exactly. I was trying to listen, but I had a tough time concentrating," Derrick said.

Akira bit her lower lip and then said, "I understand." She patted his hand. "We can team up if you would like. I've done this type of assignment before."

Derrick breathed easier. "That would be most helpful."

"We'll have to work after school," Akira said. "We can do it at my house."

"I do not have transportation," Derrick said. He remembered Akira could be a spy.

"I live close to your condo. Besides, you're on the track team. Run." She winked at him, and then jotted down her address, phone number, and e-mail on the inside cover of his notebook.

Derrick stared at the information she had written. How did she know where he lived? How did she know he was on the track team? What else did she know? Nyx knew where he lived, but he had never witnessed Nyx and Akira cross paths. It did not seem as if the two girls had anything in common. He was uncertain of the reason, but this elevated his paranoia tenfold. Students knew more about him than he had estimated. He tried to rein in his spiraling anxiety. While Potterville High was much larger than James Carver Academy, it was not huge. New kids draw attention, people talk, word spreads. Simple as that. Yet, it did not feel as simple as that. It felt dark and disturbing.

After Spanish, 55 minutes that seemed like four hours, Derrick bolted into the hall eager to get on the track and run, clear his head.

"Amigo. Hey, hold up. Amigo! DERRICK!"

Derrick turned to see Antonio Morales on crutches knifing awkwardly through the throng of students.

"Amigo, you deaf? Your head is in the clouds." Antonio tapped the side of his own head.

"I am preoccupied, I guess. What did the doctor say?"

"I tore my ACL. Thought it was a pulled muscle. Turns out it's worse. Might need surgery. They'll decide next week."

"I am sorry."

"Not your fault. Hey, why are you in Spanish, my friend?"

"Uh, I was in Spanish in Denver. I had just started before ..."

"Sorry, I didn't mean to ..." Antonio looked down and then back to Derrick. "Thing is most of the kids in Spanish are Hispanic. The white kids in class speak good Spanish too. Man, we all grew up together. No offense, but you look miserable in there."

Derrick listened, nodded, and said nothing.

"What I'm saying, man, is why don't you see if you can transfer to another class. It's an elective, right? You don't need a foreign language unless you're going to college. You going to college?"

"I am not sure," Derrick said. He had not planned on living this long after exile, so college, or anything else resembling a future, had not factored into his thinking.

"Besides, mi amigo, if you want to go to college, take Mandarin, not Spanish. Colleges love Mandarin. China is taking over the world. Plus, Akira is in Mandarin. That girl digs you. And that's a rare thing, my friend." Antonio tapped Derrick on the chest with his knuckle. "Just looking out for you. Think about it." Antonio hobbled off, hollering at another kid named Alex to wait up.

If Derrick's head was not spinning before, it was now. *Akira likes me?* He thought that was what Antonio meant to communicate. If she does, how does Antonio know that? Derrick had never seen Akira talking with Antonio. He had never seen Antonio, Akira, or Nyx speak to one another. Except for that time Antonino whispered to Nyx at lunch. But they all knew a lot about him.

Then his mind drifted back to the spy business. A conspiracy? Maybe Akira approached Antonio about getting Derrick to switch classes. Now the pieces fell into place. But what he would do about it was a mystery.

Derrick stayed fifty yards away from Nyx as he warmed up. In fact, he stayed as far from the other track team members as possible. None of them seemed to mind. He understood that. He was new. Coach let him try out after the deadline, which was a courtesy not extended to other students who lived here. Then he unwittingly made some of them look bad. Coach wanted him on the relay team. Derrick could cause them to lose at State. He understood why they did not like him, and he was okay with it. He wished more people disliked him, at least enough to leave him alone. Odds of survival might increase if he talked to no one, and no one talked to him.

When Nyx started to run, Derrick positioned himself opposite her so that every time she completed a lap, he could tell if he had fallen behind her pace. The first lap, Nyx had pulled about ten yards on him. Derrick quickened his pace. The second lap, he had pulled about ten yards on her. He slowed a little. By the third lap, he had matched her pace within a step or two.

He matched her speed. She looked over as he watched her cross his imaginary finish line. On lap five, she sped up. Derrick sped up. The mysterious barrier where he felt like quitting arrived early. He knew if he kept pushing, it would get better. Today that did not work. From out of nowhere, he thought of Jana Somersworth, her image clear in his mind. He thought of his splendid Pacific Edge bedroom with granite, hardwoods, and luxurious leather furnishings. The anthems of the Chosen played in his head as if he wore headphones. He saw his parents. He saw Miriam. A melancholy washed over him. He had lost everything. A tear traced down his cheek. He felt a powerful urge to run off the track, out of town, and back to Pacific Edge, where he would pound on the gate begging forgiveness.

When they crossed the imaginary line, he was behind Nyx, about five yards. It was hard to tell at this distance, but he thought she smiled when she looked his way. He sped up. The next lap they were even again, and Nyx pumped her arms harder. The following lap he had fallen further behind.

His lungs burned.

He looked at the stands. There sat Akira, watching.

She digs you.

He ran on.

Tears flowing.

He hoped they would be indistinguishable from his sweat. The wall did not fall today, but he was able to push Pacific Edge to the back of his mind. When he thought they were within five minutes of the bell, he gritted his teeth and picked up the pace. The next lap he was ten yards back. The next lap, he had pulled within five yards. Nyx was struggling more than he had witnessed before. He felt like his heart might burst, but he pushed harder. He was even with her at the finish line. The bell rang. He wobbled to the grass and fell to his hands and knees. When he looked up, he saw Nyx jogging into the building.

He felt as if he had won something but was unsure what that something was.

25

Thursday, March 25, 6:04 a.m.

THE MORNING AIR WAS CLEAN, DRY, CRISP, and scented with trees that seemed to have burst into full bloom with white flowers during the night. The streets were mostly empty. People had rolled garbage containers to the curb, where a mechanical arm attached to a giant blue machine picked them up, turned them upside down, and dumped their contents into the back of the machine. The sky was steel gray with pink trim at its eastern edge. Derrick ran to school in his track clothing, and his school clothing was in his backpack. The track was deserted. He did not check in with Coach Browning and hoped it was not a problem. His lap times did not improve. Every muscle in his body protested from the exertion of yesterday afternoon. He ended his workout 15 minutes early. He showered, feeling completely exposed in the large, tiled room with many showers. But he only used one shower head, and no one entered the room. When he finished, he changed into his school clothes.

He walked to the counselor's office, where he asked if he could drop Spanish and transfer to Mandarin. The counselor made the change with little comment. Derrick wondered if Akira would be in the same class. Weighing the pros and cons, Derrick had decided Mandarin had advantages. At least no one would expect him to speak Mandarin.

The rest of the morning proved uneventful until the scent of pizza drifted from the dining area. Having been up early, eaten only cereal, and running laps, the aroma, plus his hunger, made the period before lunch almost unbearable.

After filling his tray, Derrick saw Malcolm standing at the end of the serving line, waiting. "Hey, bro! Sit with me." Malcolm motioned to the center table where two large boys sat like bookends, saving two spots. "This will take care of your problem with Priest."

"Why do you think I have a problem?"

"If you keep hanging with him, you'll have a problem with me. Does that clear it up?"

Derrick stood for a moment and then followed Malcolm. "Thanks." He scanned the room, hoping Nyx would notice that he was not sitting with Jim Priest, but he did not see her.

"Guys, this is Derrick King," Malcolm said as he sat. "These guys play football with me. Nate," Malcolm pointed at the kid on the left, "is a senior. He has offers from Washington, Washington State, and Boise State. Jeff and I are juniors. Derrick might try out for football. He's on the track team already."

Malcolm did not say that Derrick was new at Potterville. No need for that. Malcolm did not add that Derrick's parents had been killed. No need for that. Malcolm did not mention that Derrick might be lying about both and was an outcast from Pacific Edge. Maybe no need for that either.

After sitting, Derrick spotted Jim Priest holding a tray, scanning the room. Jim's eyes found Derrick. Priest scowled at him and then stomped over to his friends. Priest dropped his tray onto the table but remained standing, glaring at Derrick. Priest raised his hand and stuck his middle finger in the air. Derrick did not understand the meaning of this gesture but felt confident it was not a sign of goodwill. He had acquired his first enemy, or perhaps second, remembering that Henry Clark had tripped him on the first day. Priest was the person he thought he should befriend. Malcolm, who Nyx warned Derrick to be careful around, now seemed to be protecting him. Nyx now seemed to hate him. The one thing clear to Derrick: he had no clue what he was doing.

Malcolm's friends carried on their conversations as if Derrick did not exist. Derrick ate silently. Some of the discussion was easy to follow, and some was not. They talked of girls and weekend plans, easy to follow. They talked football, steeped in jargon Derrick did not understand. The large boy on Derrick's left must play defense because he said it was a good thing Malcolm was on the same team, because if they played against each other, Malcolm would never catch a pass. This caused Malcolm to laugh, but Malcolm seemed to agree because Malcolm said, "Yeah, right."

* * *

When Derrick arrived at the Mandarin classroom, he thought he was in the wrong place. He hesitated, checking the classroom number on the slip of paper Ms. Bates had given him. A small room compared to his other subjects and only three students. Instead of desks, a green corduroy couch and three stuffed chairs with a low table in the center comprised the furnishings. On the walls hung black and white pictures of simple, yet interesting designs.

Akira came up behind him, touching him lightly on the elbow. "Derrick, what are you doing here?"

"I changed my schedule. I had Spanish, but someone told me Mandarin was better for college."

Akira smiled. "I see."

She stepped into the classroom. He followed a moment later.

"Ah, welcome to the lesson of Mandarin, Mr. Derrick King," said a small Asian man standing beside the couch. "I am Mr. Xu. Please take a seat."

Derrick sat in a green, floral overstuffed chair facing Akira. "Hi," he said to the room, but he looked at Akira. She smiled. He smiled. It was impossible not to.

Three students were Caucasian. Derrick hoped Mandarin would be as alien to them as it would be to him but soon learned that was not the case. Mr. Xu had each student introduce themselves. Pam, Mike, and Carl studied Mandarin for three years. Akira spoke English and Mandarin all her life and studied French. Akira said they were acquainted, adding that they shared other classes. She did not add that Derrick was her partner in chemistry. Maybe no need for that.

Everyone seemed comfortable that Derrick knew nothing, and each was eager to help him learn. The class proceeded in a manner alien to Derrick. Mr. Xu turned the class over to Akira and instructed her to do what she thought was best. Mr. Xu left, going into an adjacent room, a small office perhaps. The classroom was not big enough for a teacher's desk.

Akira did not stand but leaned forward, which was enough to take charge as the others turned their attention to her. "Mr. King is our guest today. We shall each teach him a word. Please choose your word so it will be meaningful. Something Derrick can use in class each day. I shall go first."

Turning to Derrick, Akira said, "Ní hǎo, Derrick. Do you know what ní hǎo means?"

Derrick thought for a moment. "Hello?"

"Very good. Now you say it."

"Ní hǎo, Akira," Derrick said. He smiled and was not sure why.

Each student took turns. Pam taught him to say "how." Mike taught him to say "you." Derrick thought the word choice was odd because Akira said to teach something he could use each day in class. Mr. Xu returned with a tray of beautiful China cups with a delicate blue design and a pot of tea, which he served to each student. Carl taught the word "are."

They had Derrick practice hello, how are you: Nǐ hǎo, jīn tiān shì nǐ ma until he was comfortable.

When the bell rang, none of the students stood except Derrick. Embarrassed, Derrick sat down. Mr. Xu stood and held up one hand and said, "Teaching others is an excellent way to learn. Derrick joining us is most fortunate."

Mr. Xu bowed and said, "Thank you for choosing our class, Mr. King."

Derrick now had Akira in three of his six classes, and for some reason, she had a free period because she was in the stands watching him yesterday during physical education. He was not convinced that Akira *dug him*. However, she was also somewhat new in Potterville and understood his situation. That was probably all there was to it. Teenagers, even in Pacific Edge, were often immature about relationships and gossip.

Derrick had watched for Nyx all day. He had not seen her at lunch. She was not at track, which convinced him she was not at school. She would have nothing to do with him, but he missed seeing her.

His run was hard again today. Jana Somersworth, New America patriotic songs, his room, family, it all circulated in his head as if it were beamed in from space. That Nyx was not there to compete with, albeit from across the track, did not help. He stopped and walked a few times. He considered giving up.

After track, he ran straight home and knocked on Paul's door, but Paul was not there. He ate a bowl of healthy cereal. He had homework, two chapters to read with questions at the end. One chapter about diverse types of rocks in Earth science. Derrick questioned that anyone wanted to learn about rocks and doubted anyone understood how they were formed. But he had to learn the answers to such meaningless questions to pass. Passing made him more invisible than failing. The other chapter was for U.S. History. This too was pointless because he was certain it was all fabricated. He knew the old United States was a complete failure.

After his studies, he felt restless, unable to shake thoughts of home. He had already run both sprints and five miles, but he decided to run again. He ran by the bistro and the music store but did not stop to admire the guitars in the window. The aroma of pastry drifting out of the bistro called to him, but he ran. He ran the same route until reaching a street named Maple, where he turned left. He did not keep track of time or distance. He just ran. It felt good, cleared his head. For a few moments, he forgot about his problems and his parents and Miriam. But it made him hungry, so when he came back to the bistro, he stepped inside.

He had no money, but Donna fixed him a ham and cheese panini sandwich and charged him half price, employee discount she said, adding that she would start a tab for him, which he could pay, or she could deduct from his check. Derrick protested, saying he had not yet started work. Donna said it did not matter. He worked there now, and she would hear no more about it. Every time someone treated him kindly, he thought about the disparity between New America Media and the reality of his current experience.

He walked home and entered the building through the garage door. For some reason, he was afraid that he might bump into Nyx in the foyer, and he was not up to seeing her, but he could not determine why. Paul's truck was not there. He did not want to see Paul either. As it turned out, he saw no one. He went straight to his computer and checked his e-mail. He was excited to see an e-mail from Miriam.

March 25

```
TO: derrickking0312

FROM: number1sis
```

Derrick, I've been thinking about what happened. I am sorry. It was my fault from the beginning. I don't understand why I did the things I did. Someday I'll figure it out.

You always wanted the best for me. I was too rebellious to listen. I'm listening now. First, I want you to know that I have tried. I've tried extremely hard. But the truth is, I cannot help you. If it were possible, I would come there to be with you. Even if I couldn't help you there, we'd be together. Please believe that I've tried my best.

But I cannot get there. Leaving here is impossible. I'm sorry. I promised and I failed. The one thing I can do for you is change. I will work hard to become the person you wanted me to be.

This will be my last message to you. I hope you can forgive me.

Your number1sis (AKA Number Six)

I love you, Number Seven

Derrick could not breathe. Tears welled in his eyes and flowed down his cheeks. He had clung to the idea that Miriam would help him. He believed that more than he believed in the Chosen ways. As certain Miriam would never give up, as he was certain the sun would rise in the east.

But there it was.

She quit.

He would never see her again.

26

Friday, March 26

THE CLOCK READ 2:00 A.M. THE LAST time Derrick checked. He awoke three hours later, turned over, pulled the pillow over his head, and decided to sleep another hour. He would tell Coach he had been sick during the night. That lasted two minutes before his competitive spirit started burning in the center of his chest. He had to improve his lap times and sleeping would not make him faster.

He showered, gobbled down a bowl of cereal, healthy oats according to the box, and jogged to school. After stretching and running a few laps, his thinking cleared. The track was empty, and the green grass of the football field sparkled with dew in the morning light. Running alone that day in the crisp morning air might have been his best experience on the track thus far. After one mile, he thought he could run all day. Not knowing proper training techniques, he decided the first lap was a warm-up, which made little sense because he was already warm, and he would not get a warm-up lap before a race. Having never been to a track meet, he did not know what to expect. He had no illusions of winning. He hoped he did not look pathetic and make the team look bad. Negative attention would not help his situation.

First lap: 62 seconds. Not his best time, 60 seconds, the last lap of his first day, remained his personal best. That notwithstanding, Derrick felt good about his first lap because he could have run faster. He jogged 50 yards and then returned to the starting line. He reset the stopwatch to zero, got into a starting position, and heard, "Hold up there, King."

Coach Browning jogged across the football field, agile for such a large man. "Let me time you."

Derrick said nothing. He handed the stopwatch to Browning.

"What was your last time?"

"Sixty-two seconds," Derrick said.

Coach Browning nodded. "Not bad, but you need to improve. It will come. I'll try to help, but I'm a football coach. Track was never my thing. Except for shot put. I did that in high school."

Derrick said nothing.

"On your mark, set, go!"

Derrick bolted from his starting position. This time felt different, but he could not say why. Something to prove, perhaps? Enjoying the audience? Halfway around the track, he was flying. His arms pumped with the fury of his legs. Marcus Carver came to mind. Derrick ran harder. At the three-quarter mark, Derrick's lungs burned. His breathing was deep but controlled. With the finish line in sight, he sprinted as if he were in a 100 -meter race. His legs burned, his heart pounded, and his lungs on fire, making wheezing sounds, as if he could not suck in enough air to feed his starving muscles.

Derrick crossed the line and slowed but did not stop, instead settling into a relaxed run, arms and legs loose, long strides and deep breaths. Twenty-five yards later, he turned, jogging back to Coach Browning.

Coach Browning whistled. "Sixty seconds was your best time?"

Derrick stood with his hands on his hips and nodded. His breathing almost back to normal.

"You ran a 55 second, 400-meter, King. That's damn respectable. After less than one week of training. Damn respectable."

Derrick ran three more laps for Coach Browning that day. He tied the 55-second lap once, but he never ran a 60-second 400-meter again. Coach gave him a few pointers, like having his hands open like knives instead of fists, which would seem strange in the beginning, but it would seem natural soon. He was not trying to break an old habit. It was not lost on Derrick that his progress was uncanny, because he had never been active, yet it seemed natural. True, he was young, but he surmised that most young people could not run like he could. It reinforced his belief that the Chosen were superior. Perhaps his Father and Mother had been athletes. Possibly genetics were at work. Still, he sensed he was missing something.

In chemistry, Ms. Albertyne asked partners to work on their scientific method projects. Akira had been on his mind, and he considered ending their friendship, but that posed problems. For one, how was he going to pass chemistry or Mandarin without her help? Maybe she was not the spy. That thinking was risky, and he had already proven he was not the shrewdest person on the planet.

"I have an idea for our project," Akira said.

Derrick nodded, focusing on keeping his mouth shut.

"It's not chemistry, exactly, but the purpose is to demonstrate using the scientific method. Right?"

Derrick nodded.

"I'll check with Ms. Albertyne to ensure our project qualifies. First, we need an observation. The observation is that light attracts insects at night."

"Okay," Derrick said, sensing too much nodding with no talking might be a bad thing.

"Next, we need a hypothesis. What would your hypothesis be?" Akira asked.

"Uh, well …" Derrick should have done some homework on this assignment. He was not sure what hypothesis meant, an idea or something. A science word forbidden in Pacific Edge.

Akira rescued him. "We have observed that light attracts insects at night. I can think of two hypotheses: one, the light attracts them, or two, the heat of the light attracts them."

Derrick nodded.

"We can devise several experiments to test our hypotheses," Akira said.

"Okay," Derrick agreed.

Akira looked down, and then her eyes returned to his. "We'd have to do the experiments after dark."

***

Derrick did not see Nyx that day. Possibly, he had been in the wrong places at the wrong times. He still had hopes of seeing her when he rushed to P.E.

"King! Dress down and then come see me," Coach Browning hollered from his office door.

When Derrick returned a few minutes later, Browning motioned him into a chair and then closed the door. Browning held the phone to his ear, rolled his eyes, and held up one finger. Derrick had been in Browning's office previously but had been too distracted by the chaos of his own life for much observation. A diploma from the University of California hung on the wall. There were pictures of a young man wearing a football uniform, pictures of the PAC-16 CAL football champions, two consecutive years. Another photo taken was of a football team on the field behind Potterville High School and written on the picture were the words California State Champions. On Browning's desk was a picture of two children: a boy who looked about 14 and a girl a few years younger, both wearing uniforms, the girl holding a soccer ball.

Browning hung up the phone. "Sorry about that. A parent who thinks he knows more about football than I do. He thinks it's all the O-line's fault that we didn't win district last year. Hell, I got four linemen who have Division-1 colleges all over them. I got a QB that will go to a PAC-16 school, and he has five PAC offers. I got a wide receiver verbally committed to Arizona. Defense is solid, but my linebackers are young. They won't be as green this year. What I don't have is a division-1 running back."

He tried to follow what Coach said while looking at the wall of framed pictures. "Coach, is this you in the photographs? You played for CAL, and you played here?"

"I played here and CAL. I know. You wonder why I'm coaching at a high school. I like the kids here. And this place probably saved my life. I was lost when I started high school. No future. Broken home. All the things that lead kids into the wrong life, but the coach convinced me to play football. I've had offers to coach at Division-1 universities. Someday, when the right offer comes along."

Derrick wanted to ask more questions, but he stopped himself and remained quiet.

"So, here's the deal. I'm impressed with your progress on the 400-meter. You'll make the mile relay team for sure, and the 100-meter sprint and 400-meter relay. How about running the 400 meters as well? I know you wanted to run cross-country, but that would be a lot to ask. What do you think?"

As innocuous as the moment seemed, for Derrick it was the hinge on which his future, perhaps his entire life, pivoted. Part of him wanted to say he had changed his mind. Track was not something he wanted to do. During his last lap this morning, thoughts of Pacific Edge haunted him as if the memories had been thrust upon him. He blocked those thoughts as best he could. Part of his brain said quit, but he could not force those words from his mouth. Another part of his brain, the part that caused him to smack Marcus Carver, the part that took a job at the bistro, the part that wanted to learn to play guitar, overpowered him, and from his mouth came these words. "I can improve on those times. But you already have runners in the 400-meter race."

"Everything we do here is a competition. We'll field the best team we can. If we have two or three people in the final, that suits me fine. If those three people finish one, two, three, fantastic. So here is my plan. Next week, you train with Nyx in the mornings. She can help you with starts and technique, teach you how to pass the baton, and time your laps. I'll check in with you both every Friday morning."

"I do not think Nyx will do that," Derrick whispered.

"Why not? I thought you two hit it off."

"She is angry with me," Derrick said. He hoped Browning did not ask what she was mad about. He was not sure himself. Maybe because he had talked to Jim Priest, which Derrick realized in hindsight was a mistake. When he thought about it objectively, he realized there was no logical reason for Nyx to be so angry with him. *Must be more to it than Jim Priest.*

"She'll do it," Coach said.

"I doubt it, Coach," Derrick said.

"Nyx may come across as a little odd, but I know three things about her: she's smart, she's tough, and she's a team player. She'll do this for the team. I know one other thing about her. She knows a hell of a lot more about running than I ever will. She's a junior and already has full-ride scholarship offers from several universities that don't give full-ride scholarships to female track and field competitors."

Derrick tried to control the stranger living in his head. The stranger thought Coach was right. Derrick was convinced that quitting track was best, but the stranger prevailed, and when Derrick opened his mouth, he said, "What about cross-country?"

"Like I said, doing it all would be tough. Cross-country should be your last priority. I won't lie. If you do them all, the 400 meters and mile relay will make it hard for you to be competitive in cross-country. Here's the deal, don't say anything about this. Okay? The others will figure it out when they see Nyx training you. You probably know that she's out sick. Some of the guys might be a little pissed, but I'll handle that. You let me know if you have any problems." Browning stood and opened the door.

Derrick walked out of Coach's office. He had not gone ten feet when behind him, Browning hollered.

"King!"

Derrick turned around.

"I almost forgot the most important thing. The reason you gotta train with Nyx in the mornings. It's because on Monday after school we start spring ball. I want you there, and I won't take no for an answer. Understood?"

"Springball?"

"Spring ball. Football, son. I've mentioned you trying out for the team." Browning winked. "I think I'm looking at the Division 1 running back we need."

Derrick searched his mind for an excuse why he could not do football. Several reasons came to mind; some of them sounded half decent. But when he opened his mouth, he said, "Okay, Coach."

On the track, Derrick ran alone. Two questions circulated in his head. *Why is Nyx so angry? What do I know about football?*

27

AFTER SCHOOL, DERRICK STOPPED AT the bistro to confirm that Donna expected him the next morning. Donna said, "be here at six o'clock." Next, he stopped by the guitar store, but Mark Grealy was showing a guitar to a man wearing a suit. Derrick looked around for a few minutes, then started for the door.

"Derrick. You ready to start guitar lessons?" Mark called out.

"Yes, I would like to do that. Tomorrow after work, if I get off early enough," Derrick said.

"Perfect. Tomorrow it is."

Derrick walked to his condo. He hesitated in the lobby and then climbed the stairs, exiting on the second floor, which was empty. He took the elevator back to the lobby. From the lobby, he retraced his steps up the stairs, hesitated at the second-floor landing, where he pressed his ear to the door, listening for sounds in the hallway. There were none. What would he say to Nyx? He had no idea.

Back at his condo, he fixed a simple meal of pancakes and eggs. After eating, he showered. After that, he checked his e-mail. Nothing.

Having no pressing homework, Derrick dug through his backpack and retrieved the book, *A Separate Peace*. He found reading it difficult because the setting was so many years ago and it referred to World War II as if it were real. The narrator, an adult named Gene Forrester, told the story, which happened fifteen years earlier when he was a teenager. That part Derrick could relate to. Central to the story was Gene's complicated relationship with a friend he called Finny. Finny was an exceptional athlete, which brought Malcolm Cross and Henry Clark to Derrick's thoughts.

The friendship reminded Derrick of no one.

His eyes grew heavy with sleep. He stumbled into his bedroom and crawled under the bedspread.

28

Saturday, March 27, 5:00 a.m.

THE ALARM SOUNDED AN ANNOYING RAPID tweeting noise in the darkness. He had forgotten to change the standard alarm to something better. Later he would change it to the rock-and-roll guitar riff he used Monday through Friday, or perhaps he would find something different for the weekend.

He gazed at the old Martin in the window of Mountain View Guitar before walking into the bistro at six o'clock. A girl who looked familiar stood smiling at the counter. She had shoulder-length brown hair, and large silver-hoop earrings hung from each ear. A colorful tattoo disappeared under the sleeve of her black blouse. The tattoo appeared to be the tail of a dragon, and he wondered why someone would want an image from a children's book inked on visible skin. She was slender, but not in an athletic way, or so it seemed, loose-fitting clothing made it hard to tell. Her hazel eyes warm, her skin tanned. She was pretty but not beautiful, or perhaps she was beautiful. He needed coffee.

"Good morning," the girl at the counter said. "What would you like?"

"Is Donna here?" Derrick asked. "I'm starting work this morning."

"Ain't that a coinkydink?" the girl said. "I started this morning, too." She turned her head and shouted, "Hey, Donna! The other new employee is here."

"Coinkydink?" Derrick puzzled.

She laughed. "Coincidence. That we are both starting this morning. I was supposed to be here at six, but I was so excited I got here at 5:30." She reached across the counter. "I'm L. Linda Maxton."

Her grip was firm, and her hand was warm. Derrick did not believe in coincidence, nor did he believe everything happened for a reason, which is what they taught him as a member of the Chosen. Now, he thought, things just happened. "What does the L. stand for?"

"Linda," L. Linda Maxton said.

"Your name is Linda Linda?" Derrick asked.

L. Linda laughed again. "Yes, it is. My parents didn't have much imagination, or maybe they thought it was funny." She still held Derrick's hand. "My grandmother on my father's side was named Linda, and my mother's name is Linda. So, I'm named after both. They thought I would go by Linda, but I like L. Linda. You don't recognize me, do you?" She let go of his hand, sliding her fingers along his with a soft touch.

"I am sorry. You look familiar," Derrick said. It occurred to Derrick that he did not know his grandparents from either his Father or Mother. Although he had never thought about it before, it now seemed odd that he knew nothing about any family members other than Father, Mother, and Miriam.

"I'm in chemistry with you. Akira sequestered you the first day, so you probably haven't noticed most of the others in class."

"To be honest," he had not been honest often here, "this first week has been a blur."

"Derrick," Donna said, bursting through swinging half doors that separated the kitchen from the dining area. "Grab yourself some coffee and then come back here. I see you've met Linda."

"L. Linda," Linda Linda corrected.

Derrick poured a cup of coffee from the large carafe, added cream and sugar, and walked to the kitchen, where Donna iced fresh cinnamon rolls on a large tray. An individual cinnamon roll sat on a plate nearby.

"I set you a fresh roll here, Hon. Don't tell me you've already eaten. They are never better than fresh out of the oven."

"I can find room," Derrick said, pulling up a stool to the counter.

"Soon as you finish, you can start on that stack of dishes and pans." Donna motioned to a large stainless-steel sink stacked with dishes, cups, and baking pans of all sizes. "Normally, the night shift cleans up the evening dishes before leaving, but we had a problem last night. It won't always be that way. The pans, however, are from my morning baking."

"You must start early," Derrick said.

"Yes, I do. Three thirty, to be exact. I've been a baker for the last 20 years here, so it doesn't seem early to me. Just seems natural. Besides, I like to bake, and I like the solitude it provides. Not going to get rich here, but I manage. Be a lot easier if they didn't keep raising the lease. I'll be here another 20 years, good Lord willing."

Derrick had stuffed a generous portion of the cinnamon roll in his mouth, so he nodded, even though Donna's back was to him. Once he had washed the mouthful down with hot coffee, he said, "You are correct. This is the best thing I have ever tasted."

"Thank you, Derrick. You help yourself to more coffee. When I get back, I'll show you where to start." Donna carried the tray of cinnamon rolls to the front.

Derrick scanned the kitchen as he ate. It was immaculate except for the pile of soiled pots, pans, and dishes stacked in the sink and overflowing onto the counter. Several times the front door chimes sounded, followed by Donna's cheery voice, often calling people by name: Eric, Sam, Suzy, Chris. Derrick finished his cinnamon roll and went for more coffee.

Donna was ladling a cinnamon roll onto a plate, so Derrick stepped to her side. "I can get started. Just wash everything. Is that correct?"

"Yes. Soapy water, hot as you can tolerate wearing gloves. You'll find them above the sink. Rinse water, same temp. Change it when it gets dirty or cools. There's a clean apron hanging by the sink. I'll be back when it slows down. *If* it slows down."

He did as Donna instructed. Pans were the most difficult because of the baked-on sugar residue. The front door chimes sounded every few minutes. He got faster, learning a few tricks, which was not actual magic, but just using a scrub brush and a rough-sided sponge he spotted on the edge of the sink. He had just finished the pots and pans when L. Linda came through the swinging half doors, pushing a cart stacked with dirty dishes.

"Donna said we are almost out of plates and silverware." L. Linda pointed to a ledge that held a small stack of clean plates and then looked at the pile of dirty dishes that Derrick had not yet started. Below the counter, a portioned plastic bin held clean forks, knives, and spoons.

Nodding, he slid a dirty dish into the sink. L. Linda pulled the plastic bin and emptied the clean silverware into three round steel containers. Glancing over his shoulder, he watched her take the last stack of clean plates. L. Linda went to and from the kitchen all morning, bringing more dirty dishes and getting clean, plus meat, cheese, bread, and soup to refill the work counter, where Donna prepared meals. The baked goods were already out front. When the baked goods were gone, that was it, but Donna kept other items in a large refrigeration unit, except for soup, which simmered in large pots on the stove.

He never caught up. He was working on the last cart of dishes that L. Linda delivered when Donna walked into the kitchen.

"What a day," Donna said.

Derrick looked at her and kept scrubbing; confident he might get fired on his first day for not getting his work done.

"Your shift is over. The next dishwasher arrives any minute. You must be starving. Sorry, you started with such a mess this morning. It won't be like that tomorrow. I'll see to it. Anyway, you get a meal each day. What would you like? How about a hot pastrami sandwich? I make the best in town."

Derrick nodded, although he did not know what pastrami was. He trusted Donna would not lead him astray on food.

"You get yourself some coffee or a soda and sit. I'll bring it to you."

Derrick sat warming in the sun on the sidewalk at a black-iron lattice-top table in front of Donna's Bistro. His new boss delivered the sandwich, thanked him again for his work, said he did a fantastic job, and that she'd see him in the morning. His fear of being fired was not well founded. Like many things he experienced the past week, pastrami, although new to him, was delightful. He wondered how much longer finding a new favorite food would continue. He wondered if Nyx had come in while he worked in the kitchen, scrubbing pots and pans and dishes.

He considered how far he had fallen from grace as a member of the Chosen. All the way to a commoner washing dishes. He understood that washing dishes was a lowly job, even in the Commoner World. He went from heaven to hell in less than three weeks. The melancholy thoughts swirled about his head, but he was learning how to keep them at bay.

The last few days, his life churned and blurred like a kaleidoscope of colors, images, people, places, thoughts, and fears. But today it slowed down, and he saw things that had escaped him. No big revelations. Trivial things. Three cars sat at the curb. He studied them. The first, a red Ford Express. A small, boxy vehicle with four doors, and on the rear of the car was a small emblem that said *Hybrid*. The next vehicle, a blue Honda Accord, looked old but in good condition. The last vehicle was strange looking. It was much older, but he wasn't sure how he knew that. The front half looked like what they called a car, but the back half looked like what they called a pickup, albeit a small one. Bright yellow and in pristine condition despite its age, as if it had been reborn. He took a picture with his phone and intended to research it on the internet. A nameplate said it was an El Camino SS.

Derrick took his dishes inside, refilled his coffee, and then returned to his sidewalk observation point. He heard birds singing in nearby trees that burst with pink blossoms, scenting the air like a girl's perfume. A man walked by with a large black dog on a leash. It was the biggest dog Derrick had ever seen. The man smiled and nodded. Derrick smiled back. The dog, he learned her name was Mia, and she was a Newfoundland, wanted to say hello too. He petted her soft, furry face. He had never petted a dog before.

What a wonderful feeling.

The man and his dog left. Steam rose from Derrick's mug.

Derrick heard the sound before he saw the source. A motor, but not like any car or pickup he had heard, some of which made almost no sound and some that were loud and raucous. A throaty sound, but not loud. He stood and turned toward the source and then saw it. A vehicle unlike anything he had seen before. Two wheels like a bicycle — bicycles were not uncommon in Pacific Edge — but bigger with a motor. The driver wore a jacket despite the warm temperatures and a covering that looked somewhat like a football helmet over his or her head. The driver's head turned, looked at Derrick, and then a gloved hand raised and gave a slight wave.

Derrick thought the rider looked free, perched on the machine. He was sure he had seen a motorcycle.

He wanted one.

From heaven to hell in less than three weeks, and that remained the fact of the matter. Derrick sat at that black metal table in front of Donna's Bistro, on a sidewalk in Potterville, California. Where he tried but failed to resurrect the fears that consumed him when he first arrived. Life as he knew it had been turned upside down. He missed his Father and Mother. He missed Miriam, and his thoughts lingered on her for a time. What was happening in Pacific Edge? How much trouble was she in? She had committed several serious crimes. Not only breaching the no-contact protocols but somehow accessing the internet. Derrick worried for her safety but knew she could handle adversity. He forced thoughts of Miriam from his head when tears welled in his eyes. Despite all the pain, for utterly unexplainable reasons, he felt alive in a way that he had never experienced.

Free.

That thought swirled in his mind like a bird gliding in lazy circles in a clear blue sky. He sipped coffee.

Washing dirty dishes.

Not merely grimy pots and pans, but dishes that contained leftover food of commoners. At James Carver Academy, they taught commoners were disease ridden creatures the Creator cursed to a status below animals.

Washing dirty dishes.

A job at the bottom of the heap of menial work, even in the commoner world.

Washing dirty dishes.

No one forced him to do that.

Free.

Or was freedom an illusion?

29

AT THREE O'CLOCK, MOUNTAIN VIEW GUITAR remained open. Derrick eased through the door. Having already exposed himself to more risks than he had planned, he did not need another entanglement. Mark Grealy was probably not the spy because who could have predicted that Derrick would be interested in learning guitar? Unless Pacific Edge Security had him under surveillance and knew that he committed to taking lessons from Grealy, in which case they might have recruited Grealy with an attractive offer. Now that he thought about it, Grealy looked like a shady character.

"There he is. Sit right here." Grealy pointed at a stool.

"I've decided …"

"Sit, sit. I need to rush this one. Sorry, but I need to close shop early because I gotta get to a gig."

Derrick did not know what a gig was and did not ask.

Grealy handed him a guitar. Derrick grabbed it by the neck. It was an acoustic, used, well worn, but not the one in the window. Grealy pushed a stack of papers into Derrick's hand and explained how to read the fingering for three chords written on one sheet of paper: G, C, D. Grealy made Derrick show he understood the instruction.

"But …" Derrick began.

"Yeah, I thought about that too. Without a guitar, it would be darn tough learning how to play with only one lesson a week. Am I right? Not to worry. I've got you covered. I'm going to let you borrow that." Grealy pointed at the guitar Derrick was holding. "It's an old beater, an import, but a good one. Can't get them nowadays with the way they've screwed things up. It plays proper. I put on new strings. It's a sweet old guitar, but not worth much money. Still a good starter. You can use it as long as you're taking lessons, which are gonna be free and once per week. It even has a case."

With his foot, Grealy slid an empty case over to Derrick's feet.

"But I …"

"No buts. Just pack it up and go. I've got to haul ass. I'll see you next week. Practice every day. Start with short sessions because you need to toughen your fingertips. They'll be tender at first."

Grealy held the door open and gave Derrick a hurry signal, twirling one finger in the air.

"Mr. Grealy, this is kind of you, but …"

Grealy held up a hand. "I hope you'll buy from me when you're ready, so it's not completely philanthropic if that makes you feel better."

Derrick wondered if it was philanthropic or the plan of a spy. Thinking hard, Derrick placed the guitar in the case. To refuse now would seem odd. A normal person would not turn down a free guitar and lessons. That would make little sense, causing the Tribunal to think Derrick knew about the spy, which might put Miriam at risk.

"Mr. Grealy, why is it called Mountain View Guitar?" Derrick asked as he reached the door.

"Have you not been outside of town?"

"Yes, I ran —" Derrick paused for a moment and then pointed "that direction."

Grealy said. "Try going east. Everyone calls me Mark."

"Okay. Thanks, Mr. Grealy."

Derrick carried the guitar along the sidewalk, thinking about how he had further complicated his predicament. Brilliant yellow flowers covered a bush at the corner of the condo. He did not remember seeing them earlier. It was as if they had appeared while he was working. Around the base of the golden bush, purple and red flowers carpeted the ground. Unprepared to explain the guitar to anyone, he walked around the building and entered through the garage entrance. Paul had returned as his truck was parked in its regular space. He did not want to talk to Paul. Not today. He did not know why he felt that way. Parked beside Paul's truck was the two-wheeled machine Derrick had seen earlier, or one exactly like it. The machine shone as if polished, white, black, and chrome, except for the frame, which was bright orange. On the side were large letters: KTM. The tires looked suited for poor traction situations.

Inside his condo, Derrick pulled the guitar from the case, and he attempted the chords Mark Grealy had taught him. It was frustrating work. Mark made it look so easy as his fingers glided into position and the strings rang clear and bright when strummed. Derrick's fingers did not seem to be under his control. Instead, some demonic force took control of them, and the strings sounded with dull thuds or buzzed when strummed. He worked at it for ten minutes. As Mr. Grealy predicted, Derrick's fingertips hurt.

He donned his running clothes, then checked his e-mail. He did not know why he checked, because he would not hear from Miriam again. He left the building, running in the opposite direction of his previous ventures. The homes looked older the farther he ran. Tall trees blocked the sun, often stretching across the street, forming a darkened tunnel under which the air smelled wet and green. An old man tended three small gardens raised ten inches above the lawn and contained in rectangular boxes edged with wood. The man smiled and raised a gloved hand. Derrick smiled and waved as if he had done it all his life, when, in fact, he could not remember ever doing anything similar. In Pacific Edge, he did not run. People did not have gardens that grew food and were rarely seen outside their homes (Miriam being an exception as she walked almost everywhere and often left the house for no reason at all.)

He could see mountain peaks over what looked like a green wall. As he got closer and without forewarning, the homes ended. On the other side of this last cross street, bushes covered with waxy, thick green leaves stood as a fortress barring his way. A path ran in both directions along the unruly vegetation. The air possessed a fresh and woodsy scent. The sound of rushing water drifted through the brush. He studied the path and tried to decide which direction to go. Without a rationale, he turned left.

In half a mile, the path turned and led up a slope. Derrick saw that the bushes concealed a mound of dirt twelve feet high. When he reached the top, he saw a footbridge that spanned a stream. He stopped in the middle of the bridge for a moment, watching the clear water tumble over multi-colored rocks. On the other side, he saw trees and above the trees, mountains rose majestically into the sky. He marveled that he had not seen the mountains before. It was possible that he was blind to them because he never looked beyond his immediate surroundings. He had been blind to many things.

Derrick had run three miles. Turning around here would be six miles. Enough distance for today. But the mountains lured him. On the other side of the stream, the path was dirt and proceeded upstream along the bank. After 100 yards, he came to a fork, with one path following the water and another leading into the forest toward the mountains. He took the path toward the highlands. The air was crisp and clean, but the path weaved through rocks, fallen trees, twisted roots, and stumps. Except for a meadow he crossed, the trees blocked the sun.

The soaring peaks were more distant than they appeared. Their size made them seem close. Lesser hills stood like sentries to the snow-covered, majestic peaks. The trees thinned as he approached the hills. The trail turned right, edging upward because the slope was too steep to ascent straight. Breathing became difficult as the incline increased. The path turned back on itself at regular intervals as it snaked up a steep hill. The rock-strewn path narrowed. As the slope grew steeper, the distance between switchbacks shrank to 25 yards. Derrick leaned forward, his legs burned, his eyes focused on the trail, because going off the side would be like stepping off a cliff. His mind was fixated on the challenge.

That is why he collided with Nyx as he rounded a switchback.

30

DERRICK STUMBLED FORWARD, NYX IN HIS arms, teetering on the edge. He looked over the side and saw nothing but jagged rocks awaiting them. He turned, putting himself between her and the drop-off. His foot slipped, sending loose rocks skidding down the slope. With one last effort, he separated himself from Nyx, pushing her to safety.

Derrick spun his arms in circular motions as he fought to remain on the trail.

Nyx grabbed his shirt; both feet planted on the trail and hauled him back onto the path.

"What in the hell are you doing?" Nyx yelled.

Derrick bent at the waist, gasping for air. "Sorry," he managed to say.

Nyx remained silent.

Derrick could not look at her. At first, that was easy because he stared at the ground in his bent position, but his breathing slowed, and he stood straight.

She glared at him, arms across her chest.

"I was not looking. Struggling up the hill." He paused, thinking, but no better words came to him. "I am sorry," he said again.

"Be more careful," Nyx said. "Don't run over me again. See you up there." She pointed up the hill, turned, and ran.

Derrick followed, but she put distance between them. It seemed as if gravity had a negligible effect on her. Her muscular legs carried her lithe body upward, graceful, fast, powerful. She wore Potterville track shorts and runner's top, which bared her shoulders. Her black hair flowed in the breeze.

Nyx disappeared when she rounded a large rock.

Derrick pushed himself up the trail. When he reached the rock where Nyx had disappeared, the trail vanished into a stone wall. He turned and peered over the edge. Fearful that she had fallen to her death. Then he heard stones skitter down the mountain behind him. Looking up, he saw Nyx climbing over the rock ledge.

The trail became a climb straight up through a fracture in the stone. Derrick had no experience climbing. Nyx made it, so he knew it was possible. He found a small ledge where he got a hold with his fingers. Then he found a place to wedge the toe of his right foot and pulled himself up a few feet. He worked his way upward. At the top of the crevasse, a hand stretched down toward him. He took Nyx's hand, her grip firm, and she helped him up. He could have finished his ascent without her, but he voiced no complaint.

Nyx stood with her hands on her hips, still breathing deeply but with less strain than Derrick.

"It's beautiful up here, isn't it?" she said.

He turned slowly. Below, the clear river tumbled and twisted along the edge of Potterville, which looked like a forest. The dwellings of its inhabitants were hidden, except for downtown, where the buildings extended above the green canopy. Straight roads crisscrossed Potterville, sometimes disappearing under the tunnel of trees, and then reappearing on the other side. Beyond the town, the orchards and farms appeared, which were an organization of clean lines that seemed as if workers used a giant straightedge to create the plantings' symmetry.

Behind them, the mountains rose dramatically. The snow-covered peaks beautiful, yet lethal. Although he knew little about snow and winter conditions, he instinctively sensed that a person would not last long in those mountains.

Derrick never felt more ill-prepared than he did at this moment. Not even the ordeal with Marcus Carver and exile had ever caused such a vacuum in his brain. Finally, he said, "I have missed you at school. Coach said you were out sick."

"I'm better, but don't tell anyone you saw me because I didn't go to school yesterday. That's why I came up here. I would be in trouble again, calling in sick and then being well enough to run the next day."

"What did you have?"

Nyx stared at him for a moment. "I don't want to talk about it. I'm okay now."

Something told Derrick this was an important moment, but he did not know what to say or how to say it. "I know you are mad at me — it is just — I don't know."

Nyx turned her back to him, gazing over the valley.

"Sorry," he said. "About running into you. Well, about everything, I guess."

With her back to him, she said, "I don't believe it."

Derrick wondered what she did not believe. That he missed her? That he was sorry? Maybe not that he said he was sorry, but that she thought he was a sorry excuse for a human. That thought had crossed his mind more than once since his 17th birthday. "What?" he breathed, not sure he wanted to hear the answer.

"First time I've ever heard you use a contraction," Nyx said.

"Oh," Derrick said, relaxing a little. "The way people talk here is wearing off on me."

Nyx walked to the edge of the rocky precipice.

Derrick remained silent for several minutes. Thinking hard. He had no experience with a girl like Nyx. As a Chosen male, they gave him a list of girls from which he would choose a bride. The girls all worked hard to gain his favor, while he did nothing. Any of them would have gladly accepted his proposal and lived a life of near servitude to him. He was out of his element here. For what was not the first time, nor last time, he ignored his advice about keeping his mouth shut. And he would regret his decision in short order.

"Why are you mad at me, Nyx? I made a mistake talking to Jim Priest. Malcolm helped me get out of that predicament. I have made a lot of mistakes since I came here."

Nyx spun on her heel. Her eyes shimmered as tears formed. "You really want to know? Because you lie, Derrick. That's why. I thought you might stop lying, at least to me, but you didn't."

She had a point. Derrick's entire life here was a lie. Well, some of it wasn't, but that did not matter. His mind raced, trying to determine which lie she meant. He lied about so many things that it became hard to keep things straight in his mind. But what lie did Nyx discover? Not his big lie, of that he was certain. How could she know? She could not know that. Unless the Tribunal approached her to spy, and she refused. If they attempted to recruit Nyx, they were not as intelligent as he assumed, because she did not fit their profile of a trustworthy person, and that struck a chord clear and bright in his mind. Besides his sister, he trusted Nyx the most.

"Okay," Derrick drawled. "What lie?"

"See! Damn it. You can't stop lying even when you're caught at it."

Derrick felt sweat running down his face. His breathing deep and ragged. Not from running. He almost burst and let it all out. He was Chosen. He was exiled. His parents were alive. All lies. But he did not say that.

Because he was a coward.

"Just tell me, Nyx. Please," Derrick said.

Nyx shook her head. Tears streamed down her cheeks. She turned, disappearing over the rocks and down the trail.

31

DERRICK SAT ON A LARGE FLAT rock overlooking the valley, his feet hanging in the open air, in no hurry to move off the mountain. The deep blue sky, marred by wisps of high white clouds, seemed more beautiful than any sky he remembered seeing in Pacific Edge. His chest tightened, but not from running up the hill. His eyes clouded with tears that threatened to spill, and he wanted to let them loose, but he fought to hold them back. He was not afraid to cry. Not so manly that crying threatened him, even here on top of a mountain ridge with no one to witness. It was the exact opposite. The Pacific Edge Derrick would have bawled and curled in a fetal position. Sucking his thumb was not outside the realm of possibility.

He refused to cry because he was no longer Derrick King — a rising star of Pacific Edge, a loyal follower of the Chosen Way — who never questioned the divine order of the world. His new reality cemented itself into his consciousness. Not only an outcast from the Chosen but questioning the foundation of what the Chosen taught. Pacific Edge Derrick King was dead, or at a minimum, on life support.

He felt alone, weak, and terrified. He had no friends. He had been discarded and abandoned. Someone had set him up. Miriam was the one person he believed would help him, and she had given up. He had trusted her. Here, he trusted no one, except maybe Nyx, and she did not trust him, and her suspicions were well-founded. Weak and alone and terrified, he realized that to have any hope, he must become strong. Reinvent himself. Become a man. Become Derrick King, commoner.

Far below, Nyx appeared on the trail, running as if she were floating inches off the ground. *What lie had she perceived?* Derrick always felt she saw right through him, as if he were a three-dimensional hologram. He told many lies. The biggest lie was that he was an orphan from Denver. *But she could not know that. Could she?* He sorted through many lies that had become his life, but none seemed enough to have caused such a sudden, irreversible riff.

The sun warmed his skin. The air, absent the pungent odor of the ocean, filled his nostrils clean and fresh. A small bird with a bright orange and yellow head and black wings flitted onto a branch of a small bush not over ten feet from where he sat. Nyx disappeared under the canopy of green that covered the river, save a few openings where the water tumbled toward the sea. Derrick sensed he had reached another turning point on which his life would pivot into an unknown future. Yet, his life also swung on an invisible thread with no clear direction of what he should do next. Part of him wanted to find Nyx and tell her the truth.

Part of him said that was too dangerous.

Adrift. He did not know what he should do. He no longer had a clear sense of his identity. He never considered himself tough or aggressive. Yet, he decked a Carver. They exiled him because they considered him dangerous.

Perhaps I am dangerous.

Of one thing, he was certain. He wished his rebellious, outrageous, offensive, unconventional, brilliant, brave, and bold sister were here.

She would know what to do.

He did not.

32

AS DERRICK NEARED THE BOTTOM OF the hill, he felt its presence before he heard the sound or saw it. He stopped and spun a circle, searching the sky. A familiar sound in Pacific Edge. But not here. He had not seen a security hovercraft in Potterville. He saw security patrols over Pacific Edge daily, mostly along the coast and perimeter walls. New America Media often showed public service announcements depicting the constant vigilance of security staff protecting their borders against attack. Sometimes showing the hovercraft in action, swooping down upon attacking hordes of commoners and engaging them with the hovercraft's superior firepower. Sometimes firing a precision laser as a sniper-type weapon. One security officer can pilot a hovercraft, yet there were often two, a pilot and a second, to operate weapons and conduct surveillance. Rarely did he see two hovercrafts at the same time in Pacific Edge.

Derrick spotted two hovercrafts above the river, about ten feet over the trees. The first craft had one officer piloting, followed by a two-officer craft. They moved past Derrick horizontally and then turned toward him, crossing his path less than fifty yards in front of him. They circled and then zoomed off to the west. There was no question in his mind why they were there. They were looking for him. This surveillance was far from clandestine. This was very much in the open. As if they wanted him to know of their presence. One question circulated in his mind: *How did they know I was on the mountain?*

Only Nyx knew his whereabouts.

His stomach knotted, and for a moment, he contemplated stopping in the middle of the river bridge to heave whatever was left in his stomach. But he moved on. He tried to suppress the thought of Nyx being the spy. He failed.

He missed his chance to tell her the truth. Maybe she took the Tribunal's offer.

He wondered how often Pacific Edge security visited Potterville. Before he came here, he assumed security forces visiting would be common. However, now he knew that New America broadcasts were greatly exaggerated if not outright lies. He ran past an older home. The front yard, surrounded by a hedge being trimmed by a white-haired man who smiled and waved.

Derrick had observed no violence here save Henry Clark tripping him. The only actual violence Derrick ever witnessed came at his own hand in Pacific Edge. Apparently, a set-up, although Marcus Carver probably did not foresee the injury he suffered if the claimed injuries were real. Perhaps they fabricated the injuries.

Derrick ran, thinking hard. Not paying attention to his location. Although he had not seen hovercraft above Potterville, it was probably not rare, which meant it would not draw attention to him. Although the hovercraft circled Derrick, no one was there to see it. He hoped. Derrick expected Pacific Edge Security would keep him under surveillance. *Watching and listening.* But he thought it would be inconspicuous. Back when he believed he would return home. Before he learned they had set him up.

Maybe surviving this long surprised the Tribunal.

Maybe Nyx told them his location.

Maybe he was just paranoid.

33

Sunday, March 30

WHEN THE ALARM SOUNDED AT 5:50 a.m., Derrick wished he had not taken the job at Donna's Bistro. Only his second day at work, and already he did not want to go. Everyone here worked, other than his fellow students. He wondered if other people ever felt this way.

Last night, he had checked his e-mail every few minutes. Despite knowing Miriam had given up and that he would not hear from her, he wanted to communicate with her. Twice he started drafting an e-mail to her but stopped when an odd, yet tangible feeling of dread overwhelmed him. For some inexplicable reason, he felt an e-mail might endanger Miriam. After he went to bed, which was after midnight, he continued checking his phone for an e-mail. Tossing and turning, he fretted about the hovercrafts, desperate to find an explanation that would eliminate Nyx as a suspect.

Forcing himself out of bed, he showered, drank a cup of coffee, but did not eat cereal, hoping Donna would give him another cinnamon roll, and then remembering he could buy one. With alertness, he remembered why he wanted the job. Money and the freedoms that came with it. The morning air lifted the weariness from his mind. Before reaching the bistro, much of the darkness had lifted. A faint pink glow lit the eastern horizon. Then, like an invisible blanket, thoughts of Pacific Edge and all that he'd lost enveloped him. For a moment, he thought tears would pour from his eyes. Pausing in front of Mr. Grealy's store, staring at the old Martin guitar, he forced the thoughts from his mind. When his playing improved, he wondered if Mr. Grealy would let him play that old guitar. That thought helped.

The next event helped more.

"There's my guy!" L. Linda Maxton exclaimed with a bright smile.

Derrick smiled back. Had to. Her smile was infectious. "Good morning, Linda."

"L. Linda." She rushed around the counter and gave him a hug. "Donna! Derrick is here."

Donna burst through the half doors, wiping flour from her hands onto a hand towel. "Linda, make Derrick an espresso coffee. Not drip stuff. Whatever he'd like."

"L. Linda," L. Linda corrected.

"Don't go to any trouble. Regular coffee is fine," Derrick said.

"Nonsense. Besides, L. Linda needs the practice. She's learning to run the machine. Tell her what you want and come sit with me," Donna said, pouring herself a coffee and walking to a table in the corner.

L. Linda sprang back behind the counter. "What can I make you, Derrick?"

"I don't know. I have not tried many coffee drinks besides the regular stuff."

"Perhaps an Americano then?" L. Linda asked.

"What's that?" Derrick asked.

"Espresso and hot water."

Derrick studied the menu on the wall. "I tasted a Mexican mocha once, but I don't see it."

"I love those." L. Linda clapped her hands. "I have not made one yet. This is so exciting."

As L. Linda busied herself behind the espresso machine, Derrick walked to where Donna was sitting. He had a bad feeling.

"Yes, ma'am?"

"Sit, Derrick. I wanted to talk to you about something. And call me Donna."

Derrick sat, dreading what was coming, although he had no idea what it was, unless she planned to fire him because of the hovercraft. Donna had apparently forgotten that she was going to stop asking him to call her Donna.

"Did I do something wrong?"

Donna made an odd expression. "Heavens no, son. We have a few minutes. The dishes are caught up, and Sundays are slow until about nine o'clock. I wanted to see how you did yesterday and apologize for the mess. Your first day and I didn't even make it back there. L. Linda needed training. I felt terrible that I ignored you."

Derrick did not know how to respond. He decided to be honest, at least about work. "It was hard. I never worked that hard." (He decided not to add that he had never worked at all.) "But I liked it. The time went quickly, and I felt — I do not know. Like I had accomplished something."

"You sure did accomplish something. Thought sure I'd have to send Linda to help you."

"L. Linda," L. Linda said from behind the counter.

Donna smiled and winked at Derrick. "So, Derrick, no cinnamon roll for you this morning."

He tried to hide his disappointment. He wished he'd eaten something before leaving the condo. "That is not a problem."

"Today, I'm fixing you a proper breakfast. No charge and you still get a meal at the end of your shift. I can't pay you what you deserve, so I can make it up a little with free food, and those bloodsuckers on the coast can't tax me on it."

"But I can pay …"

Donna held up her hand. "No, you cannot. And stop arguing with me, young man. I'll not hear another word. After the day you put in yesterday, it's the least I can do."

L. Linda brought a cup to their table. It lacked the fancy design that Nyx's Mexican Mocha had. This one had a blob of white with a daub of chocolate and a sprinkle of cinnamon. "Sorry, it's kinda ugly. I can't do the art yet."

Derrick glanced up. L. Linda's eyes seemed sad. "It looks perfect. I rather like the blob."

L. Linda smiled.

Donna stood. "Make yourself a coffee, L. Linda, and then come sit with Derrick. What do you want for breakfast? I'm treating you both." After telling Donna their breakfast orders, she disappeared into the kitchen.

L. Linda ground coffee, steamed milk, pulled a double shot, and then joined Derrick.

"I invented a new drink. It's not on the menu, an experiment. Want to taste it?" L. Linda held the cup out.

"What's in it?" Derrick frowned involuntarily as he took the cup from L. Linda's hands.

"Caramel, honey, a little dark cocoa, steamed milk, and a double shot of expresso."

He sipped it, then took a drink. "Hey. It is rather good."

"I used cocoa, which is dark but not sweet. The honey and caramel add sweetness. The idea popped into my head. I'm famous for head pops." She laughed.

Derrick handed the cup back to her. "What are you going to call it?"

"Hmmm. Good question. Perhaps, DK Double Honey."

"What does DK stand for?"

She smiled as she sipped. "You'll figure it out. Enough about my coffee creation. How are things going for you? Must be difficult. Losing your parents, moving here, living with an uncle you don't know, and separated from your sister."

Derrick took a drink of his mocha, wondering how she knew so much about him. He understood it was a small town. Gossip traveled fast, but he had not seen L. Linda talking to Nyx, and Nyx was the only one who knew about Miriam. He did not want to succumb to paranoia, but a ghost culture seemed to exist here. One you could not see. As he sat staring out the window, he felt as if he were forgetting something.

Her warm hand took his. "I'm sorry. I shouldn't have said all that. Sometimes I'm a ditz." L. Linda stared at him. Her smile gone. Today she wore her hair in braids. Instead of the large loop earrings, she wore small ones containing green stones.

"I am okay. Thanks for asking."

L. Linda jumped up to help a man who had entered. She called back to Donna, saying she had it covered. The man only wanted coffee. L. Linda handed him a cup, took his money, and returned. They chatted about school and nothing in particular. She asked no questions about his past and said nothing about the hovercraft.

After a bit, Donna backed through the half doors, spun around, carrying a plate in each hand. "Breakfast is served."

She slid a plate with two eggs, hash browns, toast, and a thick piece of ham in front of Derrick. L. Linda had asked for French toast.

"Anything else you two need? More coffee?"

"I do not need additional coffee yet," Derrick said.

"Just holler when you need one. Mexican mocha for you, Derrick? And what are you having?" Donna looked at L. Linda.

"A DK Double Honey," L. Linda said.

"What on earth is that?"

"My new creation."

"It is quite good," Derrick added.

"Okay. When you're finished eating, make me one. If I like it, we'll put in on the menu. You two enjoy. No rush. Unless you see I'm getting busy, then you can pick up the pace."

One thing became evident quickly. L. Linda Maxton liked to talk. She skipped from topic to topic, approaching every subject with enthusiasm. He had a hard time following her. Every few minutes, she stopped talking long enough to stuff a bite of French toast into her mouth. Once, she stopped talking to stick a bite of French toast into his mouth so he could taste it. Otherwise, it was non-stop talking until they both finished. He ate all of his. She ate half of hers. He never got a word in the entire time, managing only a nod or two. The exact conversation he needed. He enjoyed every minute and thought if he could bottle her energy, he might survive.

When they finished breakfast, Derrick went to the back and saw that Donna has made good on another promise. The dishwashing area had only a few pans from baking, which he finished quickly. It appeared Donna had washed several pans before he arrived. Sunday traffic never reached the crescendo of Saturday, allowing him to work steadily but not rushed.

L. Linda showed him where things were kept when she came for supplies. In case he ever had to help Donna with the front, which he did not expect because he was a dishwasher. He did not consider that he might never help Donna with the front for entirely different reasons.

At 1:00 p.m., Donna walked in. "Your shift is finished. What would you like for lunch?"

"Whatever you fix will be perfect. Something left over would be fine," Derrick said. Thirty days ago, he would have never considered eating left-over food.

In the front, he looked for L. Linda but did not see her. He got a Coke and went outside, where a pleasant day greeted him. High, thin clouds softened the harsh sun. Customers occupied two tables: one with a couple, the other with two older gentlemen. Derrick took a seat at the open table. The others paid little attention to him. Periodically, he scanned the sky for hovercraft, but all he saw was blue with thin clouds. He thought about the mountains, which he could not see from here. Although he could not see them, the mountains made him sad, because they reminded him that Nyx might have given Pacific Edge his location.

Donna arrived with a plate and a fresh Coke. "I made you a ham panini. I'm glad you're here, Derrick, despite the reasons. Don't forget that."

"Thanks, Donna. I could pay for this."

Donna waved him off. "L. Linda had to leave. She had a meeting to attend, but she told me to tell you she was sorry she could not have lunch with you, and she'd see you at school. If you ask me, she's got a crush on you."

Cheese melted from the edges of the sandwich, spilling onto the plate, which had a pile of potato chips and a pickle. Derrick did not eat pickles but knew what they were. Taking a bite of the sandwich, he realized how hungry he had become. As he ate, he thought about what Donna had said to him earlier. When she said it, he paid little attention, but as he replayed it in his mind, something struck him as odd. *I'm glad you're here, despite the reasons.*

He had eaten ham for breakfast but had not grown tired of it. Donna layered two thick slices, plus the cheese on his sandwich. It tasted wonderful, and he could have devoured it in seconds, but he forced himself to slow down. He had nowhere to go and no plans for the day. In fact, he did not know what to do next.

I'm glad you're here, despite the reasons.

Not, I'm sorry about your parents, but I'm glad you're here.

He sensed no sadness about his parents in Donna's voice, and that seemed odd, which caused him to circle back to Nyx. If Pacific Edge recruited her as a spy, then she might have told others.

Maybe everyone in town knew about him now.

I'm glad you're here, despite the reasons.

Ham sandwich and chips half eaten, he tried the pickle, crisp and sour. It went perfectly with the sandwich and chips. Now he was a pickle eater. He scanned the sky. Nothing. The silver-haired men at the next table stood to leave. One man went inside to pay, Derrick assumed.

The remaining man smiled. "I don't know you. My name is Abe. You work for Donna?"

Derrick swallowed a mouthful of sandwich. "Yes, sir. I started washing dishes here yesterday. I moved from Denver."

"What's your name, son?"

"My name is Derrick King." Derrick studied the man to see if he reacted to the name. He did not.

Abe stuck out his hand. "I'm glad to meet you, Derrick. Anyone Donna would hire is okay in my book." The other man returned. "Jake, I want you to meet my friend, Derrick King. He's new in town and working for Donna."

"Glad to meet you, Derrick," Jake said. "Welcome to Potterville. We are regulars, so we'll be seeing you."

Jack and Abe climbed into separate cars; both waved as they left. That brief encounter ruined his entire line of thinking.

And that made him happy.

Suddenly, his sandwich tasted even better. A small ray of hope warmed his heart. If Nyx had learned he lied about Denver, that he was an exiled Chosen person from Pacific Edge, then Donna would not be so pleasant, and Abe and Jake would not have been so welcoming.

And L. Linda Maxton would not have a crush on him.

* * *

At his condo, he showered, thought about running, but decided against it. His feet and legs hurt from standing on the concrete all morning washing dishes. Continuing his education about the commoner world made sense, but he was already thrust into that world, and it no longer seemed important. Learning occurred every day, and sometimes it even worked out well. Other times, he made a fool of himself.

Pulling his guitar out, he used a cloth he found in the case to polish it. On the headstock, the word Eastman was written. As he polished, the beauty of the woodgrain soothed him. He practiced for thirty minutes, fingers getting tougher, chord changes becoming easier.

At 3:30, he grew restless. Checking the weather using his cell phone, he saw it was 75 degrees out and he could not stay inside another moment. No jacket required, he slipped on his shoes, headed down the stairs, wondering if he might see Nyx, unsure what he would say if he did. Over the past couple of hours, he rationalized that she was not the reason the hovercraft found him. They watched him. He knew that but kept forgetting. They might have been passing over Potterville and then spotted him on the trail. Simple as that. Why they cared remained a mystery.

He wandered aimlessly. The streets were not busy, but a steady flow of traffic traveled the main streets. People were out in yards, children played, parks had groups gathered. The scent of food cooking over open fires drifted from backyards. People waved. He waved back. Paranoia lifted with each block walked, although he continually scanned the sky for hovercraft that never appeared.

At Potterville High, he walked to the fifty-yard line and stood for a moment, dreaming he was on the football team. He looked at the stands, envisioning a cheering crowd. Closing his eyes, he tried to hear the game but failed because he played no sports. Watching the Super Bowl with Father was the extent of his experience. Father had tried to explain the game, and he should have paid closer attention.

At 4:30, he headed toward the condo. The bistro closed at 5:00, but he decided to walk that way. He did not know why, or maybe he did but did not want to admit it. As he turned the corner, the sidewalk tables came into view. One person sat alone. He smiled.

L. Linda Maxton.

Walking up behind her, Derrick asked, "Don't you tire of this place?"

L. Linda turned and smiled. "Not yet. To be honest, I hoped you might come by."

"I hoped we would have lunch together after work, but Donna said you had a meeting."

L. Linda held a finger to her lips. "Super-secret stuff. Can you sit for a minute? I'll make you a coffee or get you a soda. What would you like?"

Derrick thought for a moment, unsure about what he wanted. "Surprise me."

"Okeydokey. Be right back."

He did not like surprises. He liked to control what he ate, what he drank, and what happened in his life. Since he punched Marcus Carver, life had been out of control, and he relished any opportunity to wrestle it back. While giving up control made little sense, he relaxed, somehow confident L. Linda would choose wisely.

After a few minutes, L. Linda Maxton returned, balancing a tray with one hand, opening the door with the other.

Derrick jumped up, tipping his chair over.

"I've got this. I've had practice the last two days."

Still balancing the tray, she set a coffee in front of him and two cookies on a single plate in the middle of the table. She placed a coffee at her chair and put the tray on the adjacent table. "I didn't know what cookie you liked, so I got chocolate chip and oatmeal raisin. We could share them, unless you don't like one of them, then you can have the one you like."

"Sharing sounds good." Derrick sipped the coffee. "A DK Double Honey?"

"I hope it's okay. Oh, no! Were you just being nice earlier when you said you liked it? I can totally make you something else."

"It's perfect. Honest."

L. Linda proved to be as talkative in the afternoon as she was in the morning. Possibly a little less scattered, perhaps a little less enthusiastic. Again, Derrick enjoyed just listening. No questions, no pressure. L. Linda did all the work.

Finally, the restless night caught up with him. Exhaustion sapped his strength and dampened his spirits. He said goodbye to L. Linda and said he'd see her tomorrow.

Unable to sleep, he spent two hours staring at the ceiling, trying to explain how Pacific Edge found him that did not include Nyx. Nothing came to mind. She remained the only person who knew his location. It was just the two of them, so either Nyx or himself contacted them, and it wasn't him. He was certain of that.

The last time he checked the clock, it was 1:55 a.m. Sleep, it seemed, would never come, but then he awoke, having missed the train. He had never been on a train. Could not remember ever seeing one.

He was back in Pacific Edge. He checked the time and saw that he was late. The train had already left. He raced out of the house naked and ran to the train station. Running so fast it caused the clock to run backwards, and he arrived 30 minutes early. Coach Browning sold tickets. A train sat on the tracks, but not his train because he was early. As he tried to buy a ticket, which he could not because he was naked, the train pulled out. Turned out it was the train he needed to catch to reach freedom. That train would never come again.

He missed it.

When he woke in a cold sweat, it took a few minutes to recognize his condo. There was no train. He did not know trains existed, yet he saw one at the station. He would search the internet to see if trains were real.

Despite knowing it was just a dream, it bothered him. He did not think sleep would return.

He feared it might.

It did.

This time, the dream started okay, pleasant even. He stood on the river bridge, watching clear water tumble over rocks toward the sea. He dropped a twig into the stream, knowing it would reach the ocean, be washed onto the shore where Miriam would find it, and she would know it was from him. One moment he was alone. The next, L. Linda Maxton stood next to him. Her arm laced through his. He recognized it was a dream. He relaxed.

Then it changed.

Nyx appeared at the forest's side of the bridge. Then she was standing next to him. L. Linda Maxton disappeared. Nyx pointed at him and said, "He's here."

The river turned blood red.

There were other dreams, but only bits and pieces remained in his memory upon awakening. None of those dreams held any meaning or even made sense. The dreams that made little sense should not trouble him, but they did.

He dreaded going back to sleep, fearing a repeat performance.

He did not want to face school.

He did not want to learn what people thought about the hovercraft.

34

Monday, March 29, 6:05 a.m.

DERRICK NEVER CALLED IN SICK WHEN he attended James Carver Academy. Miriam did sometimes, even though sickness was uncommon among the Chosen if one received the standard annual vaccines. Miriam took all the vaccines, but she got sick sometimes and did not go to the Academy. Occasionally, he thought she was faking. He never understood that either until today. Calling in sick was what he contemplated this morning.

A weight fell upon him like darkness shrouds the earth when the sun sinks below the horizon. It felt as if he were in a box and could not escape. The longer he lay there in the darkness, the sicker he became. The sickness imaginary yet debilitating. Although he never understood why Miriam would fake being sick to stay home, he thought she had a purpose for doing so. His only purpose was to avoid the inevitable: facing his peers after the hovercraft came looking for him.

Forcing himself out of bed was tough. He showered, which helped. He ate a bowl of bran cereal with raisins and drank black coffee. Finally, he felt almost human. Packing his backpack with a change of clothing, books, and laptop, which he still had not used in class — his laptop was new. The other kids' computers looked well worn, covered with stickers and smudges from fingers and time. When he got to the track, he was not alone. Nyx stood with arms crossed, glaring at him. It did not take long to learn what she thought about Pacific Edge security flying over Potterville.

"Did you see the hovercraft Saturday?" Nyx asked.

Derrick considered saying he had not seen them but decided against it. "Yes. When I came off the mountain."

Nyx glared at him. After a few moments, she said, "Coach is making me help you."

"I know. He told me on Friday."

"Why didn't you mention it on the mountain?"

Derrick shrugged. "Did not think about it. I will talk to Coach if it makes you uncomfortable."

"I'll help you, for the team. Besides, Coach did not give me options. Stretch and run a few laps to warm up." Nyx left him as she trotted off to do her own laps.

That morning, Nyx was all business. She showed Derrick how to hand off the baton. He dropped it three times but managed a decent exchange on the fourth and fifth try. He ran three timed laps. Nyx made notes on paper attached to a clipboard.

After the third lap, he took the baton, and Nyx timed him again. When he finished, she scratched more notes on the clipboard. He thought she might break the pencil, but it survived. He wanted to know his times, thinking he might have run his fastest lap yet, but she said nothing, and he decided not to risk asking.

She finished writing. "What do you think those Pacific Edge hovercrafts were looking for?"

Derrick shrugged.

"Don't you think that was strange?"

"First hovercraft I have seen here, but I have not been here long. Is it unusual?"

"You didn't answer my question. What do you think they were looking for?"

Derrick shrugged again. Seemed better than lying.

"Right. You know nothing. I'm not surprised." Nyx turned and walked away.

She seemed even madder than she was on the mountain.

Derrick smiled.

Now, he was certain she did not report his location to Pacific Edge. If Nyx reported him, she would have said nothing about the hovercraft.

During the day, students buzzed about the hovercraft. Speculation and theories ran wild. Most hated that they had come to Potterville, except for Jim Priest, who thought it the greatest event in the town's history.

Derrick did not talk with Akira during Earth science because the teacher lectured the entire class. He looked forward to chemistry to hear her opinion about the hovercraft, thinking she would not be as negative as other students.

In chemistry, after a long lecture, followed by a brief exercise, Akira and Derrick sat alone at their customary workstation. Akira leaned in close and whispered, "Did you see the hovercraft yesterday?"

"I did," Derrick whispered.

"Why do you think they were here?" Akira asked.

"I have no idea," Derrick lied. "Why do you think they were here?"

"Looking for someone is the only thing that makes sense," Akira said.

"An escapee, like from prison or something?" Derrick asked.

"Don't be silly. Probably looking for someone from a nearby Chosen Community, Pacific Edge." Akira stared at Derrick as if waiting for a reply, and then she asked, "What else could they be looking for?"

"I do not know," Derrick lied.

The rest of the day, he maintained a low profile as best he could and went straight to Coach Browning's office before P.E.

"Coach, I'd like to go home early if it's okay. I am not feeling well," Derrick sort of lied.

"Sorry to hear that. I hope you don't have the flu. Do you think it's the flu?"

"Just an upset stomach. I will be fine tomorrow, I think," Derrick said.

Derrick decided early in the day that attending football practice would be a bad idea. A catastrophe waiting to happen. A bunch of hormone-hyped teenagers looking for an excuse to declare him the causation of the hovercraft making an unwelcome pass over their town. He felt confident he made the correct decision, and it proved one of the few things that he got right that day.

35

AFTER SCHOOL, FOR REASONS UNKNOWN, EVEN to himself, Derrick walked straight to Mountain View Guitar, hoping no one saw him there because he was supposed to have gone home too ill for school. He had been practicing and was proud of his progress, but that was not why he was there, and it was not lesson day. If he were honest, which he had rarely been since arriving in Potterville, he wanted some interaction not focused on hovercraft, or on who Derrick was or who he was not, and Mark Grealy seemed like a viable choice.

"Derrick, my main man. What's shaking?" Mark beamed as Derrick walked through the door, making the bell chime.

Derrick stood just inside, confused for a moment. He did not think he was shaking. After a moment, he said, "It is not lesson day, but I wanted to show you how I am progressing."

"Pull up a stool." Grealy grabbed a guitar from the wall. "Let's hear it."

Derrick struggled through the chords, nerves getting the better of him. The changes had become more fluid, but he learned that what he could do in the privacy of his condo differed from what he could do in front of another person.

"That's darn good. You've been working. I can see that for sure."

"It does not seem like work, sir. Well, it did at first."

"Call me Mark."

"Yes, sir."

"I'm glad you came in because I gotta leave town. A little something has come up over on the coast," Mr. Grealy said.

Why would he go to the coast? To meet with someone in Pacific Edge, perhaps? Derrick wanted to ask a few probing questions but kept his mouth shut.

"I planned to cancel your lesson, but you're ready, and so is your next lesson."

Mr. Grealy handed Derrick several sheets of paper, explaining strumming instructions, scales to improve dexterity, and three new chords. He also gave Derrick the lyrics to a song. Above the words were printed chords.

"The chord changes aren't exact with the words. Do you know the song? If not, listen to it online if you can find it. Many people recorded it, but Dylan wrote it and recorded it first. Most of my stuff is incredibly old. I'm stuck on the classics. I call them classics. Especially the protest stuff, folk-rock, which are old but still applicable today. Am I right? Plus, newer stuff is exceedingly difficult to find. Then, of course, it all ended."

Derrick nodded, unwilling to show his ignorance.

Mr. Grealy lowered his voice. "You support the Resistance, don't you? I mean, I wouldn't have offered you lessons if I thought you didn't."

"Uh, sure," Derrick said, wondering if that was the correct response.

"Me, too. Most of my students do. So, you understand how it works then? Sure you do. You can find this song on the internet. It disappears but always comes back."

"Disappears?" Derrick asked and then regretted the question.

Grealy studied him for a minute and said, "You know, they block the websites, but then the stuff pops up again. They've been trying to eliminate such music for years, but The Resistance is too clever for them. They prevent new music, censor lyrics, and jail musicians, but they can never erase history or eliminate The Resistance. Am I right?"

Derrick nodded. He had much to learn.

"While you're listening to stuff, check out Stairway to Heaven if you can find it." Grealy handed him another piece of paper. "This is the intro. It's kinda advanced for a beginner, but you have a knack and willing to do the work. Every guitar player learns to play it at some point. Doesn't hurt to start earlier rather than later. Am I right?"

Derrick stared at the papers. "You think I'm ready to learn a song?"

"Ready is a relative thing, ain't it? Playing the guitar is about making music. Music can change the world. I believe that. You might as well play music from the get-go."

Derrick nodded. "Mr. Grealy, may I ask a question?"

"Fire away."

Derrick hesitated, then asked, "Why is the music so old?"

Grealy studied him for a moment. "Seems like something a guy from Denver should know."

Derrick regretted the question. "I didn't pay much attention, I guess."

"You know, the only music allowed since the fall, is patriotic crap and Carver groveling nonsense. Right?"

Derrick felt heat rising in his neck. He loved the patriotic music that played in the halls of Carver Academy, and reverence to the Creator wasn't about groveling James Carver's memory. This was the hatred for the Chosen he had been anticipating, but the first time it had been expressed so clearly. He was on a dangerous path, and he knew it. "Right, but this music by Mr. Dylan was recorded many years before the creation of New America. Why isn't there newer music? You know, recorded between, say, the 1960s and when Carver created New America?"

"You don't like Bob Dylan?" Grealy asked.

"That's not it. I like it very much. I just do not understand what happened."

Grealy said, "Digital."

Derrick stared at him.

"Digital happened. Before that, it was all analog. You know. Albums? Cassette tapes?" Grealy paused. "You're clueless. Am I right?"

Derrick nodded.

Grealy disappeared into the back room. A few minutes later, he returned with something flat in his hand, about 12 inches square, wrapped in plastic. On the front was a picture of a young girl with blonde hair, wearing a loosely knit, white cloth of some sort, and one shoulder was completely bare. In Pacific Edge, having such a photograph would be grounds for exile. Derrick was unsure of the punishment for just looking. He tried to look away but failed.

"Don't be telling nobody you saw this. Okay?"

Derrick didn't want to be part of an illegal commoner enterprise, but he nodded. If the Chosen learned he was part of criminal activity, exile would be permanent. Although his exile was already permanent, so he relaxed and studied the picture.

Grealy said, "You know who this is?"

Derrick shook his head.

"Any idea what this is worth?"

Derrick shook his head again, slower this time.

"I don't know the value either. I mean, look at it. Still in the original wrap. It's never been opened."

Derrick swallowed hard. "What is it?"

"It's analog, my boy. An album. Vinyl. You see, when she recorded this, music had gone digital. That's what makes it so rare. You understand digital, right?"

Derrick did not but nodded.

"Digital stuff lives primarily on computers. Right? So, when Carver created New America, he had to rewrite history, and when you rewrite history, you gotta wipe the slate clean. Am I right?"

Derrick wanted to keep his mouth shut but asked, "So, who does the music on this," he pointed, "thing, and how does it work?"

Grealy smiled. "You got to have a record player, which I don't have. That's why I've never opened it. It's priceless, but that don't mean nothing because nobody has money to buy much anyway. Someday, if The Resistance is successful, I'll get to hear it. I'll give it to someone who can make it available for everyone."

"Priceless, but you'll give it away?" Derrick asked.

"I sure will. Music should be shared. Don't get me wrong. I wish folks could earn a living making music, but this I'll give away."

"Who is it?" The cover read, *Happier Than Ever*, but Derrick didn't think that was the woman's name.

"Billie Eilish. Big star back in the day, but her music is hard to find. Like I said. Digital."

"But you have a record. Where did you get it?"

Grealy frowned. "You should know better than to ask. Too dangerous, ain't it?" He paused. "You don't know much about stuff for a kid from Denver."

Derrick felt short of breath. He had failed to follow his own rules, exposing too much of himself.

Grealy smiled. "No worries. I suspect you'll start understanding soon enough."

And with that, Grealy took the record to the backroom. Perhaps he had a safe or something back there. Beyond the fear coursing through Derrick's veins, a hundred questions bounced around in his head. *Why did The Resistance preserve old music? There must be more important things. What exactly is The Resistance—resisting?*

The old United States had failed. Carver corrected the errors and set the country on a better path. Everyone knew that. Being born Chosen was a blessing and one Derrick wanted back. Although Potterville wasn't what he feared, he had no intention of staying one day longer than necessary. He had to focus on survival, as Miriam had told him, not on learning to play guitar and listening to forbidden music.

Grealy returned. "Did you see them damn Pacific Edge cops circling yesterday?"

Derrick wanted to lie but saw no point. "I did."

"Reckon what those bastards want?"

Derrick shrugged. So much for avoiding further discussion.

Grealy said, "Darn funny, if you ask me. Haven't seen them for years in these parts. So, something's fishy, that's for damn sure. They are looking for something or someone, but there's nothing much happening here, and no strangers in town except for …" Mark stopped and stared at Derrick. "But we know you and Paul, so, well, anyway, I don't like it one bit."

"Maybe they were doing some routine stuff."

"Like, what kind of routine stuff?"

Derrick shrugged. "Test flights?"

"I don't buy it."

Derrick nodded, and his eyes returned to the piece of paper containing the lyrics to an ancient song he had never heard, written by a man he did not know: *Blowing in the Wind* by Bob Dylan.

* * *

Although risky because he was supposed to be sick, Derrick drifted into the Bistro and ordered coffee and a cinnamon roll.

Donna would not take his money. "They aren't fresh, but there's a couple left," she said.

After she put a dollop of butter on top and warmed it ever so slightly, it still smelled delightful.

Avoiding the sidewalk tables to reduce his visibility, Derrick took a table in the corner and listened to the conversations of the people nearby. A woman about thirty-five and two men who looked mid-forties. Neither man acted as if he were married to the woman, yet she wore a wedding ring. All were attired in professional clothing; the men wore suits, and the lady a dress. Derrick surmised they worked nearby, possibly taking a break or perhaps just meeting up after a day of work. Their discussion was not related to business unless someone paid them to speculate why a Pacific Edge hovercraft came to Potterville.

"Most people think they were looking for one of their exiles or an escapee," the woman said.

"Have you ever heard of someone escaping?" one man asked.

"No," the woman said.

"Exactly," the man replied.

"Must be an exile," the other man offered.

"How often does that happen? They don't care about exiles."

All three nodded in agreement.

How often does that happen? That question floated about Derrick's mind, circling, almost leaving, but always returning. Everyone assumed they were looking for an exile, and exiles narrowed it down to someone new in Potterville, and that narrowed it down to him. He had never heard of an escape either, but for reasons people here never considered. He could not imagine anyone wanting to escape from Pacific Edge. Although Miriam came to mind: her frequent walks to the ocean, her weekly circling the inner perimeter, and her discovery of the internet.

Exiles.

Not *an exile*. These three people did not question that exiles happen. Which meant there were other exiles in Potterville, but no one ever checked on them. He had been so focused on his predicament that he had never considered there might be other exiles here. The perfect spy would be a person exiled from a Chosen Community. An exile would know everything about a Chosen person and be able to get close without suspicion. An exile would accept the task to earn his or her way back to a Chosen Community. Derrick had never considered the possibility. He would have spotted them, would he not? He was always so absorbed in his own success that he paid little attention to his academy peers, except the girls on his list of prospective mates and those with the power to help him fulfill his dreams. People like Marcus Carver.

Marcus Carver, he remembered.

The door chimes sounded as three students walked in. Derrick did not recognize them. Freshman, perhaps? He could identify a few people from his grade and those on the track team. But the track team and the football players were still at school. One boy looked like a younger version of Malcolm Cross, although Derrick thought any brother of Malcolm's would also play sports, but siblings were not always alike, were they? Another boy was a dead ringer for a younger Antonio Morales. The girl did not resemble anyone he could remember, although she was of Asian ancestry, but not the same origins as Akira, as near as he could tell. The three friends giggled and counted their money at the counter as Donna waited patiently for their order. *Freshman*, Derrick decided.

The door chimes pealed again. Two middle-aged women walked in wearing long dresses and light sweaters. They wore their hair tied in tight knots behind their heads and stood several feet back from the three students, whispering.

The students completed their order and moved outside to a sidewalk table. The two women walked to the counter, and one of them whispered, "You shouldn't serve those people, Donna. You know what they say about them."

"Kids? I shouldn't serve kids?"

"Donna, you know full well what I mean. *Those* people." She raised her voice when she said the word those.

Donna planted both hands on her hips. Her face showed a hint of red. "What *do* they say, Martha?"

The lady leaned in and whispered, "They are unclean. Carry all sorts of diseases. They should stick with their own kind."

Donna's chest was moving visibly now. A bead of sweat formed on her brow. "Martha Becket, we've had this conversation before. I serve everyone here — young, old, black, brown, red, white, or green. But I reserve the right to refuse service to anyone. Says so right on that sign." Donna pointed to a sign behind her that Derrick had not noticed previously. "And I'm ready to not serve you or anyone like you."

"Well, I never!" The woman exclaimed. "We don't have to come here. We can go to Ed's Diner just as easily."

Donna started around the counter. "Then go there and don't let the door hit you in the ass on the way out."

Both women turned and shuffled toward the door. "You'll be sorry to lose our business, Donna Parks," the woman named Martha said as she opened the door. "I'll tell everyone at church what you did."

"You do that. Tell them if they are racist assholes like you, they aren't welcome here either."

Donna got halfway to the door as the women exited, and the door closed, ringing the chimes. She breathed heavily for a moment and then looked at the three customers sitting bolt straight in their chairs. "I'm sorry about that," she said.

One man raised his hands and clapped. The woman did the same, a little louder. Soon all were clapping, loud and rapid.

The first man said, "Good on you, Donna Parks. I hope Ed kicks them out too."

Derrick smiled, although he did not understand why, maybe because the scene distracted him from his troubles. Perhaps because he thought Donna might have taken a swing at Martha, given a chance, maybe it was something else.

Derrick's coffee had grown cold. He forced down two large gulps and walked to the coffee station to refill his cup. His momentary distraction dissipated, and the dark reality of his situation drifted back into his consciousness. Yet, with the darkness, entered a ray of light. If there were other exiles here, and Pacific Edge never checked on them, perhaps the patrol was not looking for him. He chewed on that for a while but could not soften it enough to swallow it. He felt in his gut that his situation was different. Derrick always considered himself special. Now he *was* special, yet not in a good way. What made him of interest, he had not a clue.

Another idea emerged. *If other exiles live here, and people know who they are, that meant they must be alive.* Something rose deep within his chest, and whether thought or feeling, he was unsure, yet that hardly mattered because whatever the cause, he wanted to tell someone he was an exile. Perhaps if he came clean, he would be okay. Labeled a liar. He would face some hate for that, but at least he deserved it, and in time, he could build trust and maybe gain forgiveness.

Spirits buoyed, he considered how he would go about it. Start with one person, someone he trusted, even though he was unsure who that person might be, then work outward from there. Freedom from the prison of lies he built for himself would feel like the best thing to happen to him since the morning he turned seventeen.

Still, he was not just any exile. He was an exile who brought Pacific Edge security to Potterville. While people might eventually accept his explanation for the charade, they might never forgive him for the security patrols he brought to town. He had heard enough to realize that people did not like Pacific Edge, but not in the way he had imagined. Like a rat in a maze, he traveled down every mental corridor he could envision, searching for an exit but finding none. He was locked in a losing game where all endings were not good for Derrick King.

36

Tuesday, March 30, 5:50 a.m.

A ROCK-AND-ROLL GUITAR RIFF JOLTED DERRICK awake. Memories of the white room filtered through the fog of his mind. This time, Number Six told him to stand still, and then the guitar played again. He blinked and thrashed at the blankets woven around him like a spider's web, trapping him in some alien's cocoon. He was not in the familiar white room of his dreams. He was not in his Pacific Edge bedroom of exotic stone and polished wood.

What was this strange place?

A nightmare more real than anything he had ever experienced wove through his mind in his half-awake, half-dream state. Slowly, the room came into focus, and he realized this nightmare — was his reality. Or had been, yet he did not understand it.

He ate toast, scrambled eggs, and coffee before he showered and headed to school and his track date with Nyx. He encountered Paul in the hall. Derrick realized he had failed to check the peephole before he exited. In fact, Derrick could not remember the last time he had checked the hall before opening the door.

"Uh, hi," Derrick said.

Paul stood still, studying Derrick as if he had never seen him before. While it had been several days, Derrick assumed Paul still recognized him.

"Your father's money transfer didn't come on Friday."

"Do you know why?" Derrick asked.

"No, I was hoping you did."

"I do not know what happened." Derrick paused and looked at Paul's face, which remained hard and unemotional.

Paul grunted and then walked to the stairs. Before the door closed behind him, Paul turned to Derrick and said, "Let me know if you learn anything. I can't do this without money."

Derrick ran to school, hoping it would clear his head. Between trying to decide how to admit his lies and Paul saying Father had not sent money, Derrick thought his head might explode. Nyx was not on the track when he arrived, which felt as if someone had placed a weight on his chest. He stretched and ran a few laps.

After three laps, he stopped, turned a full circle, but did not see Nyx. He was about to give up when she walked out of the school. He cut across the football field to meet her.

"No workout this morning," Nyx said as he neared. "I thought Coach would have told you."

"He did not tell me. Why not?"

"Because we are running for real this afternoon. Actual time-trials. See who makes the relay teams and which events each of us will compete in. First meet is Saturday."

"Oh," Derrick said, falling into a steady jog next to her. "I hope I'm ready. What about football practice?"

Nyx glanced sideways at him. "After time trials."

Derrick failed to suppress a smile. "You think I can make the relay team?"

"Possibly. You're not great, but you're better than nothing."

He thought he saw a slight turn at the corner of her mouth but realized that was probably his overactive imagination. They ran silently for the rest of the first lap. Derrick thought about what he might say to make things better between them but failed to arrive at any novel ideas.

"Thanks for helping me," Derrick said.

"No thanks required. Coach did not give me an option. I did it for Mr. Browning. I did it for the team." Nyx looked straight ahead as she spoke.

They ran another lap in silence. Derrick's mind churn, but clear thinking seemed impossible. Finally, he said, "I'm sorry for how things have gone with us."

Nyx stopped and turned to face him. She glared at him, but then her face softened. "I wish it had gone differently, too."

Derrick fought back a tear. "It has been so hard."

Nyx reached up and kneaded his shoulder. "I know. I hope you figure it out." And then she turned and ran to the building.

Thoughts of Miriam's final e-mail, track trials, his first day with the football team, and Nyx kept him so preoccupied, he remembered little of school that day until chemistry. He had been contemplating confessing his true origins to Akira. She was the closest thing he had to a friend, and yet, she was the most likely suspect of being a Pacific Edge spy. He weighed the risks and still wanted to tell her. He wanted, needed, to tell someone the truth. Not for moral reasons. A few weeks ago, he felt sure he held the high moral ground over everyone, but that was before he decked Marcus Carver and got himself exiled. While he might not have had a history of telling outright lies, he had a propensity for telling people what they wanted to hear for self-promotion. If lying would have helped him, he would have started a long time ago. Perhaps he had been lying for many years. Lying to himself.

In chemistry, a practical exercise or experiment would give him a chance to discreetly unload his burden to Akira. If she were a spy, she already knew he was from Pacific Edge, so what difference would it make? To his surprise, the day turned out better than he had hoped.

"Class," Ms. Albertyne said, standing in front of the room, capturing each student's gaze until the classroom fell silent. "I will give you this period to work with your partners on your scientific method demonstration assignment. You can stay here or find someplace quiet to work. I don't care which but be back in your seats before the end of the period. Questions?"

Before Derrick decided if he had a question, Akira giggled, grabbed his hand, and pulled him into the hall.

"Let's work at the bistro," Akira said.

"Can we do that?"

"She said someplace quiet, and she didn't care where." Akira walked toward the exit, smiling over her shoulder.

Derrick jogged to catch her. "We should ask if it is all right."

"If we ask, she'll say no. Better to ask forgiveness than permission."

"That makes little sense," he said. Akira did not seem like a risk taker. He marveled at the degree at which he could misread people.

Akira rolled her eyes and dashed out the front doors and trotted down the steps into the front courtyard of the school. Akira giggled as she jogged across the street. Derrick found it impossible to suppress his smile. He realized leaving the school grounds was likely against the rules. At the Academy, it would lead to a quick suspension, especially for students of his age who were supposed to know better than to pull juvenile stunts. Still, he smiled.

Akira ordered a cherry Italian crème soda. Derrick ordered coffee and a cinnamon roll for them to share. Akira produced a purse, but before she could open it, Derrick pulled cash from his pocket.

"I will buy," Derrick said.

"Thank you, but you don't have to," Akira said.

"Your money is no good here, King," Donna said.

"What?" Derrick asked, the shock in his voice clear.

Donna smiled and waved him off. "Find a seat, and I'll bring your order. It's my treat, Derrick."

Akira started for a seat near the coffee urns, but Derrick crossed the room to the furthest table in an odd-shaped corner that prevented other tables from being close.

Akira pulled a notebook from her backpack. She turned to a page of notes and spun the notebook around on the tabletop for Derrick to read. "Here's the demonstration. I hope it's okay that I roughed it out."

Derrick scanned the notes, unable to concentrate, but even in his mental fog he saw that the demonstration was well planned and written. He would not expect less from Akira, but he felt a pang of guilt anyway because he would get credit when none was due.

"It looks excellent," he said.

Donna arrived with drinks and then disappeared into the back, as if she had overheard some delicate conversation.

Derrick whispered, "You have done all the work and ..."

Before he finished his sentence, Akira said, "You've had a lot going on. I already had this worked out, at least in my head. It's no big deal."

"Thank you," Derrick said. "You have been the closest thing to a friend I have had since coming here."

Akira blushed as she sipped her soda and said, "That's not true."

Derrick looked around the room, even though they were alone. "I want to tell you something. I have to tell someone."

"Okay," Akira said, dragging out the word as if she was not sure that it was okay at all.

Derrick forked off a chunk of cinnamon roll but pushed it around in the melted butter at the edge of the plate. After a few silent moments, he looked up and said, "I have told lies."

Akira stared at him. Her eyes hard. "Everyone tells lies sometimes. It's not the end of the world."

"It might be the end of the world. At least for me. These were big lies. Bad lies. I am not who I have claimed to be."

Akira took a bite of cinnamon roll, studying him as she chewed. She cleared her throat and said, "I know who you are, Derrick. I've known since the first day you sat behind me in Earth science."

Derrick stopped playing with his fork and stuck the piece of cinnamon roll in his mouth. *What does she mean by that?* He was not sure he wanted the answer. The cinnamon roll did not taste right. Dry and bland and impossible to swallow.

He washed the wad of dough down with coffee, which burned his throat. "Who do you think I am?"

Akira pursed her lips and gave her head a little shake, as if the answer were so simple it was embarrassing. "You are not from Denver. Paul is not your uncle, and your parents are probably not dead."

Derrick drank another gulp of coffee. It burned as it went down his throat, but he tried not to wince. *How did she know that on the first day? Was I so transparent?*

"I'm not a very good actor, I guess."

Akira placed her hand on his. "You're a fine actor. You should consider theater."

Derrick paused. "Where do you think I'm from?"

"You're from Pacific Edge. You were born Chosen."

37

DERRICK STARED AT AKIRA. *How many others know?* Akira was smart, very smart. His thoughts swirled, unable to process this revelation.

"How did you know?" Derrick asked.

Akira set her soda on the table. Her expression changed, but Derrick could not determine if it was anger or something else that he detected.

"That part hurts a little," Akira said, removing her glasses. "You don't remember me even now, do you, Derrick King?"

"Remember you?" Derrick asked.

"We attended school together in Pacific Edge until the fifth grade."

Derrick looked at her and, for the first time, pictured a younger girl. There were three Asian girls in his class. He did not recall any of their names because names seemed unimportant to him then. Often, he would tell his Mother that he had made a new friend at school, and when she asked the person's name, he did not know. He did not ask for names. One of those Asian girls left Pacific Edge in the fifth grade. Akira must be that girl.

"But you moved to another Community," Derrick said.

"That is true. Pacific Northwest, where Asian people are more common," Akira answered.

"What happened?"

"They exiled me halfway through my first year there."

Derrick held his fork halfway between the plate and his mouth, and a piece of cinnamon roll dripped buttery frosting onto the table. "What happened?" he asked.

"I asked too many questions."

"Too many questions? They exiled you for asking questions?"

"You have a short memory. You never questioned things when we were younger. I assume that changed. You must have become more like your sister. Probably the reason you're here."

Derrick washed the cinnamon roll down with coffee. The flavor of both the coffee and the cinnamon roll had improved. He said, "No change in me. I believed everything New America Media broadcast and the Academy taught."

Akira's expression changed. Derrick thought he saw suspicion in her eyes.

Akira asked, "Why are you here? Some say there's a spy here. Are you a spy, Derrick King?"

"I am not a spy. They exiled me because I punched Marcus Carver."

"You did not," Akira said.

"Yes. Yes, I did. I am not proud of it. Knocked him out. Caused serious injury, at least that's what the Tribunal said."

Akira threw her hand to her mouth and laughed. "I wish I had been there. Why did you hit him?"

"I thought he was going to hit Miriam."

"Then he deserved it."

"Marcus said he was trying to help her stay out of trouble, just trying to scare her."

"Excuse me? How does threatening to hit a girl keep her out of trouble?"

"She still asks too many questions," Derrick said.

"Miriam is a smart girl. I always liked her."

"She is like a genius. Except I did not understand until it was too late. I did not like her. She embarrassed me." Derrick fought back a tear. "Now I miss her."

"I'm glad you are here, even if you didn't remember me. And Marcus Carver needed smacked when we were in grade school."

"I have ruined my life." Derrick gazed at the tabletop.

Akira placed her hand on his. "Have you? Are you sure about that?"

Derrick realized perhaps he had not ruined his life. Complicated it beyond comprehension but not ruined. Not yet anyway. Perhaps that was coming soon enough, though.

"What are you going to do now?" Akira asked.

"I have not figured that out yet," Derrick said.

Akira checked her phone. "We'd better get back."

Derrick and Akira returned to the school, trotted up the stairs, and rounded the corner into the hall near chemistry. Jim Priest's friend, the large boy with the ruddy complexion, walked toward them. The boy was even larger than Derrick remembered. As they passed, the boy came at Derrick, hitting him hard shoulder to shoulder, causing Derrick to bump into Akira.

"Hey, watch it, Red," Akira hissed.

"Oops. Didn't see you there, King. Heard you're trying out for football. I play defense. When we meet on the field, you won't be standing after I hit you."

Derrick said nothing.

Akira laced her arm through his and said, "Not worth it. Let's get back to class."

They had just sat down when the bell rang. "Good timing, Akira," Ms. Albertyne said.

Students scrabbled from their workstations. Derrick stood, smiled at Akira, grabbed her backpack, and escorted her to Mandarin. That day, Mr. Xu had tea brewed, serving each student, and then explaining the class for the day. They would watch a Mandarin movie with English subtitles. It would take two days to watch the movie.

In the hall after class, Derrick said, "Thanks for not calling me a liar."

"I'll come watch you do time trials if it's okay," Akira said.

"One person supporting me would be nice."

"There are others who support you more than you recognize."

After changing into his track uniform, he jogged to the track. His mind, clearer than it had been in weeks, feeling as if he had lost half his body weight, floating across the football field to where the team had gathered around Coach Browning.

"Glad you could join us, King," Coach said.

"Sorry, Coach. I was a little late getting back from an off-campus chemistry lab."

"Glad to hear that Mrs. Albertyne has included cinnamon rolls over at the bistro in her assignments."

The team laughed. Derrick wondered how Coach knew about that.

"It is a mix of science and art at the bistro," Derrick replied, still unable to suppress his smile, but then added, "I hope I am not in trouble."

"You've obtained a sense of humor. You get that at the bistro too?" Coach asked.

"Probably," Derrick said.

"One other thing, King. If you are ever in trouble with me, you'll be the first to know."

Later, Derrick recalled this was the precise moment when it happened. It felt good to be light-hearted and part of something. Decision made. Time to come clean, tell the truth, become Derrick King, commoner, Potterville High School student.

Coach blew his whistle. "Listen up. We'll run 100, 200, 400, and mile. The top three in each category compete in the first meet, and the top four in the 400 and 100 are the mile and 400-meter relay teams. We'll run relays to see how you are doing on handoffs and set a baseline for time. Anyone willing to take on cross-country can do so with my blessing. Questions?"

No questions were asked.

"Okay, 100 meters. Boys first, then girls. King, you need to be in this one," Coach said.

Derrick was the last one on the line. Malcolm Cross took the outside lane, which everyone avoided, as if Malcolm owned it. Henry Clark took the inside after staring down a boy named Lawrence. Derrick ended up in the middle. He had learned that everyone was supposed to stay in his own lane, which made the fall Henry Clark caused even more suspicious. Derrick did not expect any problems today. Everyone was vying for the top four. No time for immature antics.

Bracing his feet in the blocks, Derrick focused down the white lines of his lane.

"On your mark, ready, set …"

The gun fired, and the bang was much louder than Derrick expected, but his start was clean thanks to Nyx's coaching. He pumped his arms, hands flat like knives, as Nyx had shown him. Runners were tight on both sides. Halfway down the track, Derrick separated himself from the runners on his right and left. Three quarters down the track, Malcolm had two steps on him. Henry had one. Derrick pressed harder as the finish rushed to meet him. Out of his peripheral vision, he saw a body pull ahead of him, leaning into the finish. It turned out to be Larry Kinkead. Derrick had come in fourth. Henry Clark glared at Derrick. Larry Kinkead gave Derrick a nod. Malcolm Cross grabbed Derrick's hand in an odd handshake. "Good job, bro."

Browning hollered, "Boys, four-hundred-meter team as follows: Cross, Henry, Kinkead, and King. Did I mention we always win the four-hundred-meter relay?"

"Not to put any pressure on you, King," Coach Yates, who also taught history, said with a smile.

Derrick jogged back toward the center of the field, focusing on the girls' 100 meter. A puff of smoke left the barrel of the starter pistol before Derrick heard the bang. Seven girls were in the 100-meter, but he only saw one: Nyx Belos.

Nyx separated herself from the other girls and continued to pull away. Lithe and strong, Nyx's form looked a thing of beauty in Derrick's estimation. He studied her graceful, fluid, and purposeful movements. Tried to assimilate it into his mind, hoping to infuse it into his own running style. Nyx crossed the finish line in a blur of red and white.

Derrick would tell the team the truth about himself. But first, he had to tell the girl with the pink-striped hair.

Browning hollered. "Hot damn, Belos. You do that in the meet, and you'll set a new California State record!"

The team cheered. The girls surrounded Nyx, all bouncing and hugging her.

"200-meter runners on the line. Belos and King to me," Yates said.

Derrick joined Nyx in front of Coach Yates. Derrick still smiling. Nyx glanced at Derrick but did not speak.

"Neither of you will run the 200 today," Yates said.

"Why not?" Nyx burst out.

Coach Yates held up his hands. "Coach Browning's decision, not mine. He wants you fresh for the other races you are competing in. He figures we can win the 100 meters, both girls and boys, mile relay, girl's cross-country, and place in the 400 and 200 and the 400 relays, which should give us the team win. You are both alternates for the 200, should we need you."

"Still sucks," Nyx said as she turned on her heel.

Derrick shrugged. "Whatever Coach thinks is best."

Nyx jogged to the fifty-yard line, where she started her stretching routine. Derrick walked toward her, then paused when he saw Akira and Antonio Morales sitting in the bleachers, talking. That they were talking did not trouble him. There was no one else in the stands. Plus, as student body president, Antonio talked to everyone. However, he wondered how Antonio felt about Derrick taking his place.

Before Derrick reached Nyx, he heard, "King! Wait up." It was Henry Clark. "Walk with me to the 200 starting line."

Derrick wanted to talk to Nyx but fell in at Henry's side and thought: *What is this about?*

"Nyx tells me 400 meters is your best distance."

"Nice of her to say that," Derrick said. He wondered if Nyx and Henry had become a thing. Derrick had not seen them together, but that meant nothing because Derrick did not frequent the same social circles as the other students.

"Kinkead plans to win the 400. It's his best event, and he has a lot of experience."

"Okay," Derrick offered. What difference does experience make? You run around the track once. That is it. It is not complicated, he thought.

"You need to run your own race. He'll try to sucker you into running his race, and if you take the bait, you'll lose."

"Explain it to me," Derrick said.

"He'll start out too fast. It's a sprint, but he'll push too hard early and pull you along with him. Then you'll give out and won't have enough kick for the finish."

"But would not he also be exhausted?" Derrick asked.

"Yes, but he'll be in front of you, and he just has to maintain the lead. You won't have enough kick to pass him."

Derrick thought about this. He wanted to say that he would have plenty of kick, but the truth was he had never raced. Then another thought crossed his mind. He dismissed it but then asked anyway. "Why are you telling me this? I thought you did not like me."

Clark snickered. "I don't like you, King. But if you are as good as Nyx says you are, you might be our best bet of winning the 400-meter. Kinkead has never placed better than third at State. You could have beaten him in the 100 if you knew how to finish. Nyx will teach you that after watching Kinkead beat you at the line. Here's the thing: I'm a quarterback, which means I'm all about the team. So, don't assume we're friends. If you turn into a decent running back, I might reconsider."

Clark jogged to the starting line. Coach Browning frowned at him. The other runners were already in their lanes. Derrick turned and started back across the field where Nyx had been stretching, but she was no longer there. She was talking to Akira and Antonio. Something told him that this was not good.

Derrick jogged to the goalposts, where he sat with his back against the upright. He watched as Nyx and Akira talked. They seemed to argue. Not quite arguing, debating maybe, Antonio listening. Both girls stole glances his way in a manner that suggested they did not want him to notice. After a few minutes, he heard a whistle and heard Browning yelling for Belos. Derrick turned toward the commotion and saw Browning waving his arm in big circles. Nyx still had not moved, but a few seconds later she jogged across the track toward Coach.

Waiting until after track to tell Nyx made sense. He wanted a perfect setting to tell her the truth, but no brilliant ideas surfaced. He felt compelled to tell Nyx straightaway. Now felt better than waiting for the perfect setting.

He met Nyx at the fifty-yard line and fell in beside her. "There's something I need to tell you."

"Can't it wait a few minutes? I have a mile race to run."

"Yes, it could, but I cannot," he said.

"Not much time here, King," she said.

"Look, I have not been truthful with you," he said.

"No shit," she said.

"About anything," he said. He ran out of time to say more before they reached the other runners. "Good luck."

Nyx turned and looked at him. It was the first kind expression he had seen on her face for some time. "There's no luck to it, King. It's all hard work and whatever gifts we were granted at birth."

38

SIX GIRLS KNELT IN THE STARTING BLOCKS. Derrick focused on Nyx. The pink stripe in her hair glowed. Her red and white track uniform shimmered in the bright sunlight. The smell of mown grass filled his nostrils, and he wondered for a moment why he had not noticed the fragrance before. His confession to Nyx lacked details. It lacked any information at all. Yet, he felt better than ever. He had not felt this good since the morning of his 17th birthday, which seemed like such a long time ago, in another life, on another planet. He thought back to that morning, which he had considered to be the best day of his life, remembering how good he felt until that exile thing happened. Now, he concluded that turning 17 was not his best day after all.

Today was.

The starter pistol fired, bringing Derrick present. He jogged out onto the football field, watching the girls run. To his surprise, Nyx did not appear to be leading the pack, although because of the staggered start, it was hard to tell for sure. After the first lap, the girls in the outside lanes collapsed inward. Nyx was in fourth place.

Derrick did not notice Henry Clark at his side until Henry spoke.

"Watching Nyx?" Henry asked.

"Yes," Derrick replied. "How did you do in the 200?"

"Second. Someday I'll beat Cross, I swear I will," Henry said.

Halfway through the second lap, Nyx ran in third place, but she had not picked up her pace. The third-place girl had faded. First place had increased her lead by ten yards over second place. Nyx ran five yards behind the second-place girl.

"Nyx is not doing well," Derrick said.

"She's doing fine. Jenny, the girl in the lead, is trying to force Nyx into a faster pace. Same thing Larry will try with you," Henry said.

Derrick turned, following the girls. "How does Nyx determine how fast she should run? It must be difficult."

"Because she is experienced. She knows her pace. Focuses on it. But you are right. It is difficult. Larry will probably beat you this time. But that's okay. You'll learn from it."

"Why do they do that? Try to trick the other runners?" Derrick asked.

"When you're second best, all you have left is trickery," Henry said. "That's not exactly right. You could also work harder than the best and eventually be the best yourself. That's what Nyx did."

"She was not always the best runner?" Derrick asked.

"First year, she barely made the team. Coach wasn't going to let her on the team until he saw how hard she worked. She was on the track every morning before sunrise. She was last in every event at the first meet. By the end of the season, she was third in the 100. The following year, she won every event at every meet she competed in, except State. So, yeah, you can work harder than everyone else. That works, too."

On the fourth and final lap, Nyx passed the girl who had been holding second place and reeled in the leader, Jen, with half a lap remaining. Jen fought, but she was no match for Nyx, who floated by like a feather carried on a breeze. By the end of the race, Nyx had a ten-yard lead. Nyx slowed as she exited the track, jogging behind the end zone. Derrick started toward her when Coach Browning blew his whistle and then shouted his name.

"King! Four-hundred meters. Let's go. I don't want to be here all night, and we still have football practice."

Derrick noticed guys exiting the school wearing football uniforms. He ran to the track, regretting that he had not been stretching and soon regretting that he had run instead of jogging to the starting line. As soon as he was in position, Coach hollered, "On your marks!"

Derrick took deep breaths, trying to steady his nerves, trying to catch his breath, trying to manage the surge of adrenaline that coursed through his veins. He wanted to win, and it surprised him how much he wanted it.

The gun fired, and they were off. Larry was one lane over and in front of Derrick. Derrick kept pace with Larry at first and then closed on him. Larry had the inside lane. Henry was wrong about Larry. Derrick was flying, and Larry seemed sluggish by comparison.

At the halfway mark, Derrick was in trouble. He had been played the fool and did not even realize it. He had started too fast and was struggling now with each step. Henry, it seemed, was right. With 100 meters remaining, it appeared Henry knew another thing. Derrick would lose his first 400-meter race.

With 75 meters left, Derrick was exhausted. Larry looked spent too, but Derrick could not capitalize. Larry merely needed to finish. Derrick could not make up the distance between them.

Fifty meters remaining, Derrick's legs felt heavy. He considered easing up. He was already in the 400-meter relay. Second place in the 400 meters was a good first result. Especially since he had never been a runner. He had never been competitive. Never been in a fight until that issue with Marcus Carver. That little issue that got him exiled. That little issue that ruined his life. Or saved it?

Marcus Carver suckered me into that punch, but Marcus did not intend on the consequences. Larry Kinkead suckered me too. He will not like the consequences either.

Derrick had nothing left to give but gave more. Sprinting with all his strength, his chest felt as if it might burst, and his legs burned. His ears filled with an odd sound: team members yelling, King! King!

Twenty-five yards to the finish and Kinkead was now mere steps ahead, fighting to maintain his lead, but it would not work. Derrick blazed past him with ten yards remaining and fell through the finish line. He stumbled a few yards onto the football field and then collapsed onto his hands and knees, wondering if he would die. The team surrounded him, hands slapped his back, and shouts of "Amazing!" "What a finish!" and "Great race!" swirled together in a medley of noise.

After a moment, strong hands gripped each of Derrick's arms as Henry Clark and Malcolm Cross helped him to his feet. Malcolm grinned, and Henry shook his head and said, "I'll be go-to-hell. You did exactly what I told you to avoid, and you won anyway. If you get smart, you'll be mind-blowing."

Teammates who had never spoken a word to Derrick surrounded him, each taking a turn with a slap on the back or a shake of his hand. Larry Kinkead stood outside the circle. About forty-five degrees to his right stood Nyx, smiling but trying to hide it with her hand. The crowd split when Coach Browning approached.

"Hot damn, King. You were only two seconds off the state record. Holy shit, excuse my French, but we got us one hell of a team this year!" Browning put his meaty hand on Derrick's shoulder, giving it a hard squeeze. "You keep working, King. Despite your late arrival to track and field, you could still land yourself a scholarship. If you set a state record, I guarantee you'll get one."

Derrick gave little thought of a future in the commoner world. Although he had no hope of going home, he had not thought about the future. He assumed that getting a scholarship meant he could go to college. Then it occurred to him, in a gut-wrenching way, that his junior year would soon end. What did kids do here during the summer? There was no summer break at the Academy in Pacific Edge. Only three weeks for family vacations. In the summer, a few might come to the bistro from time to time, but most would scatter, and he would be alone in this unfamiliar world. Unless …

As the team dispersed, Larry Kinkead eased toward Derrick. Sticking out his hand, he said, "Strong finish, King."

Derrick shook his hand, the grip firm. "Thanks."

"I won't make that mistake again. I will beat you, King. You may break the state record, but I'll own it before year's end."

Derrick held his grip on Larry's hand. "I believe you. But I plan to break the record you set."

Larry grinned. "See you on the line, King."

Derrick scanned the field for Nyx, but he did not see her. She was not with the team, nor on the line. He saw Akira walking across the football field toward him.

"Derrick, that was incredible. I knew you had joined track. I didn't know you were like the next Potterville track star," Akira said.

"Remember, I have not run an actual race yet," Derrick said.

"True. But I have confidence that you will do well," she said.

"What makes you so confident? You know about me, and I have not been trustworthy."

"Because you are a fighter. I suspect that is why the Tribunal wanted you gone, and I don't mean just the fight with Marcus Carver."

"King!" Derrick turned. Coach Browning was waving his arm. Derrick saw Nyx had rejoined the team, who had formed a semi-circle around Browning.

"I must go," Derrick said, and then sprinted to join the others.

"Nice that you could join us, King," Coach Browning said. Several of the team laughed. "One more event, the mile relay, which you're running, King. Before you all leave, does anyone, other than the usual suspects, or should I say *suspect* — Browning looked at Nyx — want to run cross-country this year?"

Derrick scanned the team and saw no hands raised. The others seemed to avoid looking at Browning as if doing so might be interpreted as volunteering.

"I want to run it, Coach," Derrick said.

"King, I appreciate your enthusiasm, but you have enough on your plate. Besides, you're a sprinter, not a distance runner."

"Nyx is a sprinter and a distance runner," Derrick said.

"No offense, son, but you are not Nyx."

"That is true. I am Derrick King."

Browning studied Derrick for several minutes but said nothing.

"Let him run it, Coach," Nyx said.

Browning turned to face Nyx. "And why should I do that, Belos?"

"I've run with him. He might be a better distance runner than he is a sprinter. Let him try it today and see how he does," she said.

Browning turned back to Derrick. "Okay, King. You run it today with Belos, which means you'll miss football practice, again. If your time isn't good — and I mean podium good — then you won't run cross-country at the meet. Fair enough?"

Derrick, uncertain what podium-good meant, said, "Fair enough."

"Ladies and gentlemen, on the line for the mile relay. We'll run both teams together. Same runners are in the 400-meter relay, so we'll skip that one. Belos and King, stick around afterward, and we'll run the cross-country."

The mile relay proved tougher than Derrick expected. The 400-meter had sucked more energy from him than he had anticipated. But he did not drop the baton, and Coach was happy with the results, although he did not give runners their individual times. Browning talked to the team one last time and told everyone they could go except for the football players, who were told to suit up.

"If it's okay with you, Coach," Larry Kinkead began, "everyone wants to see how Nyx and Derrick do in the cross-country."

"Okay, fine. But no one misses football practice tomorrow. And be prepared to work tomorrow cause I'm going to work your butts off for missing today," Browning said.

Derrick and Nyx stood side by side in front of Browning as the team members made their way to the bleachers closest to the stadium entrance. The football team was warming up at the far end of the field with Coach Yates.

"King," Browning began, "What is the distance for the cross-country?"

"I do not know, Coach," Derrick said.

Browning grunted and shook his head. "It's 10 kilometers. That's about 6.2 miles. Like the name implies, it's cross-country, so you leave the track, run west on Broad St. to Maple, turn left on Maple to Broadway, left again, and return. One lap around the track, then out to the course, back through the entrance, two more laps to the finish. Questions?"

When neither Nyx nor Derrick said anything, Browning said, "At the meets, there will be course observers to ensure no one cuts the course. Today, you're on the honor system. I hope we can trust you."

Browning looked at Derrick, not Nyx. Derrick wanted to say that he was trustworthy, but it seemed a shallow statement at this point.

Browning described the route again and asked Derrick if he understood. Derrick confirmed that he did.

Derrick took the line beside Nyx. This would give him a chance to tell her the truth about himself. The gun sounded, and they were off. Nyx set a pace faster than Derrick had expected. He remembered trying to keep up with her when he first started running.

"Nyx, I am sorry I have been dishonest with you," Derrick began.

Nyx said nothing.

"I wanted to tell you, but I did not know how to begin," Derrick said.

"Tell me later. We are in a race here. So, shut up. Just so you know, men are faster than women. If you don't start running like a man, you won't be in the cross-country."

Derrick did not detect any sarcasm or animosity in her voice. Only the facts, nothing more, nothing less. So, he ran. He pulled ahead of Nyx and did not look back. He suspected she would blaze past him at some point on the course, but for now, he ran like a man.

39

AT 4:35, DERRICK REENTERED THE SCHOOL track. He felt as if he floated on air, running smoothly, breathing effortlessly. The entire course had not been so easy. At about the halfway mark, he went lightheaded and thought he might heave the rest of the cinnamon roll from the bistro. It was as if someone had strapped a gallon of milk to each ankle. He struggled to maintain his speed and expected Nyx to fly by him at any moment. It took all his willpower to not turn and look for her. She must be close. Nagging homesickness threatened him.

He turned left on Elm and then left on Broadway.

But at about the three-quarter mark, something happened. He had experienced this before. Nyx called it a second wind. He did not know what that meant, yet the name fit. Derrick assumed Nyx would experience the same thing. Still, he was confident he could hold her off and picked up his pace. But then, looking ahead through many people, he noticed Nyx was a block ahead of him. He must have been so focused on pushing through his rough patch that he did not even notice her pass him.

When they had reentered the football stadium and were halfway around the track, he pushed hard, pulling closer to Nyx, but he could not catch her before the finish. She was running at a brisk pace, her perfect form on display. He ran like a rag doll.

He heard voices at the finish line. The team members had gathered and were waving arms and shouting at Nyx. Coach was staring at a stopwatch held in his right hand. Derrick sprinted toward the line with all the strength that remained in his seventeen-year-old body. He crossed the line and then jogged to where Nyx had stopped. She was bent at the waist, hands on her knees, and catching her breath.

"King, you're a dumbass," Nyx said as he stopped at her side.

"Yes, I am. I'm sorry. I expected you to pass me. At the halfway point, I was exhausted, but I did not even see you go by," Derrick said.

Nyx stood. Her breathing deep but controlled. "I didn't pass you, stupid. You didn't turn on Maple. You ran another block and turned on Elm. Stupid male stuff for sure, big lungs, but can't follow simple directions."

Before Derrick could say more, Malcolm Cross slapped Nyx on the back, and Henry Clark gave her a hug.

"Frigging awesome," Malcolm said.

Coach shouted. "Cross! Watch yourself."

Malcolm held up his hands. "What, Coach? That's not swearing."

"What—is that we've been down this road before."

Malcolm shook his head. "Lighten up, dude."

"Sounds like someone wants to run a few laps."

Malcolm said nothing for a moment. "Sorry, Coach."

Browning said, "That's better."

"Still want me to run laps?"

"No. There's more to learn here."

Coach Browning faced Nyx. "Did you stay on the course?"

"Yes, sir. You know me better than that."

Derrick noticed that Akira had eased up behind the group, listening.

"I apologize," Browning said.

Nyx stood straight. "Why would you even ask?"

"Girl, you broke the state record."

Nyx smiled. "About time."

"King, no cross-country for you," Browning said.

"Coach," Nyx began. "He didn't run the course."

"King, I'm double disappointed now. You cut the course, and you still couldn't hang with Nyx? Son, I'm considering cutting you from the team. I won't tolerate a cheater."

"Coach, he didn't cut the course. Derrick didn't turn on Maple. He went to Elm. He added distance."

Browning said nothing for a moment. He stood with his mouth halfway open, looking at Derrick and then at Nyx. "Is that true?"

Derrick felt stupid and was sure he looked stupid too. "She is correct. I ran right past Maple. Not sure why? Not paying attention." Derrick looked at the grass. "Sorry, Coach. I have no excuse. I screwed up."

"Holy shit, King. Pardon my French, but you added that much extra and still ran a respectable time. You're an animal. You know that?"

Derrick smiled. He thought this might be the best day of his entire life.

Then he heard it.

A hovercraft flying in from the west.

40

DERRICK KNEW ABOUT HOVERCRAFT, at least a little. This one slowed to a stop, floating mere feet above the goalposts at the south end of the field. A two-trooper machine, both men dressed in black pants, black shirts, black blast-jackets, black helmets, black face shields. Derrick learned where the security officers lived when Paul drove out of Pacific Edge. Where they lived had meant nothing to him, and he never contemplated going to their town to disrupt their lives. But they had traveled to Potterville to ruin his.

In Pacific Edge, Derrick saw hovercraft every time he ventured outside or had the transport windows set to transparent. They patrolled the seaward side of Pacific Edge because it did not have a massive wall for protection, and they made periodic passes around the perimeter and over the town. New America Media often showed how Chosen Security officers used hovercraft, protecting Chosen Communities and reporters often described the weapons being used. Although no attacks had ever happened near Pacific Edge, which was the sort of thing Mirriam recognized, yet he had been oblivious to.

For those reasons, Derrick knew the standard equipment. This machine had additional gear. They had mounted a military weapon on its right side that he recognized from New America Media coverage of the war with Mexico. In the center of the machine, stood a large camera or telescope. One trooper wore an odd-looking set of goggles. Both troopers wore stun blasters on their hips.

The hovercraft moved closer and then circled the team from 20 yards, always facing the runners and their coach. The team moved in unison, watching the circling machine. Derrick smelled the odd odor produced by the machine as it defied gravity. It stopped again in front of the northern goalposts, where it remained for what felt like hours, but it was scarcely thirty seconds, and then it rose straight up and rocketed west, toward the coast, toward Pacific Edge.

"I'll be damned," Coach Browning said. "What the hell are they doing?"

"Looking for someone," Henry Clark said.

"Or looking at someone," Larry Kinkead said while staring at Derrick.

The team members noticed Larry's gaze and turned their attention to Derrick.

Derrick knew this would not be good. As he had focused on the hovercraft, like everyone else, part of his brain processed why it was there. It was there because of him, but he still did not understand the reason. Miriam warned him that things had grown worse in Pacific Edge. She said something bad would happen. Another part of his brain hoped that none of his teammates would correlate the hovercraft with him. That was wishful thinking. He was the new kid at Potterville High.

Before anyone else spoke, Derrick said, "They are here because of me."

Forcing his way between Malcolm Cross and Henry Clark, Kinkead shoved Derrick. "I told you he was a lying SOB!"

Derrick rocked back but did not move. His hands clenched into fists. He noticed Larry take a step back. Derrick felt the heat rising, and this had happened before. This time he managed it instead of it managing him.

"Larry is correct. I am from Pacific Edge," Derrick said.

"Some sort of spy," Larry said.

"Run him out of town," someone shouted.

"I am no spy," Derrick said.

"Then why all the lies?" Larry shouted. White foam formed in the corners of Larry's mouth, and his face turned red.

"I was afraid," Derrick said.

"Afraid?" Kinkead squeaked in a shrill voice. "What's there to be afraid of? This is a small town in the middle of farm country, not a war zone."

"You do not understand," Derrick said.

"And what are we supposed to understand? You come here, tell us a bunch of lies, make friends, happen to be a great track star, and we're supposed to believe you're not a spy?" Henry Clark said, pushing past Larry.

Derrick sensed he could not explain how they brainwashed the Chosen. He was only now coming to terms with it himself, and he had lived it. He had seen firsthand how New America's propaganda about the commoner world had been so deceptive. No one here even referred to this as the commoner world, which was the only title the Chosen ever used to describe the world outside the walls of Pacific Edge.

Emotions ran too high for reasoning and lengthy explanations. "You have every reason to distrust me, but I am telling you the truth. I am not a spy. They exiled me."

"He's telling the truth," Akira said, forcing her way to Derrick's side. "He punched a Carver at his school."

"How could you know that?" Henry growled. "Or that Derrick even went to school with a Carver?"

"Because I attended school with Derrick and Marcus Carver in Pacific Edge before I was reassigned and then exiled," Akira said.

Henry thought about that for a minute and then said, "Maybe you're a spy too, Akira. Or maybe they set you up to vouch for Derrick's story."

"Right!" Akira shot back. "I've lived here for four years. They booted me out so that years later they could send Derrick here and hope that I would remember him and vouch for him so he could spy on us. And spy on us for what reason? They don't care about us as long as we keep growing their food, building their machines, paying their rent, and fighting their wars. You're letting conspiracy crap run wild in your head."

Over Henry's shoulder, Derrick saw Browning walk into the building. Derrick's confidence that he could handle the situation faded. Coach would not intervene before this got out of hand. Perhaps Coach wanted it out of hand.

Everyone is worried about spies, including me. Isn't that interesting? Derrick thought.

Funny how quickly he had gone from hero to villain. These kids had no love for the Chosen. Yet, they had accepted Akira when she came here, not hiding who she was or where she was from. Why had she been unafraid of the commoners, whereas he had been certain they would kill him and eat his carcass for dinner the day he arrived, or at least before the second day ended? Akira was the only person standing up for Derrick. He searched the group for Nyx and found her standing toward the back. Her brow knitted in a tight knot, her eyes penetrating.

"Whatever," Henry said with a wave of his hand. Henry's face blazed red and sweat formed droplets on his forehead. "Malcolm and I will handle this. The rest of you leave. Now!"

"What do you think you're doing?" Akira shouted as Larry grabbed her from behind and started dragging her toward the school.

"Getting rid of the problem," Henry growled.

"Stand down, Henry." Nyx stepped in front of Henry. Hands on her hips.

"Not now, Nyx," Henry said.

"I mean it. Stand down and leave. We'll discuss this later."

Malcolm put his hand on Henry's shoulder, giving him a gentle tug away from Nyx. Henry shook him off. "I don't think she's kidding, Henry. Don't make us take you out of here by force."

Two other team members moved to either side of Henry. Larry and Akira returned and stood by Nyx.

"Do it now, Henry," Nyx hissed.

What was happening? Derrick wondered. *Stand down? Was not that like a military term?* Nyx had taken command of the situation, and he could not envision what hold she had over Henry or the others here. Nyx was not military, none of them were, he was sure of that, but there was an order here he did not understand. He thought he had seen Nyx angry. However, he had seen nothing like this.

"Let's go," Malcolm said. Henry turned. The others had formed an escort around Henry as they left the field.

Nyx turned. "Let's talk. Over there." She nodded toward the bleachers.

They walked in silence across the field to the bleachers. The football players had left; only Antonio lingered near the goalposts, watching. A thousand thoughts swirled in Derrick's mind: where to start, how to explain. He tried to harness his collage of thoughts but failed. His stomach twisted like a snake. Breathing became difficult.

When he saw Browning had abandoned him, fear gripped Derrick, but he had put it off quickly enough. Even if there was a fight, he could make things difficult for Malcolm, Larry, and Henry. But now, fear gripped him again and refused to let go. He could not shake it. He could not, would not hurt Nyx. He was certain that what was coming would be more difficult than a three against one fight.

"Sit." Nyx pointed at the first-row bleacher. She remained standing and faced Derrick. "Start talking."

"I am so sorry, Nyx," Derrick began.

"Not that crap." Nyx cut him off. "Tell me why you are here. And it better make sense, or I'll let Henry and the others take care of you. Their way."

Derrick had never heard Nyx sound so cold, calculated, and candid. He had no doubt that she meant what she said. Just as he knew, she had some mysterious authority here.

"I am from Pacific Edge. I am a Chosen. Well, was Chosen. In fact, I lived and breathed being Chosen. I loved everything about it. Then I got into trouble at school. I hit a kid named Marcus Carver." He paused. "You see, the Carvers..."

"I know who the Carvers are. Do you think I'm stupid? I knew you were from Pacific Edge the first day I met you."

"Sorry," Derrick said. "I do not think you are stupid. How did you recognize I was from Pacific Edge?"

"I'll ask the questions. You give answers."

"Right. Sorry." Derrick studied the ground at his feet.

"Why did you hit this Carver kid?"

"I thought he was going to hit my sister," Derrick said.

"Miriam?"

"Yes." Derrick looked up.

"She sent me an e-mail," Nyx said.

Derrick sat open-mouthed. Staring. Finally, he stammered, "How?"

"That's what I want to know. How does she know my name or that I know you?"

"No idea. I never told her about anyone here. I'm not lying." Derrick looked at Akira and then back at Nyx.

Nyx paused, bit her lip, glanced at the ground, and then continued. "She asked me to keep you here and to keep you safe."

Tears flowed from Derrick's eyes down his cheeks. "She must be in trouble, and it's my fault." He bent at the waist, head in his hands, and wept.

They all remained in silence for several minutes. Derrick gradually gained control of himself. He looked up at Nyx. Her stare remained hard, fixed.

"Tell me why you hit this Carver kid."

"Marcus raised his fist to hit her. I snapped. Before I knew it, I was there, and I hit him. Just once, but it put him in the hospital. Broke his jaw and knocked out some teeth. The Tribunal said that at my hearing."

"You must love your sister?"

"To be honest, I did not even like her. She embarrassed me. I was all about being the perfect Chosen person. She wore her hair black, black clothes, bright purple fingernails. She argued with teachers. After the fight, well, it was not exactly a fight. After I hit Marcus, it was like I saw her for the first time. She is smart. Way smarter than me. Smarter than her teachers. Smarter than anyone."

"Argues with teachers? I like her already."

"In an e-mail, she said that Marcus set me up. It was all planned. They wanted me out of Pacific Edge. I do not understand why. I never had a problem with the Carvers. I was a whole-hearted supporter. Now, someone wants me out of Potterville. None of it makes sense."

"You stood up when she needed you."

"She is amazing," Derrick said. "I wish I would have understood that sooner. I am scared, Nyx. I do not know why security patrols are here. I mean, I realize it is because of me, but I do not understand what they want."

"Why didn't you tell us who you were in the first place? Why all the lies? The pretense of Paul being your uncle? All of it?"

"I was afraid, terrified."

"Of what?"

"All of you. You do not understand. In Pacific Edge, we do not have access to the internet. I had never heard of it. They show us news every day about the commoner world …"

"Commoner world? What's that?"

"That is what they call this. Everything outside Pacific Edge is called the commoner world. We have no contact with anything outside Pacific Edge. And the news we see is not what this is." Derrick swung his arm in an arch. "We see fires, fighting, death, destruction, squalor, disease, drug wars, poverty. I was certain I would be killed and lying was my only hope of survival. It was not just me. My Father paid Paul to pretend to be my uncle."

"You understood that your food, clothing, and machines came from outside Pacific Edge, right?"

"Well, yes," Derrick admitted.

"Did it ever occur to you that those things could not come from the world they showed you on TV?"

Derrick studied the ground again. "No." He scraped the ground with his foot. "I was stupid. Miriam understood. That must be why she often challenged her instructors."

Nyx paced.

41

DESPITE ALL DERRICK HAD EXPERIENCED SINCE HIS birthday, the rage, the exile, the terror, the despair, he had not felt more hopeless than he felt now. Nyx remained quiet, pacing. Akira stood nearby but had not spoken. When the Tribunal exiled him, he feared for his life, but his fear was unwarranted. Now fear seemed warranted, but not for himself. He feared for Miriam's safety. He was not special. Miriam must be why Pacific Edge watched him, but he wondered if he should keep that thought to himself.

As for his safety, Henry Clark's threat was no illusion. Nyx seemed to be the only barrier between Derrick and some violent end. Beyond Miriam's safety and Henry Clark's threats, the worst fear percolating in Derrick's head surprised him. Loss. Miriam was lost to him. Now he feared losing the friends he had made here and the new identity he had begun to develop.

He feared losing Nyx as a friend.

Wiping tears from his face, he looked up to find her staring at him.

"Something's fishy," Nyx said.

Akira sat next to Derrick. "She is right. Things don't make sense."

Derrick was not sure what fishy meant and appreciated Akira translating. He said, "I am telling you the truth. I understand why you do not trust me, but I am telling the truth."

"I wish you'd use a contraction or slang sometimes."

"I'll try."

"Better." The corner of her mouth turned up just a little. "Why the patrols? Lots of people get booted out of the Chosen Communities. That's common knowledge for us *commoners.*"

Nyx drew out the word commoners.

"And how did your sister know to contact me? That's weird, Derrick. Spooky."

"I do not know. How could she even know about e-mail? How does she know anything about you, or why you would be a person to contact?" Derrick looked at his shoes again, having almost blurted out something stupid about how he felt, and then said, "You're right. It is weird."

"The Chosen don't care what happens to the people they've removed from their sanctified world. It's like they never existed. Good riddance, if you know what I mean. Why do they care about you?"

Derrick shook his head.

"What are you not telling me?"

Derrick believed he was special most of his life. Special because he was Chosen. Special because divine intervention created a plan for his life. Special because he was better than everyone else. Even after being exiled, deep down, he clung to that belief. When Miriam told him the Carver incident was not an accident—that they had set him up—his first twisted thought was: *Because I am special.*

He would not tell Nyx that he used to consider himself special.

He no longer felt unique. All the justifications for his superiority were delusional. He was not special. He was gullible and stupid. Yet Nyx was right. There must be a reason Pacific Edge hovercraft came here. But he did not understand why, and at this point, he did not trust his thinking any more than Nyx trusted him.

"I do not know why. I'm not special," Derrick said. "But here's another thing. A few days ago, Miriam sent me an e-mail. She said she had given up and that I would not hear from her again. So why did she contact you?"

"I gotta think about that. Those patrols are here for a reason, and that reason centers on you. Rumors spread fast in a small town. I hate to say this, but it's not safe for you now. You'd better get home. At least until I work some things out." With that, Nyx turned and walked toward the school, Akira in tow.

What does that mean? "Until she works some things out." After she works some things out, then what?

Nyx looked over her shoulder. "Well, get your ass in gear."

Derrick sprinted to her side. "I'll shower and meet you in the gym."

"No time for that. Grab your stuff. You can shower at home," Nyx said.

"But I thought I'd see if Mr. Grealy would give me another lesson." Derrick stared at Nyx. "I cannot go smelling like this."

"You're not listening," Nyx said with the cold tone she had used earlier with Henry Clark.

"But …"

Nyx held up her hand. "We are going to my place until we can get your condo checked for bugs. Akira can do it. Give her your key and apartment number."

"I'm on it," Akira said. "I'll be at your place soon as I finish."

They neared the locker room door. "I assume you are in your own condo, right over me. You're the stranger I've heard knocking around up there. Right?"

Derrick stared at her. "Uh, well, yeah. But I do not have bugs. I have not seen any, that is. Just a few flies, but I swatted them."

"Not bugs! BUGS! Sometimes I think you're the densest person I've ever met. Which I kind of like in a strange way. Electronic bugs." She looked at him. "Listening devices? Video? Surveillance?"

"Oh. I worried about that at first, but I saw nothing unusual. Then, I kind of forgot about it." He thought about Miriam's emails and how they would have put her in danger.

He stood there, staring at Nyx, but not seeing her. He wondered what else he had missed. Miriam would have made better decisions. Nyx was right. He was dense, stupid in fact. He wondered how transparent he had been since he arrived in Potterville. When did others recognize he was Chosen? How they must have marveled at his lame attempt to deceive. Even Jim Priest must have suspected and coveted being close to a bona fide member of the Chosen, albeit a rejected one. Perhaps that explained Priest's vehement reaction to Derrick ditching Priest's cult of Chosen worshippers.

"Grab your stuff." Nyx pointed toward the boys' locker room, walking alongside him to the entrance. "If anyone gives you trouble, call out for me." She stared at him. "Got it?"

"Got it."

The team members were still in the locker room. They fell quiet when he entered. Every eye followed him to his locker. He grabbed his clothes and stuffed them into his backpack. He started to say something but could not think of anything that might make the situation better.

Derrick waited outside the girls' locker room while Nyx retrieved her backpack. He handed Akira the key to his condo.

Akira said, "Nyx is the best friend you could have right now. Trust her." She gave him a kiss on the cheek and left.

Nyx led him through a door marked employees only, down the stairs into a concrete basement, past a furnace, and other machines that Derrick did not recognize, through a metal door, which came out the side of the building in a stairwell that emptied into the street.

Nyx eased up the stairs, searching the sky. "Looks clear."

And then she ran.

42

NYX RAN THREE BLOCKS IN THE wrong direction and then slipped into a malt shop populated with teenagers. Nyx walked to a corner booth. No one was sitting near them. Derrick hoped he had money in his backpack and then realized how unimportant that thought was.

Nyx pulled her phone from her pocket. "Hi. Yep, he is with me." She looked up at Derrick. "Good. See you in a few."

"Akira should be there in an hour. That gives us time to talk." Nyx swiveled out of the booth, swung her backpack over her shoulder, and headed for the door. She paused at the window, scanned the sky, and then motioned him to follow.

Derrick followed her, weaving through folks strolling, some arm in arm, others with small children in tow, and a few gazing at window displays. Nyx continued to weave a random course through the streets and alleys of Potterville. He doubted anyone who followed them would have a clue where they were going because it was perhaps the most indirect route to the condo imaginable. Since they both still wore their track uniforms, everyone probably thought they were out training, except the backpacks seemed out of place. Many people gave them a thumbs-up as they passed. Some shouted, GO BEARCATS! Derrick smiled and waved to the Bearcat fans. Nyx ran on, scanning the sky every few minutes.

Derrick knew that Nyx had circled back toward the condos but did not recognize they were there until they crossed the street. He had not even been on this side of the building because there were no entrances far as he knew. Nyx took a stairwell down concrete steps, much like the steps that led them out of Potterville High 30 minutes earlier.

"Good, it's still unlocked. Charlie, the maintenance man, locks it when he leaves for the day."

Nyx's condo on the second floor was smaller than his by half. No hardwood or granite. The floor covered with worn beige carpet that might have been a cream color at one time, old furniture, and a cat lying in a sunbeam on the windowsill. A faint scent of spiced meat lingered. The place was clean.

"Put your backpack anywhere," Nyx said.

He swung it off his back and set it on the couch.

Nyx kicked off her shoes and glided to the kitchen. A counter separated it from the living room. She pulled two sports drinks from the refrigerator, opened one, took a long drink, and then set the other on the kitchen table. She motioned for Derrick to sit.

Derrick sat at the table, popped the top, took a drink, then said, "You think my place has electronic surveillance?"

"I'd bet on it," she said as she sat.

"That's not good," he said.

"No, it's not. But you haven't had a lot of parties there for them to watch. Have you?"

Derrick sighed. "True. But I was thinking about Miriam's e-mails. She was sure they were safe. Maybe on her end, but not on mine. I feel so helpless."

Nyx said nothing.

A knock came at the door.

"It's open," Nyx hollered.

Akira walked in carrying two black bags that swung from straps around her neck. She waddled over and hoisted one of them onto the table. Derrick, slow on the uptake, managed to get a hand under the second bag.

Akira studied Derrick and then looked at Nyx. "What?"

"He's worried about his sister," Nyx said.

It was as if some secret code passed between them. Derrick knew he was not smart like Miriam but wondered if he was something worse. Perhaps he had an unsmart disability he was too dumb to know about.

"Can you find them?" Nyx asked.

Akira sat silently at the table and pulled a laptop computer from one bag. While it booted, she got other gadgets from the second bag. One appeared to be a small gray bowl that stood on three short legs.

"Perhaps not. The Chosen must have sophisticated stuff," Akira said.

Derrick was more confused than ever because he thought Akira was going to his condo first. "I thought ..."

Akira held up her hand. "Not now. I need to concentrate."

"If you find them, can you defeat them?" Nyx asked.

"That's the plan, Stan."

Derrick wondered if Nyx had a middle name he had not heard. *Stan is a funny name for a girl.*

Nyx rolled her eyes. "No shit, Sherlock."

Perhaps odd middle names are common here, Derrick thought.

As Akira worked, she said, "I was thinking on the way over. If we find anything, we nuke it."

"Sounds right to me," Nyx said.

Derrick hoped he would understand this conversation at some point.

Akira clicked at the keys, adjusted the dish, and twirled her long black hair around the fingers of her left hand. After a few moments, she moved both hands to the keyboard and hammered at the keys.

After a few minutes, Akira closed her computer screen. "Well, crap. Nothing."

"Seriously?" Nyx said.

"Yep. Let's get coffee," Akira said, standing.

"Huh? We ran three miles out of our way to get here undetected, and you want us to stroll back out for coffee?"

"Yes. I really want to do that." Akira grabbed Derrick's hand and started toward the door.

Derrick could have stopped Akira dead in her tracks, but instead he followed her. Looking over his shoulder at Nyx, he said, "I think she means it."

Nyx followed, complaining all the way to the street about how stupid it was to leave. When they hit the sidewalk, Akira said, "Three bugs in Derrick's place."

"Why didn't you tell us at my place? Why are we out here?" Nyx grabbed Akira's arm and spun her face to face.

"And two in your place. That's why," Akira said.

For the first time, Nyx looked unsettled. "My place. Why my place?"

Akira's eyes moved from Nyx to Derrick and back again. "I guess they noticed what everyone here has."

Nyx's face reddened. "What's that supposed to mean?"

Akira rolled her eyes. "Whatever. Another important question: who planted them?"

"Guys," Derrick interrupted. "What are we going to do about the bugs?"

"Akira, can you defeat them?" Nyx asked.

"Yes. In a few different ways. But that might not be a smart thing to do."

"Where are the bugs at my place?" Nyx asked.

"One in the dining area and one in your bedroom."

"Wait. What? Why my bedroom?"

43

NYX TURNED AND WALKED TOWARD THE bistro but said nothing. Derrick walked by her side. At the cross street, a car slowed. Jim Priest, halfway out of the passenger's side window, raised his hand, made a fist, and extended his middle finger. Priest's fat friend was driving. Red Badowski was not in the car. Derrick understood Priest meant the gesture for him.

Nyx started across the street and said, "I need a drink."

Akira skipped to catch them. "We need clear heads. This is not a time to be drinking."

"Coffee, Akira. Remember?"

At the bistro, they ordered coffees. Out of cinnamon rolls, Nyx ordered a blueberry scone and two cookies to share three ways. They sat outside, and a breeze cooled the air and wafted fragrance from blossoming trees. The sun neared the western horizon, casting the sidewalk in shadow.

"So, any ideas?" Nyx pulled out a chair opposite Derrick and sat.

"We act normal, so they don't know that we know," Akira said.

"Easy for you to say," Nyx said.

"Not really," Akira said. "Two cameras in my house. Same as yours, Nyx."

Nyx looked at Akira and then back to Derrick. "Derrick must have been quite a ladies' man back in Pacific Edge."

Akira blushed. "That's not how it works in Chosen communities."

"How does it work?"

"Another time," Akira said. "Derrick has not been to my house. Honest."

"How long have you known?" Nyx asked.

"Since this afternoon. I scanned my house soon as I got home. I figured it best to check."

Nyx sat back, folded her arms across her chest. "More in our building and on the street?"

"Probably," Akira said.

"We are so screwed," Nyx said.

"Derrick is who I'm worried about," Akira whispered.

Nyx looked at Derrick. He could not discern her thoughts.

"Why?" Nyx asked.

"Why what?" Derrick asked.

"Why do they care? What makes you important?" She paused a moment, her eyes narrowed. "Or dangerous?"

Derrick lowered his head, shut his eyes, pinching his fingers together at his nose. "Good question. I still do not understand." He exchanged looks with both girls. A strange thing happened as he did. He realized there was a relationship of which he had been unaware between Nyx and Akira. That struck him as odd. Had they hidden their friendship on purpose? Did Akira befriend him on Nyx's instruction? He also realized that he liked them both in different ways he could not explain. What a weird time to have such thoughts. "Maybe I am not their concern."

"Explain," Nyx said.

"Perhaps it's Miriam."

Nyx said, "I don't understand. Miriam is still there. Right? Has anyone ever escaped from Pacific Edge? Is that even possible?"

"I have never heard of it," Derrick admitted. "And when I left with Paul, from what I saw, it seems impossible. Still, if anyone could do it, it would be Miriam." He thought about all the time Miriam spent in her room or out walking around. *What had she been doing?* Then he thought about the times Miriam had e-mailed him since the exile. Then he remembered that she had given up. *She was not coming. She wasn't even trying.* He and he alone had brought Pacific Edge security here.

"Maybe it's not about her escaping," Derrick said.

"I'm not following your logic," Nyx said.

Derrick thought for a moment, still trying to avoid accepting that he was responsible for Pacific Edge security's presence. "What if they staged the entire thing to monitor Miriam's response?"

The scone and cookies sat uneaten.

Nyx kicked Derrick's shin under the table. "Eat."

"What? Oh, I'm not hungry," he said.

"I'm not concerned with your stomach. It looks abnormal for a teenage boy to be sitting in front of a perfectly good scone and not eating."

Picking up his fork, he took a small bite and then a larger one, followed by another.

"We still have a major problem we haven't talked about," Nyx said, glancing at Derrick.

"True," Akira whispered. "Any thoughts?"

"Not really," Nyx said.

Derrick glanced from one to the other, still not following their conversation.

"Maybe it won't be a big problem," Akira said.

"It's a big problem," Nyx said.

"But I didn't have any problems when I arrived here," Akira said.

Nyx held up one finger: "One, you weren't a teenager." Then she added a second finger: "Two, you were honest from the beginning." Then she added a third finger: "Three, no security patrols ever came here looking for you. Mister King has lied to us, and there have been several patrols, the most recent one rather threatening."

"But only the track team knows about Derrick."

"Come on, Akira. You're smarter than that. The whole town knows. If you haven't noticed, people are avoiding us even now." She pointed to a group of people crossing to the other side of the street mid-block before reaching them.

"Guys, I'm sitting right here," Derrick said.

Nyx picked up a chocolate chip cookie and broke off a chunk, sticking it in her mouth.

"I'm afraid Nyx is right, Derrick," Akira said, placing her hand on his knee. "People will be pissed about this. Most people here don't like the Chosen. And we've had little direct contact with them, except a few that come here as I did. Plus, people hate being lied to. We must depend on and trust each other here."

Derrick hung his head. "I messed up. I messed up in Pacific Edge and now here. Not long ago, I thought I had it all figured out. Now," he paused. "I don't know anything."

Nyx punched him on the arm. "That's better."

Akira withdrew her hand and sat back. "Do you think Henry and Malcolm would hurt Derrick?"

"Hurt would not be the word I'd use. We can control them, but we can't control everyone," Nyx said.

"I realize it may not help, but I want to apologize to everyone. I guess I can't apologize to the entire town. But I can to the team and the students."

"I'm not sure it will help," Nyx said.

"I'd not be doing it to get myself out of trouble. But I would feel better. You have no reason to trust me, but I hated lying." Derrick looked down. "Especially to you."

Nyx nodded.

They sat silently for several minutes. Derrick watched people and noted that Nyx was correct. When people saw him, they crossed the street or turned around. No one had walked by that he could remember since they had been there. Three older boys, probably graduates from Potterville High a year or two ago, stood on the corner staring.

"Let's go," Nyx said.

"Nyx should walk with you," Akira said, looking at Derrick.

"Then who will walk with you?" Derrick asked, still watching the three boys across the street.

"We'll walk Akira home first," Nyx said.

They walked two blocks, then turned down an alley shortcut to Akira's. Large waste bins lined the alley, and a stench of garbage hung in the air. The shortcut was a mistake. Later, Derrick would consider how taking shortcuts had been his mistake all along. When they reached the middle of the block, two of the three boys who had been stalking them at the bistro appeared in front of them.

Nyx hooked Derrick's elbow. "Crap."

They pivoted and saw the other boy walking toward them from the opposite direction.

Derrick backed the girls against the wall. The boys formed a semi-circle in front of them. Derrick studied them. One was smaller than he was, one was of equal size, and one had him by six inches and fifty pounds. They should have terrified Derrick. He had avoided conflict his entire life, except for berating Miriam daily, which in hindsight was not the least bit brave. But he was not afraid. An unexplainable calmness overcame him. Everything slowed down. Details popped into his senses. He sensed Nyx coming forward before she appeared in his peripheral vision.

"So, this is the Chosen jerk who's brought the Pacific Edge thugs to Potterville," the boy Derrick's size said.

"Back off, Brian," Nyx said.

"We have no quarrel with you, Nyx. You and Akira are free to go. We'll take it from here," Brian said.

"I said, back off." Nyx stepped forward.

Derrick placed his hand on her shoulder to ensure she did not go any closer. Nyx shrugged it off.

Before Derrick could move, he sensed Akira at his side.

Standing on tiptoe, Akira whispered, "Let Nyx handle it."

A familiar sensation started deep in Derrick's chest, burning and churning and growing. The heat rose from his neck to his cheeks, radiating so hot Nyx must have felt it on her neck. It was that same rage that consumed him right before he punched Marcus Carver not long ago in Pacific Edge. Yet, it seemed a lifetime. Now, he could not distinguish which version of his life seemed most real?

Derrick King, a Chosen vessel in Pacific Edge,

or

Derrick King, commoner, budding track star in Potterville, California.

Notwithstanding all that had happened, he struggled to denounce being Chosen in his heart. Every morning, he awoke with profound loss. He ran a mental checklist of the Tribunal's actions against him. Despite everything, he had still entertained an unrealistic daydream that the Tribunal would reverse its decision. They would send a special escort to Potterville to carry him home. The Tribunal having issued a proclamation: a full restoration of his rights, privileges, and status. A crowd would be gathered at the entrance of James Carver Academy, where the transport would land. As Derrick walked out of the craft, he saw the student body there to greet him. Jana Somersworth would run to him with a bouquet of enhanced red roses. Rebekah Ford would be there, standing in the front row, her hand to her heart. Even Marcus Carver was there. After Derrick hugged Jana, Marcus would step forward, holding a microphone in one hand. "I apologize, Derrick. It was my fault. You did the right thing, protecting Miriam. I hope you can forgive me."

Derrick understood this was what commoners called bull. Yet, it was there, always there, every morning, his incomprehensible loyalty to the Chosen as if it were sent to him from above. Most pronounced in those early morning hours as he stirred from sleep, surfacing at odd times during the day, but always there. He had tried but failed to shake his longing to be Chosen.

However, rage pushed those thoughts from his head. It was as if he thought clearly for the first time since that fateful punch. Now, he felt loyal to Nyx, who stood between him and three men. She displayed no fear. Ninety-five pounds of confidence he could not explain. The frontal lobe of his brain, the analytical problem-solving part, told him that fear was an appropriate response. The primitive part of his brain, wired for fight or flight, should have been switching itself to flight, but he felt pure fight. Any wrong move by any of the three boys would break the thread holding Derrick at bay.

"Brian, we have this. Believe me, we're pissed too, but we have protocols, and it's my job to see that we follow them," Nyx said.

"We don't answer to you anymore, Nyx," Brian said.

"True, but Derrick is still under our authority. Don't test me, Brian. You'll regret the day you did. I'm asking you to follow the rules. If that's not enough, I can get a direct order if that's what you need."

Brian scuffed at the ground with one foot. "What are you going to do with him?"

"Still trying to figure that out," Nyx said.

"Shouldn't be too tough a decision," Brian said, the menace back in his voice and eyes.

"Not as simple as that, Brian," Nyx said.

"Seems simple enough to me. The guy comes here, lies to the entire town, then brings Chosen's goons here to spy on us, or worse."

"Exactly," Nyx said.

"What is that supposed to mean?" Brian asked.

"What makes him special? That's what we must figure out. He might be of some value to us." With that, Nyx took Derrick by the arm and walked away. Brian and his friends remained rooted in the alley.

44

THAT NIGHT DERRICK COOKED A FROZEN pizza he found in the freezer compartment of the refrigerator, drank a thing called Dr. Pepper (it might replace Coke as his favorite should he live long enough). He had grown accustomed to being alone in his condo, but tonight he did not enjoy it. For a moment, he wondered if Nyx would come up and share dinner. Then he remembered the cameras. So, he concentrated on acting as if he were not on camera, being studied like a lab rat. He tried to act natural but felt sure he failed to do so. He checked his e-mail, and for the first time since arriving in Potterville, he prayed there were no new messages in his mailbox other than the junk he received for no reason. He had homework but knew he could not concentrate, which would be unnatural for him, so he stared at his books as if he were reading. He showered, even walked through the house naked, as was his custom here, which gave him a sense of freedom he had never experienced in Pacific Edge. Now it made him uncomfortable, and he hoped it made the people watching him uncomfortable too. Were people watching him, or was it some sophisticated autotron that looked for irregularities? Probably a combination of the two. He thought autotrons with a little random human observation.

Guitar practice helped. The more he focused on playing, the more he relaxed to the point he forgot about the cameras, at least for a moment. Mark Grealy had given him a song to learn. Mark said it was a classic, a blast from the past. Derrick found the song and a video that displayed the words over pictures that cycled every few seconds. The singer, Bob Dylan, did not have a great voice in Derrick's estimation. Yet Derrick liked Dylan's sound, and the more he listened to the song, the more he liked it.

Mark said it was not a difficult chord progression. When Derrick thought he had the melody in his head, he struggled to play the song while humming the tune. As the chord changes became easier, he tried singing. Not that he was a singer, but neither was Mr. Bob Dylan. After several times through the tune, he had the chords and most of the words memorized.

Then he found the paper containing the second song Mark Grealy provided. Mark did not tell Derrick who wrote the song. A computer search found a band named Led Zeppelin. He did not know what a Zeppelin was and was sure this was a joke of some sort. A band named Heart, which sounded like it might be real, also played the song. Before he listened to it, he studied the paper that Mark had given him. It was written differently than the other songs. After studying it for several minutes, Derrick decided it was showing him notes on the neck. It did not, however, tell him which fingers to use. It looked difficult. After listening to the song, Derrick found himself captivated by the melody and vowed that he would master it, beginner or not. As he played it, rather well he thought after his umpteenth attempt, he wondered if Miriam had heard *Stairway to Heaven*.

Stairway to Heaven took him past midnight.

He lay in bed, but he did not sleep.

A question Mr. Bob Dylan had asked drifted through his thoughts.

Had he ever heard people cry?

Not that he could recall.

That haunted him.

45

Wednesday, March 31, 6:15 a.m.

MORNING CAME EARLY. DERRICK PULLED THE covers over his head, unwilling to face the cameras, watching his every move, dreading the day at school. Yet, a part of him was eager to get there. Before going to sleep, he contemplated how to address the student body. His only connection was Coach Browning. Derrick would go to him first thing, tell the truth, and ask for his help. Derrick wasn't sure Coach would help, because he walked away when the team turned on him yesterday. Yet, he was also sure Coach *would* help. All he needed was a few minutes on the school PA system during morning announcements.

Derrick needed to do more with the track team. He could apologize at practice but decided he could not wait that long. They deserved something better than an et al. confessional he would make over the school PA system. The team deserved face-to-face contact. He would seek each out individually, although it was more likely that he would apologize to two or three at a time because team members were also friends.

He wanted Nyx at his side — not because she seemed to have some power to protect him, which he still did not understand — he just wanted her close. He had to face whatever was coming alone, which frightened him, but seemed his best way forward.

Lying there, he sensed that something had changed, as if he had not been through enough change already, but he could not determine precisely what this change entailed. Perhaps because he no longer lived a lie, waiting to be revealed naked to the world, like one of those dreams where you arrive at school and then discover that you have forgotten your pants. Everyone had those dreams, or at least Derrick assumed they did. He had also assumed that other people experienced dreams where they were known by a number instead of a name. Now, he was sure only he and Miriam shared that dream.

But this was not the same as arriving at school half-naked. He sensed fear, but that was not right either. Maybe if he lay there long enough, it would come to him. Maybe if he lay there long enough, he would awaken to learn that this entire episode from his 17th birthday until today was a long-playing nightmare.

And maybe if he lay there long enough, the sun would burn itself out, and his problems would be moot.

What am I missing? Something important.

***

Derrick pounded on Paul's door.

"It's open!"

In Pacific Edge, Derrick never left doors unlocked. Despite the tight security surrounding him, the house sealed itself and armed the security system after each family member entered. Derrick even locked his bedroom door because he feared hordes of commoners were amassed outside the walls of Pacific Edge.

"Hi, Paul. It's me, Derrick," he called as he stepped inside the empty great room, which comprised the living, dining, and kitchen area. The odor of shower soap and shaving cream drifted from Paul's master bath.

Paul walked in shirtless, wiping his face with a towel. "Who else would pound on my door this early?"

"Point taken," Derrick said. "I suppose you heard."

"I hear a lot of things," Paul said, tossing the towel back through the bedroom door without looking. "If you mean, did I hear about Pacific Edge showing up at the school? Yes, I heard about that. Hell, the whole town, no, the entire state, has heard about that by now."

"Right. Nyx said news would travel fast."

"What are you going to do about it? That's what I want to know. I'm out here on a limb that's all but cut in two."

"I'm sorry, Paul. I never meant …"

Paul cut him off. "You owe me no apology. I took the job. You didn't force me. Hell, you didn't even ask." Paul studied him for a moment. "So, what are you going to do?"

"I'm going to tell the truth at school. Apologize to everyone for lying to them."

"That's it?"

"What else can I do? I'm open to suggestions."

"Not about the school." Paul waved his arm. "What are you going to do now?"

"I don't understand," Derrick said.

Paul shook his head. "The gig is up, my friend."

"Gig?"

Paul waved both arms. "This. All of this. You, me. They changed the deal on you, Derrick."

Possibly this was the disturbance Derrick sensed earlier, but he didn't think so. Still, he should have seen it coming. He had already learned that the Tribunal was not above making up rules as they went. "Changed the deal?"

"Your father called," Paul said. "I'm fired, so to speak. Services no longer needed."

"I'm sorry, Paul. I have said nothing to Father about you. Honest! And I know you need the money."

Paul shook his head. "I'm not blaming you. You don't understand. They're coming to get you. They are moving you."

"Moving me. Why would they move me?"

"Hell, if I know," Paul said.

Derrick felt lightheaded. He made his way to a barstool and sat. "I do not understand. I am exiled, and I know they will never let me return. Why won't they just leave me alone?"

Paul pulled up a stool, looked into Derrick's eyes, and put a hand on his shoulder. "I can't answer that. I'm sorry."

Tears welled in Derrick's eyes, but he was determined not to cry. Pacific Edge security people were likely watching him. Measuring his reaction. Deciding his fate. Damned if he would let them see him cry. "What if I stay?"

"Your father said he can't pay for the condo anymore. You'll have no place to live."

"Did Father say when?"

Paul stood. "Not exactly. Soon."

Derrick stood, walked to the door, and then turned and said, "Thanks, Paul. Thanks for everything."

Paul nodded.

Before Derrick walked out, Paul said, "One more thing your father asked me to tell you."

Derrick stood in the hall, his hand on the door, ready to close it on Paul, maybe for the last time.

Paul hesitated and then said, "Your father said that security caught your sister trying to escape. She was in the ocean when they found her. Almost drowned. She's okay, but they have her confined to the house."

There it was. What he felt earlier. He gave a slight nod, hoping it was not perceptible to those watching. Not that it mattered.

***

Panic started deep in Derrick's chest and threatened to overwhelm him. Before he could ring the bell at Nyx's door, it opened. Nyx jumped back.

"Damn it, you scared me. Why didn't you ring the bell?"

"I just walked up," Derrick managed.

"You're late."

"I was talking to Paul," Derrick said.

Nyx nodded, closed the door, and walked to the stairs. She said nothing, and neither did Derrick, yet he was about to burst. He struggled to walk down the stairs and out of the building. When they had walked what he estimated was a safe distance, he leaned down and whispered, "Bad things are happening."

"Bad things? You mean worse than yesterday?"

"Much worse. They caught Miriam trying to escape. She was out in the ocean."

"What do you mean out in the ocean? Like in a boat?"

"I don't think so. Paul said she almost drowned."

"Is she a good swimmer?" Nyx had stopped and looked into Derrick's eyes.

"I didn't know she could swim. Seems crazy. Swimming out of Pacific Edge is impossible. She would have drowned if they had not caught her. Now, they confined her to the house." Tears formed in Derrick's eyes despite his best effort to prevent them. "I am freaking out, Nyx. I must do something, but what can I do? Miriam said she had given up. That she could not help me. What if — she wasn't trying to escape?"

Nyx took a deep breath and gave Derrick's arm a squeeze. "You will not freak out, and there is nothing you can do for Miriam, except do what you need to do here." She paused, bit her lip, glanced at the ground, and then continued. "She called me."

"You talked to Miriam?"

"I did not. She left a message. My phone was on, do not disturb. She sounded out of breath, like she had been running, and whispered as if she was hiding from someone. She said, no time to explain and begged that I keep you here and I keep you safe, no matter what happened."

"Did she say where she was?" Derrick felt his chin quiver. He looked away.

"I heard something in the background that made her difficult to understand. Might have been the ocean."

"In her last e-mail, she said I would not hear from her again. What if she meant she had given up on living?"

"I don't think so," Nyx said.

"You cannot know that."

"She's alive. Hang onto that for now."

Derrick nodded and wiped his face with his sleeve. "I don't think I can do this. Not today. Maybe tomorrow."

"You're doing it today, and you're going to be fine," Nyx said, and then she did something that surprised him.

She threw her arms around his waist and hugged him.

They stood like that for several minutes, and Derrick wanted to stand there several more, but Nyx released him and stepped back.

"There's more," Derrick said. "Paul said they will make me leave here."

Nyx stared at him.

After a moment, Derrick said, "It would make your life easier if I were not here."

Nyx shook her head. "Derrick King, you're an idiot."

46

Wednesday, March 31, 7:05 a.m.

AKIRA SAT WAITING ON THE GYM bleachers when Derrick and Nyx entered through the field-side door. The gym had aired out during the night. Later in the day, the place would smell of pine, sweat, and teenage hormones. Now only the scent of dusty pine remained. The wood floor glistened as if to welcome young people to bounce balls, run, compete, and laugh. Derrick felt as if no good feelings existed for him. Not anymore.

Akira looked different to Derrick, but he wasn't sure why. Her hair, long, straight, shiny, and brilliantly black, had not changed. As was her custom, she wore no makeup — he knew what makeup was now — or if she did, she applied it in a manner that looked natural. She didn't need makeup. Her skin was a smooth, flawless olive color. But what Derrick saw afresh was not that Akira was attractive. He noticed that the first time he saw her in Earth Science. What he noticed was no less startling than if she had cropped her hair short, bleached it blonde, and painted her face a rainbow of many colors. Why he saw this for the first time baffled him. Akira was Chosen. His peer a few years ago. Akira told him this yesterday, but the significance of the revelation sailed over his head like a flock of geese headed south.

Akira stood. "It might help if I go to the principal's office with Derrick." She paused, looked at Nyx, and said, "I'm in better standing."

"True," Nyx said.

"What does that mean?" Derrick asked.

"Another time," Nyx said, turning on her heel and walking toward Coach's office.

Nyx rapped on Coach's door.

"It's open."

Derrick, Nyx, and Akira filed into the small space between the old wooden desk where they stood shoulder to shoulder in what passed as an office for the Potterville High School head coach.

"Well, to what do I owe this honor?" Browning asked as he pushed back from his desk.

"We need a favor," Nyx began. She explained Derrick's situation with a precise efficiency that would have made any debate coach proud.

Derrick studied Browning's face for a reaction. Occasionally, Browning shifted his eyes from Nyx to Akira to Derrick. Derrick's eyes fell to the floor rather than meet Browning's gaze.

Browning remained silent. Working his jaw. Staring.

Now Derrick met Browning's eyes. Neither wavered.

Browning asked, "Why is Nyx talking for you, Derrick?"

The question was not unanticipated. Yet Derrick did not have a decent answer. "I don't know, Coach. Nyx presents herself better than I do." He paused. "She has your respect, too."

Browning pinched his lips together and gave a slight nod. "I respect Nyx. No question about that. But that does not mean that I don't respect you, Derrick. I respect you more now that you're ready to end this charade."

Browning turned to Akira. "And why are you here, young lady?"

"She has pull with the principal," Nyx said before Akira could speak for herself.

"Are you speaking to the students, Derrick, or will the girls be doing that for you?" Browning asked.

"I will speak for myself," Derrick said.

"In that case, I have a little pull with the principal myself," Browning said, standing. "Let's go."

The trio followed Browning across the gym floor to the exit doors that led to the main hall. Before he hit the door's exit bar, Browning turned to them. "Girls, I'll take it from here. Derrick needs to face this by himself."

Derrick felt a weight deep in his chest, not unlike the feeling he had when the Tribunal announced his sentence.

Nyx protested.

Coach raised his hand. "It wasn't a question, Nyx, and it's not open for debate." He paused and said, "Trust me."

Coach took Derrick by the arm, not angrily. More like a father might guide his son, although Derrick's Father never did anything similar. Browning took two steps and turned back to the girls. "Derrick is lucky to have you two as friends."

The halls were full. The first bell would chime within minutes. Derrick could feel the eyes following him and thought any moment a book might clunk him on the head. Coach kept his grip on Derrick's arm, which may have been the only thing preventing a confrontation. Derrick felt queasy and, if he were honest, terrified. But not of a fight. A fight he could handle. Speaking to the student body, he was not sure he could handle that.

During the night, as he tossed and turned, he concocted several scenarios of how this would go. All of them included Nyx and Akira doing the work. Nyx making the first introductions, Akira explaining how the media bombards the Chosen with bleak images and vivid stories about the savage world outside their protective walls. How New America controlled all the news, all the communications, all the programs.

In his favorite versions, Nyx would step in before Derrick could speak. She would say how she had come to know Derrick, his contribution to the track team, and how he'd become a close friend. In his secret, secret version, the one he had not admitted even to himself, Nyx said he had become more than a friend. Derrick would then simply, yet sincerely, say he was sorry. The end. They would go on to win the state track championship and live happily ever after. His dreaming got away from him sometimes, out of control, run amuck.

Inside the principal's outer office, Browning pointed to a chair. "Sit. I'll talk to him first. If his admin assistant returns, her name is Gail. Tell her I brought you and I'm talking to Mr. Snapp. Got it?"

"Yes, sir. I mean, Coach."

Derrick sat, thought about what he would say. "I am from Pacific Edge. They exiled me." Well, that was true, but every student would ask why. He would try to explain, and then the story would pass from student to student, and each time they exchanged it, his story would change. Eventually, his version would be unrecognizable. "Hi, I am Derrick King. I did not grow up in Denver. My parents are not dead. I am from Pacific Edge. I got in a fight." *Well, it wasn't much of a fight.* "I hit a kid." *No, that sounded even worse. Like I am some sort of psycho.*

"I said, hello." A white-haired lady, standing at the door, said in a loud voice. "You're a million miles away, son. Can I help you?"

Derrick stood. "Oh, sorry. Yes, I mean no, I mean yes, I was preoccupied, but no, you cannot help me. Sorry, not that you are not capable of helping people ..."

"Slow down, son. We don't bite. Despite what you might have been told."

"Sorry. You must be Gail. Coach did not tell me your last name. I do not mean disrespect calling you by your first name." Derrick searched Gail's desk for a name placard but saw none.

Gail followed Derrick's gaze to her desk and said, "That's because everyone calls me Gail and I'd have it no other way. Now, how can I help you, Mr. ...?"

"Derrick King, ma'am." Derrick gathered himself. "Coach Browning brought me here. He is inside talking to Principal Snapp. He told me to wait here."

"Oh my. So, you're the legendary Derrick King. Well, it's a pleasure to meet you, Mr. King." Gail stuck out her hand.

"Legendary?" Derrick asked.

"It's a small school, Mr. King." Gail went to her desk and as she sat, she said, "They're right. You do speak in a rather formal manner."

"Sorry," Derrick said. He had not recognized that he had slipped back into his — what? Chosen manner of speaking?

"No need to be sorry, Mr. King. Spending all day around teenagers, it's refreshing to hear someone talk without using slang that I can scarcely keep up with."

Legendary? I am in a worse predicament than I ever imagined.

47

AS HE SAT WAITING, DERRICK STUDIED the walls, covered with photos of teams, graduates, students holding plaques, pictures spanning decades, and formal documents too far away to read. The room smelled of mint over a musty odor of age. The floor was old but gleamed from the night crew's efforts. He checked his phone, hoping Miriam had escaped and found a way to contact him. That thought sent a deep chill into his chest because reality dictated that she did not escape. They imprisoned her, but she was safe. Sadness washed over his fear. He had, unrealistically, hoped she would escape. That she would come and help him solve this mess he had created for himself. But he was on his own. He would never see her again.

Although he expected no e-mails, two text messages awaited on his phone, one from Nyx, another from Akira. Akira sent emoticons: a thumbs-up and a smiley face. Nyx wrote: "You can do this."

The door to Principal Snapp's office opened, creaking on old hinges. Coach Browning smiled, gave a gentle wave of his hand, and said, "We're ready for you, Derrick."

Derrick walked on unsteady legs into Principal Snapp's office. Mr. Snapp stood to the side of his desk, offering his hand, which Derrick shook, but he did not get his grip right, resulting in an anemic handshake. Mr. Snapp's office was modest by any standard and downright pitiable compared to the Pacific Edge Academy's Headmaster.

Mr. Snapp waved at a chair in front of his desk. "Sit, Mr. King. Let's discuss your situation."

"Yes, sir." Derrick sat and then glanced at Browning for encouragement.

Browning nodded and offered a feeble smile.

"Coach Browning explained things to me, Derrick. Not that it came as a surprise. But before I turn the school PA system over to you, I have a few questions." Mr. Snapp stopped.

When the silence became uncomfortable, Derrick sensed Mr. Snapp was waiting for a response. Derrick did not know what response the principal wanted. After a few moments, he said, "Sure."

"Tell me, Derrick, why did you concoct this elaborate lie?"

"I was afraid, sir," Derrick offered.

Mr. Snapp waved him off. "That's not what I'm looking for. Why were you afraid? Derrick, this isn't a trick question. I want to understand."

So, Derrick told him. Told him in as much detail as fifteen minutes could offer. He told of the daily news of arson, riots, shootings, rapes, and murders. Every image he had ever seen of the world outside the gates of Pacific Edge depicted an active war zone where the combatants were not military but drug lords, gangs, and strongmen vying to wrestle territorial control from other strongmen who had stolen it from someone else. He told of how any travel outside Pacific Edge, until Paul drove him to Potterville, was in a windowless air transport because officials told them that seeing what was happening below was far too violent for children and not advisable for adults.

"I believed every bit of the information they provided," Derrick said. "I thought I would be murdered as soon as Paul and I left the Pacific Edge compound." It occurred to Derrick that it was the first time he had referred to Pacific Edge as a compound. That term described it perfectly. A compound that contained what? The thought of a cult came to him. And if it were a cult, exactly what purpose did Pacific Edge serve?

Mr. Snapp listened, leaned forward, hands clasped on his desk. When Derrick finished, Mr. Snapp straightened, looked at Browning, and said, "I never heard a story like that. And we have a few kids here from Pacific Edge or other Chosen communities."

Derrick wondered how many *few* amounted to, and besides Akira, who were they?

"True," Browning began. "But they came here when they were younger. Grade school, maybe a couple in middle school. Kids don't pay attention to issues at that age."

"Humph. Maybe not. That's disturbing, Derrick. If it's true," Mr. Snapp said.

Derrick had not considered that Snapp and Browning would not believe him. Akira knew that what he said was true. Nyx had no knowledge of Pacific Edge and had not questioned that part of his story. *Why did Nyx believe me?*

"It is true," Derrick said. "I have lied enough. No more." *Well, mostly no more.* Where did that thought come from? He considered telling Mr. Snapp about Miriam. How she'd tried to escape, got caught, and locked up, but he decided against it. Then another thought he had never considered before. *Maybe New World Media tailored those broadcasts for just me.*

"Do you plan on telling the entire story to the student body?" Mr. Snapp asked, sounding skeptical.

"I want to tell them where I'm from and apologize for lying to them."

"Well, I can't see the harm in that," Mr. Snapp allowed. "What do you think, Coach?"

"Seems like the right thing to do. Maybe the only thing Derrick can do," Browning said.

"There's something else," Derrick interjected. "They plan to move me."

Mr. Snapp leaned forward. His brow furrowed and his eyes narrowed. "Who will make you move?"

"Pacific Edge, well, the Tribunal."

Mr. Snapp rubbed his chin. "Then your apology might be unnecessary. Perhaps this is premature."

"I'm not leaving," Derrick said. By the look on Mr. Snapp's face, Derrick's statement was a shock.

Why did Mr. Snapp seem surprised? Derrick considered that for a moment but then admitted he surprised himself by blurting it out. Part of him did not want to start over. Part of him did not want to leave Nyx and Akira or the track team. But he also realized that starting over would have advantages. He could avoid all the mistakes he had made the first time. Part of him felt relieved with that prospect. Part of him wanted to go home to Pacific Edge.

Going home was what he wanted from the start of this entire experience.

Yet, suddenly, and somewhat unexpectedly, he resolved to stay. Miriam had told him to stay, but she was no longer coming. The real surprise is that it was not coming from Miriam's instruction. It came from his heart.

"Can you do that?" Mr. Snapp asked. "I mean. The Chosen don't bother us much. They leave us alone if we pay and do what they require of us. But we all understand that if they came here and said jump, many people would *ask how high* and get to hopping."

Derrick felt rage boiled in his chest, but he controlled it. "I don't know. But I am not leaving."

Mr. Snapp drummed his fingers on his desk. After a few moments, he slid a silver-gray device about six inches tall, with a dirty flat button embedded in its base, in front of Derrick.

"Let's get this over with then," Mr. Snapp said as if they were about to do something wicked. He pushed the device in front of Derrick.

Derrick stared at it.

"It's the PA microphone. Go ahead. Make your announcement."

He stared at it for a moment and then took a deep breath and began. "Hello? My name is Derrick …"

"No, no, no," Mr. Snapp interrupted. "Press the button while you talk. And move closer to it."

Derrick studied the button. He hesitated. It was once white. He assumed but was now yellowed with a brown spot in the center, years of fingers poking at it, collecting oil and dirt. Derrick had rehearsed in his head dozens of times what he would say. Now, he couldn't remember a word beyond, *Hello, my name is Derrick King.* Six words. That was all he had. Staring into the middle distance, he pushed the old plastic button. "Hi, this is Derrick." He couldn't even get the first six words right.

"Derrick King," he continued. "Most of you don't know me. Well, maybe most of you know who I am. Uh, because I am new. Not new, but a new student at Potterville."

"Breathe," Browning whispered.

Derrick paused and took a deep breath. "Here is the thing. I have lied to you all, and I am sorry. I am not from Denver. I am not an orphan, at least not as far as I know, but maybe I am now. I do not know, actually. Anyway, as I was saying, I am not from Denver. I am from Pacific Edge. I was a Chosen. I was exiled. See, I got into a fight. Not what you think. I did not start it. I was protecting my little sister. I hit a kid. Hurt him pretty bad. Sent him to the hospital. The kid's name was Marcus Carver. That is all. I am sorry."

Derrick released the microphone button and fell back into the chair. No one spoke. Mr. Snapp busied himself rearranging things on his desk as if it were the most important task of his day. Browning leaned over and patted Derrick's knee. Then Derrick heard something odd. It started low, creeping through the walls. Voices. Many voices. The angry cry of a mob.

Then Gail threw open the door. "Are you hearing this?"

That sound of many voices careened down the hall. Gail then went to the outer office door and held it open. The voices were clearer now, angry, threatening. Then another sound became evident below the din. It grew louder. First, equaling the angry noise, then rising above it, and then drowning it out.

Cheering.

48

THE NOISE DISSIPATED AS IF SOME had better control of the class than did others. Mr. Snapp and Coach Browning stood, and Mr. Snapp said, "You may go to your class now, Mr. King. A written excuse is unnecessary given the circumstances, but if your teacher — who is your teacher this period?"

"Alice Schilling," Derrick said.

"In that case, you'll be fine." Mr. Snapp walked to the door, signaling to Derrick that it was time for him to go. "Coach, stay a moment if you will," Mr. Snapp said.

The hall was empty as Derrick anticipated, except for one person Derrick did not expect.

"Amigo," Antonio said, giving Derrick an unexpected hug. "You make your life interesting, my friend."

"Interesting is not the word I would have used, but it works. I understand people might not like me. Because of all the lying. But I do not understand the cheering."

Antonio released Derrick and walked at his side. Antonio was getting around easily on crutches now. "Walk with me to my class. When the teacher sees you, she'll assume I'm just doing the duties of my office. Even the student body president has a limit on how much tardiness is deemed acceptable, and I'm skating on thin ice, if you know what I mean."

Derrick did not know what Antonio meant. He had not seen ice in Potterville, thin or otherwise, and if there was ice, why would Antonio want to skate if it were thin? Besides, he couldn't skate. He was on crutches. Whenever Derrick thought he was starting to understand things, something like this illustrated how illiterate he was here.

"The angry reaction came fast because the believers don't distinguish shades of gray. Understand? Soon as they heard you had hit a member of the royal family or godhead, if you like, their response was fast and compulsory. That group makes up about a quarter of the population. The second group, a little over half, thinks hitting a Carver was a good thing. You will have a little stardom with them, which is good, right, amigo?"

"I guess. But I am not trying to be a star or famous or anything like that," Derrick said.

"Well, what you want and what you get are two different kettles of fish, as my grandpa would say."

"I guess." Derrick wondered what fish had to do with it, but he did not ask. "What about the others?"

"What others?"

"Twenty-five percent and fifty percent do not equal one hundred percent," Derrick offered.

"Right you are. The rest don't care. Or they might care, but they aren't going to choose sides," Antonio said.

They turned right and headed up the stairs. Antonio carried his crutches with one hand, hopped on his good leg, and winced with each step taken.

"So, I understand two of the squad were ready to take you out yesterday."

Derrick said nothing and must have looked confused because Antonio continued, "Deal with the problem, which is you. Understand?"

"Yes, I understand," Derrick said, yet he was not sure that he did. Squad seemed like an odd term to use. Teammates sounded right or track team.

"Word is that Nyx has your back. That true?"

Derrick wanted to be honest, but he was not sure what Antonio meant. He was struggling to speak more relaxed English. Jargon and slang used here were still unfamiliar. He either remained silent or took his best guess. "Maybe that is true," Derrick said.

"You can't have a better friend right now than Nyx Belos. Seriously."

"I do not think Nyx is my friend. I mean, I would like to be friends. Uh, but I am not sure she even likes me," Derrick said.

"Dude, you are the most naïve person I've ever met," Antonio said, stretching the word naïve out.

They had been standing at the head of the east stairway for a few minutes. Antonio turned and headed down the stairs. "Come on, Amigo. I gotta get to class."

Antonio stopped in front of Derrick's English class.

"Here you are, mi amigo," Antonio said.

"I thought we were going to your class first," Derrick said.

Antonio opened the door, motioning Derrick inside. As Derrick passed, Antonio smiled and said, "I have completed my assignment. For now."

Derrick walked in, and the room grew silent. Mrs. Schilling wore a smile, which was not uncommon, as she seemed to enjoy the subject and particularly enjoyed the occasional spirited debate that might occur over a reading assignment. He thought about how Miriam would thrive in this environment, which made him feel empty and angry at the same time.

Other than Mrs. Schilling's smile, Derrick remembered little of what happened in English that day. When the bell rang, it was like he had awoken from a deep sleep.

"Derrick, may I speak with you a moment?" Mrs. Schilling stood at the door, motioning students into the hallway.

Derrick felt certain that she would send him back to the principal's office for being absent while present in class. She might have called on him to answer a question, which he did not hear, did not respond to, and would seem to have been sullenly ignoring her.

Mrs. Schilling closed the door and touched Derrick's arm. "I'm proud of you, Derrick. What you did this morning was difficult, I'm sure. Things may become challenging for you. At least for a while. Some people will try to make you a celebrity. Some will be mad because of the lies, and some will dislike you because of what you did to get yourself sent here. But remember, most people will get over being mad at you. You will have support from many. Still, some people will never like you." She paused, her eyes searched his and then said, "And some will try to destroy you."

Derrick had to rush to his second class. He heard whispers as he passed people in the hall. A girl's voice rose above the buzz. "I love you." Another voice said, "You rock, King."

Another voice said, "You're dead, King."

49

DERRICK SPENT THE DAY IN A FOG. For some reason, the song of Mr. Bob Dylan circulated in his head and the words haunted him. How often had Derrick turned his head, pretending he did not see?

During the day, either Akira, Antonio, Nyx, or Malcolm was always at his side, each taking a turn escorting him in the hallways until he was inside a classroom. He ate lunch, consisting of junk from the vending machines, on the bleachers with Nyx and Akira. No one spoke much. He studied the field and wondered what it would be like to play football. That brief daydream was the only time when he was not fretting about what would happen next.

He did not have to wait long to find out.

As they finished their lunch, three men exited the gym and walked in their direction. Two Derrick recognized: Coach Browning and Paul. The third man wore a tan uniform with a thick black belt that carried several things Derrick did not recognize. He did, however, recognize one item, a gun, and on the man's chest, was a gold-colored star.

Derrick stood as the three men approached. A patch on the third man's sleeve read, Sheriff. A name plate on the man's shirt read, Bill Collins. Derrick asked, "What's going on, Coach?"

"Sorry, son. Bad news is coming," Browning said.

Paul shrugged. "Sorry, kid."

"Why is the sheriff here?" Nyx asked, stepping down from the bleacher, positioning herself between the lawman and Derrick.

"They asked me to be here. Make sure there was no trouble," the sheriff said.

"Who asked, and what sort of trouble? We aren't bothering anyone," Akira said, stepping to Derrick's side.

Before any of the men answered, a Pacific Edge hovercraft, followed by a sky transport, appeared over the school. Derrick watched as both vehicles descended, landing in the middle of the football field. A security officer from the hovercraft and a man from the transport walked toward the group. He sensed Akira standing beside him, her hand placed on his shoulder.

"Derrick King?" a man from the transport asked, smiling.

"I am Derrick King."

"Of course, you are." The man extended his hand. "Bruce Bolden, special assistant to the Tribunal." His hand remained outstretched for a few moments, and then he withdrew it when Derrick made no movement to return the greeting.

"Good news, Derrick. The Tribunal found additional information that proves you were not the aggressor in the incident with Marcus Carver. The Tribunal wants you home. A welcome home celebration is waiting for you."

Derrick felt an overwhelming sense of loss. A yearning for home washed over him, and he wondered if it was a dream. Everything seemed too tangible for it to be a dream. Things around him faded. He no longer felt Akira's hand on his shoulder, nor did he see Nyx staring up at him. The sheriff, Coach Browning, and Paul faded like ghosts in the fog. Derrick glanced at the transport that would take him home. Back to Pacific Edge, to the life promised him, to a devoted bride picked from a group of deserving candidates to a city-wide welcoming.

Back to his life.

So, it was no small surprise to Derrick when he said, "Tell me what happened to Miriam?"

The man named Bruce Bolden continued to smile and nodded. "We understand your concern. You must love her a great deal to protect her as you did. A noble act, the Tribunal plans to reward and compensate." Bruce Bolden paused. His face drew dour as he surveyed the sheriff, Coach Browning, Paul, Akira, and Nyx. Then he continued, "For your, shall we say — unfortunate exposure to all of this." He waved his hand.

What sort of compensation, Derrick wondered? Cash? Status upgrade? Both? How much money?

"You did not answer my question," Derrick said. A voice in his head asked what he was doing. His surroundings snapped back into focus.

"She took your exile hard. We found her in the ocean and just in time. Saved her. She is fine. She's getting counseling, and for the time being, for her own safety, she is confined to …"

Derrick interrupted. "I want to talk to her."

"Of course, of course. We will fly you straight home. You will be there soon and see for yourself."

"I mean right now. You can contact her on your device," Derrick said.

"But I do not …"

"I said, NOW!"

Bruce Bolden took an involuntary step back as Derrick stepped off the bleacher.

"Okay, well, irregular, but sure we can do that," Bruce Bolden said.

Bolden turned his back and whispered something to the security officer. The security officer jogged back to the hovercraft, where he conferred with the pilot. The pilot appeared agitated, pointing toward Derrick. Finally, he spoke into a microphone clipped to his collar.

The group waited in uncomfortable silence. Derrick studied those around him. Akira remained at his side. The sheriff stood relaxed, as if he had experience waiting. Paul fidgeted, twisting his head and neck every few seconds as if he had slept wrong. Coach Browning stared at Derrick. Derrick was not sure how he would explain Coach's expression. Determined, perhaps. He could not see Nyx's face, because she was standing in front of him, facing Bruce Bolden. She looked tense in a relaxed sort of way, not wasting energy, coiled like a snake ready to strike. He wished he could see her face.

Again, the yearning for home washed over him like a wave and threatened to overpower him.

After about fifteen minutes, the security officer returned, whispered to Bruce Bolden, and handed him a communication device. Derrick thought they called it a tablet. Larger than a cell phone, but not a laptop.

Bruce Bolden turned, holding the tablet, and smiling. "Here she is now, Derrick."

On the screen, Derrick saw Miriam. He squinted against the sun and raised one hand to shield his eyes. Tears blurred his vision. He recognized she was in their dining room, although the image on the tablet was cropped close. It did not appear that she was holding a phone-like device, which meant someone else was holding the camera. He wondered who else might be in the room. He realized that what he saw might be recorded, so he needed to talk to her to confirm it was a live feed. Because there were no doubt others in the room, not to mention Bruce Bolden holding the tablet, Derrick knew Miriam could not speak freely.

Derrick moved around Nyx and closer to the tablet, and to Bruce Bolden's right, forcing him to turn 90 degrees. "Hi, Sis. Are you okay?"

Miriam nodded, her eyes moving to the left and then to the right as she did, but she did not speak.

"I heard they found you in the ocean?" Derrick asked.

Miriam nodded again and shifted her eyes.

What did the eye shift mean? Probably that someone was standing there just out of sight. Not Mother or Father. Someone else.

Derrick needed a question that could not be answered yes or no. And every question that came to mind was one Miriam could not answer truthfully. "Why were you in the ocean?"

Miriam's eyes shifted to the left. "It's a long story. Someday, I'll tell you."

"They say I can come back to Pacific Edge. Right now. I can be there soon."

"I know," Miriam said.

Derrick thought he detected an almost imperceptible shake of her head, but he might have imagined it. *Focus.* Derrick's mind churned. Every word and movement meant something. He was sure of that. Miriam was too smart to let this opportunity pass. *So, if she knows I will be back today, why did she say that she would tell me someday? Maybe because they will not let me see her. Maybe because there are too many listening devices in the house.*

Maybe it is something else.

Bruce Bolden said, "Let's wrap this up, Derrick. There's a ceremony forming up as we speak in Pacific Edge to recognize your return and we don't want the guest of honor to be late, now do we?"

Derrick held his hand up, palm out. "I have missed you, Sis." He felt a tear trace down his cheek.

"You haven't been gone long," Miriam said.

This time, Derrick was convinced that Miriam had given a slight shake of her head as she spoke. Her lips were drawn tight, teeth clenched.

"I'm so sorry I was such an awful brother. I'll make it up to you."

"No need. You've always been the best brother a sister could ask for."

Her image faded.

The screen turned black.

50

TWENTY-FIVE YARDS SEPARATED DERRICK FROM the aerial transport that would fly him to Pacific Edge. He could not subdue the excitement that raced through his mind. Home, safety, future. Chosen again. Special again.

Yet something opposite burned in his chest. Leaving Potterville High, the track team, Nyx. A war waged between his heart and his head, and something else wormed its way into his thoughts: Miriam.

Was she trying to send me a message? She would try to, but did she? Am I smart enough to understand? She glanced to the side. That meant someone was there, out of view. Not Mother or Father. Did she shake her head, which universally meant no, but no what? No, don't come back? But why would she not want me home? That made no sense. If she knows I would be back today, why did she say she would tell me about her venture into the ocean sometime? Why was she in the sea in the first place? To escape? But that made little sense because she was not a swimmer, and the likelihood of escape by way of the sea was slim. She was too smart to do something that had such a low chance of success. Unless she was desperate. And why did she say I had always been the best brother a sister could ask for? That makes no sense at all.

"Derrick, Derrick, DERRICK!"

Derrick blinked. Bruce Bolden was holding out a hand toward him.

"We must leave now, Derrick. We must be quick. I am sorry there is no time for goodbyes. Someone will gather your things, although we cannot allow most of it in Pacific Edge. But come now. We must leave to get to your homecoming ceremony," Bruce Bolden said.

Derrick surveyed Coach, the sheriff, and Paul. He could determine nothing from their expressionless faces. A few weeks ago, he did not think he could survive outside Pacific Edge, and since coming here, he did not think he could live without Miriam. Now, Miriam was but a short flight away. If he were there, he could help her earn freedom again. Ensure that she was safe. He had to go back.

Nyx turned to face him. He thought he saw a tear welling in her eye.

Not taking his eyes off Nyx, he took a deep breath and said, "I'm not going."

"What? Well, that is unexpected," Bruce Bolden said. "But that is not an option. The Tribunal hoped you would be overjoyed with your pardon. However, I have my orders. I am to bring you back to Pacific Edge."

Bruce Bolden's smile faded, and a stern, frightening face took shape. "You are going back one way or another."

"I'm not going," Derrick said again.

Bruce Bolden laughed. "You do not have a choice, Mr. King. You have no citizenship here, and you have no home. Being an undocumented person with no means of support, no home, means you have no rights here. Do you understand?"

Nyx had turned around to face Bruce Bolden again. Her muscles coiled tense. Akira tightened her grasp on Derrick's shoulder. Derrick noticed the sheriff's hand had moved to the pistol at his side.

Derrick looked at Paul.

Paul shrugged. "I'm sorry, Derrick. I would like to help you, but I can't. I don't have room, and my wife wouldn't stand for it. Not now with what has happened."

Coach Browning nudged Paul to the side as he stepped forward. "He will stay with me."

The sheriff looked at Browning. "You sure about that, Coach? Why would you do that?"

"You're looking at the running back we need to be state champion. I'm not letting that slip away. Besides, I've taken a liking to the boy."

"I heard the boy is fast, but he's never played football," the sheriff said.

"Bill, I know a running back when I see one. But I would take the boy in even if he could not run. I ain't letting these bastards take him if he doesn't want to go. There's something wrong with this entire scenario," Coach said.

The sheriff stepped between Bolden and Derrick. "You heard the boy. He doesn't want to go, and he has a home. You have no jurisdiction here." With that, the sheriff keyed his microphone and said, "red dog."

"Sheriff Collins, I have my orders. You can file a complaint through proper channels. Derrick, you can walk to that transport, or we will carry you." Bruce Bolden gave a slight wave to the security officer.

The security officer pulled his weapon, which might be set to stun. Or to kill. Bill Collins, the sheriff, pulled his firearm, which Derrick understood had one setting: kill.

Nyx started for Bruce Bolden, and Derrick grabbed her from behind. She was strong for her size. Derrick did not want to hurt her. He wrapped his arms firmly but gently around her waist, and he whispered in her ear, "Let the sheriff handle this."

"Now, sheriff, do not do anything you will regret." Bruce Bolden looked back to the hovercraft, where the second security officer aimed the mounted weapon toward the sheriff.

"My thinking exactly," Collins said, giving a nod toward a booth built at the top of the stadium.

Everyone glanced up. A deputy stood in the booth aiming a rifle. When Derrick looked back down, another man stepped to the open door of the transport with his firearm pulled and pointed at whoever was inside. A third man, weapon drawn, moved behind the security officer on the transport.

"Don't be rash. There has not been a conflict between the Chosen and the commoners — I mean the United States — in twenty years. You do not want to start a fight over this, boy," Bruce Bolden said.

"You're right, I don't. But I will, and one thing is certain, if I do, none of you are going back to Pacific Edge today."

Bruce Bolden looked at the sheriff, and then at the deputy in the booth aiming the rifle and then turned to see the other two men. "Derrick, last chance to make a good decision and come home. The offer will not come again."

"I made a good decision. I'm not going," Derrick said, surprised at the tone in his voice. He felt Nyx relax, but she held onto his arms, keeping them around her.

Bruce Bolden motioned the security officers to lower their weapons. He eased back to the transport. Both machines rose into the air, and they were gone.

Bill Collins holstered his weapon and spoke into his radio microphone. "Martinez, stand down but stay alert and thank Hank and Fred for helping. And I want you to stay at the school today." He turned to Coach Browning. "State champions, you say?"

"Trust me," Browning said.

51

WHEN THE BELL SOUNDED, NYX REMOVED herself from Derrick's arms and stood beside him. Akira stood at his other side. Paul said he had work to do, shook Derrick's hand, wished him luck, and said he'd see him at the bistro sometime, acted as if he wanted to say more, but walked away.

The sheriff extended his hand and said, "I'm Bill Collins. Don't believe anything this old fart tells you about me." Bill Collins nodded toward Coach Browning. "I'm glad to meet you after all that I've heard."

Derrick shook Bill Collins' hand and said, "You've heard of me?"

"Son, it's my job to know about people new to this town." He nodded toward Nyx. "I see you've picked the right people to hang with. That's important right there. And if Coach Browning says you're okay, then you're okay in my book, until proven otherwise."

Bill Collins reached into his shirt pocket and pulled out a card. "Here's my personal cell phone number. Call me if you ever need help or if those guys show up here. In fact, you best program it into your contacts and speed dial."

Derrick was not sure what a speed dial was and wondered about the book the sheriff kept, but only said, "Yes, sir. Thank you, sir."

"Call me Bill."

"Yes, sir."

Bill Collins looked at Browning.

Browning shook his head and said, "It takes a while."

The assembled group laughed.

Sheriff Collins said, "I hope he's a quicker study at running back."

"You want to help? I still need another assistant coach," Browning said.

Sheriff Collins studied Browning for a moment and then looked at Derrick. "I'll take you up on that this year."

The two men shook hands as the second bell rang.

Browning turned to the trio of students, and, with a smile, he said, "Nyx and Derrick, do your track stuff in P.E. and then be in my office to get Derrick's football gear. Now, get to class, you slackers."

"Want me to go easy on him?" Nyx asked.

"Hell, no. Work his ass off. He's got a meet coming up," Browning said, still smiling. "And if he isn't throwing up before the end of football practice, I'll take it as a personal failure."

"Thanks, Coach," Nyx said. "For everything."

"Now, get," Browning said, pointing toward the school.

The three started toward school at a pace short of a fast walk. Before they had crossed the track to the football field sideline, Browning hollered, "Derrick, we'll talk further about your new living arrangements after football practice."

Derrick turned, unable to suppress a smile. "Thank you, Coach."

As they walked toward the building, Derrick's smile did not fade. He could not say why he felt so pleased. He had passed up a chance to go home, had an uncertain future, and he understood little about football and believed it was Coach Browning's motivation for helping him. The longing for home still hung over him like a cloud, but a cloud that no longer penetrated his mind. He identified one thing that made him happy. He eliminated Coach Browning, Akira, and Nyx as the Pacific Edge spies.

What he did not know was that the spy was closer than he ever could have imagined.

52

DERRICK DID NOT REMEMBER MANY EVENTS from the remainder of the day. Later, people would mention things that should have been significant but that he did not retain. He recalled L. Linda Maxton saying she was proud of him and giving him a kiss on the cheek. He also remembered the look he got from Nyx when that happened but believed it best to say nothing about either event.

His thoughts circulated from one thought to another all day, considering Bruce Bolden's offer to take him to Pacific Edge, deciphering Miriam's clues, worrying about Miriam's safety, wondering about living at Coach Browning's home, fretting about his first football practice, L. Linda Maxton's quick kiss, and the subsequent look on Nyx's face. Akira would later laugh about the day, telling Derrick the teachers cut him a lot of slack because sometimes he failed to hear when his name was called as he sat staring out the window.

At track, he functioned on autopilot. Even Nyx struggled to get his attention. They had only run a few laps when Nyx jarred him from his mental fog.

"Earth to Derrick King." Nyx said.

"Huh?"

"Your head is in outer space."

Derrick said, "I know. Sorry. I keep thinking about Miriam. Not just Miriam, lots of things."

"Understandable, but you gotta clear your head. You'll be in a football uniform for the first time in your life. Coach won't let you run any live stuff today, so you'll be safe. But the thing is, football is a violent sport. If you're daydreaming, you could get hurt."

"I'll try. And thanks."

"No thanks necessary. We need you healthy for the track meet on Saturday."

"King," Browning hollered from across the field, waving for him to come. "I've got him now," Nyx," Coach yelled.

Derrick ran to catch Browning, who had already turned his back. Derrick caught up to him in an area Derrick had never entered behind the basketball court. On his right, Derrick saw a room full of things he did not recognize but assumed they were training devices because students were using them, lifting bars with large round disks affixed to each end and other machines that appeared to allow one to exercise all parts of the body. He saw Malcolm Cross, Henry Clark, and the red-faced friend of Jim Priest. This explained why Malcolm and Henry were not present during P.E. and track on certain days. Most of the kids were large boys Derrick did not recognize. Coach Yates walked around the room, holding a clipboard and taking notes as each student lifted.

Coach Browning walked into a room and turned on the light. The room was full of sports equipment. Browning stepped to a pile of items — helmet, pads, pants, jersey, and a small black box with a big red check mark that Derrick now recognized to be a well-known sporting equipment manufacturer.

"I gathered your football equipment. You're expected to take care of it, keep it reasonably clean. The jersey is a practice jersey. I'll order you a game jersey if you make the team."

Derrick had forgotten that making the team was not guaranteed. He felt an odd sinking sensation in his chest. His ability to stay here hinged on the football team. At least, that is what he believed. "I'll do my best, Coach."

Browning studied Derrick for a moment, picked up the box with the red check mark, and said, "I bought shoes. I guessed the size, hope it's right. If they don't fit, don't wear them, because we'll take them back and get the right size after practice."

"I can pay you for them, Coach. I have a job."

"I know about your job, King. I'll talk to Donna about your schedule. You might have to work fewer hours. And you don't pay me back for something I want to buy. Got it?"

Derrick nodded his head. He hoped he could live up to Coach's expectations.

"Keep your track clothes on for now. We need to get a baseline in the weight room. Gather your gear and meet me in there."

Derrick struggled with the equipment until he devised a way to carry everything at once. Browning had already left the room by the time Derrick waddled to the weight room.

Browning was shaking his head as Derrick entered. "You could have made two trips, King. Stow your stuff over there." Browning pointed at the wall. "Coach Yates will take you through the stations. He'll explain each station to you. Goal is to see how much you can lift. Lift as much as you can, but don't hurt yourself. It's not a competition. Understand?"

Derrick nodded as Coach Yates walked up. Yates surveyed Derrick from head to toe and said, "You're a lifter, I see."

Derrick assumed Yates meant weightlifter. He was becoming more accustomed to how people here rarely talked in complete sentences. "No, sir. I have never lifted weights. I have been running a lot though. Oh, and I wash dishes at the bistro."

"Dishes, huh?" Yates chortled. "You must do something. Pushups, chin-ups, something. And call me coach."

"Yes, sir. Nyx has me do pushups during warmups."

Yates looked at Browning. "You think that's true?"

Browning shrugged. "I told you, didn't I?"

"Yeah, you did." Yates looked at Derrick. "Natural athlete, Coach Browning says. We'll see."

"Clark! To me." Browning waved his hand. "You spot for Derrick, as Coach Yates gets a baseline. Then help Derrick get into his football gear. Something tells me he don't have a clue how to get into his stuff."

"If you say so, Coach," Henry Clark said, glaring at Derrick.

Yates walked to a metal bar on a rack positioned over a bench. "We keep this simple. Two lifts: bench and deadlift. Based on how much you can lift, we pair you up with another player for weight room workouts. You're probably like other kids: busy, but we'd like you in here three times a week in the offseason. If the team is serious about going to state, they will be here at least three times a week and once on the weekend. Because you're on the track team, you'll have to pair up with a team member."

Derrick nodded and looked at the bar perched above the bench.

"Two tests on the bench. First, we set the weight at 225 pounds. You lift it as many times as you can. If you can lift it that is. Understand?"

Derrick nodded his head. How to perform the lift was less clear.

"Clark, show him how it's done," Coach Yates said, and then added, "Whatever you're thinking, leave it out of my weight room and off the field. Got it?"

"Yes, Coach."

Derrick was starting to understand another thing, coaches liked last names. Henry Clark laid down on the bench so that his shoulders were under the bar.

"Stand up there, King. In case he needs help." Coach Yates motioned to the head of the bench.

When Derrick was in position, Coach Yates said, "Begin."

Henry Clark removed the bar and lowered it toward his chest and pushed it straight up. Coach said one. Henry Clark continued to lift the bar, and Coach counted each lift. At ten, Coach said enough, but Clark kept lifting. At the count of 14, Clark returned the bar to its perch.

"Fourteen, Clark. Your best mark. Maybe I'll pair you up with King. He seems to motivate you."

Clark got off the bench, glaring at Derrick. "Your turn."

Derrick got on the bench.

"If you can't lift 225, don't worry. We'll move to the next round and see how much you can lift there," Coach Yates said. "Before you start, I need your weight and height. How much do you weigh?"

"I do not know, Coach. Is that important?"

"Of course, it's important. We'll weigh you when we get done here. How tall are you?"

"About six feet, I guess."

Coach Yates shook his head and laid his clipboard down. "Start whenever you're ready, King."

Derrick adjusted his hands on the bar. He was not sure that he could lift it. It looked heavy, and when Clark did it, he turned red-faced, grunted, strained, and veins popped up under his skin. Derrick pushed and raised the bar into the air. It was heavy, balancing it somewhat difficult. Unlike anything he had ever done before. But it was not too tough. So, he began.

"One, two, three, four," Coach Yates counted in a steady cadence.

Derrick realized he had not been paying close attention. He could not remember if Coach Yates said to do a certain number or as many as he could. Henry Clark did 14, and Derrick wanted to match that number. He heard Coach Yates say ten. The bar felt heavier now. Derrick was not sure how many more he could do. He had never done anything like this where he worked his muscles to complete exhaustion, although it was somewhat like running the 400-meter, except with his arms, so it felt the same, except different.

"Thirteen, fourteen."

Derrick stopped with his arms extended straight up. "Should I keep going?"

"That's the idea, King. Can you do more?"

"A few."

Derrick did a few more. He was not counting, focusing on each lift. When he could not lift it again, he concentrated on landing the bar on the perch. He missed it on one side, and Clark helped guide it into the holder.

"Nineteen. Are you sure you never lifted before?" Yates asked.

"I am telling you the truth this time," Derrick said, sitting up and shifting his eyes from Clark to Yates.

"Don't get bent out of shape," Coach Yates said.

Derrick thought he was sitting straight but adjusted himself to be sure.

"Maybe he should play linebacker," Clark said.

"He's got a lot to learn if he's going to play at all. Let's focus on one thing at a time. Browning thinks he's a running back. You have a problem with him being in the backfield?"

Henry Clark stared at Derrick, breathing deeply, red-faced. "No, Coach."

"Good. After we get your height and weight, we'll do deadlifts and then come back to the bench to get your last number," Yates said.

Yates walked a scale, pointing for Derrick to step up. "Six one and 196. We'll try to add a few pounds to your frame before season starts."

Yates walked to another station where the bar was on the floor. "What are you lifting, Clark?" Yates asked.

"Three ninety, Coach," Clark said.

"Set it at 325. He's a runner. He should be able to do that much," Yates said.

After Henry Clark removed weights from each side, Derrick stepped to the center of the bar, bent at the waist, and grasped it with both hands.

Coach Yates yelled, "Stop! Good grief, King! You'll hurt your back like that. Show him, Clark."

Henry Clark moved to the bar, squatted, stood up, then dropped the bar to the floor.

"That's how you lift, King. Think you can do that?"

"Yes, sir." Derrick realized his mind drifted, so vague were his thoughts that he could not even identify what he had been thinking about. He managed to remember he was supposed to squat to lift the bar. He thought Clark was being rude by dropping it like he did.

Yates shook his head.

Derrick moved to the bar and squatted. He looked up at Clark, and Clark nodded his head. Derrick stood. And lifted the bar over his head. Once the bar was overhead, he didn't know what to do with it, so he eased it back waist high and lowered it to the ground.

Half-way to the ground, Coach Yates said, "That's not how it's done."

Derrick stopped and stood again, still holding the bar. "How should I do it, sir?"

Yates shook his head. "Just drop it but step back a little so it doesn't hit you."

Derrick looked at Henry Clark. Clark gave one nod of his head downward. Derrick dropped the bar. It landed with a heavy thump on the thick rubber mat.

"King, did anyone tell you to lift the bar over your head?" Yates asked.

"No, sir."

"Did Clark lift the bar over his head?"

"Uh, I'm not sure, but no? Sorry, I kind of drifted off."

Yates's brow furrowed and his eyes narrowed. "I will only say this once, King. There's a lot to learn here, and I don't need a smartass or goof off. You got that?"

Derrick nodded.

"What you need to do is listen and do what you're told. You don't need to think. We'll do all the thinking for you. Got it? And for the last time, call me coach."

"Yes, sir. I mean, Coach. Sorry, sir."

Yates' lips became thin lines. He gave an almost imperceptible nod and said, "What you did is called a clean and press, except you didn't do it right. We don't do that here. Understand that? It's too dangerous. We use the machines." Yates pointed to the contraptions with bars and cables and weights. "I never want to see you lift a free-weight like that again in my gym."

"You will not see me do that again," Derrick said.

"That was a lot of weight for your size to lift like that, and it didn't look like it was difficult for you."

Derrick looked at Clark but saw no indication of how he should respond. "It was heavy, but not too bad."

"Clark, put 390 on the bar."

Derrick moved to the bar and lifted it.

"Put 425 on it."

Derrick lifted it.

"We don't have all day. Put 500 on it."

Derrick lifted that too. This time the effort, etched his face.

"Holy crap," Yates said. "We'll call that good enough. We have a few linemen lifting that much weight." Yates wrote on the paper on his clipboard, turned, and walked back to the bench press.

Yates studied Derrick for a moment. "Put 325 on it."

"Seriously?" Clark asked.

Yates did not answer. Derrick moved to the side opposite of where Henry Clark was adding weight and copied the process. When they had finished adding the weights, Derrick slid under the bar, grabbing it with both hands. Simple math was not a problem for him. One hundred pounds more than he had lifted before. But he wasn't sure what an extra hundred pounds would feel like. He took a deep breath, exhaled, and lifted the bar off its perch, holding with arms extended for a moment. Turns out 100 pounds added to 225 is quite a lot. Derrick lowered the bar and pushed it back up. One, two, three, four, five. On the sixth repetition, Derrick heard Coach Yates yelling at him.

"Stop!"

Derrick returned the bar to its perch and sat up.

"What did I tell you, King? Did anyone tell you to keep lifting?"

"No, Coach," Derrick said, with eyes cast to the floor. Looking up, he added, "No one told me not to either, Coach."

A smile spread over Yate's face. "Good point, King. I should also add, if you have questions, don't be afraid to ask." Yates looked at Henry Clark, whose mouth hung open. "What are you thinking, Clark?"

Henry Clark folded his arms across his chest. His jaw muscled flexed. "I'm thinking he needs to learn the offense fast so we can teach him defense. He's an animal."

"My thoughts too," Yates said. "But he hasn't taken a handoff yet. Coach Browning says he's the key to State. So, you and I better get him up to speed fast. Take him to the field and teach him some basics — handoff, dive play, and see if he can catch. Grab Winslow so you can take snaps."

Derrick worried about making the team. Now, Yates wanted him to learn two positions. His hope of pleasing Coach Browning grew dimmer with each passing minute.

The three of them left the gym and walked onto the field, where Derrick and Henry separated from Coach Yates. Henry called out "Winslow" as Yates walked toward Coach Browning, still writing on his clipboard.

The boy named Winslow trotted to the end of the field where Derrick and Henry stood. "This is Sam Winslow," Henry said. "He's about the finest center in the state. He has, what is it now, Sam, 30 college offers?"

"It's six." Sam Winslow stuck out his hand, about twice the size of Derrick's, making for an awkward handshake. "Call me Bull."

"Okay, Sam," Derrick said. "I'm Derrick King."

"I know who you are. What I want to know is why you're here."

"Well, see, I am from Pacific Edge, but I got kicked out because I …"

"I know that. Why are you *here?*" Bull stressed the word here while pointing to the grass at his feet.

"Browning thinks he's running back material," Clark said before Derrick could reply.

"Humph," Bull grunted.

"Let's work on handoffs first," Clark said. Henry showed Derrick how to form what he called a basket with his arms. Bull did the handoff with Henry a few times as a demonstration. Not as challenging as the baton handoff. Henry practiced with Derrick a few times in slow motion.

"Not bad," Henry said. "Now for the plays. You're a halfback, which means your plays will all be a 20 series. So, when the line is here, the holes on the right are even numbers, and the holes on the left are odd. If you go up the center, following Bull, which is not a bad way to go, it's zero. We use two primary formations: pro and spread. There are others, but let's stick with those for now because they make up about 80% of the playbook. If we do a sweep right, it's called a tango. If we sweep left, it's called a foxtrot. For example, say you're the third halfback, your number will be 23. So, if I call a pro 23 1, you're going to run through the hole between Bull and the left guard. Got that?"

Derrick nodded and said, "No."

Bull and Henry Clark laughed hard. It took a few minutes for them to recover.

"Coach will give you a playbook. You'll need to put in extra work until you know all the plays. Until then, your time will be limited. Let's walk through a few plays. You don't have to worry about knowing them. I'll call the play number and explain it to you. Plus, we will go slow. Coach won't let you run plays with the team today, that's for sure."

Clark was doing a good job. It surprised Derrick that Clark was not making life difficult, at least not at the moment. Yesterday, he was ready to kill Derrick, and Clark did not seem thrilled to be helping in the weight room. Nyx had said she would take care of things. Derrick wondered again what magical power she possessed.

Clark was a patient teacher. He did not get upset when Derrick messed up and praised Derrick when he came close to getting it right. Derrick did not know how good of a quarterback Henry Clark was, but he thought Henry would make an exceptional coach one day.

After running several plays, Clark said, "Okay, let's see if you can catch the ball." Henry showed Derrick how to hold his hands and how to hold the ball to throw it back. He put ten yards between them and tossed Derrick the first pass of his football career.

The ball sailed through Derrick's hands.

Derrick chased the ball down and ran back to his place and threw the ball back to Clark. It went high, right, wobbling like a bird with a broken wing. Sam Winslow laughed so hard he went to one knee. Derrick was smiling too, but he did not understand why.

The next two balls also sailed through Derrick's hands, although he managed to touch the third pass. His throws back improved enough that Clark was able to bat them to the ground but not catch them. Derrick grabbed the fourth pass, which was a little high.

After several catches, Clark moved back, placing fifteen yards between them. Derrick caught five in a row, and Henry waved for him to come back. Henry showed him how to catch the ball when he was running away from the line of scrimmage. "This is a timing pass. You understand what that means?"

"No," Derrick admitted.

"Means it's all about timing. In other words, I throw the ball before you turn to look for it, which means if you aren't in the right place at the right time, it's incomplete or worse."

"Worse?" Derrick asked.

"Interception," Henry Clark said.

"What do I do?" Derrick asked, a little worried, a lot excited.

Henry walked him through it. "First, you come up like it's a run. Then you hesitate behind the line and take a quick look to see if anyone is blitzing …"

"Blitzing?" Derrick interrupted.

"Rushing at me. If you see that, you need to block them instead of running the pass route." Henry Clark stared at Derrick for a moment. "Block means you stop them. Coach will teach you more about blocking."

Derrick nodded. Seemed like a lot to decide with so little time. He never knew football players had so many things to process in seconds.

"If no one is blitzing, you run right between the guard and the tackle." Clark pointed to where the guard and tackle would be located and walked through the hole, simulating the play. "Then you sorta sneak five yards, but you need to be running by now. Here is the tricky part. If the linebacker, that's the guy right behind the line, is on your right, you're going to turn left after five yards. If the linebacker is on your left, you turn right. As soon as you make your cut." Clark showed Derrick the degree of the turn. "You look for the pass. If we are on the same page, the ball will be right here when you turn."

"Then what?" Derrick asked.

"Then you catch the ball and brace for a wicked hit." Clark smiled. He thought for a moment and added, "The goal is to run to the end zone. I assume you know that much."

"I do now," Derrick said.

Clark waved Malcolm Cross over. "Malcolm is a corner, but he can sub for a linebacker for this drill."

Derrick had not seen a drill or anything that looked like one. He assumed drill meant something different in this scenario.

Malcolm trotted over. "What do you need?"

"Play linebacker. Let's see if King can catch the ball."

Malcolm glared at Clark for a moment. "Why me? Can't you get a linebacker over here?"

"Maybe because I need to see if you understand the situation," Clark said.

"Right. I understand it well enough," Malcolm said.

Derrick wished he understood the situation.

Clark looked at Derrick. "You can't do this slow. Go full speed, but there won't be any tackles. When Cross touches you, you stop. Means you're down. Questions?"

Derrick thought for a minute, rehearsed what he was supposed to do in his mind, and asked, "What if Malcolm doesn't touch me?"

"Run to the end zone. But you won't have to worry about that happening. We all know that Malcolm is the fastest kid at Potterville High. He might be the fastest guy in California."

The first play, Malcolm lined up on Derrick's right, and Derrick turned left. Soon as he turned, he looked back, and the ball was right there. He did not even get his hands up. The second play was the same as the first. Derrick missed that ball too, but at least he got his hands on it.

"Sorry," Derrick said as he lined up for a third try.

"Don't be sorry. You're making the cut right. You'll get there."

Malcolm moved when the ball was snapped on the next try, and Derrick cut right. This time, he snagged the ball, and Malcolm knocked it out of his hands.

"Hey," Derrick shouted.

Malcolm laughed. "Oh, this is going to be fun."

"Sorry," Derrick said again as he lined up next to Clark.

"Stop saying that. You did great. Cross did what he's supposed to do to break up the pass. No matter how good you get, sometimes the other guy makes a good play. It's what makes the game fun. Just be ready for it and try to get the ball secured soon as you catch it."

On the next try, Cross moved to the right after Derrick crossed the line of scrimmage. Derrick broke left, and the ball was right at his shoulder when he turned. Derrick snagged it, made a hard cut toward the end zone, and ran. He ran to the end zone at the opposite end of the field. As he ran, it occurred to him that Malcolm had let him go and was having a good laugh as he ran almost the full length of the field. But Derrick did not care. He had run for his first touchdown. It was a feeling, unlike anything he had ever felt before.

Derrick slowed as he crossed the finish line and made a slow turn, expecting to see Henry Clark, Malcolm Cross, and Sam Winslow on the ground, laughing. Instead, he saw Malcolm Cross about seven yards behind him.

"Holy crap, King. Coach Browning's right. I don't know how he sees this stuff. It's like he's a time traveler or something."

Derrick slowed to a trot.

"Fastest man in pads," Malcolm said. "It's a thing. Some people are fast on the track, but they get faster in pads. You've never run that fast in the 100. I had an angle, and you still pulled away. I might become a believer after all."

"Believer?"

"Never mind," Malcolm said.

The two boys trotted back. "What do you mean about Coach Browning?" Derrick asked.

"He sees talent that no one else sees. Like Henry. Henry was an average linebacker all the years we played together growing up. Might not have been a starter in high school. But two weeks after we started in fall camp with Coach, he called Henry over and said he was going to play quarterback. Gave him a playbook and told him to have it memorized by Monday. Henry worked his tail off his freshman year and got on the field a few times in the fourth quarter when we had a blowout. Coach let him attempt one pass, and it was intercepted. Would have been a touchdown, except Henry flattened the guy near the sideline. Got flagged for unnecessary roughness. That turned out to not be such a bad thing because every defense in the conference heard about it." Malcolm laughed.

"That summer, Henry drove the running backs and receivers nuts because he wanted them to run routes every day, sometimes twice a day. He studied film all summer. By fall, he knew the playbook better than Browning. He beat out our senior QB last year. We lost in district to the team that won state. Henry has two years left and already has half a dozen college offers. No one saw that talent in Henry. Only Browning. He's a football wizard, I tell you."

"What happened, Cross?" Clark asked.

Cross shrugged his shoulders. "Fastest man in pads, dude. Fastest man in pads."

Before Clark could respond, a loud whistle sounded, and Browning yelled, "To me!"

53

DERRICK THOUGHT PRACTICE WAS OVER, but errors in his thinking were common and did not appear to be slowing down. They were just getting started. Coach Browning told them to line up, and everyone knew how to do that except Derrick. A hand grabbed his elbow from behind, and a voice said, "Over here, King, with the other RBs." That voice belonged to Larry Kinkead. Coach Browning barked commands, and every player responded. Derrick was a step behind because he had to watch the others, except for running in place — that command was self-explanatory, as was down and up. Browning pushed them hard. Sweat ran into Derrick's eyes, his muscles burned, and he fought for breath. He saw two kids vomit, but they returned to the workout soon as they finished.

Just when Derrick thought he could take no more, Coach blew his whistle. "Catch your breath and first-string offense and defense line up. Except for you, Kinkead. I'm running King through some plays."

Kinkead leaned close to Derrick and whispered, "You're not taking my spot, King. You got that?"

Derrick was not sure what he should say, but he maintained eye contact with Kinkead. Derrick said, "Not my choice, is it? I'll do my best, and you do the same. Coach will decide."

Kinkead gave a slight nod of his head but did not seem to endorse Derrick's statement. "You'd better line up, Chosen boy."

Coach Browning lined up the offense and the defense. Gave them instructions on how scrimmage would work. First, Coach would tell Derrick the name of the play, then he explained the play, and then he walked Derrick through it. Derrick heard groans from several players. It seemed clear they were not used to this repetitive slow-motion process. He needed to learn that playbook. They ran the same play, between the center and the guard on the left side of the line and on the right side of the line several times, each time a little faster than the last.

"Okay, gentlemen. We are going full speed now. QB and RB are still touch only. We are not live. Questions?"

"Why no contact on the RB, Coach?" Red Badowski, Jim Priests' ruddy-complexioned friend, asked.

"Two reasons, Badowski. First, because this is King's first practice, and he hasn't been coached on any contact elements of the game. Second, because I said so. You have a problem with that?"

"No, Coach," Badowski said under his breath.

"On three," Henry Clark said.

On three, Derrick broke hard for the line. He took the handoff, and a nice hole opened where it was supposed to be. Sam Winslow pushed Badowski to one side. Derrick spotted the linebacker. For now, he was supposed to cut one way or the other when he reached what Coach called the second level. As Derrick was even with Sam Winslow, an arm the size of Derrick's leg caught him below the neck and slammed him to the ground. Derrick was certain the blow killed him.

Coach Browning stood over him, pulling on the belt of his pants. "Breathe, son. You got the wind knocked out of you. You'll be okay in a minute. Relax and breathe."

Coach was right. Derrick got air back into his lungs and recovered. After a few moments, he felt fine. It seemed quite amazing.

When Derrick stood, Browning spun around and said, "What was that, Badowski?"

"Uh, sorry, Coach. Reflex, I guess."

"Don't 'sorry' me, Red."

Derrick would later learn that when Coach stopped using one's last name, it meant trouble.

"To the bench, Red. Later, I'll decide if you're still on the first string." Coach Browning pointed to the sideline.

Derrick looked at Coach, then at Badowski, and then at Clark.

"Coach, I'd like to have him stay," Derrick said, confusing himself with the statement.

"King, I'm the coach here," Browning fumed.

Derrick's confusion dissipated. "No disrespect, Coach. Seems that tackling the running back is the standard practice. So, Badowski was doing what he had been taught. And if I'm to make the team, if I can help the team, I must learn fast. I would like to run it for real, if that's okay with you, Coach."

Browning looked at Yates. Yates shrugged. Browning turned to Badowski and said, "This does not get you out of the doghouse, Red. Got that?"

"Yes, Coach," Badowski said. "Uh, you still want me on the bench?"

Browning looked at Derrick and said, "No, stay. King might as well test himself against the best. Seems like that's what he wants. Huddle up. We are live. Except the QB. I suppose you remember which player that is, Badowski?"

A few snickers coursed through the offense.

Derrick stood near the line of scrimmage, unsure what to do. The other offensive players turned their backs and grouped 10 yards from him.

Badowski crossed the line of scrimmage and leaned in close to Derrick and said, "I hear your sister doesn't swim well." Badowski chuckled. "This will be great."

"King!" Clark waved for Derrick to join the group.

"You don't understand what you opened yourself up to," Clark said.

"I will find out soon," Derrick replied. It should have scared him, at least made him anxious but it did not. That odd calm overcame him. He did not understand it. The small voice of the old Derrick King, the Pacific Edge Derrick King, tried to raise the alarm in his head, but the new Derrick King, this stranger in his head, the Potterville Derrick King, refused to listen. However, he wondered how Red Badowski knew about Miriam.

Clark called the play and gave Derrick a few pointers. "You can use one arm, like this, to shove a defender off you. That won't work with Badowski. He's too big, too strong, too fast. And the most important thing is to protect the ball, which means you can't risk not having both hands on the ball when you hit the line. Main thing is, keep your legs moving. You want to go forward, not backward. Questions?"

Derrick had many questions, but this was not the time to ask them. At the top of the list: *Why am I doing this?*

"We going to run the play today?" Browning hollered.

Clark yelled break, and the team members took their positions. Clark motioned Derrick into his place. Winslow snapped the ball, Derrick bolted toward the line, missed the handoff, and the ball bounced on the ground, and Clark fell on it.

Browning blew his whistle. "Again. Hang onto the ball, King."

Badowski met Derrick at the line and said, "Good decision, King. You don't want to run through my line with the ball in your hands."

The offense didn't huddle. Clark said something to Derrick that no one else could hear. This time, Derrick took the handoff, but where he was supposed to run was blocked with bodies. He ran into the guard's back, where he stopped until Badowski burst through and tackled Derrick five yards behind the line of scrimmage.

"You want to go the other direction, King. Pay attention. If that hole isn't open, look for one that is." It was Yates this time. He had positioned himself behind the offense.

"Yes, sir," King said. "I did not understand that was allowed."

That made everyone laugh, including Browning. Browning did not seem mad. Derrick understood why everyone laughed. It sounded stupid the moment the words left his mouth. Two plays, both for lost yardage, from the guy Browning was sticking his neck out for. Derrick did not understand why Browning was not fuming.

Henry Clark lined up the offense a third time. Derrick did two things right, taking the handoff and securing the ball. It occurred to Derrick, even at that moment, how things slowed down in his mind, watching the ball coming from Clark as if in slow motion. A slender opening appeared between the center and the guard that he thought he might squeeze through. Sam Winslow pushed Red Badowski in a magnificent struggle. Then everything changed. Badowski pushed Winslow aside like a toy and came at Derrick, shoulder lowered. Derrick braced for the collision, wrapping both arms around the ball, lowering his shoulder, churning his legs as Clark had told him. Things got worse.

Badowski walloped Derrick hard from the right, and a split second later, a linebacker smacked him from the left. Then someone hit him head-on. He ended up at the bottom of the pile with clumps of grass coming through his helmet. A muffled whistle sounded. Derrick felt the weight that pinned him to the ground lighten as players removed themselves from the pile.

Derrick stood and found himself face to face with Browning. "Sorry, Coach."

"What are you sorry about, King?"

"I got tackled, Coach. I'll do better." Derrick fought back a tear.

Browning shook his head. He smiled. "King, they're going to tackle you on most plays. Times that you'll take it to the house will be rare."

Derrick did not know why he would take the ball home but decided now was not the time to ask.

"King, where was the ball before the play?"

Derrick looked around, realized he had not been paying much attention to that and understood that not knowing was not good. "Uh, on the 20-yard line, I think."

"Correct, King. Where is the ball now?"

Derrick studied the field for a moment. "The 26-yard line?"

"Correct again, King. Son, there was nothing there. Not your fault, mind you. Badowski here is an animal. Winslow is getting better all the time, but he rarely gets Badowski blocked out of a play. Not to mention, Van Burton," Browning pointed at the linebacker, "met you at the line of scrimmage too. Then Cross joined them. You pushed three of the best defensive guys I have ever coached six yards. If we gain six yards on every play, we are state champions. Understand, King?"

Derrick gave a slight nod. He was not sure he understood. He got tackled, and he thought he was supposed to not be tackled. Six yards did not seem like much.

"You did great, King. That's what I'm trying to tell you." Browning turned to the defense. "You let the RB push you guys six yards. That, gentlemen, is not acceptable."

Derrick felt more confused than ever. Browning wanted that six yards. Browning was unhappy about those six yards.

Browning said, "One more play, Clark. Your choice."

"Huddle!" Clark called.

Derrick joined the huddle. He noticed Akira, Nyx, and Antonio Morales watching from the bleachers.

Clark called the play by number and explained it, which Derrick recognized was for his benefit.

"King, this is the pass play I taught you a few minutes ago. The defense will not think we'd try throwing you a pass so soon. So, remember how it goes. Act like you're taking a handoff. Check for a blitz. Next slide between the guard and the tackle, five yards, cut right or left depending on the linebacker's position. Soon as you turn, the ball will be there. On two. Break."

This time, Derrick was nervous. Lots of things to keep straight in his head. Lots of things could happen. Most of them were bad. This time, Clark stood back several yards behind the center. On two, Derrick saw the ball fly between the center's legs. In flight, spinning toward Clark, Derrick counted each time the laces came into view. Clark caught the ball. Derrick broke for the line. Slowly, Clark reached the ball out to Derrick, paused for a moment before pulling the ball back in and disappearing out of Derrick's field of vision. As Derrick watched the fake handoff, he also surveyed the defense and saw no one coming hard toward him. So, he trotted through the line, as if he were merely completing the ruse. The linebacker was to his right, which meant Derrick turned left. Then he broke hard. He had done something wrong. The ball was high and sailing past him. Derrick sensed the linebacker coming hard from the right. Derrick slowed things down more.

With one hand, Derrick stretched for the ball, snagging it at the last moment. Then he ran.

A defensive player was coming fast on his right. As the player dove for Derrick's legs, Derrick moved left, and the defender grabbed arms full of air before hitting the ground. Another defender was coming on the right, and Derrick had run out of room on the sideline for another dodge. Before the impending impact, Derrick stuck his arm straight, placed his hand on the defender's helmet, and pushed him hard to the ground. Only green grass between him and the goal line.

It was one of the most beautiful things he'd ever seen.

54

AMONG DECISIONS DERRICK WOULD LATER regret was not showering after practice. He stuffed helmet, shoulder pads, and football shoes into his locker, and crammed everything else in his backpack. He put on running shorts, shoes, and a t-shirt and kept his phone in a pocket, but not his wallet. He should have been exhausted but thought he'd go for a run and then go home and shower. As he left the locker room, he remembered he did not have a home.

Nyx was waiting in the gym. "That was quick."

"I did not shower," Derrick said. "I hope Coach Browning doesn't mind me showering at his house."

"He'll accommodate that. You'll need to shower if you're living there." Nyx pushed Derrick's shoulder. "Everyone will need to make a lot of adjustments with you there. It won't be easy. It doesn't even seem real."

Derrick considered what Nyx said. She was right. This was all crazy. He should have gone home. That is when things got worse.

Outside the gym, Jim Priest leaned against the building. One of his buddies, not Badowski, stood nearby. "Here's the big man now, Josh," Jim Priest said. "Plus, his bodyguard, the runner."

Derrick felt fear and then anger. Both at Jim Priest and at himself. Nyx was *the runner*. When they called out the runner and threw a bottle against the condo building, he thought it was about him. Everything was about him. Center of the universe. He hated that about himself.

"Ignore him," Nyx whispered as they approached the pair.

"Shove it, Nyx. I don't take orders from you. Now, why don't you run along home and let us take care of this little problem here?" Jim Priest pushed off the building.

Derrick thought Priest's hair looked greasier than usual if that were possible.

"Leave her alone," Derrick said, dropping his backpack to the ground.

"Oh, King to the rescue. Big man from Pacific Edge. Blindsides a Carver and now he's a big deal," Priest hissed.

Nyx grabbed Derrick by the elbow. "Fighting will get you kicked off the track and football teams. Ignore him."

"So, King is a football player now? It would be too bad if Mr. Big Shot got kicked off the team, wouldn't it?"

Priest circled one direction, and his buddy, Josh, circled the opposite so that Derrick could not see them both at the same time. Derrick turned and twisted his neck, trying to track both.

Things got worse. From the gym door, came a familiar voice that sent a chill up Derrick's spine.

"Priest!"

It was Red Badowski. Derrick realized how difficult it would be for him to stay in Potterville. His optimism faded. Living in Potterville might not work after all. It might prove impossible.

"Red," Jim Priest said. "Join us. King is trying to start a fight."

"I doubt that," Badowski said. "There will be no fight."

Jim Priest's expression changed to a blank stare, but his face grew deep red, and his lip curled into a snarl as Badowski stepped in front of Derrick. "Red, we've been friends since the first grade. You're siding up with this infidel?"

"He's on the team," Badowski said.

"That erases years of friendship?"

"It means he's on the team. Our team. And we need him. We can win State this year."

Priest spit on the ground. "Big deal, Badowski. You can go to State without this traitor."

"Maybe. Maybe not. Either way, I may not like him, but he's on the team. There won't be a fight. Not today, or any other day."

Priest said, "Maybe there will still be a fight, and you'll both get kicked off the team."

Badowski said nothing.

"You and King beat me up. That would get both of you off the team."

"I need a scholarship to go to college, Jim. You know that," Badowski said.

"You will get a scholarship, even if the team doesn't go to State," Priest said. "Besides, forget college. Join the military with me like we have talked about."

"Like you talked about. I'm going to college," Badowski said.

"Why? What will you do in college? Try to hook up with some cast-off Chosen chicks?"

"Play football. And get an education. Become an engineer. Learn something so I can help people here," Badowski said.

"Like that's going to happen. We will never be Chosen, so the military is the best life for us. Room and board, plus you get to keep your money. Here, they just suck you dry. Besides, your dad was in the military. He would be proud of you," Priest said.

"I never met my dad. He died in the Middle East when I was a baby. Fighting so the Ones stay rich. I've told you before, I'm not interested."

Derrick heard a quiver in Badowski's voice.

Badowski said, "I need a scholarship. Better offers if we go to State."

"Who cares? That means nothing to me," Priest said.

"Means a lot to me. If you go after King, you gotta go through me. And that would be a bad idea."

Priest paused and said, "Screw you, Red. You can't protect him all the time. And our friendship is over. You hear me? Over!"

Derrick watched Jim Priest and his friend Josh turn the corner of the school and disappear. "You did not have to do that," Derrick said.

"Don't read too much into it. I still don't like you. But you're a teammate."

Derrick nodded. "Thanks, anyway."

"Everything okay?" Coach Browning asked as he came out of the gym door.

"Everything is fine," Badowski said. He turned to Derrick. "See you on the field tomorrow."

"Count on it," Derrick said, not knowing he was wrong.

Browning walked up to Derrick and Nyx. When Badowski was far enough away, Browning asked, "What was that about?"

Before Derrick could speak, Nyx said, "Just that jerk, Priest. It's okay. We took care of it. And Red was being helpful."

Browning smiled. "Good enough. Follow me to my car, King. I'll introduce you to the family and get you settled in."

"Coach, can Derrick come with me to the bistro? I'll walk him to your house when we are done."

"Okay. I suppose you two have a lot to talk about." Browning winked.

"Thanks, Coach," Derrick said.

55

NYX AND DERRICK WALKED IN SILENCE to the bistro. The sun warmed his face. Birds sang in the trees. Flowers of red, yellow, pink, and purple sprang out everywhere. Although she was silent, he sensed no coldness from Nyx. The encounter with Jim Priest kept circling back into his mind. He was not afraid of Jim Priest, but he feared he could be removed from track and football should a conflict occur.

"Would Coach remove me from the team even if I did not start a fight but was protecting myself? I have a right to protect myself. Don't I?"

Nyx remained silent for several seconds and said, "Depends."

"What does that mean?" Derrick asked.

"A lot of things. How hard did you try to avoid the fight? How many witnesses? Did you break the other kid's jaw? To name a few," Nyx said.

"I don't want to fight. I want to move forward. You know what I mean?"

Nyx remained silent.

Derrick held the door open for Nyx as they stepped into the bistro. Another fragrance replaced the scent of spring. Food. Freshly baked bread, soups, meats, pies. Derrick realized he was starving.

"If it isn't two of my favorite people," Donna said.

Derrick smiled. "Hi, Donna."

"Perfect timing. I pulled a fresh batch of cinnamon rolls from the oven. I had a special order. I rarely make them this late in the day. Want one?"

Derrick looked at Nyx and said, "Yes, we do."

"Is it true what I heard?" Donna asked.

"Maybe. Depends on what you heard," Derrick said.

"I heard that people from Pacific Edge came to take you back, but you said no. I also heard you would live with Coach Browning. Lord knows where he's going to fit you in with that house full of kids. That man has a big heart."

"Both are true," Derrick said. "I am sorry I have lied to you, Donna. I wanted to tell you, but it sounds like news travels faster than I can get around to make amends." It felt good, telling the truth. "House full of kids?"

"Apology accepted. You didn't know? Coach has five kids ranging from two to fourteen. It will be quite a change for you, I suspect."

Derrick nodded, opened his backpack, and pulled out his wallet. "Two sodas also, please."

"Your money's no good here, Mr. King." Donna winked.

"No, please let me pay, Donna. I'd like to do that."

Donna nodded, took a ten from Derrick's hand, and gave him change.

"Grab your drinks. I'll bring the cinnamon roll," Donna said.

Derrick and Nyx went to a table outside.

"Five kids? What if Mr. Browning's wife says no?" Derrick asked.

"I doubt that will happen," Nyx said.

"Why do you say that?" Derrick asked.

"Because she likes you. At least that's what I hear."

"But how …"

Donna came through the door with a plate weighted down with the largest cinnamon roll Derrick had ever seen.

Donna set the plate on the table. "Don't worry. This is an extra."

After Donna left, Nyx said, "Alice Schilling is Browning's wife. She kept her maiden name. Kids say it's obvious that she likes you."

Derrick paused, his fork speared through a chunk of cinnamon roll, frosting dripping on the table. "But Ms. Schilling is Caucasian, and Coach is …"

Nyx glared at Derrick. "Is what, Derrick?"

Derrick saw fire in Nyx's dark eyes. He considered her perfect olive-colored skin and realized he did not know her ethnic heritage. He also realized he had never thought much about the color of her skin, or the color of Akira's skin, or the color of Antonio Morales' skin, the color of Malcolm Cross's skin, or the color of Coach Browning's skin. Suddenly, he recognized the subliminal messages of New America Media that had shaped his thinking. So far, he had been too scared and self-absorbed in his own problems to worry about skin color. He realized the people who had first accepted him, the people who befriended him even when they knew him to be a liar, were all people of color.

Derrick paused. "I would have never guessed that they were married in a million years. And, well — it's marvelous."

Nyx's face softened a little. "You're dripping."

"I'm what?"

Nyx pointed at the frosting as it dripped onto the table.

Derrick took a bite and then another. The cinnamon roll was disappearing. Nyx took a few morsels, leaving most of it to Derrick. When the roll was almost gone, she said, "You're not out of the woods yet. You understand that, right?"

Derrick had not given it much thought. Not that he hadn't been thinking, but for him, coming clean was the biggest hurdle. His life would not be easy, yet he was excited about the challenges ahead of him.

"What's next?" Derrick asked.

"Not sure," Nyx said. "Some decisions need to be made."

"Decisions?" Derrick said.

"Yes. I can't explain it to you now. You'll have to face Malcolm and Henry, and many others, but not on the football field. However, what you did today on the field won't hurt you. I can tell you that much."

After finishing their roll and drinks, they walked back toward Coach Browning's home. Derrick remained silent, his mind spinning on Nyx's last statement about decisions, wondering what decisions remained. He decided to stay in Potterville. Maybe Potterville had to decide if he could. He wanted to stay. So many things were important to him here that did not exist in Pacific Edge, purpose, friendship, freedom. The thought of Potterville rejecting him frightened him, yet he also recognized a deep-seated confidence that he would be okay even if he had to start over.

His thoughts swirled around these two possibilities, preventing consideration of a third.

Part Three

1

COACH BROWNING WAS IN FRONT OF his house playing catch with a boy who looked to be 14. The eldest son, Derrick assumed. A white picket fence, typical of homes in the area, surrounded a lawn strewn with brightly colored toys. Derrick and Nyx stopped outside the gate.

"Delivered as promised," Nyx said. She turned to Derrick. "I'll see you in the morning."

Derrick swung his backpack off and set it inside the fence. He glanced over his shoulder at Nyx as she walked away.

Coach Browning trotted to the fence. "Derrick, this is Terrance, my oldest. Terrance, this is Derrick King."

Terrance came to the fence and shook Derrick's hand. The handshake was pleasant, but Derrick sensed some animosity, which seemed normal under the conditions. "Glad to meet you, Terrance."

"Want to toss a few balls before dinner?" Browning asked.

Derrick should have been exhausted, but the sugar must have caused a burst of energy. "Coach, I'd like to go for a run if that's okay."

"Seriously? You haven't had enough for one day? Are you nervous about meeting the family?" Browning waved his hand toward the house.

"It's not that, Coach, but I have a lot of things on my mind. Running helps me sort them out."

"Dinner is at seven. Don't be late. Okay?"

"Yes, Coach. I will be back," Derrick said, and he added, "I am looking forward to meeting your family. Well, I guess I have met your wife, but the kids, except for Terrance, who I just met. Well, anyway, what I am trying to say is thanks for taking me in, Coach."

Browning nodded, gave Derrick a slight smile, and said, "You are most welcome, son."

Derrick ran toward the river and the mountain path. He checked his watch: 5:30 p.m. He wanted to run to the top of the mountain ridge where he sat overlooking the valley with Nyx, but he would not have time for that. He wanted to get up the mountain far enough to contemplate things for a moment. It would upset Nyx if she learned he was unescorted, but no one knew his whereabouts. No spies, no Pacific Edge cameras on the mountain.

What could go wrong?

Derrick stopped on the footbridge and gazed at the water for a moment. The clear stream rushed over multicolored rocks the river had polished. Looking upstream, he saw a bend where the water slowed, turning deep blue, which he assumed meant the water was deeper. He wondered why he had failed to notice such things before. He wondered how he knew the water was deep.

Derrick ran through the woods. The trail twisted and turned. Occasionally, he hurdled a log in the path.

Free.

It occurred to him that his mind was clear. Maybe that was the point all along. Just running. Muscles and lungs and heart all working together in harmony.

Free.

Not thinking, no worries, at least for a brief time. He had plenty to worry about, but not right now.

Free.

He turned a corner. The forest gave way to a small meadow, where the trail laid a straight course toward the mountains.

That is when he saw it.

A Pacific Edge hovercraft blocked the trail.

2

A PACIFIC EDGE SECURITY OFFICER STOOD in front of the hovercraft. Derrick did not see a second officer. That seemed strange. The officer took two steps toward Derrick. The man held a long black rod in his hand. Derrick did not know its purpose.

"Derrick, I'm Officer Jarvis," the man said. "I am here to take you back to Pacific Edge. I am afraid you never had a choice. Tribunal's orders."

"You have no jurisdiction here," Derrick said. "The sheriff said so."

The man laughed and said, "The sheriff isn't here. Seems like he does not understand reality."

"I am not going." Derrick took a step back. Thinking hard. The officer could not outrun him. The hovercraft could not maneuver through the trees. Once he reached the river, the hovercraft would be visible to the people of Potterville. If he made it across the bridge, he had a chance.

The officer smiled.

Before Derrick turned to run, he heard a crackling sound. Then a thunderbolt, unlike anything he had ever felt, struck him in the back.

White hot, muscles frozen, and then, nothing.

3

WHEN DERRICK AWOKE, EVERY FIBER OF his body ached. His head pounded, and his vision blurred. He remained still, trying to determine where he was. His head rested on a black rubber-like surface, and a black steel bar inches from his face. Wind ruffled his hair. Beyond the black steel bar, pine trees rushed by. He was on the hovercraft. *How long have I been out? How far are we from Potterville?*

He heard voices, jumbled at first, as if his ears were filled with cotton. Gradually, the voices became clear.

"You should not have hit him with that much voltage." Derrick recognized the voice of Officer Jarvis.

"Asshole deserved it. Refusing the offer to return to Pacific Edge like that. Who does he think he is?"

"Still, it will be our heads if he's hurt. You heard the orders."

"Yeah, yeah. He'll be all right. I think." The man laughed.

Derrick moved his head to take in the craft's orientation. He saw the back of a man's boots. Jarvis must be piloting the craft, which meant Derrick had one man to fight. Lifting his head, a little, peering between the man's legs, he saw they were flying over the river. Slowly, cautiously, silently, Derrick rose to his feet. Up ahead, Derrick saw a bend in the river where dark blue water swirled. Not much time.

"You should have used more voltage," Derrick said.

Both officers twisted their heads, shock on their faces. The back-sneaking officer turned toward Derrick and reached for the device he must have used earlier. Unwise decision.

Derrick hit the man once. His head snapped back, and he crumpled to the floor of the craft. Blood streamed from his face. Derrick looked at Jarvis. Jarvis turned white.

"I said, I'm not going." Derrick climbed over the railing.

And jumped into the dark blue water.

4

THE WATER RAN DEEP, BUT WHEN Derrick's feet hit the bottom, he pushed himself to the surface. The current carried him downstream. Turning in the water, he saw the hovercraft following him. His chances of escape were nil like this. They would keep him in sight until reinforcements arrived and that would not take long. Escape required something different.

He turned, swimming downstream with no delusion that he could elude the hovercraft. Ahead, he saw thick brush overhanging the river. Derrick took a deep breath and dove deep. He fought hard across the current, the water dark and cold. His lungs burned, and his limbs ached.

He surfaced under the bush, and branches scratched his head. The current dragged him through the limbs and would soon carry him back to open water. Driving his hands into the brush, he grabbed at the thin branches, which collapsed in his grip and slipped through his hands but slowed his progress downstream. He grabbed a thick branch that allowed enough purchase for him to stop.

Derrick could not see the sky, but the water twisted him toward the bank, and he did not know how well he was hidden. He could not hear the hovercraft above the rushing water. Switching the position of his hands, the current turned him toward open water. He could not see much, which meant they could not see him. At least, that was his theory.

Something appeared a few inches above the surface of the river. The black platform of the hovercraft inched along a few feet from where he held tight to a limb. His feet now numb. He could not stay in the water much longer. The hovercraft moved out of sight, but Derrick did not know its location. The cold overcame him. He may have waited too long. Thrashing toward the other bank, his legs almost useless and his arms felt like rags. Halfway across, he knew he would not make it.

No strength left.

At least I did not let them take me.

Will anyone find my body out here? I told Red Badowski that I'd see him on the field tomorrow.

Nyx, I'm sorry I left Coach Browning's without you.

He gave up and sank into the stream.

A remarkable thing happened.

His knees scraped along the rocky bottom. Derrick stood waist-deep in the stream on unsteady legs and then stumbled out of the river. Wilderness survival was not his strong suit, as he almost drowned in three feet of water. Making his way up the bank, he spotted a tall pine tree whose large branches stretched out low and hugged the ground. He crawled under the branches and leaned against the trunk, and his entire body shivered. His feet and hands burned. Wrapping his arms around his chest, he studied his location. Only the edge of the riverbank closest to him was visible. He was out of sight, for now.

Warmth spread over his face. A most unnatural feeling. He reached up and touched his hair and then looked at his hand. Bright red. His head became light. Then, nothing.

When Derrick awoke again, his head rested against the tree trunk. *How long was I out?* No way to know. He touched his head again and felt something tacky. Leaning forward, he removed his shirt and wiped his head. It came back red. He rubbed more, grimacing as he touched his wounds. The shirt was redder still. An idea came to him.

He eased from under the tree and glanced up and down the canyon. Nothing. The sun disappeared below the mountain crest, the sky glowed orange. The time spent in the icy water must have cleared his mind because despite passing out, his thinking cleared. Weird as it seemed, he felt different.

He found a large stick, threaded his shirt onto it so it would not drift away and waded into the stream to a large snag of drifted limbs and trees. The cold water swirled around his waist as he lodged the stick with his blood-stained shirt into the snarled deadwood, watching for a few minutes to ensure it remained visible. The water did not seem as cold now. Still, he knew staying in the water was dangerous.

Back on the bank, deciding to go upstream, he worked his way into the woods until he found a trail. Not a trail like the one he ran on outside of Potterville. This trail was narrow, primitive. Maybe only animals used it. He wondered what sort of animals. Brush had overgrown the trail and where there was no brush, the tall grass made it difficult to see. Often, when forced to duck under a bush, the branches scratched at his bare back. When the trail opened, he ran. Running warmed him.

He watched the sky and listened to the sound of the river, trying to decipher any change to the noise that might denote an approaching hovercraft. The trail took him away from the river about fifty yards when he heard a hovercraft mix with the sounds of the forest. He ducked behind a tree and watched. A hovercraft appeared over the mountains and dropped into the canyon. A second machine, like the one that came for him yesterday, trailed the first. He watched the machines ease downstream until they paused above where his blood-red shirt drifted in the water. They moved on. Derrick waited until both machines were out of sight. He smiled as he ran along the trail. He did not know where he was going but felt confident it was the right direction to escape from the hovercraft, yet he sensed he was getting farther from town.

The trail continued up the canyon, sometimes next to the river, sometimes closer to the canyon wall. It concerned Derrick that he might not hear an approaching hovercraft, so he kept his eyes on the sky, sometimes stopping to turn a full circle. As the sun edged behind the crest of a mountain, colors faded to gray, rocks and roots blended together. He tripped a few times but caught himself before falling.

Derrick's hope of getting back to Potterville faded with the light. He would spend the night out here, cold, wet, and shirtless. The Pacific Edge Derrick King would have been distraught about his personal discomfort. Different things worried the Potterville Derrick King: that Coach Browning would be worried and that he would not be at football practice as he had proclaimed to Red Badowski. But mostly he wondered if he could get back to Potterville without being captured. He wondered if Nyx would worry about him. Maybe not. A relief to have him gone. Problem solved.

Running slowed to trotting, trotting slowed to walking. Not because he was fatigued, but anything faster than walking became unsafe, the trail difficult to see. The darkness fell fast. The trail ended at the base of a large pile of boulders strewn from the canyon wall to the river. No way around them. The previous mile had provided little cover. He hoped to find shelter for the night. Leaving his blood-stained shirt spinning in the river seemed like a great idea. Now he wished he had it back.

Crossing this mound of stone did not appeal to him because it provided no cover should the hovercraft return. It would be slow going and a wrong step might cause a twisted ankle or worse. He did not like it, but he had to make it to the other side to find shelter.

Turning a slow circle, he inspected the sky before starting over the rocks. Light radiated from the horizon. He looked but saw no good cover. He scurried to the closest scrubby tree and crouched behind it. The light on the horizon grew brighter but not at the speed of approaching hovercraft. *Perhaps a flying armada? What on Earth?*

The light grew brighter still.

Then he saw it.

The first sliver of a full moon materialized over the mountain crest.

Idiot. He chuckled and shook his head.

Shivering in the darkness, watching the moon rise. How much time had he wasted? He made his way back to the boulders. Moonlight made the mound easier to see. It sloped upward toward the canyon wall and tapered down to water's edge. Part of the canyon wall may have fallen, but there was no missing section of canyon wall that accounted for the huge pile of rocks. It made little sense. The rocks varied from about three feet to over five feet in diameter. Some boulders he could climb over without difficulty, and sometimes he maneuvered to work around a larger stone. Once on the pile, he saw some boulders were not rock but chunks of concrete, which often had pieces of steel rods protruding from them. The steel rods made for good handholds but were dangerous if he were to slip, and the concrete's presence made little sense. He knew very little about geology, but he knew concrete wasn't a rock. It was man-made. The climb was slow going. He scanned the sky every few minutes. When he had reached the pinnacle, the other side came into view.

The moonlight reflected off an unnatural sight.

A road.

No road existed on the side from which he came. The road ran straight to the pile of rocks. He breathed a little easier. The road might lead him out. He turned a circle, checking the sky before heading to the road. Although shadows made it difficult to make out details, he reached the highest point of the misplaced rocks and concrete.

He took one last look over his shoulder before starting down to the road. That's when he saw a light coming. Going backward, forward, or toward the river was useless. He could not get off the rocks before they spotted him. He headed toward the canyon wall, which was closer than the river, plus there was no place to hide by the river. The machine grew louder. The lights moved back and forth, casting brilliant circles of light. When he dared move no further, he scrunched behind the biggest rock he could see. For a second, everything around him was lit as if it were day. But the light moved on. He watched the machine move farther downstream. When the light moved almost out of sight, he started toward the road again, but this side of the pile proved more difficult because the rocks were in the moonlight's shadow. He felt his way, worried about stepping on a steel rod or into a hole. Twice he stepped wrong, and his leg slipped between the rocks, once scraping his shin. Warm blood trickled down his leg and into his shoe. The second wrong step twisted his ankle.

He slowed. A broken leg would be the death of him — right here, right now. Just out for a run before dinner. Thinking he was free. *How could I be so stupid? No time to feel sorry for yourself. Keep moving. Stay focused.*

When he glanced to check the hovercraft's location, he saw it had turned back toward him. He reversed course toward the canyon wall. When the hovercraft grew close, he laid on his side with his back toward a large stone. He watched as the light crawled over the rocks. Near the canyon wall, he saw a black spot. A hole. Perhaps a place to hide for tonight. Or until the patrols gave up.

If they gave up.

With the light moving away, he started moving again. They would look at where the light was shining, not back into the darkness. He made it to the black spot. The hovercraft crossed the river, moving downstream. The bottom was not visible in the blackness. He did not know if it was five feet deep or fifty.

Something occurred to him.

He touched the back pocket of his shorts. It amazed him he had not lost his cellphone in the river. It probably would not work. The hovercraft moved slowly about fifty yards away. If he laid flat on the rock, the hovercraft was out of his sight. So, he crawled to the rock's edge and pushed the button on the side to wake it up. A faint light indicated the phone still lived, and the light from the screen showed a rock about four feet down. Putting his phone in his pocket, he lowered himself over the side until his feet reached a solid stone. Then he turned his back to the rock and sat.

He pulled his phone out, shielding the screen with his hand. In the upper left-hand corner, small words said: NO SERVICE. *Great.* But he had a light, so that was something. And if he got out of here, he would find service. Then he could call for help. Patience became the key to survival.

Standing, he peeked over the rock. A second hovercraft had joined the first, passing over the river. Both machines moved side by side, searching. A third machine appeared and joined the others. Soon they would be right on top of him. Exposed for sure. He scrambled to the edge of the rock and tried to peer into the darkness.

He smelled the harsh odor of the machines. Using the light from his screen, he tried to see the next landing, but the light did not reach far enough into the darkness. The flashlight feature was too bright to risk using. Nothing should be deeper than the largest stone, which was about five feet. That meant he would not fall far. That was his theory. He didn't know much about theories. They didn't teach them at the academy.

He lowered himself over the side. His toes touched the surface below, which meant that this stone was about seven feet in diameter. His size estimate was off a little. No big deal. Next ledge, same problem. The light could not penetrate the darkness. He was within five feet of the canyon wall. A black hole below him. Once he was at the bottom, however far that was, they still might see him when they flew over. But he would be difficult to see. At least that was his theory.

No place else to go. His lone hope was that a fissure existed down there into which he might crawl.

Light blazed above him onto the canyon wall.

No time.

He eased over the side. His feet dangled in the air.

A light moved above him.

No choice.

He let go.

He fell.

5

DERRICK DID NOT KNOW HOW FAR he fell. It seemed like forever but was only a few seconds. It wasn't a free fall because part way down, he slid along a large stone and then fell again. But the moment terrified him. He had no control. When his feet hit the ground, pain shot through both feet and into his legs. He crumpled on the ground as the white-hot light passed overhead. He saw an arched outline above him. The ground beneath him was flat but not dirt. He moved away from the light, scooting back on his butt. The lights did not reach him but reflected off the rocks enough to dimly illuminate the surrounding space.

A cave.

A very large cave.

He moved back further until he reached the edge of darkness. He watched as the lights tried and failed to penetrate the hole into which he fell. He stood and turned. Behind him was total darkness. He held his hand to his face and could not see it. One more step might send him into a hole hundreds of feet deep.

Or he might step on a snake.

Snakes had not occurred to him.

Time to activate his phone flashlight. With the light on, he saw the surface of a road. But caves did not have roads. He scraped at the ground with his shoe. It still looked like a road. He moved the phone up. The top of the cave was a uniformed arch. He swept the light from side to side. He saw enough to know it was not a cave but a tunnel. Big enough for two large trucks side by side. His light did not penetrate to the other end.

He started walking, trying to estimate how far he had traveled. He thought about the length of the football field, picturing it in his mind as he walked. One football field. Two. Near the end of the third football field, he saw something. As he moved closer, he found a massive metal door that looked as if it could withstand a powerful blast.

Why he thought of an explosion puzzled him.

Off to one side, stood a small room. A standard size door, made of the same metal as the large door, embedded in the rock, led to whatever was hidden in the mountain. The entry door to the room stood open.

The room had a desk and an old chair that the fabric had rotted off of long ago. Near the metal door, embedded in rock, he saw a pad with numbers. A locking mechanism. The ground looked safer than the chair and more comfortable, too. He walked to the larger door and saw a similar pad off to one side. Nothing else. Dead end.

Turning a slow circle, he studied the tunnel. A walkway ran down both sides along the walls. On the ceiling, he saw light fixtures. By the size of the lights, he thought they would make the tunnel as bright as day. If they were on, which they were not.

He turned his phone's light off and stood in the darkness. No light appeared at the far end of the tunnel. He did not know if the patrols were still outside the entrance. He had never been in a cave or tunnel and did not know what to expect. Because he did not know what to expect, his thinking made no sense, so he dismissed his thoughts. He turned on the light to find a place to sit. The sides of the tunnel were scarred as if an enormous machine clawed its way through the mountain.

He stopped shivering. Untying his wet shoes, he kicked them off and hoped they would dry before morning. Sitting against the rock would be rough on his bare, scratched back. He walked to the large metal door. It would be cold but smoother than the rocks. He touched it with his fingertips. Not as cold as he expected. He placed his palm against it. Not cold at all. That seemed odd. But not unwelcome.

Many thoughts circulated in his head. When should I leave? Which is better, day or night? Travel would be faster during the day, but I would also be visible. That road must go somewhere. But is it somewhere safe to go? I must get to Potterville, to Coach, Akira, or Nyx. Damn, I promised Mrs. Schilling I would not be late again. Once I get out of the canyon, there might be a cell phone signal, but I'll still be lost. Maybe work my way across open country. That would make it more difficult for Pacific Edge to find me. But which direction should I go?

He took a deep breath. Safe for now. Unless Pacific Edge security knows about this tunnel, in which case, they might appear at the other end at any moment.

With three machines patrolling the canyon, best to stay put. How long he should stay remained a mystery. The adrenalin rush subsided. He yawned.

What is on the other side of the door?

Sitting with his back against the door, his eyes grew heavy. He might never get out of this place alive. He wished he could tell everyone what had happened to him. How he felt about them. Before he nodded off, he unlocked his phone and opened a notepad app Akira showed him one day in chemistry. He had Akira's and Miriam's e-mail addresses and their phone numbers from their text messages. He opened a new note and linked Akira's and Nyx's phone numbers to the note. He titled it: Derrick King's Journal. If someone found the phone and powered it on, the message would send, and his friends would learn what had happened to him.

He sat in the darkness.

He wrote.

- The End -

Escape
A Derrick King Novel:
Book 2
Miriam King

In the Beginning

This is the story of Miriam King.

Miriam felt responsible for Derrick's exile to the commoner world.

She promised to help him.

Circumstances evolved faster than she anticipated, forcing her to act before she was ready.

But she had a plan.

On March 31, when curfew lifted, Miriam walked out the front door, putting her plan into action.

Things didn't go well.

Now she's under house arrest.

But she promised Derrick she'd come.

Author's Note:

Thank you for reading my books. If they gave you a bit of an escape, I'm pleased. Please consider writing a review. To sign up for my newsletter, visit my website daniellcopeland.com.

Acknowledgements:

Thanks to the love and support of the love of my life and partner, Liz. She is also a writer and illustrator. Check out her books on Amazon Libby K. I couldn't do any of this without her. She is also my best editor and critic.

Special thanks to Rod Leonard for providing feedback and guidance.

More books from Daniel L. Copeland:

Available at Amazon.com in paperback, eBooks for Kindle, and audiobooks.

The Derrick King Series

3

About the Author:

Daniel is a lifelong Idahoan and grew up on a small farm in Southern Idaho. He worked in the criminal justice system for 35 years and is now retired. Daniel has published nine novels. In addition to writing, he and his wife, Liz love to travel on their BMW motorcycle. They have ridden in most of the US, including Alaska, the Great Lakes, and Florida. They have also ridden in Canada, New Zealand, and Australia. Daniel is an award-winning home brewer and a certified beer judge.